SWEET EMBRACES OF A STOLEN MOMENT

With a groan that seemed to rend his very self, Fahne lifted Dione's face to his own for a long, devouring kiss, his hands exploring her silken shoulders and her arms, tracing the sweet arcs of her breasts, learning the frail concavity of her narrow waist, the grace with which it swelled on either side, so gradually, into that bewitching curve of slender hip.

And the touch of Dione studied the firm, hard splendor of the arms of Fahne; his muscular, vast expanse of torso; his leanness.

"To leave you is to tear away my skin," Fahne whispered in her ear. "But you shall soon have word of me; and we shall meet in Erdem~~""

"In Erdemar," Dione replied . . .   ~~hed Fahne disappear into the darkness~~

PAT WALLACE

The WAND and the STAR

A KANGAROO BOOK
PUBLISHED BY POCKET BOOKS NEW YORK

Another *Original* publication of POCKET BOOKS

 POCKET BOOKS, a Simon & Schuster division of
GULF & WESTERN CORPORATION
1230 Avenue of the Americas, New York, N.Y. 10020

ISBN: 0-671-81240-8

First Pocket Books printing August, 1978

Trademarks registered in the United States and other countries.

Interior design by Cathy Carucci

Printed in the U.S.A.

For "the Maeden"—
DAVID LATNER,
the Sorcerer
and
my cousin
ERMA BENNETT DUNCAN

THE OLD STAR-RACES

SABBIANS (FIRE)	ERDEN (EARTH)	BRISEN (AIR)	MARIN (WATER)
Multun (Mar. 22-Apr. 20) (Aries) ♈ (prima-Sabbia)	Bole (Apr. 21-May 21) (Taurus) ♉ (erst-Erde)	Twisan (May 22-June 22) (Gemini) ♊ (premier-Brise)	Crabba (June 23-July 23) (Cancer) ♋ (prime-Marin)
Ruler: Ares	Ruler: Aphrodite	Ruler: Hermes	Ruler: Artemis
Leun (July 24-Aug. 23) (Leo) ♌ (mezza-Sabbia)	Maeden (Aug. 24-Sept. 23) (Virgo) ♍ (mittel-Erde)	Bilance (Sept: 23-Oct. 22) (Libra) ♎ (moyen-Brise)	Escorpiun (Oct: 23-Nov. 22) (Scorpio) ♏ (middle-Marin)
Ruler: Helios, Apollo	Ruler: Hermes	Ruler: Aphrodite	Rulers: Ares, Proserpine
Kani (Nov. 23-Dec. 22) (Sagittarius) ♐ (fine-Sabbia)	Capra (Dec: 23-Jan. 19) (Capricorn) ♑ (endlich-Erde)	Waetergyt (Jan. 20-Feb. 19) (Aquarius) ♒ (dernier-Brise)	Peisun (Feb. 20-Mar. 21) (Pisces) ♓ (latter-Marin)
Ruler: Jove	Ruler: Chronos	Rulers: Chronos, Ouranos	Rulers: Jove, Poseidon (Kun, Ea, Ler)

AUTHOR'S NOTE
ON NAMES OF GODS

The old star-races named their ruling gods, or planets and lights, as follows:

The Sun—Helios, Apollo
The Moon—Artemis
Mercury—Hermes
Venus—Aphrodite
Mars—Ares
Jupiter—Jove
Saturn—Chronos

These were the ancient planets and lights. The following so-called modern planets, though not discovered as physical facts until the following dates, were felt intuitively and therefore acknowledged by the ancient Marin and taught to the other old star-races:

Uranus—Ouranos: actually discovered 1781
Neptune—Kun, Ea, Poseidon, Ler: discovered 1846
Pluto—Proserpine, Hades: discovered 1930

PART I

THE STAR
OF EA

(Illusion and Dream)

CHAPTER 1

Dione of Mar, shadowing her sea-green eyes with a white oval hand, looked up at the sinister clarity of the sky. Above the city's turrets, auger-sharp and gleaming, a feeble patch of gray struggled to pierce the harsh expanse of blue.

For long oppressive moons, the silver port of Mar, center of the world where one heard by night and day the tongues of many lands, had lain in drought. The water streets, nourished for centuries by a continuing small mist of rain, were sunken. The winding stairs that led from the riverways to the palaces of bloodstone and greenstone, beryl and jasper, on the banks stood naked above the lowering waters. Makeshift stairs had been devised to let the women, in their wide-hemmed robes, reach their homes unsoiled.

The gray-green trees and vines lining the riverways shriveled to a shade of pewter. Already the Marin, the inhabitants of the city, forbidden by Kun and Ea to slay the higher beasts, were feeling the lack of the salty fruits that grew on the trees. Even in the wealthy houses, strange flora from the sea were being served at table.

But the Peisun, the more imaginative Marin, for whom food was a matter of some indifference, were beginning to know a greater discomfort—a darkness of the spirit.

It was as if, Dione reflected, Mar was dying—Mar, the soft, silver city of a thousand tongues and myriad faces, variable with the colors of distant lands; Mar, the beautiful! The thought gave Dione a stab of pain.

"Look there," said Earla to Dione, pointing with her stolid finger to the surface of the riverway.

Dione followed the gesture of her nurse's broad hand: a small deep Peisun, the fish that never showed its eye to day, was surfacing. The watery Peisun were easily swayed and as fragile as the foam of the sea. As the women watched, the creature rose above the water, and, with one

3

convulsive gasp of the burning air, was still. It floated like a leaf of tarnished silver as their craft waded slowly through the riverway.

Earla was silent, regretful, Dione saw, for it had been her nurse's custom to shelter her from harsh realities, Dione thought with affection. Now that I am a woman, Earla still shelters me—she touched her nurse's hand and looked again at the sky.

The nurse studied the pale, slender woman beside her, whose green sleeves were flowing like waves. Dione's soft face, under the wimple of silk hiding her blue-black hair, was as open as a child's. Dione's pale hands, with their moonstone-colored nails, were squeezed together tightly, as if her divided selves were comforting each other.

She saw the death of Mar in this Peisun, thought Earla. Sensuous and calm, the nurse was not born to such thinking. She reckoned that her nearness to Dione these many circling years must have begun to make her so. She watched Dione's tender mouth tremble as the girl looked back on the shriveling trees along the water banks; the castle turrets of abalone, in whorling shapes of shells, glared in the alien light.

Earla's fears were far more practical than Dione's: the fruit and fish, staples of the Marin diet, were dwindling. To obtain the weeds and creatures from the sea was slow and perilous, and soon even they would be dear. But, worst of all, the neighboring warlords hovered like vultures, waiting for the fall of Mar, the great city, with its commerce and treasures. And the violent desert lords to the West had friends among the people of the mountains, their heaven-fated lovers from antiquity.

Earla glanced swiftly at Dione, almost afraid the girl could read her somber thoughts: there had been times, indeed, when the nurse had wondered if her charge had "the sight."

But Dione, she noted with relief, had not appeared to notice; her green eyes were still studying the trees and sky.

How fortunate, Earla reflected, are the travelers to Mar. The airy people from the North and the calm brown kinsmen to the South could withstand the drought. Northerns seemed indifferent to any weather beyond the windy climates of their minds, and the earthy ones, whose lands were warm and dry, could almost be merry, were it not for their sympathy for the pain of their companions in Mar, the watery country.

It was now the star-month called the Circle of Yod, and the Marin were weary of the unremitting brightness that assaulted their sensitive eyes and worn by the endlessness of the heat.

Earla and Dione sat lost in their thoughts now, as a craggy-browed servant poled them down the riverway. They heard music in the distance, growing stronger as they drew closer to the river bend. Music was alien to Mar, a blend of the ethereal handbells and rebecks of the northern air-land, Brise, with the earthy piping and drums of Earla's native land, Erde. Dione caught the twang of an Erden psaltery, and the coldly sensual harp of the children of Bacchus, the people of the South.

Something in the sound struck at Dione's nerves; she could feel, low within her, a serpent of longing uncoil.

And then around the river bend they saw emerging a motley barge, definitely not a boat from Mar, for its prow, instead of being trident-set, was hewn in an ambiguous form that might have been an emblem of any of the other nations—a form like a gust of air, for Brise; a growing leaf, for the earth-country of Erde; or the lapping of a tongue of fire, for Sabbia, the far-off, hot nation to the West of Mar.

"Who are they, Hathor?" Dione called to the servant at the prow.

"I know not, Madame," Hathor replied in his thicker, less-singing Marin. Hathor was a Crabba, the summer-born Marin of brooding temperament and more material nature; Dione was a Marin of the spring. "They are so mingled," Hathor continued, "they could be a band of minstrels . . . or traveling healers. And they are brave," he added, "to breast the troubled winds from Brise and Sabbia."

Dione looked puzzled, and Earla shook her head at Hathor, frowning. It had also been the order of the Lord Mayor Chiton to keep from Dione any mutterings of war.

Earla feared her charge's questionings, but soon she saw that Dione was distracted by the strangeness of the barge. "They are of every land," she murmured. "Look there, Earla, look upon their hair! There is the flaming hair of the fiery Sabbian. There are some Brisen, with their heads like yellow flowers! And a Maeden, of Erde," she said with a peculiar change in her melodic speech, a hesitancy of breath that caught the inner ear of the cautious Earla.

She glanced sharply at Dione, whose green look was on a tall figure in teal-blue, standing in the point of the barge, apart. And there was in Dione's eyes a light Earla had never seen—a glow like the passage of the moon across the waves, a look of awakening desire that was almost pain. Then Earla turned to watch the nearing barge.

Among the men and women with hair of copper and of gold, of night-black and leaf-brown, wearing the tunics and robes of foreign places, the one that drew the eye was the tall, strong man in the teal-blue tunic of the Maeden —those Erden born in the last of summer and the first of autumn, the race of healing and magic. On his face was an expression of great gentleness and power; his nose was hawk-like, and his generous lips bore the traces of laughter and of hurt.

Around his sinewy neck he wore on a pewter chain the caduceus of Hermes, or Mercury, the fleet messenger of the gods, the caduceus twined with serpents that was the rod of all wisdom. But on the medallion's center, surmounting the customary entwining snakes held by winged hands, was the six-pointed crystal star of magic, the Seal of Solomon.

His eyes, however, seemed the brightest part of him—at once clear and kind, far-seeing and piercing.

"He is a sorcerer, this Maeden," Dione said softly, raising her small oval hand to her beating throat; the green sleeve went flowing away from her arm.

"And yet," Dione added, "there is something in him like Vanand." A shadow fell upon her face as she pronounced the name.

Why, Earla asked herself sadly, does the thought of Vanand the Escorpiun always fill her with this darkness?

But there was no time for inner questioning; the barge of motley strangers was very near. And Earla was curious about the tall man with the piercing eyes and the gentle face.

The golden brown of his hair and beard was indeed that of the Place of Magic. Even Merddyn, the incomparable magician, Dione had told Earla, was a Maeden. In truth, as Dione had thought, the massive strength of this stranger's arms and shoulders was kindred to the power of Vanand the Escorpiun, of the fierier race of Mar.

"I wonder on his parentage," Dione said with that pretended coolness Earla had learned to suspect.

She is up to something, the nurse reflected, and she said to Dione, "It is unseemly that you wonder on this man. Have you forgotten that you are promised to Vanand?"

As soon as the words were said, Earla felt a great dismay. For the white face of Dione had clouded over and the moon-like light had darkened in her eyes. Dione smiled her odd Peisun smile, which was almost a grimace of sadness, and she answered hollowly, "It is something I never forget."

Suddenly, like a miracle, the sky turned wholly silver and a light drizzle began to fall. With the very entrance of the barge, Earla thought, the rain came down! And a peculiar excitement chilled her skin.

The servant Hathor ceased his plowing labor and looked up at the graying sky.

"Ea!" he cried with reverence, calling out to the Marin god. "Ea, son of Kun, we send our gratitude." He made the sign of the trident, the emblem of Mar, and of the crescent Moon that ruled his own Crabba race.

Earla's hand rose in answer as she made the gesture of horns, for the Bull of her own birth. But she had the strangest feeling that it had not been Ea who had sent the rain—that the miracle was somehow connected with the stranger in the barge.

Yet Dione, Earla noted with amazement, had hardly seemed to feel the rain, for whose caress she had been praying for nights on end to Kun. The girl was powerless to look away from the tall man in the prow of the motley craft.

As their barges neighbored, Dione could look directly into his eyes: they were the clear eyes of the Maeden. But their color, instead of the lucid blue-gray of that race, was hazel, and reflected in their wondrous depths were the lore and tinctures of other races. In them Dione saw the quicksand of the Thinking Sabbian from the land of fire, the winged look of the air-ones of mountainous Brise, the dark horns of the Erden, to the South, and last, the mordant knowledge of the deep-seeing, autumn-born Marin called Escorpiuns.

Dione looked shyly at his muscular bare arms; they were as powerful as oaken branches, and the hair on them was so light they seemed as smooth as fruit in the overcast. His

long-fingered hands were broad, yet sensitive, the hands of
the healer.

Shaken and amazed, Dione knew a wild desire to kiss
the great hands of the Maeden, to taste his heavy forearms
with her tongue.

And suddenly down into the crystal eyes, reflecting many
things, Dione felt herself descend, awhirl and shattering,
caught in grasping hands of light. Like the Drops of Yod,
she thought, the drops of heavenly light that were the
Tarot symbol of the Maeden. And as the sorcerer's eyes,
for a sorcerer he must be, locked once again with hers,
Dione saw in them a fatal greeting.

Beholding what went between them, Earla was stricken.
Neither Dione nor the stranger seemed to care that the
drought, at last, was over; neither seemed to hear the
clamor of the motley strangers. To the still, tall man their
voices might have been the wailing of a cloud of gnats, for
all his notice.

Even when a lean, yellow-clad Brisen moved toward
him, crying, "Fahne! You have done it! Feel the rain!"
the man called Fahne stayed motionless, keeping his steady
gaze on the face of Dione.

Dione began trembling and sank to a little padded stool
behind Hathor and covered her face with her hands.

And as the boat with the ambiguous insignia passed
them, Earla looked back. The man called Fahne, alone
with the polesman on the deck of the barge, had turned
and was staring at the huddled form of the woman on the
stool.

Venus protect her, the nurse prayed soundlessly, protect
her from the fire that passed between them. And Earla
wondered at the fervor of her own petition.

The barge was drifting to a halt before the ancient
greenstone on the shore that was the house of her uncle,
Chiton, when, without warning, Dione fell forward in a
faint. Earla ran to her with a moan and, looking up, she
saw Vanand the Escorpiun, glowering.

Earla knew then that he had seen it all—the meeting
of Dione and the stranger; the quicksand of the Maeden,
where Dione the Marin had been drawn.

What manner of man was this stranger? Earla questioned silently. Could the sorcerer, in truth, have given
them the rain?

CHAPTER 2

Fahne the sorcerer, watching Dione's barge draw in to the ancient greenstone on the shore, had also seen her fold into herself like a small green bird and crumple, senseless, on the deck.

All Fahne's pleasure in the rain's coming vanished utterly; at once he could see nothing but the little figure in the robe of green.

A flash of scarlet on the winding stairs caught the edge of Fahne's vision: a tall, broad Escorpiun, the only race of Mar affecting violent color, had stepped with two long strides into the barge. Fahne heard him order the servant to bring a healer.

The sorcerer Fahne held up his broad, long-fingered hand and said quietly to the polesman, "Halt."

The polesman, a Capran with night-black hair, gave Fahne a quick glance from his oblique eyes, but the impassivity of his face was unchanging as he obeyed.

Fahne saw the older woman, the russet-clad Earla, scramble up from the barge and watched, with a raging pain, the powerful Escor gather the little Marin woman in his arms and bear her up the winding stairs and through the shadowy entranceway.

Giedi, the polesman, looked questioningly at Fahne. Gemelle had pressed him to pole them swiftly out of Mar.

"A moment." Fahne nodded at the gray pronged barge; already the Crabba servant of Dione was poling strongly toward the city's heart and would soon approach the strangers' craft. When the trident-set boat was drawing alongside their own barge, Fahne waved his strong, slender hand at the Crabba, motioning him to stop.

"Crabba." Hathor, his deepset eyes turned straight ahead, labored on to find a healer, unheeding the stranger's cry.

"Crabba!" Fahne's deep-throated greeting belled. "I am a healer."

Hathor abruptly ceased his plowing motion and stared across the narrow belt of water dividing them. He examined the blue-clad Fahne with suspicious eyes.

"I am a healer," Fahne repeated in Marin. "Take me to your lady."

After an instant's pause, the Crabba Hathor said in his soft, thick tongue, "Come, then, messire."

Giedi maneuvered the barge nearer to the one with the trident prow.

Vanand thundered at the uneasy Earla, "Why have you disobeyed me and the Mayor? She has been stricken by the unclean air. And if she dies, you die."

Earla was silent, trembling. She stared at the marble floor.

A little mollified by her demeanor, Vanand the Escorpiun said more quietly, "Stay with her. I will await the healer in the entranceway."

His muscular body strained at his tunic as he rose from the chair, shaped like Varuna's chariot, next to Dione's bed. He strode from the chamber, softly closing the massive door.

Earla sighed with relief, but her face was anxious. She bent again to Dione and put a broad, gentle hand on the heart-shaped face. Dione was burning with fever.

Earla drew the dragonfly silk to Dione's neck and slipped from the room, returning with a basket of fresh-smelling leaves. Delicately she lifted Dione's small head and slipped the silken pillow from under it, sliding the neighbor pillow below Dione. Earla began to stuff the vacant pillow with leaves, then repeated the process with the other.

Once more Earla left the chamber and came back carrying a gray dish of seaweed poultices, which she applied to Dione's neck and wrists and face. The girl's breathing, Earla noted with dismay, was very shallow.

There was a gentle tapping on the massive door, and Earla, bidding the caller to enter, looked up into the dappled, lucid eyes of Fahne the sorcerer from Erde.

So great was Earla's astonishment that for a moment she was silent. It was not until the blue-clad stranger had twice greeted her in Erden that she could stammer, "Good evening." Her wide brown glance flew to the face of Vanand. Apparently Vanand had not yet connected the man in the barge with this quiet stranger, for his stony face revealed nothing but his concern for the little Marin.

Earla expelled a little sigh of gratitude, but when she saw Fahne looking at the still-white Dione, small in the ocean-colored lap of the canopied bed with its dolphined feet, it seemed to Earla that she and Vanand were suddenly invisible, that the stranger was alone in the room with Dione.

For his clear look arrowed to the girl like the flying rays of light from the bow of Eros, god of desire. Soundlessly, he crossed the marble floor and bent to scrutinize Dione the Marin.

Dione's green eyes were open now, and she was staring back at the sorcerer with the same enchanted stare Earla had noted so coldly in the barge a little while before.

The man sank down into the chariot-shaped chair and put his broad, long-fingered hand, the healer's hand, upon the forehead of Dione. Under his breath he began to murmur an alien rune.

"What is he saying?" Vanand muttered to Earla.

So intent upon the picture that at first she could hardly grasp Vanand's query, Earla faltered, at last: "An . . . an Erden healing rune." Earla herself was a Bole, a spring-born Erden, whereas the sorcerer Fahne was an Erden of the autumn.

Vanand took a tentative step toward the bed. "This is barbarous!"

Undisturbed, the clear-eyed sorcerer kept his powerful, long fingers on the white brow of the girl. As if Vanand had never spoken, the alien whispered rhythmically in his narrow Erden. Earla the Bole could catch only random meanings; her many years in Mar had made her strange to her native Erde, and Vanand the arrogant Escorpiun, though lettered, had never deigned to learn the Erden tongue.

Earla glanced again at Vanand: he had not taken his mordant look from Dione. And in his grim expression Earla saw the dawning of an angry recognition: he recognized the stranger as the man in the barge.

A flicker of a smile had touched Dione's mouth; her breathing was more normal, and the glaze had left her green, dreamy eyes.

"Why, the child looks well!" Earla exclaimed.

Vanand's face was a study: in its stoniness were blended

his relief and the dismay of owing Dione's recovery to the man from Erde.

Earla moved to the bed and touched the girl's cheek; a dew of fleeing fever had moistened her skin, but it was cool now. Amazed, Earla turned to Vanand and said, "She is well."

"Yah," said the healer softly, "she is well . . . for now."

Vanand raised his black-winged brows. "For now?"

The sorcerer nodded. "Please apply the poultices through the night and morrow," he said to Earla. "We must leave her now to sleep."

With an air of quiet command, Fahne waved the other two from the chamber. Earla was surprised to note that Vanand obeyed.

But once in the windy corridor, he addressed Fahne the Maeden curtly: "What is her illness?"

A veil fell over the sorcerer's clear eyes. "A mild Marin fever, arising from the drought."

"What do you ask in payment?" Vanand queried coldly.

A peculiar smile lit the dappled eyes of Fahne. "I ask no reward." He stared into the steely eyes of Vanand and thought, the man looks angry.

"I care not for your jousting, Maeden," snapped Vanand the Escor.

"Fahne does no jousting." The smile in the crystalline glance was brighter now. "I will return this evening."

"You will no longer attend my spoken wife," Vanand replied icily. He lay a suggestive hand upon his sword.

Fahne made no reply. White with anger, Vanand the big Escorpiun strode away down the echoing hall. Fahne and Earla heard the clanging of the massive entrance door.

"Your care was excellent." Fahne bowed to Earla.

"How did you know I used poultices?" Her brown eyes widened.

"And hops," he added, smiling.

"You are indeed a magic maker," said Earla the Bole in a low voice. Yes, she thought, I believe he did bring the blessed rain!

"I am a healer. It is no bodily thing that troubles your lady—no bodily thing alone."

Earla waited interrogatively.

"It is a sickness of the soul." He stared at her; the woman swayed dizzily, beholding the depths of his stare. "I am more than a healer of the flesh," he said.

Earla asked shyly, "Will you take some wine?"

Fahne nodded once and descended with Earla the Bole to a chamber below the level of the corridor, sunken like a Peisun-pool. Fahne had seen an ancient chamber like it once, in Sabbia, built by the pagan Desert people.

Moving to a heavy carved chest fitted to the curving wall, Earla gestured to the beakers and bottles gleaming there. "May I offer you some maiglöckchen?" she asked, indicating lily of the valley, pressed from a flower of Hermes. Earla's voice was low as she listened nervously for the step of Vanand the Escor.

"Please." He smiled; a tender expression was on his lean face. "Your lady is a friend to all the races." He tasted the delicate wine with appreciation.

"Yes." Earla gestured again to a high-backed carved chair, padded in velvet; its gray-green flesh had a subtle dusting of silver, like light upon the sea.

"It is all beauty," said Fahne, sinking into the chair. The nurse wondered at his wistful tone but thought with a pang of guilt, I have not asked him about my lady. "What is the sickness of her soul?"

"The shadow of her marriage," Fahne replied, "a famine in the body's core."

Earla sat down on a neighboring stool the shape of a shell. "I have long feared so," she sighed. "Whenever I say his name, her face is dark."

"Who is he?"

"Is it possible that you cannot know? He is Vanand the Minister of Mar."

"Vanand. Of course." The sorcerer Fahne set his fragile goblet on a bloodstone table at the elbow of the chair. And the crystal sight of the sorcerer took him beyond the boundaries of the sweet, rich chambers of Dione. He could see, as through a mist of azure, the steeds of a host of men in mail; could hear the warriors' armor clang, their bloody bellows, their screams of pain. And then he saw the terrified small face of the white Marin; she turned to him for succor and for calm.

"What is your lady's name?" The sudden question startled Earla.

"She is Dione—Dione of Mar. And she is promised to Vanand," Earla repeated.

Fahne made a careless gesture with his long-fingered

hand. "The skies have destined her for me." Again his bold self-confidence struck Earla almost dumb.

"But you . . . you . . ." she protested, "are a . . . wanderer . . . a wanderer lacking property or land, a gypsy without title, with no roots. What can you offer to my lady?"

Fahne smiled. And Earla heard the paltriness of her own question, for she saw again quite clearly the fateful meeting of Dione the Marin and the man from Erde. In their meeting look had been a wind that would feed a fire to burn a city, the storming of a sea to rock the cleaving oval of the earth.

And Fahne, Earla the Bole observed, though he sat so tentatively in the high-backed chair that he sat as a gladiator rested, ready any instant to arise, was serene and certain.

"Your lady will come with me," he said quietly.

From some far chamber now they could hear the sweet music of a cithara of Mar.

"Vanand will not release her," Earla the Bole said somberly. "Nor her uncle, Chiton, the Lord Mayor of Mar. You know the latter's ire against the Erden."

Fahne raised his golden-brown brows. "I have encountered it—Mar for Marin, Erden in Erde. There are more ancient laws."

"Vanand is not concerned with ancient laws."

"The ancient laws are deeper than Vanand's concerns," the sorcerer retorted. Rising, he began to pace the naked stone. "Ever since the dawn of knowledge, since the first Chaldeans saw the whirling of the primal wheel of stars, the sea has always sought the calm of land, and the earth has thirsted for the water."

How true it rang, thought the Bole. She remembered her strong Erden mother, like herself a placid, sensuous Bole, singing a little air, "of the Marin that long for Erde, and the Brisen for Sabbia."

And time after time the truth that was hidden in the song revealed itself to her: the watery Marin read the Erden's thoughts like seers. The strong, solid Erden, who built, conserved, and healed, were charmed by the soft and changeable Marin, the water people, who gave the world its arts and mysteries. And the inevitable direction of their loves—like the compass's needle swerving to the Pole!

Earla recalled the enchantment of her Marin Crabba father for her mother, the Erden Bole.

The people of the Fire Land, Sabbia, with their flaming hair, their brassy lays, and brutal jousting, were drawn to the fair, cool air people of Brise, who lived in the mountains. The Brisen and the folk of Sabbia were "shadowless," like fire and air, the Bole had learned long ago, whereas the Marin and those of Erde had in their souls the darknesses of land and ocean.

"She must come with me," Fahne said abruptly.

Again Earla was astounded at his temerity.

"Her uncle, the Lord Mayor of Mar, has given her to Vanand." Earla attempted to sound severe.

"She will never marry Vanand." Again, as she had in the barge, Earla caught that strong, indifferent knowledge of his own power, as if he were repeating a lesson to a child.

She sighed. "Vanand will kill you. I know him as the land knows tempest winds. He is mad to have her." When the sorcerer did not reply, she went on. "He is a triple Escorpiun, with roots in the Erden Capra. You saw."

Fahne nodded. "I saw the star-wheel of Vanand."

After a moment, he added, "My own, which it is no longer politic to show"—a hard smile creased his full, sensuous mouth—"has mightier stars: the Thround, the Escorpiun, was also rising at my birth. And Chronos, the old Erden god of time, has thrust with Capran horn the weakness from my soul. Moreover, I am touched with the Sabbian's chariot, the symbol of the overriding, subtle will, from the place of quicksand and magic."

"You do well to hide it," Earla said dryly. "For all those things, to the mind of the Lord Mayor and Vanand, are signs of impure blood, the soul awry."

Fahne did not answer, listening to the cithara. Earla wondered if he had heeded her at all. "You will persevere," she said sadly, and it was a statement, not a question.

"Forever." Fahne, who had seated himself tentatively again, stood up. "I must go. My companions are waiting to proceed to the air land of Brise. I must tell them to go on without me."

"There will be no one to aid you," Earla said.

"I need no aid. I have the spirits and the *Vau*."

Dimly from her childhood Earla recognized the word— the ancient word for the Eye, kin to all light and brilliancy, a name adopted by the Maeden, the Erden from the place of magic.

"I can say naught to move him," Earla reflected.

As if she had spoken, Fahne smiled and said, "Naught. I give you thanks. See to your lady. And tell her that I will return." His deerskin shoes were soundless on the flags; suddenly, he was gone. At last Earla the Bole heard the clanging of the massive entranceway.

And Earla returned to the silver-green chamber to sit in the shimmering chair in the form of an ocean-car; to wait for the awakening of Dione the small Marin, resolved that she would never belong to the dangerous gypsy from Erde, with his terrifying powers.

CHAPTER 3

Vanand the Minister of Mar felt grateful for the drizzle and buttoned the neck of his crimson tunic, with its broidered emblem of the golden scorpion, badge of the High Escors. The blessed rain! Like all the moisture-loving Marin in the tall silver city, Vanand had suffered in the drought. Only his Erden planets had kept him from sickening, for the Erden were friends to heat; this fortune of his birth had served him well.

But not so great a fortune now, he thought darkly, remembering the sinister visitor from Erden—and thinking of the peaceable Marin, who, no longer threatened by the drought, would most certainly revert back to their customary thoughtless ways! Vanand's green slanted eyes, made even more oblique by the Capran in his wheel of stars, looked at the oval arch above him as he entered the city-palace of Mar.

There, grinning amiably in the center of the arch, were the insignia of the Mar—the forms of Varuna, Ea, and Poseidon, the rulers of the sea. Below the arch, set in a square on the floor of the green marble terrace, were the symbols of Erde—Bull, Goat, and Maeden, and the great god Pan, king of the hooved and fur-eared creatures, caressing the body of Cybele, the goddess of the earth.

Vanand the Escorpiun smiled now as he trod upon the image of the Maeden. The symbolic gesture filled him with bitter joy. He seemed to be treading on the body of the sorcerer, whose ruler was this harvest figure. "Mar will rule them all," he whispered. But he had caught the attention of a Crabba guard, and reddening, he clamped his thin lips tightly shut.

The deep-eyed guard saluted the big Escor with great respect and stood aside for him to enter.

A score of petitioners for the Council's grace lined the verdigrised benches along the corridor—the Peisun, with their trident-shaped hats and doublet and hose of ocean green; the shadow-eyed, more earthy Crabba, wearing a silver-green akin to the Peisun, but with the glyph of the Crab, the stylized claws, decorating their tunics or caps. And the Escorpiuns, in scarlet, Vanand noted with satisfaction, were waiting most regally, with the least patience of all.

But he strode by without a further look and stopped at the pewter door of the Council chamber. The guards bowed low and, tapping the ornately chased pewter with their spears, opened the doors with a flourish.

Chiton, the Lord Mayor of Mar, was rapping his silver gavel on the table of green Celtic marble, his Crabba face more irritable than usual. Behind him the Prime Chair of the Sea, with its pewter emblems of the subaqueous gods, gleamed in the rain-dimmed light from the oval windows.

On either side of the long marble table, where Chiton sat at the head, were five men of the races of Mar, numbering four Peisun, three other Crabba, and an equal number of Escorpiuns. Their dress differed subtly from the clothes of the petitioners in the halls. These Peisun wore, instead of tunics of heavier, duller stuff, clothes of soft and shining ocean-green with a patina of silver like evening mist; their symbols were not merely embroidered, but worked in aquamarines, bloodstones, or moonstones, gems of the Fish. And their faces were even gentler than those of the men in the hall—more dreamy and far-seeing, for their greater fortunes had enabled them to fulfill their true Peisun natures.

The Crabba, dressed similarly in a silvery ocean-green,

wore hats in the form of the crescent moon, embroidered
with moonstone and pearls; and the Escors, their hats in
the form of the phoenix's flames, wore a more vivid crimson. None of them, however, bore on his breast the golden
scorpion that was on the breast of Vanand; their insignia
were pewter, mingled with the opals or topaz of their October or November births.

The Sea Chair facing the Lord Mayor was empty.

"Milord Vanand," said Chiton sourly, "has deigned to
join us, now that we have settled the business of the
drought." The old Crabba's hooded eyes looked disap-
provingly at the bare head of Vanand. Sullenly, Vanand
the Escor put on his hat with its image of the Eagle, the
lion of the air, bird of the High Escorpiun.

Vanand restrained his rising anger—were this crabby
old insect not the uncle of Dione . . . He replied, "I was
in attendance on the Lady Dione. She was unwell."

"Unwell! Unwell? She was left in your hands; I charged
you with her well-being."

"I am not a sorcerer," Vanand snapped, "nor yet a
nurse." A cold sickness assailed his stomach-pit when he
pronounced the former word. He saw again the hated face
of the stranger, on whom Dione had looked with such
longing. "I beg your pardon, Your Worship," Vanand said
grudgingly.

"And my niece, the Lady Dione?" asked Chiton.

"She has recovered, through the efforts of . . . she has
recovered."

"Very well, then," the old Crabba Chiton said sourly.
"Will you be seated so the Council may proceed? Else we
shall all be sitting here until December, the Circle of the
Goat."

Fuming, Vanand sat down in the high-backed, eagle-
carved chair opposite that of Chiton. His royal pride was
stung. Yet, glancing about the oval table, Vanand saw that
the others had barely seemed to notice the interruption:
in his chair with the pewter fish, Fomalhaut, Peisun star-
brother of Dione, looked weary and dismayed. There were
lilac circles under his dreamy green eyes and he held his
arms close to his body, like the fins of the fish, a posture
habitual to Peisun.

Again Chiton tapped his silver gavel, shaped like the
body of a crab. "Shall we resume, my lords?"

Madimiel, one of the sharp-eyed Escors, spoke quickly.

"As I was saying, I do not believe the Prince of Erde is seeking peace."

"I am in accord," said Zuban, another of the Escors.

And Nur, the fourth Escorpiun, nodded his agreement, murmuring.

They are good men and true, thought Vanand, examining the hard, strong faces in which the piercing eyes were set so like his own. But what of the others, those old women of the Peisun and Crabba?

"I am grateful," said Vanand in his growling voice, "that my star-brothers resent on my behalf the Erden slur, the offering of Monoceros' hand to my chosen wife."

He glanced reproachfully at Chiton, who spluttered, "The Lady Dione need not accept such overtures."

"*Need* not accept?" cried Vanand. "And it does not rest with the Lady Dione, sire. It rests with you."

Chiton looked shamed. "Will not accept, that is to say."

"Then what," interjected Litor, a Crabba, "is our quarrel with the Erden?"

Nur the Escor snorted. "How many times must I repeat that this proposal, insult that it is, is only a blind? The Erden mean to overcome the Marin through this alliance."

"And the Erden's friendship with the fire-land Sabbia is warming."

Vanand looked with surprise at Mollis, another Crabba member of the Council. Here was help from a new quarter! The Escor's oblique green eyes began to gleam, and he smiled at Mollis.

However, looking about the Council table, Vanand saw that the other Peisun were glaring at Mollis, as were the Crabba. We are still a minority, the big Escorpiun raged silently.

"And therefore, it follows," said Fixas the Peisun ironically, "that Erde and Sabbia—and, by extension, Sabbia's ally, Brise—are plotting to conquer Mar?" His Peisun jowls quivered with anger.

"It is no matter for jesting." Nur the Escorpiun said repressively. "I have never trusted Monoceros, or the Erden, for that matter."

"You have the planets of Erde in your own star-wheel," Desmos, the Mayor's nephew, retorted, nodding at the pewter-and-topaz medallion that dangled from Nur's massive neck on a heavy chain. The garnets of the Erden's

Capra and the emeralds of the Erden's Bole were shining among the larger topaz.

"And so have most of us," said Chiton, his fingers touching the sapphires of the Maeden that gleamed darkly among the moonstones of his own silver wheel. "But of late I have begun to question our beliefs in the ancient laws."

Vanand's sea-colored eyes glittered, and a half-smile stirred his thin, hard mouth. So the old crustacean was beginning to think! Vanand gloated.

Litor the Crabba said in a shocked voice, reflecting the reverence of the worldly Marin for custom and tradition, "I am full of wonder at your meaning, sire. Since the stars were read in Babylon, the truth of astral law has flamed like a beacon through the ages. The Erden have ever been our chosen mates and friends; the sea and earth have been destined to mingle. The land contains the waves, bounding them for the good and pleasure of men; the sea makes fertile the land, causing it to blossom and bring forth the fruits of our necessity."

"Are we to suffer a sermon from the ancient school of stars?" inquired the Escor Madimiel. He was thinking sourly that Litor's wife and her Erden kinsmen were behind this noble-sounding outburst. "Yes," Madimiel went on, "the Erden have been our chosen mates in the past; the airy Brisen and the fiery folk of Sabbia were likewise destined. But we speak now not of custom and romance; we are dealing with what is real. Apparently," he continued with heavy irony, "the heavens are awry, for now the Erden have unlikely friends in the Sabbia and the Brise, and they are banding together with an eye toward conquering Mar! We are the treasure-hold of the world: our port is the only port accessible to other lands; our city bears the gold and silver and the precious gems of a universe inside its palaces! In the quality of our life, the knowledge of our scholars and seers, lies power—power that the other star-lands wish to own."

"You are insane!" cried the Peisun Desmos. "It is by openhandedness and freedom that we have *made* our quality of life!" The others looked at him in some surprise; generally, the Peisun were the most soft-spoken, least violent of Marin. "The jealousies of Vanand have infected you, my friend!"

"Hold!" Vanand the big Escor had leaped to his feet

and had his broad, oval hand on the pewter scabbard at his hip. Unwillingly, but with a dreadful calm, Desmos the Peisun had also risen. Vanand looked insane with rage.

"Milords, milords! Contain yourselves." Chiton, the Lord Mayor, was banging at the marble with his hammer of silver as the other nine Marin began to get to their feet.

"Are we to slay each other now, and save the Erden the trouble?" The soft, sarcastic voice of Fomalhaut the Peisun fell into the sudden silence. His race's hatred of violence was evident in his tone.

The big Escor removed his heavy hand from his scabbard and sat down. The others followed suit.

"Now, then," said Chiton sourly, "may we continue?" There was a sullen stillness over the assembly. The Lord Mayor said to Madimiel, "You feel certain, then, that Monoceros seeks to war on us?"·

"I do, my lord."

"And you?" The Lord Mayor nodded at Vanand, Zuban, and Nur. "Aye, my lord," each said in turn.

"The Peisun, and my brother Crabba?" Chiton addressed himself to the other seven.

"No, my lord," Fomalhaut said firmly. "I speak for all the Crabba and Peisun in this chamber."

But there was a muttering from Mollis.

"Is this true, Mollis?" Chiton asked.

The previously dissenting Crabba hesitated a moment, then said slowly, "No, my lord. I am leaning in the direction of the Escors. In Erde now even the minstrels of the alleyways are mocking Mar. And there have been many traveling from Sabbia to Monoceros, the Capran Prince of Erde."

"Why was I not apprised of this?" cried Chiton.

"We have attempted to . . . apprise you, sire," Vanand broke in angrily, "but you would not give us your ear."

"Truly, the matter grows more serious." Chiton's face had turned solemn.

There was a worried murmur among the Peisun, the Crabba Litor, and Jana, who had looked askance on the traitorous pronouncement of the Crabba Mollis.

"But, my lords," protested Myrtillus the Peisun, "the land of Sabbia contains more wealth, in metals and in slaves, than any other. Why should it desire to conquer Mar?"

"To own more slaves," said Nur the Escorpiun coldly.

"If Milord Myrtillus would stick to his verses," the Escor added, "and leave the governing of Mar to soberer men . . ."

Myrtillus flushed darkly. The Escorpiuns perpetually chided the Peisun, the minstrels of Mar, about their womanish pursuits.

Chiton, infuriated at this attack on the ancient custom of racial balance—tradition called for four men of each Marin star-race to serve—shouted, "Milord Nur! You will observe the decorum of the Council of Mar, or suffer contempt!"

Chastened, Nur was silent, glowering.

Wearily, Chiton put his graying head in his soft, oval hands, the hands of the Crabba, for an instant, then removed them, looking up at the eleven men.

"I must think on this," he said at last. "The Council is adjourned until the morrow."

Zuban the Escor opened his thin lips to protest, but Vanand the Minister of Mar frowned and shook his massive head.

As the twelve men dispersed from the rain-dimmed light of the Council chamber, Vanand said in an undertone to Zuban, his fellow Escor, "It matters not. I have a plan. Come to my quarters with Mollis. We have much more to say to you."

Hearing, but giving no sign of his knowledge, was Desmos the Peisun, cousin and long-years' companion to Dione of Mar.

CHAPTER 4

Dione opened her eyes. The chamber was full of shadow; the rainy light from the oval windows was lilac with dusk. She heard the murmuring of the Marin cithara, the melodic tenor of the minstrel, Volan.

"The small rain down doth rain," he sang. Dione could see his fragile silhouette in the corner by the fire, its blue-green glow the only lamp. The air, sharpened by the rain, was cool for the star month called the Circle of Yod, and the little Marin breathed it gratefully. There was an edge of autumn there, she thought drowsily, wondering why she had slept so long.

Then, quite suddenly, she remembered, and her heart gave a sickening thud. She lay back on the silken pillows.

At last, she said very softly, "Volan."

"Madam?" His gentle reply had something in it of the bird-song, for he had been of questioned birth, his parentage both of the airy Brise and the watery Mar.

"Please sing 'Plasir.' "

Volan turned his narrow head and smiled. Dione could see his face more clearly now, and the look of his clear affection.

The singer delicately struck the cithara, and his melodic tenor rose in the haunting song, precise and courtly in the tongue of the air land, Brise.

"The joys of love are but a moment long. . . ."

Both the Brisemarin and the woman in the bed were lost in dream, until the sudden torch, the stolid steps of Earla entering broke the web of music.

"Why are you lying in the dark?" The matter-of-fact tones of the Bole grated on the Marin's ear. "Volan, what are you about, to let your mistress lie here in the shadow?"

Volan abruptly ceased his singing.

"Go on, Volan," Dione said gently. Then, imperiously to Earla, she said, "Please leave us so, and take the torch away."

Already she addresses me like a queen, Earla thought. More quietly, she replied, setting the cresset on its stand, "It is time for your poultices. The . . . healer has so directed."

At the mention of the man from Erde, the little Marin's heart leaped in her throat; the Bole saw her pale.

"You must eat now," said Earla. She set a steaming bowl upon the small table by the bed of Dione. "I have brought you a broth of quercus to give you vigor."

Dione shook her head, frowning. The bitter aroma of the quercus broth, brewed from the oak that was a tree of the Peisun, filled her with loathing.

"I cannot," she said quietly. Volan had again struck up on his cithara, playing a wordless air that sounded like the wind of the profoundest woods. Dione recalled it as a melody of Erde, and again in the depths of her body she felt such a sick coldness of longing that she feared to faint, for the air recalled so clearly the tall strength and the wise, gentle face of the man from Erde.

"Please leave us, Volan." The Bole's voice shattered the spell of the Marin. "I must have private speech with the Lady Dione."

Stubbornly, the little Marin said, "Stay, Volan, and play to me. There is nothing," she commented to the Bole, "that must be hidden from Volan."

Earla sighed. "Very well, very well, my child. But kindly strum your instrument more softly," she added severely to the Brisemarin.

He grinned good-naturedly and complied, the rippling of the cithara almost a whisper in the shadowed room. For a moment there was no other sound, except the steady falling of the rain, heavier now, and a random whipping of the flames, like velvet curtains flapping in a mighty wind.

"And what have you so solemnly to say to me?" Earla saw a look of mischief on the white face of the Marin; she shook her head. How changeable the child was—always!— she mused; her moods are in constant motion, like the waves of the sea.

"Your uncle is coming to you tonight, with news of great import and happiness," said Earla.

Dione sat up in the wide silken bed, throwing back the sea-green coverlet with such force that it fell with a soft susurration to the marble floor.

"He is releasing me from Vanand, releasing me!" she cried.

Clucking, Earla retrieved the coverlet and smoothed it back on the bed.

With a fey and happy smile, Volan began to play a lively dance of Brise. "This is happy news, my lady," he said in his gentle tenor.

Earla smiled. "You will be released from Vanand to marry a far greater man."

Dione, who had risen with an impetuous motion, sank back onto the bed. "A greater man?" There was a wary puzzlement in her question.

"I have already said too much," the Bole replied ruefully. "Your uncle will give you to a prince."

"He is a prince, the man from Erde?" Dione was incredulous.

"The man you are to marry is a prince, but not a Maeden," said Earla. "He is a Capran."

"A Capran." Dione's pallid face had grown even whiter. "Monoceros!"

"You must lie down," she said. "You are not yet strong. Please," the Bole pleaded, "have some of the broth."

Dumbly, the small Marin lay back on the sea-green pillows and replied in a cold, almost inaudible voice, "I will eat hemlock. That is a plant of Capra, I believe."

Beseeching, the Bole leaned to Dione and put a broad hand on her cheek. "My dear child, it is best. You know my love for you, and the devotion of your uncle."

"Devotion!" Dione cried. And she began to weep, with great, tearing sobs that fairly seemed to rend her narrow body. "He is returning, Earla. I know it. How can I give myself to another? He told you, did he not, the sorcerer, that he was returning to me . . . and charged you to tell me?"

Earla hesitated. Now in the shadowy chamber—for Volan had abruptly ceased his playing—there were only the sounds of the rain and the fire, the incessant flowing of the riverways.

"No," Earla said at last. "He gave me no such message."

"You are lying! You are lying!" the Marin cried out again, and the pain in her voice was unbearable to the Bole. But obdurately she repeated to herself, again and again, I know what is best for her.

The Marin turned and hid her face in the pillows, sobbing and sobbing until the Bole feared she would become ill.

Earla moved to her and smoothed her tangled blue-black hair, spread like the wings of night on the sea-green silk. "Hush, hush," the Bole whispered, as if she were soothing a wild creature.

At last the rending sobs were spent. Dione turned in the wide silken bed and looked up at the Bole with a cold, fixed stare. "Look, Earla," she said, and her voice had a woefulness that Earla, in all their years together, could not remember hearing, "look there, upon my wheel of stars."

Puzzled, Earla the Bole said, "You know I know it well, as I know the lines of my own hand."

"Look upon it again," Dione said with an imperious air.

Bewildered but indulgent, Earla took the cresset from

its stand and held its fire near the great medallion on the wall above the bed, wondering what she would see that she had not seen a thousand times before.

Everyone in the world they knew was given, at birth, his star-wheel that set out the position of the heavenly planets for the hour of his coming. The star-wheel was a circle divided into twelve sectors, one for each of the races of stars.

On the left side of each circle, at the nine-o'clock position, was the sector of the Ramm, signifying the birth period beginning with the spring equinox, from late April to late May; counterclockwise around the circle proceeded the other eleven star-races, or signs: the Bole, the Twisan, the Crabba, the Leun, the Maeden, the Bilance, the Escorpiun, the Kani, the Capra, the Waetergyt, and, last, the Peisun of Mar, Dione's birth-race.

The Ramm, Leun, and Kani, or Centaur, were races of Sabbia; the Bole, Maeden, and Capra, of Erde; the Twisan, Bilance, and Waetergyt were races of Brise; and the Crabba and Escorpiun shared the Peisun's water country, Mar.

The star-wheels of the nobles, of course, were wrought in precious metals and gems; Dione's was one of these. Earla stared at its ornately chased silver, with the forms of the planets in white-gold and jewels. In the sector of the Peisun, in Dione's star-wheel, the smiling Sun, or Helios, was set in aquamarine and moonstone, indicating Dione's March birth.

"But what is it?" Earla repeated. "I have known your wheel for many years."

"Something for you to behold with newer eyes," Dione said in the same strange tone that so discomfited Earla.

"Look upon the figures of Ares, the god of urgent direction, and Jove, the god of fortune, in the Maeden sector opposite my Sun—look upon the aspects of the Houses."

And Earla the Bole looked again upon the forms of Jove, also called Jupiter, and Ares, another name for Mars; upon the aspects of the seventh house of fate. The planets were set in sapphire within the sector of the Maeden figure, the Queen of Harvest and Fertility. The race of the sorcerer of Erde!

Despite her firm resolves, Earla felt a little chill of unease. This was a weighty matter—to defy the very order of the skies! It may have been that the very pattern of the ancient stars had decreed Dione for the sorcerer. What terrors awaited those who broke these sacred, timeless laws? And she, Earla the Bole, was she to aid the Mayor in this wrong, abet him in his dreadful sacrilege?

Slowly, she returned the cresset to its stand. Dione's green eyes were fixed on her irresolute face.

"You lied to me, Earla."

Again the Bole hesitated, but said at last, "No, my lady, I did not lie. The man from Erde is gone, and he will not return."

"I do not believe you." Dione's clipped words reproached the Bole. "Leave me."

"My lady . . ."

"Leave me."

Earla opened her full lips, about to speak. Then, sighing, she shook her golden-brown hair with its threads of gray, and taking up the bowl of quercus, left the chamber on slow, heavy feet.

With her going an oppressiveness was lifted from the air, and Volan began to play his cithara, very softly.

For long moments Dione was silent. Then she cried out to the unmanned Brisemarin, "Oh, Volan, Volan, what am I to do?"

Volan rose from his stool by the fire, and cradling his instrument tenderly, he came to the chair by the bed.

He sat down and began to play again, this time with such incredible softness that the air was almost that of stillness.

"Have faith in the goodness of the skies," Volan replied in the bright, optimistic manner of the race of Brise that colored him.

Or "tainted" him, Dione thought now, as Chiton, her uncle, would say.

They both looked up at the star-wheel over the immense bed: the hour of her ascendant had almost touched Dione with Brise. The little circle with the cross within it, indicating the ascendant, was perilously near the border of the Twisan, the airy twins ruled by Hermes, messenger of the gods, and that of the Bole, the Bull under Venus' reign.

"That, perhaps, has made us kinsmen of the soul." Volan smiled affectionately at the Marin. "And it cousins you to the Hermes-colored sorcerer of Erde," he added, bold in the absence of Earla. The sorcerer's Maeden sign was also ruled by the fleet, silvery Hermes.

Startled, Dione examined the narrow face of her friend, pallid under its bowl of strangely colored hair, black with glints of Brisen gold. "You have seen him, then?" she said with eagerness.

"Oh, yes," Volan replied, "I have seen him before now —when your cousin Desmos took me that summer to Brise. You remember?"

She nodded. "He was much younger then, of course, and I was only a boy. But I will never forget the wonders he performed on an ailing woman of Brise. There seemed to be magic streaming from the crystal star he wore."

"The Star of Solomon," Dione murmured. "Do you think he is . . . of questioned birth?"

"Yes," Volan said. "He, too," the Brisemarin added in a dreamy voice, "has the star-wheel of questioned birth—the birth that lends, it is whispered, especial glories to the person and the mind."

"Is this so?" The Marin's pulse quickened.

"Oh, yes, my lady, it has always been so. It gave me this." Volan caressed his instrument. "To you, it gave great beauty and a heart that understands all in this world, and the things above and below it. To the sorcerer from Erde, it gave the wisdom of the ancients and the magic sight."

Dione was silent, listening to the fire. Then she turned to her friend and whispered, "I love him, Volan. I love him."

The singer bowed his brindled head and answered in a low voice, "I know, my lady. Had I been such a man . . ." He ceased abruptly and a painful color flooded his white cheeks. He looked down and struck a tentative chord on his cithara.

Dione felt an overpowering sadness for the slender boy. "Dear friend," she whispered, and leaning over, she touched his head.

"I beg you, lady," he said, and his voice was choked with tears, "oh, touch me not."

"But I thought . . ." She stopped in confusion.

"You thought," he said bitterly, "that my being no more a man has made me but a gust of air, purified of all hot feeling. It is not so, for still, in my mind, is the memory of what I have never known."

Dione felt wetness gathering in her eyes and gushing down her face. "Volan, Volan, I never knew. I ask your forgiveness."

The slender Brisemarin smiled through his tears and answered tenderly, "You need not beg for my forgiveness. I have ever loved you as a brother and a friend."

"Oh, then, my dear Volan, will you help me? Will you help me to go from this place?"

"I have no power to help you, my lady." The minstrel's thin lips were set in a grim line. "What can I do?"

"You can aid me in my deception—of Earla and my Uncle Chiton."

Trembling, Volan took her small hand in his and kissed it. "I will do all that I can." Then his dancing gaze, blending the sky-color of Brise with the sea-green of the Marin, flicked toward the massive door.

"But I must leave you now," he whispered, "for if I mistake not, that is your uncle's tread. And you know he likes me not."

Dione made a rueful face. "Because he knows that you are privy to my thoughts, and I love him less than you. Take heart from that." She smiled her odd Peisun smile that almost looked like a grimace of pain, crooked and childlike.

Volan smiled in answer. "I do, my lady, I do ever." And the Brisemarin slipped from another door, even as the corridor door was parting to admit the Lord Mayor of Mar.

CHAPTER 5

The others had gone to sup at the inn. Giedi was afire with curiosity, but he asked no questions as he poled Fahne down the riverway to join the others in The Cup and Crescent.

"Thanks, Giedi. I shall find my own way back." And with an agile leap, disdaining the steps, the sorcerer landed on the bank.

The reticent Giedi gave Fahne a probing glance from his flat, black, slanted eyes. There was a leashed excitement in the man that puzzled him sorely, but he only nodded and began to guide the barge away.

Fahne had supped before in The Cup and Crescent, the largest inn of Mar, where Marin of all stations mingled.

Now in its smoky depths the sorcerer saw the jeweled star-wheels of the landed, mingling with the single-broidered glyphs on the tunics of servants and polesmen come to spend their mathale for the wines of Mar, or the ales from Erdemar, the border settlement between the lands of earth and water.

However, this evening Fahne the sorcerer could feel a difference, an edge of bladed air; there were looks of malice as he threaded the crowded room, seeking Gemelle and Kaus.

A comely Crabba with the heavy breasts of her race studied Fahne with deepset eyes, commenting to an underEscor she was serving, "The air is blue tonight."

The sorcerer knew she was referring to the teal-blue tunic of his race, but he passed them by without expression. The underEscor sneered, "The King of Gypsies is above the likes of us."

Still expressionless, the sorcerer Fahne turned back and stood like a statue before the table of the Escor. Fingering the medallion around his neck on its heavy pewter chain, the sorcerer caused it to pendulum to and fro; the soft light caught the crystal Seal of Solomon in the center of the caduceus.

Staring, the slack-mouthed underEscor seemed transfixed by the light of the star. He soon began to nod and fell face forward on the driftwood table.

His Crabba companion, awkwardly made in the manner of the under-race, started to roar with laughter. "Sargas has taken too many cups," he mumbled drunkenly in his thick Marin.

But a timid underPeisun at the table with the indeterminate features of the ill-aspected Fish said in a softer voice, "Sargas drank only two cups." And then: "It is noised that the Maeden brought the rain."

He stared at his Crabba companion and they fell uneasily silent. The heavy-breasted server gave a nervous laugh and, looking with respectful fear at the sorcerer, scuttled away.

Fahne had caught sight of the alien heads of Gemelle and Kaus in the rear of the smoky chamber. Their red and golden hair, the only patches of color in the inn except for the garish crimson of the Escors, stood out as alien as strange flowers on a bed of darkness. Even at this distance, Fahne could see that the fiery Sabbian, Kaus, had taken much wine. Gemelle, the yellow-headed man of Brise, was as usual in complete command of his equilibrium, befitting an acrobat and mime.

With them, the sorcerer saw then, were the night-haired Bock, the gloomy Capran, and the sleepy-eyed Bole, Veris.

Shouldering his way good-naturedly among the bibulous polesmen and the tipsy lords of Mar—many of whom moved quickly aside; the sorcerer's height and breadth of shoulder made him an adversary to respect, and already the strange indisposition of Sargas the Escor had been noised among the serving-women—Fahne reached the table of the players.

The saturnine Bock was the first to speak. "Aben," he said in his brassy Erden, "is our business concluded in Mar? You have obtained the Council's permit for our passage through to Brise?"

Fahne, with a repressive glance at the Capran, pulled out a driftwood chair with his broad, long-fingered hand and sat down next to Gemelle.

"Our business is concluded; mine has just begun."

Veris the Bole examined Fahne with puzzlement in his heavy-lidded eyes, and Bock the Capran's dark brow grew darker. Kaus had barely heard; he was staring at one of the buxom servers in her low-cut bodice of green.

But Gemelle of Brise, cousined to the sorcerer by their common ruler, Hermes the god of the mind, read his words instantly. "You mean to tarry in Mar?"

Fahne nodded, his dappled eyes bright. The randy laughter of the drinkers about him might have been, Gemelle thought, the whisper of the newly falling rain. Fahne seemed to sit in a self-created silence, apart from them all, as was his wont.

Gemelle made no answer, but Kaus the Sabbian, awakening to the import of their words, cried, "Tarry? For that little Marin? Why, she's not enough for a mouthful, far less to fill the arms." Gemelle recalled the like fragility of the Lady Shabatu. He put a restraining hand on the arm of Kaus and whispered, "Be still." For the brow of Fahne was lowering and there was a dangerous glitter in his peculiar eyes.

"And what of the troupe?" Bock the Capran asked

curtly. Veris, the Venus-ruled Bole, ever in the sway of beauty, had said nothing. He felt a great compassion for the sorcerer.

"You will go on without me," Fahne said softly, seeing again the small white face of Dione. Grotesquely, an underPeisun, almost a caricature of Dione, approached their table.

She gave the big sorcerer a seductive glance. Kaus smiled meaningly, and Bock the Capran colored, but Fahne did not look up.

Offended, the plump server leaned to Bock. Her lips almost brushed his flat, shapely ear as she crooned, "Another round for you gentlemen?"

Bock's face darkened with the heat of her nearness. He looked at Gemelle and Kaus. Both nodded, but Fahne, still looking down at his hands, murmured, "Nothing."

"Your belly, like your center, will dry up. You take your wine as seldom as your whores." Kaus the Sabbian, laughing his coarse laughter, twitted the sorcerer.

Fahne replied with one blank look, and the flame-haired Kaus could see himself reflected like a tiny, gibbering insect in the profound crystalline eyes of the other. Kaus fell silent.

But Fahne the sorcerer was thinking of Kaus's metaphor. There was indeed within him such an aridity: the thought of Dione was like a clear, bubbling fountain. He had seen her at once as the symbol of his lost, enchanted land of infancy, the center of his dreams, the fountain in the center of the garden of himself, the hallowed area that would feed again the long drought of his years alone.

How many had there been? How many, when for the lack of a woman he had choked back his groans in the darkness; when, sickened by the grossness of a woman's flesh or speech, he had, again and again, turned away . . . or in the blackest desperation thrown himself upon a random jade to empty like a dog and awake from the momentary frenzy to an even greater sadness?

"Fahne," Gemelle said gently. "Fahne." The sorcerer seemed to awake from a dream. He felt the anguished beating of his loins aroused by the memory of the small white Dione. He turned to Gemelle.

"How can we manage without you?" Gemelle asked.

"You will manage very well," Fahne said gently. "You will serve in my stead, as director. There will be your music and dance, and Veris and Bock have become conversant with my healing methods."

Gemelle shook his narrow golden head. "You know full well the people follow us for you, and not our entertainments. You are the central light, and we but shadows. Look what you brought today—and only a fortnight ago, in Erde . . ."

"Be still a moment," Fahne said quickly, laying a firm hand on the wiry forearm of Gemelle the Brisen.

At the table next to them, a server was seating two lords of Mar. One of the lords had said a name that rang in Fahne a bell of clear recall—Chiton. Chiton, the Lord Mayor of Mar, the uncle of the little Dione!

Out of the corner of his eye, Fahne examined the two lords. The one who had pronounced the name of Chiton was a handsome, well-aspected Peisun, wearing the gemmed star-wheel of the privileged.

The other was a genial-looking Crabba, dressed with equal richness. The heavy-breasted server who had spoken so pertly to Fahne was hovering over the lords.

"Strawberry and lunar," said the Crabba lord and waved the server away.

The Crabba turned to the Peisun lord and said, "I wish you would use more discretion, Desmos." And the Crabba lord glanced at the table of aliens where Fahne sat with the night-haired Bock and tawny Veris, and Kaus and Gemelle with their respective heads of fire-color and narcissus-yellow.

"Discretion!" Desmos cried. "Dione is my beloved cousin and my friend; we played together as children. I am like her brother! And now our Uncle Chiton is playing with her happiness; whether he gives her to Vanand or Monoceros, either course will be disaster. Do you wonder that my blood is on fire with anger?"

Fahne sat quite still, and the observant Gemelle's goblet was arrested halfway to his lips.

"Are you sure it is true?" the Crabba lord asked the man called Desmos.

"Of course," said Desmos. "Volan, my cousin's minstrel, brought me word not a quarter-hour gone. Look, you, there he is now, about to sing for fleur-de-lys."

Desmos turned and gestured toward the alcove of ales and wines. Very slightly Fahne altered the angle of his chair and saw among the serving-women a slender boy with peculiarly dappled hair, dark as a Marin's but with a touch of Brisen gold.

"Is the singer safe among these ruffians?" the Crabba lord inquired of Desmos the Peisun.

"As safe as my hands can make him," Desmos declared.

The Peisun of Mar, like the men of Brise, the country of air, and the Maeden of Erde, shrank from killing. But they were skilled with their feet and hands in combat, using the martial arts that stunned opponents and rendered them senseless. "He has been for many circles the friend of my cousin Dione," Desmos added.

"Need you name her?" the Crabba exclaimed, looking around cautiously again. His suspicious eye lighted on Fahne; the mittel-Erden stared blankly ahead.

"And that is your final word, Fahne?" The Capran's brusque question smote the thick air.

The sorcerer slowly turned his head and met the flat, black look of the Capran Bock.

"That is my final word."

Veris the Bole said urgently to Gemelle, "Speak sense to him!"

The red-haired Sabbian Kaus chuckled. "There is no sense to move a man in love. I offer you my felicitations, Fahne; I had thought you a man of magic . . . and of stone."

All the fieriness of the Sabbian's nature smoldered in the phrases of Kaus.

Just then they heard the strumming of a cithara from the shadowy alcove of wines, and the countertenor of the boy with dappled hair rose like the wings of a golden bird in the ancient air of "Greenfire."

"Hark!" Gemelle whispered to the sorcerer. "The boy has the voice of the very spirits."

Fahne nodded and listened to the melancholy little air; he saw again the gleaming green sleeves of the small Dione, recalled the fatal greeting in her wide, dreamy eyes as they had met his that afternoon across the narrow waters between their passing barges.

"Gemelle," he said in a low voice, leaning to the Brisen's ear, "I must see her tonight."

The Brisen smiled sadly and shook his head. "You heard the lords at the neighboring table. She is promised now not only to one noble, but to two. Whoever enters her

house will be accounted an enemy of one or the other—
or both. Do you want to battle the nations?"

Fahne smiled in reply. "A whim," he said evasively.

"A perilous whim," Gemelle returned with suspicion.
"Her palace will be a fortress now. How do you mean to
gain ingress?"

"You will fit me out," Fahne whispered urgently. "Please,
Gemelle. You know that only you have the skill with paint
and putty, the hand with draperies, to make me a credit-
able guise."

Gemelle thought, I would do as much for Shabatu, in
truth. He sighed. "You are incorrigible. Return, then, with
me to the barge, and I will fit you out."

Bock and Veris watched them rise; Kaus was sporting
with a serving-woman and did not notice.

Gemelle tossed a pewter coin onto the driftwood table.

"I will say sense to him," Gemelle said lightly to Bock
and Veris. But they answered his chafing tone with worried
faces.

"We will follow soon," said Veris. "We may be bearing
Kaus upon our backs," he added in his deep Venusian
tone.

As Gemelle and Fahne passed the shadowy alcove of
Marin wines and Erden mead, the latter noticed that the
boy with dappled hair, despite the protests of the serving-
women, was gathering his cithara under his cloak and soon
was but a step behind them.

When they stepped outside into the misty night and
Fahne beheld again the lanterned bridges of stone, innumerable, spanning the city's waterways, he felt the familiar enchantment of Mar. Some years ago, when he had
been almost a boy, he had taken a ship to Oriens, where
he had seen, bewildered by its loveliness, the city of Kinsai.
And that antique city had been very much like Mar, its
silent, black-haired women almost as exquisite as Dione,
the little Marin.

"Let us go on foot a ways," Fahne said softly to
Gemelle.

And nodding his assent, the Brisen fell in step with the
sorcerer, gratefully sniffing the newly moist air. The Brisen,
like those of Mar, thrived upon the damp. And Fahne, with
his brindled birth and the ascendant of the Escor, breathed
more freely now that the drought was over.

They were passing through one of the great squares that broke, every few miles, the vastness of the city. Fahne's deerskin buskins made no sound on the wet flags, but the wooden soles of Gemelle—the Brisen, used to the softness of snow, protected their feet from cobblestones in wooden shoes—resounded with a clopping measure.

The square and the broad streets were very still; the merchants had shut up shop for the night and only the scarlet weskit of a random Escor guard lit the gray shadows here and there.

All at once the sharp ears of Fahne, who could hear grass growing, caught the faintest echo of the step of Gemelle. The footfall was very light, almost like that of a woman or boy, and careful. Now the Brisen heard it, too.

Fahne and Gemelle exchanged a wary glance. If it were a cutpurse, he was very frail, Fahne thought wryly, and wore very noisy shoes.

As one, the men stepped into the shadow of an empty passageway. The steps grew louder, then ceased. Peering out, the sorcerer caught sight of a slender figure silhouetted in mist.

In two strides, the sorcerer catapulted from the shadow and grabbed the stranger from behind; his massive arm maintained a stranglehold upon the hooded figure's neck.

"Who are you?" Fahne's voice was hard and threatening. "What is your business with us?"

"Please, sire"—the choked words of the hooded stranger came in gasps—"unhand me. I can do you nor your friend no hurt."

"It is the singer!" exclaimed Gemelle. "The boy from The Cup and Crescent!"

Fahne loosened his hold but kept a grasp on the boy's thin arm. "What do you want?" he repeated.

"I am Volan, the minstrel of the Lady Dione. You are the sorcerer Fahne, of the place of magic?"

"I am."

"Please, sire, I wish to speak with you—about my lady . . . and other matters."

The sorcerer felt the relentless hammering of his own pulse in his ears. "Your lady?" he repeated, and his voice was thick with excitement.

"Yes, sire. Please let me go with you and this gentleman. Please."

"Come, then, boy. We are bound for the minstrels' barge."

The boy Volan fell in between the two tall travelers, trying to match his stride to theirs. Companionably, Gemelle put a narrow arm around the shoulders of the slender singer.

As they emerged from the square and traversed the broad, rain-silvered street, Gemelle peered down the black canal, wearing on its surface the reflected lantern lights like beads of gold.

"The barge is there," said Gemelle in surprise, pointing to the craft with the ambiguous sigil bobbing on the waters near the second arching bridge. "Why has Giedi dropped anchor there?"

Fahne replied with a look of consternation at Gemelle. "Has he been driven downstream, do you suppose?"

The Brisen nodded. "I think that is the case."

"Sires." They turned to the timid minstrel. "Vanand the Minister of Mar ordered your craft away from the sight of the Mayor's palace."

"I see." The sorcerer's eyes were hard and bright, like crystal. "The fine Escorpiun hand of Vanand."

"Come," said the Brisen, quickening his lithe stride. "One of the red throunds"—he cocked a dancing eye at an Escorpiun guard—"is about to descend. And I have been told their sting is powerful."

The man from the place of magic took the slender Volan by the arm and hurried him to the escalade descending to the canal.

With an agile bound Gemelle was on the deck. Like a powerful coursing hound, Fahne leaped after, catching the flustered Volan, who had nearly fallen, hauling him aboard.

"And now," said the sorcerer when his breathing had slowed a little, "come with me to the cabin, and tell me of your lady."

CHAPTER 6

The last red rays of the August sun had barely faded from the sky in lower Erde when Beta lay down wearily by Aspel. He was already fast asleep, exhausted by the hand work and field work he had done since sunrise.

Beta's back was paining her, all the way from neck to haunches. Awkwardly, she turned, the coarse coverlet rasping her chin, and sought with a blunt-fingered hand to rub away the ache without disturbing her husband.

Yet, aching and bone-tired as she was, the Capran could not forget what she had seen that morning, in the men's work chamber of the steward Dabih's house. She had not dared mention it to Aspel; he would have beaten her for spying on the prince, as he called it.

Beta felt a nervous sweat begin to trickle down her side, a moisture owing more to fear than to the oppressiveness of the August dusk. For Dabih the steward had nearly caught her! Thanks to Chronos, she whispered to herself, she had been able to run away before he saw. She had cracked two of the eggs in her basket, though, meant for the egg-rent and chicken-rent that morning. It had meant the long return home, the searching for two extra eggs, and the hen cackling in discomfort all the way as she squeezed it tightly under her sinewy arm.

Drowsily, the serf recalled the strangeness of the day. It had begun ordinarily enough.

Beta had risen with the sun, put on her coarse stuff dress and shoes of straw, screwed up her tail of thick black Capran hair, and fed Aspel and the children. Then, leaving the second child to see to the baby—the others went with Aspel to the fields—Beta had carefully chosen five of the brown eggs the steward favored, gathered up the chicken under her arm, and set out for the house of Dabih.

The great square castle of the prince Monoceros brooded upon the rise, but Beta barely gave it a second glance. The doings of the gentry seemed as unreal as the posturings of puppets at the fair. Beta had never been inside the castle; only the house serfs and the privileged freedmen ever trod its mysterious chambers and halls. It was the house of Dabih the steward that loomed large in her life, and in Aspel's, for it was to Dabih that they made account; it was he who ordered the hand work and the field work to be done, and the weaving for the servants of the castle. The garments of Monoceros and his sister came from the mountains of Brise, said Aspel, through the gleaming city of Mar.

Beta had stopped at Selvia's hut to see if she were going along. But her neighbor's third child was ill and Selvia was attending it frantically. Selvia cried out to Beta, "I shall be late with the chicken-rent! What am I to do?"

Kindly, Beta had consented to carry Selvia's eggs, but she could not for the life of her manage the second hen. "I shall speak to Dabih," Beta said with a confidence she did not feel, and Selvia's flat black eyes rolled with fear.

With reluctance Beta left her neighbor with the feverish child and trudged on up the dusty path to the steward's house.

The yard, she saw, was quite deserted, and the wooden door to the men's workshop gaped ajar. "Dabih! Sire!" Beta called.

There was no reply, only the whisper of a slight wind in the barley field beyond, and the creaking of the door as it moved inward in the breeze.

Timidly, Beta, grasping the chicken under her sweaty armpit, moved forward on awkward feet to the workshop door.

Again, she called out Dabih's name, but there was only silence. Beta took three cautious steps to the opening door. And then she saw it; she saw the saddle.

It must be the new saddle for Monoceros. In the women's working room it had been said that the prince had ordered a saddle of unmatched magnificence for his night-black steed, for the day when he rode into the square before the palace of the Lady Dione with his betrothal gifts.

This must be the saddle! Dazed, Beta conjectured that it must have come from the lands beyond the distant desert, in the place called Sabbia, a name that Aspel had heard Dabih say. Slowly, Beta entered the men's workroom and drew near the magnificent thing, resting on a horse of wood.

Still grasping the chicken closely and hearing its agitated cluck, Beta set her basket carefully upon the floor and touched the polished leather with her work-roughened hand. The saddle was a flaming grün, the fire-green of the higher race of Capra, and it was as smooth as a baby's skin, perfectly wrought without an apparent seam or break anywhere on its glazed surface. It shone like a great magic apple, and from it were hung black stones and stones of dark blood-red. Could these be real?

Beta had seen the paste gems of the players at the fair, and they were not like unto these. Beta had never seen anything like this, except once at a distance, when she and three of the children had hidden in a thicket to watch the hunting party of Prince Monoceros pass. And on that day Beta had seen the jeweled women. But their jewels were not as big as these! Why, every one of them would cost as much as . . . Beta could not calculate it.

She rubbed the great smooth saddle with her hands, thinking it was softer than her own skin, even her skin that was shown only to Aspel. For Aspel had said that even the soap the horsemen rubbed the saddles with was fine, far finer than the stinking tallow soap Beta washed her body with.

Then she had heard the footstep on the flags, and full of fear, she had gone racing from another door and hidden in the barley field, holding the chicken's beak together to muffle its squawking, and breaking the two precious eggs, Selvia's eggs, that had to be replaced from Beta's own small store.

But I have seen the saddle, Beta thought stubbornly now, grinning in the twilight. It was real, because I touched it with my hands. I have touched the saddle of the prince and will remember, always. My children's children will remember this.

The month called the Circle of Yod was cool in Mar, and Chiton the old Lord Mayor, the uncle of Dione, had felt an autumn in his bones that day. Now, as he reclined in his tall velvet chair before his study fire, the well-nourished Chiton sighed with satisfaction.

At his elbow was a small green marble table in the shape of a crescent moon, and on the table reposed a tall gray jar of the Mayor's favorite saxifrage wine. Brewed from an herb of his Crabba ruler, the Moon, the decoction was an excellent way of ridding the kidneys and bladder of stones—a matter of some import to the portly Chiton, whose dedication to the table was intense.

Earla the Bole entered the study, bearing in her broad hands a little pewter dish of sweetmeats for the Mayor.

"Ah!" said Chiton, as delighted as a greedy child. "And what are these, my good Earla?"

"My own handiwork, just for Your Worship." Smiling, the Bole set down the dish beside the half-empty jar.

"You do well. You are a good woman, Earla." Chiton tasted one of the sweetmeats and made an approving sound. "I should say *we* do well, in arranging the affairs of Dione. You are aiding me, of course, in pressing Monoceros's suit?" He examined the servant keenly with his deepset green eyes, embedded like small hard emeralds in the doughy expanse of his mottled face.

Earla hesitated, then smiling, said, "Certes, sire. The Lady Dione does not always . . . understand these matters at first. But I am sure that she will see reason in time to receive the prince with joy."

"What in the name of Artemis are you saying, woman?" Chiton's content was evaporating.

Before the uneasy Bole could make a reply, a slender little page, clad in the gray-green of the underPeisun, came soundlessly into the chamber.

"Kindly make your advent noisier!" the Lord Mayor said irascibly to the page. The boy, whose large fish-like eyes were already round with fear, widened almost to circles.

"Is he a halfwit?" Chiton bellowed at Earla.

"He is an underPeisun, sire," the Bole replied dryly, "and they are the minnows in the world of fish."

"I am not blind. Well? Well, what do you have to say to me, you little minnow?"

"Please, sire . . . please, sire," the page stammered, "there are three gentlemen . . ."

"Three gentlemen? Three gentlemen where? On the roof? In the sea? On a boat in the waiting-lobby?" Chiton's intake of wine had been sufficient, Earla reflected.

"Who are they?" she interposed gently. "Give the Lord Mayor their names."

"Va . . . Vanand," the boy gasped out, "Vanand the Minister of Mar . . . and his kinsman . . . and . . . a member of the Council. They are all . . . Escors," he concluded gloomily.

"Well? They will not devour you. You are not their mother," the Crabba said with a nasty inflection. "Get this halfwit out of my sight," he ordered Earla, "and show them in."

Grasping the big-eyed Peisun by his protruding ear, the Bole pulled him out of the chamber.

Hearing the page's yowls, Chiton broke into ill-natured laughter.

But his laughter died on his lips when, through the parting door, he saw the grim face of Vanand the High Escorpiun.

In response to the Lord Mayor's mumbled greeting, the great Escor only nodded. He was wearing the full panoply of his race and station: his stiff, domed hat of black velvet, folded at his lofty brow, bearing the emblem of the Eagle, lion of the air; and over a silken shirt of topaz color, gathered at the shoulders, he wore a slit tunic of heavy crimson. On the breast his star-wheel glowed like a stormy heaven with the somber topaz of the Escor and the shadowy garnets of his Capran positions. The tunic, exposing his powerful legs several inches above the knee, revealed the finest hose of crimson and gold.

And over all he wore a voluminous cloak of black with a lining of scarlet velvet; the cloak was clasped at his massive throat with a smoky topaz the size of a pigeon's egg.

Behind him were Zuban, an Escorpiun member of the Council of Mar, and Venand's uncle Sinapis, who wore, like his nephew, the golden thround of privilege.

Yet neither of the other two, for all their splendor, could match the splendor of the Minister of Mar. Where gems glittered on Vanand, the accouterments of his companions were pewter and silver, the traditional metals of Mar.

"Gentlemen"—with difficulty, Chiton rose from the depths of the soft, wide chair—"to what do I owe this pleasure?" Despite the smoothness of his greeting, Chiton the Crabba's fat face had a foreboding look.

Earla hovered at the door.

"Bring in the wines of Hades and Mars," said Chiton to Earla with an uneasy cordiality.

She nodded and disappeared, returning in an instant with a heavy pewter tray of red goblets and decanters.

"We are here on a matter of grave import," Vanand said heavily.

"Grave?" Chiton's voice was chaffing. "I hope you do not mean to announce someone's demise."

The Escor made a face of disgust, not deigning to answer.

"Will you not be seated?" Chiton said.

Zuban and Sinapis sat down, but Vanand, tossing his great cloak to Zuban, remained where he was.

With trembling hands, Earla poured out three goblets of artemisia, brewed from the Martian wormwood, the wine that only the Escors could drink without fear of poisoning. She then withdrew.

Chiton, smarting from Vanand's reception of his little joke, said more curtly, "Are you here on a matter of state? Surely that could be brought up in the Council Hall."

"Your tone is not hospitable," Vanand said coldly. "It is a matter both personal and political. It is your traitorous performance, your breach of honor regarding the Lady Dione—my promised wife." He added the last words solemnly.

"Traitorous? Breach?" Chiton spluttered, sitting forward in his chair. "Surely the hand of my niece is mine to bestow."

"Not," Vanand thundered, "when you had given her to me. And not when it affects the state of Mar. I have been informed, in the most roundabout fashion, of your encouragement of the Capran Monoceros."

"This is more than a private matter now," Zuban commented. "The union of your niece with Erde could place us in Erden power."

"And we are leaving aside," Sinapis said angrily, "the matter of our family honor . . . the choosing of an inferior being for your niece's husband. The blood of the ancient star kings pulses through my nephew's veins. And yet you mean to mate her to a barbarian!"

"The Crown Prince Monoceros can hardly be described as a 'barbarian'!" Chiton cried.

"His lands are worked by slaves," Vanand persisted, "and his dearest joy is the slaying of every beast that breathes!"

Chiton returned ironically, "I have never known you to take such a noble stance before. And the blood of 'barbarians' mingles with your own royal strain." The Crabba stared pointedly at the Capran garnets on Vanand's star-wheel.

The big Escor was fuming.

The Councilman Zuban held up his strong, oval hand, the hand with the shape of Vanand's and Sinapis's. "Barbarian or no"—his voice was hard as steel—"both the family honor of Vanand and the primacy of Mar have been assaulted by your countenancing Monoceros." Zuban put down his goblet hard upon the stone table before him; it made a snicking sound as final as his words.

"When my niece Dione is Princess, living in the castle of the Capran, wherein will lie a threat to Mar?"

Vanand, still pacing the bloodstone floor, cried out, "You muddleheaded fool! Monoceros will not place a crown on her head for love! She will then be in the slant-eyed goat's sole power. And you will see the Erden trampling over Mar—seizing the Council's power, gaining supremacy over the sea, the sea whose wealth and loveliness the Erden have ever lusted for. He will lead us by the noses back to serfdom, and into a feudal destiny!"

The rage of the big Escor had blazed to such a height that Zuban intervened. Zuban could not forget the madness of Vanand's father.

More quietly, the Councilman said to Chiton, "Do you believe that in this alliance there will be peace?"

"Of course I believe it!" Chiton replied with vigor. "Do you think that I would sell my kinswoman for a jeweled crown?"

There was an awkward silence. Then Vanand returned boldly, "That is exactly what I think, milord."

The Crabba now was puffed with ire.

Calmly, Vanand continued, "This is a matter to be discussed before the Council. I shall take it up there, at a special convening."

"A special convening," Chiton repeated. "Only the Lord Mayor of Mar can call a special convening."

Zuban said, "I think, milord, you will find that there is a new and growing majority in the Council."

"What do you mean?"

"He means," said Vanand, "that the frost of age upon your hair has also, apparently, shriveled your brain. The Council may try to unseat you."

Chiton was shaking so with rage that he was speechless.

Then, at last, he said in a choking voice, "How dare you? How dare you?"

Sinapis said in his quieter tone, "You are as unfit to rule the Council as you are to arrange the fate of Lady Dione. Why, even this afternoon, my nephew tells me . . ."

"What about this afternoon?"

Vanand cut in. "Your niece was exchanging hot glances with a gypsy on the public canal."

"You dare!" bellowed the Crabba. "You dare! When my niece the Lady Dione was properly accompanied by her waiting-woman? You dare to slur her name?"

"I do not slur the lady's name," Vanand protested. "I only say what I saw with my own sight."

"Earla!" Chiton shouted. "Earla!" Turning to the Escors, he said, "We shall see if your words are so."

The trembling Bole reentered.

The Crabba repeated to her the charges of Vanand. "Did you see her look in such a way at the gypsy?" the Crabba asked.

Not daring to meet the eyes of the great Escor, the Bole said calmly, "Why, no, milord, I saw no such thing. The Lady Dione was in my keeping and would not have been permitted to look so." So much for His Arrogance, she thought with spite.

Chiton turned and stared at Vanand. "So, you are lying, my friend."

Vanand said coldly, "Your servant is lying. I saw."

"Get out of my house!" The Crabba pointed to the massive chamber door. "Get out of my presence now, and take your lethal companions!"

The big Escor snatched his splendid cloak from the hands of Zuban and threw it around his shoulders with a swirling gesture. As he clasped the huge topaz clasp, as large as a pigeon's egg and as dark as the clouds of a stormy twilight sky, he repeated to Chiton, "We shall meet in the Council, milord."

Without further speech, he strode from the chamber, followed by the silent Zuban and Sinapis, his kinsman.

As the Bole was opening the massive entrance door, Vanand asked, "Why did you lie to him?"

"I lied not. The Lady Dione thinks of no one but the Prince Monoceros. How could she have looked with favor on a gypsy?"

"If you were a man," Vanand retorted, "I would slay

you for less. And you are too old to be given to the guards for their pleasure. But go cautiously, Bole. I shall not forget."

And the Escor strode from the Lord Mayor's palace, followed by his companions.

On the shadowy stairs at the end of the palace square, near the Lady Dione's water garden, an ancient beggar was crouching.

As they passed Vanand said carelessly, "Drive him away, Zuban."

But his Uncle Sinapis, annoyed at Vanand's threat to the servant and stung, perhaps, by his earlier references to age, intervened. "Why?" Sinapis demanded. "He is old and can do no harm. Throw him some pewter, Zuban."

Zuban complied. The mendicant cried out his feeble thanks in Marin. But none of the Escors noted that he was not a Marin or saw the keenness of the crystal eyes that stared at them from inside the tattered hood.

CHAPTER 7

Eleven-dark, the hour of the Waetergyt, was late for Marin women of high degree to wander in their gardens.

But the water garden of Dione of Mar was as private as a dressing room, its only door being the one that led directly to her chambers. The gate upon the square was always firmly locked but for the rare occasions when workmen came to tend the pools or wash the statues, prune the water vines, or, with a healer of the beasts, attend an ailing creature.

The magical enclosure, devised by Dione's late grandsire, an inventive High Escor, was a grotto domed in glasses stained the hues of Mar, thick with massy water vines.

Only the unmanned minstrel Volan and her cousin Desmos accompanied Dione into the water garden; the matter-of-fact voice of Earla discomfited the fish, and somehow her presence jarred the delicate balance of the grotto.

Therefore, when the Bole complained of the dim and moisture of the garden, saying the damp brought an aching to her bones, Dione did not demur; she was happy enough to be alone there, or with the sensitive Volan, whose narrow songs and Brisemarin ways were so attuned to her nerves.

And this eleven-dark Volan was with the Marin, seated on a chair of Celtic marble made like the chariot of Ler, the Irish emperor of the sea. The Brisemarin lightly strummed his cithara, crooning the "Song of Distant Wind" for his friend the Marin.

When the last, sad, silvery strains had died away, the Lady Dione smiled her thanks to Volan. But something in his mutable face aroused her wondering. How easily he could be read! she reflected. His face was like a silver mirror reflecting countless moods and things: sometimes the sudden wings of merry thoughts, at others, somber waves of feelings, like the washing over sands of twilight seas.

"What is it, friend?" she asked gently, turning with reluctance from her dreams of the man from the place of magic. "You seem as tightly drawn as the string of a bow this night."

"Do I, my lady?" With careful casualness, Volan looked down at his instrument and began to tune the strings.

"Come, come, Volan. Your harp does not need tuning. You adjusted it a quarter-hour gone." There was a smile in the Marin's voice, but a persistent undercurrent, too, the Brisemarin knew well—the obdurate insistence of her rising Bole.

Volan looked up to meet her dreaming eyes, and in the dusky light she could see his dancing with nervous mischief. Again, she wondered what was afoot. But disliking to press him, Dione was silent and wandered away to the little coral bed beyond him, where the gem-like fish were flashing to and fro.

She thought she heard an alien, rasping sound, a sound like the scraping of the gate that led onto the square. Impossible! The gate had been latched for many circles, so long, in point of fact, that when the healer had last entered to medicate the fish, the opening of it had taken two workmen's strength. How could it open now—and by whose hand?

Apprehensively, Dione exclaimed, "Volan!" But, astounded, she saw that the boy had disappeared. How could he leave her to face this peril alone?

A chill of terror ran like some dread mercury along her veins: there was the sound again. "Volan," she gasped, but her fear had made her call so weak that it echoed like a murmur in her ears.

She was about to flee into the door that led up to her chambers when she heard the deep, gentle voice pronounce her name, and, amazed, she saw the tall, hooded figure step into the water garden, approaching her down the path of marble forms.

"Who are you?" Dione cried out, relieved to note that now her speech was clear again, imperious.

"Do not fear me, lady," said the hooded man in the soft Marin of the Peisun. He sounded very old. "I am a friend of Fahne." He had paused by a statue of Triton, the god that blew, forever soundless, upon his shell-encrusted horn.

Dione could feel her pulse beating like trapped birds in her ears. Fahne! Fahne—the sorcerer from Erde.

Heartened by the kindly tone and tentative manner of the person in the tattered robe, and noting that its color was that of her Peisun race, the people seldom violent, Dione said, "Come and be seated, stranger."

The man moved forward, she noted now, with a vigorous motion. He stood by a little bench bedighted with shells, waiting for her to sit down. When she did so, he sank down beside her. There was something in him, she thought, something in him young and full of the trembling hardness that was passion leashed—the eager steed reined in that quivered for the chase; the waiting of the taut-drawn bow.

She felt his star-wheel must contain the quicksand of the horsemen of Sabbia; the piercing horn of the slant-eyed Capra that even in the hated Monoceros could prick her with peculiar longing; the enchanted stillness of the Seeing Escor; the Maeden with the crystal sight. Even the winged perception of a Twisan of Brise, akin to Volan's!

She knew he was not old.

And in a trembling, shy way, she repeated his words: "You are a friend of Fahne's."

It seemed to her heated fancy that she had pronounced the name with tenderness, and that the stranger felt it, too; his hood began to quiver almost imperceptibly. How in tune he is! she thought. Surely he *is* a Peisun.

"You must be very close to him." Apparently, this had been the last thing he expected, for his hooded head snapped up, as if in great surprise, and now Dione glimpsed the keenness of his stare.

"Peisun are always unexpected," she heard the soft voice say with muffled humor. "Why, my lady, must we be?"

She hesitated, then painfully, afraid of her own boldness, answered, "Because you are so alike."

"So alike?" he said in a thickened, excited tone, and Dione, who seemed aware for some mysterious reason of each quiver of his sleeves, saw now that the very cloth above his breast was moving with the heightened beating of his heart. The stranger moved a fraction nearer to the Marin on the little bench.

"Yes." She looked up at his shadowed face, and he stared hard upon her heart-shaped little face, as smooth and white as the lilies of the pools; her small, petal-like mouth, with its brief upper lip—it looked, the hooded stranger was thinking in his fevered delight, as if it had been stung by the sweetest golden bees, the little mouth was so delicately pillowed out. He longed to press it inward with his own.

And her eyes! Never in all his dreams had the stranger seen such wide softness, such openness of longing. Her mouth and eyes, he felt, were like the flowers widening to light that made such an enchantment of his land of infancy.

"The land of infancy," he said aloud, "the fountain in the center of my garden of the self."

Astonished at this lyric outburst from the tattered Peisun, Dione stared at him, speechless.

"Your grotto is *temenos*," he said then with quiet urgency, "like the ancients' holy sanctuary, the hallowed place that gives you strength."

Weakly, she asked, "How do you know these things of me? Who are you?"

"The courier of him who loves you," he answered in a muffled voice. "He, who could not reach you through the guard, and who is known to the High Escors, sent me in the raiment of a mendicant to seek out his hope."

Her heart was beating so that Dione's reply had a throbbing tone. "But how did you get in?" When he did not answer, she said, "Volan! My minstrel!"

She thought of this a moment, then added tenderly,

"Volan and your . . . friend are known to one another, then. I might have guessed. The singer is as near to me as my very flesh. He said that he would help me," she concluded, half to herself.

"Are you . . . his brother?" Dione asked then.

"Why do you feel that?" He sounded as if he knew the answer well, but it appeared that to make her say it would give him an excruciating pleasure. All this Dione could read into his brief words.

So she told him then of what she had intuited of his star-wheel a short time before, of the qualities in him that sang at once of a brindling of Sabbia and Mar, of Brise and the land of Erde.

"You are a sorceress of questioned birth," the stranger commented.

"Why, that is what Volan . . ."

"Yes. The boy with dappled hair knows, too. Your web of wheeling stars has given you the sight his wheel gave to my friend."

Then all at once Dione felt an overpowering emotion she could not comprehend: a leaning of her flesh unto the stranger, as if a mighty wind drew at the feather she had become, pulling, pulling her helpless body into the tunnel of his being.

And she realized that, in her dualistic fashion, all the while they held their low converse, her glances had taken in his breadth and strength, unlikely for a ragged man of many years. His hands, she saw quite clearly now, were ungloved, revealing themselves as the broad, long-fingered hands of a Maeden in his lusty prime. The shoulders below the cloak were firm, and the keen eyes were seen as dappled now when a sudden, rash movement of the stranger's head disturbed the hood.

Then Dione knew. A wave of rasping heat, an aching languor, clawed at her center, gathered itself into a quite unbearable burning, and began to flow in a manner she had never known and could not understand.

Hardly knowing what she did, the little Dione gave a mourning cry, like the cry of a small animal in pain, and leaning forward lay her head upon the knees of the hooded stranger, her soft mouth pressing many kisses on his strong, long-fingered hands. And in a kind of madness, with closed eyes, Dione saw before her inner-vision clouds of redness and fires of night as her tongue caressed the stranger's wrists and hands and arms.

With a groan that seemed to rend his very self, the man cried out her name quite loudly once, then softly, again and again, raising his hands to cradle her silken face; to lift it for his long, devouring kiss as his tattered hood fell away to show her his noble face below its tousled thatch of gold-brown hair, the hair of the Magic-Erden.

Breathless, she withdrew an instant from his kiss, but he was relentless, clasping her to him again and covering her mouth with his until she feared her lungs would burst for air.

Feeling her timid struggle, the sorcerer took his full mouth away from hers. Breathing like a man at the end of a grueling race, he managed to gasp out, "My love, my love! Forgive me. I am sorry. Have I hurt you, have I hurt you?"

With an anguish of tenderness, she heard his words tumble out with the eager openness of a child's. "No, no," she whispered, feeling all of a sudden a glorious power. This great, broad man, she thought with exultation, this man of knowledge and wisdom, this one with the air of command, has become so different in my arms. And she drew his hard face with its hollowed cheeks down to hers again, and she kissed him as his hands explored her silken shoulders and her arms, tracing the sweet arcs of her breasts, learning the frail concavity of her narrow waist, the grace with which it swelled on either side, so gradually, into that bewitching curve of slender hip.

And the touch of Dione studied the firm, hard splendor of the arms of Fahne; his muscular, vast expanse of torso; his leanness.

"You are like the oak, the quercus tree," she whispered shakily when she could speak again.

"I drown in you." His soft reply had almost the quaver of her own whisper. "I drown my book," he added in tender irony. Then, tucking her dark head between his hard-muscled arm and his sinewy chest, Fahne said in great solemnity, "You are the Lake of Life, where earth and heaven meet. When I looked into your eyes this afternoon, I knew that all my endless seeking was done; that forever and always, should I never have the blessed sight of you again, you would burn within me like a fire of green, and burn away my lust for any other."

Dione burrowed more deeply into the Erden's shoulder, having no words at that moment, content to feel the vibrating of his speech against the cheek that pressed itself against him.

"You treated me," she said at last, "when I was ill. Did you . . ."— she hesitated, in an agony of shyness— ". . . realize the . . . nature of my malady?"

"Yes. But I wish that you would say it so I might hear."

She felt her face flame. But obediently she answered, "I was . . . ill with . . . desire for you." Misreading his silence, she said quickly, "I am unwomanly to speak so." And she gazed up at him. She was touched to see that his eyes were wet.

He held her in a bruising grasp. "Unwomanly! Unwomanly!" he said in a voice of amazement. "You are . . . an angel to speak so." And he kissed her again, more hungrily than before.

"I told your nurse," he said then, "that your malady was the shadow of Vanand."

"Oh, do not name him!" she cried piteously.

He caressed her flowing hair. "But now," he said firmly, "there is another—this . . . Monoceros."

He recalled the words of the kindly looking Peisun in the inn: "They will rend her between them." And his arm tightened protectively around her small, vulnerable body.

"You will marry neither," he said with calm.

"You spoke of this to Earla?"

"Of course. And I told her I would return for you. Is she not your ally?"

"I had thought her to be," she answered bitterly. "Volan, now, is my only ally . . . in this house." A dim smile lit her small mouth, and she kissed the beating space below the sorcerer's neat ear. "For Earla lied; she did not tell me that you would return."

Hearing the desolation in her voice, the sorcerer held Dione nearer. "Use guile with her for the nonce," said Fahne. He added consolingly, "It will not be much longer —if, that is," he said in a beseeching tone, "you will consent to throw your lot in with a gypsy."

There was something wild and unbearably stirring in the name he called himself; in it she heard myrrh and samphire, the ivories and silk of the distant East, mysterious small bells and swarthy faces in a ring around an open flame.

"Life offers me no other way, that I can see," she answered solemnly. "I care not if our castle is a wagon or a barge or a cave; without you there is neither breath nor light nor hope for me."

Fahne gathered her close again and kissed her deeply. "I think," he said with gentle humor, "it will not be so primitive as that."

But now a nearby wheel of hours sounded its watery chime: twelve-dark, the time of Capra.

"I hate this hour," the little Marin whispered against the Erden's collarbone. He knew she was thinking of the dark Prince Monoceros.

"Never mind," he said softly, stroking the white silk of her bare arm, from which the gleaming sleeve, slit almost to the shoulder, had fallen away. "There will come a day when all the hours are sweet for us. But listen, now, my love, for soon I must be gone. Your uncle or your woman may seek you out. Volan has told me that the Mayor plans to take you soon to his house in Erdemar to receive Prince Monoceros."

Sadly, she nodded. Her uncle had decreed a tryst in the border-castle of Erdemar as a symbolic gesture of meeting the Capran halfway.

"This will be our hope," Fahne went on urgently. "When you are on the road to Erdemar, where the four roads meet before the Church of Stars, I shall come to take you away. You will feign illness and swoon; your woman and Volan will bear you to the church. From there you and I will flee to safety."

Dione looked up at him with new hope in her wide, dreamy eyes. "Can it be? You will take me from them, away with you?"

"It can be." With great reluctance now, the sorcerer arose, drawing up the small Marin with him. He towered above her, his craggy face solemn but exultant in the aqueous light of the domed garden, where the early autumn moonlight cast soft shades of green and rose, of blue and lilac, over them.

The colored shadows, thought Dione, gave the hour the character of a dream, bringing strange values to the sorcerer's tawny hair and dappled eyes that had in the depths of them the hues of Mar and Brise, of Sabbia and Erde. His Maeden pallor, darkened by years of wind and sun, reflected all the sea shades of the dome.

"I almost fear to take you from these splendors," he whispered somberly. "I fear that someday you will sicken for this loveliness, this colored garden where one seems to live inside sequestered waves, and know the quiet of the deepest sea."

The Marin moved nearer to the tall man in the tattered robe and put her slender arms around his body. Their length was just sufficient to circle him, and he was overcome with tender laughter. His great arms drew her close, so close their bodies promised to flow into each other.

Breathless, for his hold was like a vise, the Marin answered, "There is no loveliness for me but you."

He gave her one last desperate kiss. Twelve-dark was chiming now its last long bell and they could hear approaching the hesitant, light steps of the minstrel Volan.

Without releasing Dione, Fahne the sorcerer turned to greet the boy.

"Thank you, my friend," he said, smiling.

But the face of Volan, in the watery light, was tense. "You must make haste, milord Fahne! The Mayor approaches!"

Dione gasped. Her uncle had never before come into the water garden. "Could he know?" she cried to Volan.

"I know not, lady, but, oh, sire, make haste!" the boy said again to Fahne.

"To leave you is to tear away my skin," the sorcerer whispered in the little Marin's ear. "But you shall soon have word of me; and we shall meet in Erdemar."

"In Erdemar," she repeated, the tears coursing down her white face.

And she watched Fahne disappear into the darkness, just as the heavy steps of Chiton fell on the other path of forms and Dione began to frame an answer to his prying query.

CHAPTER 8

Monoceros, Prince of lower Erde, the land of Caprans, threw back his black, close-shaven head in its crown of steel and howled with raucous laughter. The crown was formed in the horns of an ibex goat.

"Good, good, very good, Mahar!" said Monoceros, and he clapped his young companion on the shoulder.

Mahar inclined his narrow head.

Monoceros had the look of an arrogant young stallion; his neat nostrils flared proudly and his pointed ears lay flat to his head in the manner of the Caprans. Over the ears his stubble was cut in a perfect square. His onyx eyes glittered and flicked to the other end of the quartz table, where his sister, the Princess Shira, sat among the women. She was staring into her flame-green goblet.

Mahar leaned to the Prince, whispered something.

Where Monoceros had the look of a stallion, his leaner confidante had the lines of a gazelle. There had in recent circles been strange whispers of Mahar, which the arrogant Prince, who prized his friend's quick mind and humor, would not allow.

Had not, the Prince reflected now, his friend proven again and again his manhood, between the thighs of whores and on the jousting fields and at the hunt? Monoceros smiled now, both at the jest of Mahar and at the memory of something his friend had said a night or two gone. "Women? They are all very well in their place. But why stay in their place so long when it takes but a moment to thrust them and empty?"

Mahar was a sensible man. Only the fools and women lingered over tales of love and fluttered up their eyes like slaughtered calves, showing only the eyeball whites, as the minstrels played their silly lays. Monoceros wondered idly what the fleshless Marin would expect.

55

He whispered his wondering into the flat ear of Mahar. "Expect? Nothing . . . she has no thrusting to compare."

Monoceros saw a glint of mischief in Mahar's malicious eyes. "She will run to your tether," added Mahar. "The Peisun are like children, next to Capran women."

Monoceros' hard glance returned to Shira. There was a pouting droop to her small, sensual mouth and her white lids covered her fiery eyes as she continued to gaze into her goblet of violet.

"Sister, sister!" Monoceros called. His guttural voice chafed the air. "Sister, why is your face so dark?"

Shira looked up, startled, her hot eyes meeting the cold ones of her brother.

"I am . . . not well," she answered in a husky voice.

"Not well!" Monoceros' comment rang like steel on steel. "Will you sicken before the joining feast?"

Shira did not reply. She tossed a crude smoke-garnet with a careless motion to the Bole musicians surrounding the end of the table.

The genial-eyed minstrels, touched with the smile of Aphrodite, the goddess of love, that made the Boles the musical folk of Erde, raised their horns and lutes. They began to dance.

Diverted, the prince nodded his close-shaven head in time to the music, reminiscent of the heavy sound of the steeds the warriors rode into battle.

The horns were low but nasal, hardly softer than the earthen's hunting blasts; the thick strings of the lutes, made of ibex gut, gave forth a deep and throaty twang. The pallid face of Monoceros had darkened; he had drunk a good deal of mead, Shira reflected.

She raised her glass of violet; her eyes were blank when they met the hostile eyes of Mahar.

What was there in that snake that angered her so? Perhaps he had learned of Fahne! Shira's blunt fingers trembled as she lifted her goblet again to her sensual lips. Perhaps he knew that she had thrown herself almost at the feet of the Maeden that mad spring night before the wagon of minstrels had left on its northern journey.

Fahne. As Shira soundlessly said the name, a weakness washed her shapely arms and she could feel the star-wheel on her breast almost leap with the forceful pounding of her heart. He was like no other man, she mused—elusive and withdrawn, he seemed to be forever listening to unheard voices, speaking quietly to the servants' hounds, which, to Shira's annoyance, always cowered back from her, showing their dagger-like teeth in a growl.

"His very strangeness makes a slave of me," she murmured, finding that her words had been aloud.

Shira's face flooded with shame as her brother questioned, "What are you saying, sister?"

The Princess gave an unintelligible reply, lost in a sudden swell of music, and turned her thoughts again to Fahne, the sorcerer from the place of magic. Yes, his very strangeness lent a spice no other man had ever had—the sharp sweetness of a kind of alien mead she longed to roll around her seeking tongue. It made her long for him almost beyond enduring. Well, she was not defeated; she would find him again someday.

And he would raise her thin kid gown and see her smooth, pearly nakedness, shining as the very moonstone itself, and bite her breasts until they bled and then finally enter her.

Mahar seemed to read her thoughts; he lowered his oblique black eyes to the shining table and put his fingers to his mouth. Mahar's gaze lingered on her moist red lips, watching them quiver. His hard eyes dropped to her perfect breasts, plainly outlined by the thin green kid.

He watched Monoceros watching him. By Chronos, it is a child's game to fool them! thought Mahar. Continuing the game, he said to Monoceros, "The Princess is comely, right enough."

"Do you want her?" the Prince countered in a low tone. "The price is marriage."

"A price too high," Mahar said carelessly, and Monoceros' black brows drew together.

"Someday you'll go too far, my friend," he said coldly, but Mahar laid a soothing hand upon his heavy forearm The Prince, for no reason he could name, felt a sudden quiet, as he always did when his companion touched him so.

Then, seeing the ironic eye of the lute player, Mahar removed his hand. He felt his loins start beating with desire and knew the awful swelling of his need, glad that he had worn this full robe tonight above his skin-tight breeches. The pressure of the leather was agonizing.

Soon he would go seek out a kitchen jade to render the

caress he craved. The serfs could not talk back, Mahar
reflected cynically.

"I beg your leave to retire," Shira declared suddenly.

"Retire?" her brother repeated. "Why, it is only nine,
the hour of the Ramm! This is no hour to retire and leave
our guests."

The nations' clocks had hours that were named for the
various star-races, and followed the position of the races
on heaven's wheel. Therefore, the heavenly position of the
Sabbians' Ramm was nine upon the earthly clocks, followed by the Marin's Peisun at ten, the Brisen's Waetergyt
at eleven, the Erden's Capra at twelve, and so on around
the dial.

"Very well." Shira nodded her sleek black head and
shrugged. Motionless, she stared at Monoceros, her face,
over the flame-green of her high-necked gown, so pale it
shone like the lances of the Titans.

All at once, however, every member of the company
stopped in place: the clang of mailed feet, with an urgent
rhythm, was heard in the corridor. The Prince held up his
blunt, square hand for silence. The horns and lutes died
and Shira abandoned the notion of rising.

The double doors of lead, beaten with the sigil of the
Ziege, the Capran goat, were parting. Between the doors
stood an ancient man with long, coarse hair in ragged
curls the color of trodden snow. He was wearing a
voluminous robe sewn of the coats of hooved creatures.
His gray face was stern and in his night-black eyes, deeper
than the other Erden's, was a look of consternation.

Beside him, in armor the hue of pewter, stood a man of
magnificent height, impassive as a stone. On his face a
livid scar zigzagged from chin to brow. Below his brief
gray shaggy tunic was an immense codpiece of armor.

The diners murmured and the servants whispered behind their blunt-fingered hands. "Gonu, the highest Pfarrer.
Polyg."

The two men in the doorway bowed to Monoceros.
"Polyg," said the Prince. "Gonu. Enter."

As the two moved forward, the old man taking short,
mincing steps, the Prince asked, "And what is your business?"

Gonu was silent, but Polyg answered in his clipped,
metallic tone, "We ask a private audience with Your Highness."

Monoceros said brusquely to the room at large, "Leave me." But to Mahar he added, "Stay."

Polyg raised his jagged brows; his hard eyes locked with Monoceros'.

Zune, Prince Monoceros' directing slave and bodyguard, lingered. The others were taking their leave, their rough-soled buckskin slippers shuffling on the crude granite floor.

"Leave me, Zune," said Monoceros. "Mahar will serve."

The slave inclined his shaven bullethead and took six backward steps. Then he, too, was gone; the vast entrance doors of tarnished lead rang shut.

The Prince waved at vacant chairs. "Sit down. A drink?"

Polyg the warrior poured himself a heavy glass of mead; Gonu the priest shook his ancient head.

"Well, what is it?" Monoceros, through long habit, had turned to Polyg, his warrior chief.

"This," said Polyg bluntly, and he thrust into Monoceros' hand a scroll of vellum tied with green, vellum that the prince recognized as a substance of Mar, made from weeds of the sea.

Opening the greenish scroll, Monoceros let his onyx eyes flick down the ornately written message to the seal at the bottom, the seal of the Escorpiun, or Thround, that lethal race of Mar. The signature was black and many-legged and sinister, like the scorpion that symbolized the race.

"Vanand," the Prince repeated sourly. Then he laughed his metallic laugh, which had no amusement. "He challenges me. And the Marin know fighting as I know . . . verse."

Polyg the warrior did not smile, and the priest Gonu trembled. Polyg the warrior chief commented, "The Escors aren't like the other Marin, you know. Their vengeance is death."

"You are saying that this rash fool can hurt *me?*" Monoceros demanded.

"I am," Polyg returned.

Monoceros was silent a moment. Then he asked, "How did you get this scroll, Polyg?"

"I found my lieutenant on the way to you. He had gotten it from an underCrabba scuttling toward the moat."

The Prince laughed aloud at the contemptuous words of the stately Polyg describing the Crabba, his star-opposite.

"Well, then, my friend," said Monoceros, "I will meet Vanand as he asks. I'd like to unseat this impudent bastard."

"I . . . I believe it would be impolitic, messire."

Timidly Gonu had spoken. Monoceros turned to him, amazed. "What are you doing here, anyway? Acting the statesman?" he demanded in a scathing tone. "Why don't you attend to your own business—nourishing the peasants' legends—and leave the men's business to us?"

The old priest's gray face darkened with humiliation. But doggedly he continued: "The people of Mar will not look kindly on the slaying of their Minister."

"The people of Mar can look any way they please when I have wed the Lady Dione," the Prince retorted coldly.

Gonu's deep, ironic eyes rested on the face of Monoceros. "The King of Erde has always kept the peace between our peoples."

"The King is dying. He lies without sense or thought upstairs, waiting for the darkness of the end."

Gonu the Pfarrer bowed his head, saying nothing.

Monoceros glanced at Polyg, who raised his heavy, jagged brows and shrugged.

"Why have you come with Polyg?" the Prince snapped at Gonu.

The old priest raised his shaggy head and looked at Monoceros. "Last night in sleep I saw the truth of all my trauminitions."

The Prince snorted at the fanciful word; the Pfarren saw, they claimed, by dream-intuition. It was a word that had maddened the Prince ere now—more like to wine-dreams, for all their protestations of abstinence . . . or vaporings of women!

"Well? Get on with it."

Gonu hesitated. "I have seen a terrible thing, a thing that galls my tongue to say."

"What have you seen?" the Prince cried.

"A darkness in the sky, where always the sun has shone, above the point where four roads meet near the Church of Stars in Erdemar."

"The trysting-point of Marin and Erden trains," Polyg said slowly.

Monoceros held up his blunt hand, with its club-like thumb, for silence. "Go on," he said to the priest.

"I saw the frail form of the Lady Dione, falling, and delivered into the hands of monks. And then . . ."

"What care I of the Lady Dione?" Monoceros interjected. "What, then?"

"I saw you slain, sire—slain by the hand of Vanand."

"What is this babble?" Monoceros turned to Polyg. "Can any man unhorse me?"

"It seems laughable, sire," said Polyg. "And yet . . ." He paused, his scarred visage solemn.

"Do you mean to tell me you believe these tales . . . these dreams?"

Polyg looked uneasy. "Never, sire. Yet a kinsman of my orderly in Mar, a Crabba who imports implements of steel, has remarked that many weapons have remained in Mar. And ere this they had been dispatched to Erde and Sabbia."

Monoceros rubbed his hard jaw with his blunt hand, looking thoughtful. "So?"

"And Vanand, my informant said, is forming allies with an evil-looking band of Escors," Polyg added.

"You think we should go to Erdemar armed?" the Prince asked Polyg.

"I do, sire."

"No!" The thin voice of Gonu startled them. The Prince was too amazed at his temerity for an instant to speak. Then his black brows drew together over his hard, flat, slanting eyes and he rose, thundering, "How dare you take this posture with the crown?"

The old priest said stubbornly, "The King wears the crown."

His onyx eyes flashing with anger, Monoceros returned, "I have said the old King is dying. He has countenanced you too long. Be careful; the new King may not."

Summoning all his courage, Gonu said relentlessly, "What if the Escors come only as seconds to Vanand, and not as a band of lords of war?"

" 'If'?" bellowed Monoceros. "The women speak of 'if.' A warrior takes no chances. Polyg?" He turned to his chief.

"I think you are right, messire. We should be ready."

"So be it," said Monoceros. "Arm troops to see me to Erdemar."

Polyg stood and saluted.

A mournful sigh escaped the withered mouth of Gonu the Pfarrer. The dark hour of the Goat had struck, dyed the color of death, the ending of the light.

CHAPTER 9

Twelve-dark, the hour of the Capra, reverberated from the many towers over Mar as Ocimum, captain of the Marin guard, led his lieutenants down the escalade to the motley barge of travelers.

The captain, catching sight of the bizarre figure on the deck, stopped dead. "Prince of darkness, madness has overtaken one," Ocimum muttered to the red-clad Escor behind him.

For there, in the light of the ripening moon, they saw an agile Brisen, in raiment as yellow as his flying hair, cartwheeling like a whirl of wind and loudly counting to himself.

"An acrobat," the second Escor said foolishly.

"I know, you dunderhead," spat Ocimum. "But whirling at this hour, all alone, and talking to himself?"

Cat-like, Gemelle had landed on his stockinged feet, and called out amiably to the guards, "Good evening, gentlemen." He made a mocking bow to them, examining them with his pale-blue, dancing eyes. "How can I serve you?"

Heavily, the captain sprang aboard, his scarlet escort grunting after. "For whose amusement do you perform?" Ocimum asked suspiciously. The fellow must be drunk, he thought.

"For mine only, and the moon's." Gemelle laughed. "I keep my limbs in tune, for Brise," he said more soberly.

"You are going to Brise?"

"Yes, Captain. We pole away as soon as my . . . companions return from the inn."

One of the Escors had wandered away and was trying to see into the cabin.

"Where is your . . . leader, Fahne?" Ocimum rapped out.

Without an instant's hesitation, the Brisen replied, "Why, carousing with his fellows at the inn, my captain."

Ocimum did not care for the alien's tone. Looks as if a puff of wind would blow him down, the Escor concluded with contempt.

"Are you not aware of the curfew in Mar, Brisen?" It was the third Escor who snapped the question.

"Curfew, messire?" Gemelle inquired with innocent respect. "Why, no, messire. We are but strangers to the city of Mar."

"Who is in . . . command," asked Ocimum, "in the absence of this . . . Fahne?"

"I am, I suppose, my captain." Again Ocimum chafed at the Brisen's air of subtle insolence.

"Chiton, the Lord Mayor of Mar," said Ocimum, "has ordered your barge from the city. You are to leave at once."

Gemelle looked at him with surprise. "At once?"

Ocimum nodded grimly.

"As soon as my fellows return . . ." the Brisen began.

"And when will that be, Brisen?"

"Why, momently, messire . . . momently," Gemelle said, laboring to keep the panic from his voice.

Capra struck the quarter, and the rippling chimes echoed along the black canals, with their beads of lantern light. The Brisen wondered uneasily what was keeping Fahne. If the Escors saw him emerging from the plaza of Dione . . .

Then, unbelieving, he heard the unmistakable baritone of Veris, raised in drunken song, proceeding from the direction of The Cup and Crescent. And blending with Veris' was the voice of Fahne—Fahne, who never took a more than modest swallow!

With difficulty, Gemelle the Brisen controlled his rising laughter. When he had mastered his lungs, he said calmly to the Escors, "I believe those are my companions."

The rowdy singing was louder now, and as they came into the light, Gemelle saw that Veris and the sorcerer bore on their broad backs the limp body of Kaus the Sabbian.

"The Sabbian has taken a little wine," Ocimum commented sourly. Raising his voice, he called, "Ho, gypsies! Quit that racket. You will rouse the town!"

Fahne and the Bole, staggering under the weight of Kaus, looked up with fuddled eyes.

"We ask your pardon, Captain." Fahne's speech was so thick that the Brisen could hardly make out the words. "We were making music for Mar."

"You will make music in the dungeon if you do not be still," said Ocimum. "Come aboard."

Gemelle had sprung forward to assist. Stumbling and laughing, Fahne dragged the unconscious form of Kaus onto the barge. Overcome with fresh paroxysms, Veris narrowly missed falling into the canal.

"Allez-oup," Gemelle cackled, as he and the sorcerer drew the stolid Veris onto the deck.

"Welcome, Captain." Fahne smiled at Ocimum, swaying on his strong, slender legs like a young tree in a gale.

"Silence!" The chief Escor glared at the sorcerer. "You are the leader of these . . . gypsies?"

"Indeed, messire." Fahne smiled a vacuous smile and tugged at a forelock of his thick golden-brown hair.

"You are to leave the city at once," said Ocimum in an imperious manner. "It has been decreed by Chiton, Lord Mayor of Mar."

"The Lord Mayor himself!" Veris exclaimed, satirizing terror.

"Enough!" Ocimum had had his fill of the jesting varlets. "Be gone, and do not let the dawn light shine on you in Mar."

With one last look at Fahne, the captain signaled to his red-clad escort and leaped upon the escalade.

"At once, messire!" With great solemnity Veris saluted the glowering Escors. Ocimum hesitated; he seemed about to board again.

But Giedi the Capran, who had heard the commotion and hurried from the cabin, had already begun to pole the barge toward the exitway from Mar.

"I think we have seen the last of them," said Ocimum's lieutenant; his hard green gaze followed the barge downstream.

"For their own skins' sake that had better be so," the captain returned. "I know not why, but Chiton and Vanand are hot against Fahne and his gypsies. The only thing they see eye to eye on these days," he added with bitter humor.

"I have heard it said that the Maeden are more abstemious than the sorcerer appeared," the third Escor commented. He sounded puzzled.

Ocimum stared suspiciously after the parting boat. "And so have I, my lad. So have I." He turned and peered at the green dimming lanterns of The Cup and Crescent. "The landlord has not yet gone. Let us have a word with him."

"Gods," said Gemelle, wiping the nervous dew of sweat from his pallid brow as the Capran poled them toward the harbor. "You appeared like the ancient *deus ex machina*," he said to Fahne. "I could fairly hear the creaking of the pulleys as you descended. How did you lose your guise with such speed?"

The sorcerer, staring eastward absently, recalled himself and answered, smiling, "I learned from you, my friend, these many circling years. You have instructed me well in chameleon ways."

They were alone now with Giedi on the deck; Veris had borne the limp Kaus to the cabin, where they were snoring soundly among the others.

The deep night had an edge of autumn chill: Gemelle the Brisen sniffed it gratefully, picturing the mountain of his homeland and the lilac-shadowed snow, the beauty of the Lady Shabatu.

At last he said to Fahne, "Then you are coming with us to Brise?"

The blue-clad sorcerer shook his stately head. "In the harbor I will take ship to the inlet of Erdemar."

"Erdemar? And what of . . . the little Marin?"

"That is where we shall meet," the tall man said quietly.

"Are you certain of this course, my friend?" The slender Brisen studied the man at his side.

"Quite certain, Gemelle." Fahne's reply was solemn. Then he said, more lightly, "For a pledge, I have left her a star."

Gemelle heard him with puzzlement, but he was silent for a time as the dark-windowed palaces of Mar slid by in the moist and peaceful dark; at intervals they passed below an arched stone bridge that roofed them for the nonce from the gentle drizzle.

"The small rain is like a wide caress," Fahne said to Gemelle the Brisen in a low voice, and they listened to the splash of the Capran's slowly plowing pole. The sorcerer spoke again. "I would have liked to linger one night more in this silver place."

The sorcerer's deep voice was blurred with pain, and Gemelle, because of his own passion for Shabatu, felt his pity stir. He laid a narrow hand on the sorcerer's arm.

"When shall we meet again?" he asked softly.

"When the time comes, Gemelle." And the Brisen, who knew of old the shadowed manner of Fahne's speech, accepted his answer.

They were nearing the harbor now; excitement beat through the veins of the motion-loving Brisen. He could smell the sea beyond. Soon they would behold the towers of Mar against the dark gray skies—tall and sharp as auger shells, the towers that shone silver in the day, but now, by night, were mere black shapes half-lit by the lanterns of the many boats and smaller ships riding at anchor.

He glanced again at Fahne: the sorcerer stood straight and still as an oak tree in a windless forest, staring back at Mar. With affection, Gemelle remembered their circles together, and the first day of their meeting, long ago.

Seven years, seven full turnings of the Great Wheel of the Stars, had intervened since that drowsy afternoon. It had been, like now, the month called Circle of Yod, or the Maeden. But there had been no coolness then, or silver drizzle, or lapping sound of quiet water. For they had been in lower Erde.

Hermes, the winged-footed god! Gemelle said silently. His pallid, moisture-loving Brisen skin had almost shriveled in the oppressive heat as the minstrels' wagon jogged the rutted, dry, brown, dusty road to the castle.

Kaus the Sabbian, he remembered, not Veris, had been with him then, and Kaus, of course, soaked up the heat like a lizard of the sands! Letting his mind drift backward now, Gemelle could hear again quite clearly the clopping of the *Erdenpferd* upon that dusty road.

Erdenpferd! Even now the clumsy Erden name for horses amused the Brisen, born to the precision of the courtly tongue. And the country had been like the horses' name, to him—heavy and dry, plain as the black bread the serfs had shared with them; the Erden language clopping like the hooves of the patient mare.

The troupe had been summoned to the castle of Icorn the King of lower Erde to play before his heirs, young Monoceros and Princess Shira.

Gemelle recalled the words of the hot-eyed Kaus that day: "I have heard it even in the fields that the Princess has a lusty nature. The King would see her soon wed. And I would see her bedded, friend." Kaus' turquoise eyes had glittered with anticipation.

Kaus the Sabbian, Gemelle had reflected sourly, would make love to anyone, star-race or comeliness no object. He himself, in his infrequent lusting, moved only toward the fragile Brisen women, or the vivid Sabbians, with their flaming hair and laughing manner. Gemelle the Brisen found no temptation in the Erden women, and he longed for Brisen heights and the cities of Sabbia.

Therefore, he had merely grunted in reply to Kaus that afternoon, and then complained, shading his blue eyes from the sun, "I can endure this climate no longer. It has none of the delights that leaven Sabbia."

And then, quite suddenly, they saw the tall, blue-clad figure before them, trudging patiently forward at a steady pace in the unremitting sun.

Gemelle blinked. "I saw him not before."

"Nor I." Kaus stared at the strong, slender man. "He must have emerged from the thicket."

And the sun wheeled redly in the Brisen's eyes as he examined the stranger. "A Maeden," he said to Kaus before his heat-drained strength began to fail him wholly and he fell unconscious from the wagon to the dusty road.

When Gemelle the Brisen had awakened, he found himself in the wagon's rear, among the Sabbian's implements of magic. And staring down into his eyes, blurred from sweat and weakness, were the lucid eyes of the Maeden.

But their color, instead of the blue-gray of the race, was hazel; shining in their crystal depths were the colors and wisdom of other lands—the quicksand of the Sabbian Kani, the dark horns of the Caprans of his country; even the mordant lore of the Escorpiuns, and the winged look of the Brisen that was Gemelle's own heritage.

The man with the strange, magnetic eyes smiled at the

Brisen. "How do you fare now, friend?" he asked in a deep, bell-like voice. He spoke precise and perfect premier-Brisen, to the amazement of Gemelle. Generally only the Brisen of his own race were so proficient at tongues.

His surprise must have shown on his wet, pallid face, for the Maeden laughed. "You will be thinking deeply of phenomena on your very deathbed," the stranger said, but there was no sting, only understanding and amusement in his words.

Gemelle smiled weakly in answer. He made as if to sit up. "Not so soon," the stranger cautioned. "The sun has greatly weakened you. Your pulse still races like a captured bird."

The Brisen lay down again. "You are a healer?"

"My name is Fahne. Healing is one of my trades," the man answered evasively.

And the Brisen saw then the unique sigil on a heavy pewter chain about his sinewy neck—the caduceus of Hermes, rod of all wisdom. But it was a caduceus like none the Brisen, Hermes-ruled himself, had ever seen: on the medallion's center, surmounting the customary entwining serpents held by winged hands, was a six-pointed crystal star of magic, the Seal of Solomon.

The stranger Fahne put a broad, long-fingered hand—the healer's hand—on the Brisen's forehead. "That is better," he said quietly.

And Gemelle had fallen fast asleep, to see, perhaps to dream of, lilac-shadowed snow that lay on the high, clean peaks of the mountains of Brise. And as he dreamed, or lay in his pleasant trance, the Brisen had known a coolness of brow and limb he had not known for countless circles.

That had been his first meeting with his friend the sorcerer. As the barge drew now into the Marin harbor, Gemelle recalled the rest of their stay in lower Erde.

Before that afternoon had waned, he had engaged the sorcerer in their band. Gemelle smiled and glanced at Fahne, who still stood unmoving while the barge breasted the stronger waters of the bay. He had directed Fahne, only to find a few months later that they all needed Fahne's direction.

How he had enchanted Princess Shira! Her mooning had set the very peasants of the field to snickering. And Fahne would have none of her, Gemelle remembered, though at last the lustful Kaus—or so he said—had paid profitable visits to her chamber.

Well, Gemelle thought darkly, now he was fairly caught. The Brisen had never seen such yearning on his companion's face—or on that of any man, for the matter of that. He wished them well, the sorcerer and the little Marin, although he could not, for his life, see how they could ever live in peace. The very lands of Mar and Erde conspired against them, with Vanand of Mar and Monoceros of Erde both vying for her hand. . . .

Sadly, the Brisen gave it up. Sighing, he shook his yellow head and inquired of Fahne, "You have told the others?"

The sorcerer turned his stately head and nodded. Gemelle was pained to see that his dappled eyes were wet. "I have," he said to the Brisen. "Soon I must disembark and say farewell."

"Fahne," the Brisen said urgently, "there is still time."

"Time?" The mittel-Erden raised ironic brows.

"Time to alter your course."

Swift anger fired the sorcerer; then he smiled forgiveness at Gemelle. "The course is laid, dear friend. I know I cannot make you understand, with your limbs like wings that live only for your flying dance, and in the Twisan's ever-seeking motion." Gemelle had not yet told Fahne of Shabatu.

Fahne stared into the water and then went on: "We are like and not like, you know, Gemelle. We have both been touched by the quicksilver staff of Hermes, our common ruler; yet in me the night-side rules, in you the day. And where you are cool and free as wind, I am rooted in the warm earth that craves the balm of the sea. I have a fever in my body; it runs through my being in the flooding heat of wine. I can feel at every moment the pounding of desire for her that is like the never-changing rhythm of the waves upon the shore. I must be with her."

Staring into the mittel-Erden's earnest eyes, Gemelle could understand but a single thing—that indeed he would never understand. Even the gleaming Shabatu was not, at this moment, Gemelle's whole world; if he saddened to lack Shabatu, it was the sadness of a moment, for there was always another to gladden him. Yet this imminent parting tore at him in quite another way.

Giedi the polesman turned to Fahne and called, "There is your craft, sire."

Fahne gripped the Brisen's slender hand in a fervent signal of farewell, gripping with his other hand the deceptive forearm that had the tensile strength of finest steel.

"Until we meet, Gemelle."

Astonished at his own mist of tears, the Brisen blinked and watched the sorcerer leap like a great agile hound into the sideboat of the neighboring craft that would take him to the inlet of Erdemar.

CHAPTER 10

The echoing of twelve-dark, Capra's final chime, came dimly to Dione in her water garden. She stood transfixed by the gleaming form of Triton, sounding his soundless conch, as the heavy step of Chiton struck the path.

She saw her uncle emerging through the arch of water vines and composed her expression.

"It is a black hour for wandering," he greeted her in his panting fashion. The abalone colors cast by the moon through the dome of glass were grotesque on his wine-veined face. "I had thought you sleeping." Puffing, he set his bulk upon the bench of shells. "And all this while," the Crabba chided, "I have had splendid news."

The Marin, standing before her uncle, steeled herself for his next words.

"Why do you stare so?" he demanded. Chiton was made uneasy by her pallor, annoyed by her vulnerable air. She looked like a wild thing waiting for its death, he thought sourly.

But forcing a genial tone, he said, "Sit by me, child. I have something to say to you."

Reluctantly, Dione sat down on the bench of shells in a rustle of gleaming silk. She did not look at Chiton, but stared down at her hands.

"The stars," Chiton began in a blaze of pomposity, "have decreed a crown for the head of Dione." She was still silent. Irritated but determined, the Crabba went on: "The Crown Prince Monoceros of Erde has offered you his hand. And with it," he said meaningly, "there will come eternal peace between the lands of Erde and Mar."

Dione found her voice. "Do you mean to . . . sacrifice my happiness to Monoceros?" she asked piteously.

Chiton was so startled by the desperation of her tone that at first he could not reply. Then he spluttered, "What foolish, unwomanly prattle is this?" Why, he questioned silently of the heavens, have I been cursed with this sad water-sprite for a child . . . when there are other men whose own nieces are the cozy, full-breasted Crabba, trained to the cooking pot, or the hot-eyed Escors so lusty for a mate they would leap at Monoceros?

"What objection can you have to the castle of a queen?" he cried.

"Monoceros could never read my heart."

Again the Crabba was amazed at the calm objections of the fragile-looking girl. And it annoyed him doubly to have her speaking in terms he could never comprehend.

"Why do you say such foolish things?"

"Monoceros is forever on the hunting field. I cannot bear the smell of men who smell of blood."

Chiton was placating. "But these ways, my child, are the ways of the Erden."

"Not the Maeden race." Instantly she regretted her rashness.

The Crabba turned and stared at her suspiciously. "What do you know of the Maeden of Erde?"

"Only what I have read," she replied softly.

Chiton sighed. There lay the rub! "I have let you read too much," he snapped. "You have had too much freedom."

When she did not answer, he added, "You will do as I say. The day following tomorrow, Monoceros and his train will call at our mansion in Erdemar. And he will bring with him betrothal gifts to gladden the heart of any natural girl. You have never seen such magnificence."

Dione replied, "There is magnificence in this garden, and in the singing of Volan, that is greater than anything Monoceros could offer."

He repeated, "You will do as I say."

She answered sadly, rising from the bench, "I have no choice. May I go to my chamber?"

Chiton nodded and watched the slender, green-robed girl walk down the path of forms. She had such grace that she moved with almost a swimming motion.

The Crabba sighed. His lunar temper, half-shell, half-softness, was frayed. He looked morosely about the water garden, thick with masses of water vines, dotted with shining forms of the creatures of the sea.

I have never understood her, he reflected, listening to the water murmur. "She seems to have no love for what is real, for what touches the rest of us," he muttered. And rising heavily, the Lord Mayor of Mar departed from the shadowy garden for the consoling enclosure of his rooms.

"You have been too long in the garden," Earla scolded as Dione entered from the corridor. "If your slumber is too long broken, you will be pale and wan in Erdemar."

She moved to the little Marin and began to unfasten her silken robe, drawing it roughly over the girl's small head. A strand of satiny black hair caught in the sleeve; Dione cried out and began to weep uncontrollably.

"There, now!" said the Bole, untangling the lock of hair. "What a cry for such a little pain!" Clucking, she shook out the gleaming garment and hung it in the great walnut press by the wall.

I can bear no more, thought Dione, wiping her wet cheeks, trembling. Like most Peisuns, her emotions were overpowering, and the force of them this night had left her weak and shaken. Her legs and arms felt as insubstantial as foam.

"Please, Earla," she said weakly, "you are right. I am very weary, and I must sleep now so that I may look . . . well in Erdemar." She managed a mendacious smile.

The Bole stared at her in pleased surprise. "You have come to your senses, then!"

Dione nodded and said in a low voice, "I have at last come to my senses." She gloried in the secret double meaning.

"Splendid," the Bole said heartily, chafing the Marin's nerves. "Sleep now. The skin below your eyes is black as a Crabba's cave. I will brush your hair on the morrow."

Gently, she undressed the girl and slipped a gray-green nightrobe, fragile as smoke, over her white body and turned down the ocean-colored coverings of the bed.

"A good night, my child," said the Bole, then left the chamber, extinguishing the taper by the door.

Dione expelled a loud breath of relief and, tiptoeing to the door, relit the taper on the table. With its flame she touched the wick of another candle and set it in a candlestick. Throwing around her a rustling nightcloak that matched her gown, she took up the candle and hurried to the door of her dressing chamber.

"Volan! Volan!"

The minstrel, blinking sleepily, emerged through the half-open door. His brindled hair was very tousled.

Dione began to laugh softly, her laughter touched with weariness' hysteria. "You have been sleeping in my closet!"

Volan put a narrow finger to his lips and grinned. "Yes, my lady. And I have a message for you from him."

Eagerly, she watched as the minstrel drew from a recess in his tunic a glittering small object on a delicate chain, a chain so web-like it was almost invisible. "He has left you a star, he said," Volan whispered, handing her the bauble.

"Hold the candle here," she said in high excitement. By the flickering light, Dione saw the bauble clearly: on the chain of white-gold, the metal of Mar, was an exquisitely wrought star of crystal with six sides—the Star of Solomon.

"It is so lovely," she said in a trembling voice.

"He said to tell you"—Volan's whisper was urgent and quick—"that it was the star of his mother; wear it to bring him near and gain the Sight." The young minstrel giggled and said then, "He was in such haste that he flung this to me, racing from the garden, with his words of direction."

Dione held the delicate bauble in her hand for a moment, then clasped the chain around her neck.

"Thank you," she said softly to Volan. "Thank you."

They heard the rasping whirr of the great clock in the corridor, about to strike, and then its deep-throated gong.

"Oh, lady, I must be gone," the minstrel whispered. "Even my estate," he said jocularly, "will not excuse my being here at such a darkness."

Dione smiled and squeezed his slender arm. "Go, then. And thank you, my dear companion."

She watched him disappear into the shadows of her dressing closet, then heard the snick of the closing door beyond.

Wide awake and trembling with tense excitement, Dione went to the oval window and examined the star again by the glow of the ripening moon. The star was part of him, a piece of the heavens!

The little star, a quarter of the size of Fahne's, glittered like a flake of Brisen snow; at one instant, it was clearer than water, and at another, peculiar shadows appeared.

Was it true? she thought. Could the star bring Fahne near her, as he had been for those fleeting moments in the garden?

Dione put her small hand to her throat, and clasping the star, she felt a sudden, deep exhaustion. She moved on heavy feet to the canopied bed and sank into its wide, ocean-colored lap.

She ached for sleep, yet feared to close her eyes, for then she might lose the stealing warmth that now enveloped her. The little Marin had begun to feel the presence of the sorcerer, and with his presence, the mysterious sensation of riding the moving waters—first, upon a surface of calm, like the Marin canals, but then below her she experienced a stronger motion, a rhythm of harbor waves and sea waves under her feet. It was true, then; the star could bring him near.

And as she fell asleep the Marin seemed to hear the distant voice of Fahne that cried "Until we meet!"

CHAPTER 11

Marin in armor, even the vengeful, warlike Escors, was an uncommon sight. The many years of amity between the lands of Erde and Mar had given the forgers of breastplates and swords, knee-protectors and helms, little custom in the tall, silver city of Mar. The arms and coats of mail rested in the warehouses of the Marin before they were shipped to Sabbia, or to the jousting lords of Erde. The ironic Maeden of Erde, devoted to the arts of scholarship and healing, scorned the weapons of their brother Erden, which the Maeden deemed childlike and absurd.

The Maeden bore with good grace the other Erden's comments on their manliness; but when their tempers were frayed beyond repair, the Maeden could surprise opponents with hands and feet long skilled in the martial arts of the distant Oriens.

So strange was it, however, to see a Marin wearing mail that the herdsman of Erdemar, catching sight of a broad Escor and his little army on this twelve-light in the month called Maeden Circle, stopped dead on the over-looking hill. The herdsman was a genial, sleepy-eyed Bole, that race of the Erden best suited to the cultivation of plants and beasts. Uneasy with the Escors, his star op-posites—unless they were hot-eyed women of that race!— the herdsman stared down at the small band in crimson. They wore from foot to head close-fitting suits of blue-gray pewter mail; their knees were shielded in armor, and on leathern straps over their shoulders were hung newly enamelled oval shields, bearing the signet of an ebon eagle and a golden scorpion. They must be lords of high degree, the herdsman concluded.

Leathern belts similar to their straps were buckled loose-ly at the Marin's waists and held wide-bladed swords to the left of their bodies; to the right, each wore a sheathed and shorter-bladed dagger. The faces of the armored men were set and pallid.

The herdsman on the hill spoke in melodic Erden to his wandering sheep, and with his crooked staff he pulled them in line and hurried them to another grazing ground beyond the Marin's sight.

On the road below, Vanand, riding next to Madimiel, said in answer to the latter's question, "We will reach them by two, the hour of the Escor—a fitting hour to down the slant-eyed bastard."

"Shall we unfit him for the bed of *matermoine,* or simply slay him?"

Vanand replied, "It matters not; in either form he will be a less than lusty husband for Dione."

Madimiel's answering laughter, loud and brutal, echoed

to the disappearing herdsman. The young Bole shuddered at its sound.

Monoceros, riding next to Polyg, wondered why he had bothered with a gambeson. The padded leather tunic of flame-green leather, worn to give extra protection in the games of war, seemed superfluous against the novice Marin.

The Capran smiled with contempt. He rode as straight as a tree upon his massive night-black stallion, his eye-slit helm slung from a great staple attached to his fire-green saddle hung with the onyxes and garnets of the Chronos-born.

Polyg glanced at the Prince, thinking darkly that his confidence seemed high. The deep scar that zigzagged from the warrior's chin to his brow was livid in the cooler air of Erdemar. His wide-bladed sword and companion dagger, with their jeweled hilts, bore stains of long use that could not be sanded away—stains that, Polyg reflected, the young Prince's arms did not yet bear. He had seen too many reversals in his time to take a skirmish lightly. And then, Polyg mused, there was that cursed prophecy. . . .

Accustomed to the lukewarm air of lower Erde, Monoceros shrank a little from the chillier noon of Erdemar. At least the gambeson, he thought wryly, will serve for warmth while I unseat Vanand.

The Capran's shield was square and bore the device of the royal line of endlich-Erde, the emerald-green sea goat in its crown on a ground of onyx. Like Polyg and the Escors approaching from the North, Monoceros was wearing the wide-bladed sword called a falchion and a shorter-bladed knife.

"I hope," said Polyg in his deep, brassy voice, "that we dispose of Vanand before we meet the lady. Women go vaporish at the sight of blood."

Monoceros shrugged. "She must get used to it. It will train her not to shriek over the corpses of my field prey."

He would endure no Marin vaporing, Monoceros resolved. They had warned him that the Marin ate no flesh, except that of sea creatures, and that the Lady Dione would protest his sport. Protest! he scoffed silently. He would teach her the ways of a man.

The warrior chief stared at the Prince; this was no match of love! Then he said tentatively, having discovered that bluntness did not sit well with the Prince, "The other Marin may go more than vaporish."

Monoceros laughed. "No fear! Her uncle the Crabba is an old woman; he travels only with those of his own star-race, and with Peisun." The last word was spat out with condescension. A stiff smile creased the Prince's hard, full mouth. "The Escors, it seems, have fallen from His Worship's grace, since the quarrel with Vanand. The Mayor will not mourn him. And what kind of warriors can the Escors be, who cannot even kill a rabbit?" There was deep scorn in his metallic tone.

Polyg was silent. He was not so sure as the young Monoceros. Despite himself, the warrior chieftain could not take lightly the black predictions of Gonu the priest and seer of lower Erde.

Earla's wide brown gaze slid left again to scrutinize the tense expression of Dione. Strange, thought Earla the Bole, the child had not let her own waiting-woman dress her for the journey! She had insisted on arraying herself, and alone. Earla burned to know what Dione concealed, both on her person and in her heart.

Even with the Brisen tinge of her questioned birth—the Brisen were cool and changeable creatures—it was unlike Dione to swerve so wholly from a cherished goal. And she had not mentioned Fahne again, not since the day of their meeting. In point of fact, since yestermorn, she had not seemed herself at all, alternately agreeing with the Bole on the splendors of Monoceros, in a hard little voice, and lapsing into sudden, mysterious silences.

Yestermorn, when Earla had entered the Marin's chamber to array her and brush her hair, Dione had clasped her rustling night-cloak high about her slender neck before she sat down to submit to brushing.

Earla had inquired if she were cold. The Marin, looking at her blankly an instant, at last said "Cold?" in an absent way. "You know I am rarely cold."

Not a moment later, the little Marin had shuddered and declared that the air was very chill for September.

It was very peculiar indeed, Earla reflected with suspicion. She would be glad when the girl was wedded.

And the tension of the Marin seemed to have infected Volan the minstrel as well; the shadows of it raced across

his transparent brow, and Earla noted that he rarely met
her eyes. Volan and the girl had always been like a glove
and a hand, but these few days had seemed to bring them
closer, as if they were bound in some childish conspiracy.

Moreover, Dione had chosen to go mounted to Erdemar,
rather than in the wagon, like a proper lady, with the
Bole. "There are too many trunks and bundles to accommodate us all with ease," Dione had said quickly to Earla,
ordering the men to saddle her small mare and to mount
Volan.

"Mount Volan!" her uncle protested. "A servant need
not go mounted. He will think himself a lord. He can ride
in the wagon with Earla."

The little Marin had said with an imperiousness that
amazed the Bole, "You have chosen to make me a queen.
Well, I must habituate myself to ordering."

And chastened, the old Mayor had complied.

The Bole leaned forward now and peered again from the
wagon at Dione, stiff with tension on the back of her
cloud-gray palfrey. The days of her confidence are gone,
Earla thought with sadness. Well, she was paying now for
throwing in her lot with Chiton. The servant sighed and
leaned back again in the wagon. It made no matter, she
concluded. The gypsy was gone for good and all, driven
with his raffish companions forever from Mar.

Guiding her sleek Marin horse that moved with the
grace of water, Dione of Mar stared ahead along the road
that took them farther from Maringate and deeper into the
border country of Erdemar.

She lowered her silken hood; already the silvery drizzle
of Mar had given way to the warmer air of Erde, the
strange transition from moisture to the dry half-sunlight,
half-cloud of the borderland.

The memory of her interval with Fahne shone now like
a steady beacon to the eye of her mind, blotting out all
other images. She smiled, remembering the simple Earla's
happy words: "You have come to your senses."

Indeed, I have come to them, Dione reflected, for the
first time in my life! Never had she known this bright
astonishment of flesh, the flowing and the burning that she
had known at his touch! This, she thought, was what the

stories in her beloved books had meant—the books that, with Volan, had been her sole companions for so many circles.

The little crystal star of Fahne was a blessed weight in the small hollow of her neck, hidden from sight this hour by her modest, high-necked robe, with its cowled draperies. The peacock color of the gown emphasized her pallor and lent an almost turquoise color to the green sparkle of her eyes.

Her pulse began to thud more swiftly as she recalled the last sweet words of the sorcerer, and the feel of his lean, hard body melded to her own. And she knew again the ghostly roll of waves below her on the night before the last, when the star of Fahne had let her take ship with him, standing near him, clasped to him in the dark.

It had been true, then! she sang to herself, and she caught the pale eye of Volan, who was riding next to her on his dappled pony.

It was so, Dione said to herself; the little star had brought them as close in spirit as they had held each other in the garden!

The spell of his enchantment, since she had watched his tall robed figure disappear into the dark, had been so overpowering that she had moved through the last long days as if in a dream.

The morning after their meeting in the garden, Dione had risen with a sick reluctance, longing in the manner of the Peisun to linger in her bed, continuing her sleep. Of all the Marin, Peisun were happiest in the veiled realm of dreaming; and how many years had she escaped in it, Dione thought now—fled from the stern direction of her uncle, the puzzling disciplines of Earla the Bole, from all that was less beautiful than the world of her books and her sleep! But now, since Fahne had touched her, Dione had hardly known whether she had slept or had been wound in a cocoon of semiconscious witchery that simulated sleep.

She had been cold with apprehension to face the prying Bole, and she steeled herself to taking food and making civil answer. She chose with unseeing eyes the garments Earla had prepared for the journey. The gowns mattered little enough, the Marin thought dazedly, when Fahne would never see a single one.

Now, guiding her gentle palfrey ever nearer to the Church of Stars, Dione could not help smiling despite the tremble of her excited nerves.

All that would greet Monoceros would be a trunkful of empty gowns. She could picture the Bole's dismay when the hard-eyed Monoceros rode into the courtyard of their house at Erdemar, his lackeys bearing coffers of jewels and silver and gold for betrothal gifts. Dione had to restrain her giggles; she could not resist the sharing of her thoughts with Volan.

"To think," she leaned to him and called softly, "that I will be dashing away into the afternoon without a bundle to bless myself! And Monoceros waiting with his jewels!"

The singer looked warily over his narrow shoulder, then ahead at the broad back of Chiton. No one had seemed to notice.

He grinned at Dione and answered rashly, "You will have a better covering than silk." Then, realizing the indiscretion he had committed, he blushed deeply.

Dione's cheeks turned the shade of coral. But she glowed with such a patent joy that Chiton, glancing backward at his niece, knew a vast relief.

Perhaps, he thought, the girl is warming at last to Monoceros.

"This is the spot, Madimiel." Vanand held up his massive oval hand and waved the mounted men behind him to follow.

The little army of Escors cantered into the thicket and dismounted. About a hundred yards ahead, above the trees, could be seen the auger-like steeple of the Church of Stars.

"What trickery is this?" Madimiel asked the High Escorpiun.

"Trickery?" Vanand gave Madimiel a steely glance over his broad shoulder as he led his restless gray stallion into the underbrush. "What foolishness makes you inquire?" he retorted.

"I had understood we were to meet Monoceros and the Caprans head-on in equal combat."

"I have appointed a child as my second in command," Vanand said coldly. "The Caprans are too old in combat for Marin to defeat except by stealth."

"But all our shields and other gear . . ."

"Were purchased to satisfy the childish love of show in others like yourself," Vanand snapped back. "We will need only daggers, if all goes well. Here is what we will do. . . ."

"Be still," Polyg ordered suddenly. The Prince and the men behind him reined in at once, murmuring low to their skittish mounts.

"I heard the neighing of an *Erdenpferd*," the scar-faced Polyg muttered. "I had not thought them wily enough to come in stealth, but I looked for the childish panoply of novice warriors riding to be slain. Listen."

From deep within the forest Monoceros could hear a horse's nickering. "Yes. They are there."

Turning, Polyg called softly to his lieutenant, "Dismount. And lead the men on foot into the wood just there."

Dione of Mar could see the tower of the Church of Stars. Her heart began to flutter so alarmingly that she feared that she would tumble from her horse.

She trembled and looked at Volan. The narrow minstrel's face was pale.

"I do not think my illness will be feigned," she murmured weakly as their beasts started up the rise that would lead them down to the crossing roads, in the full view of the Church of Stars.

"Quickly!" hissed Vanand. "Into the trees. You take Polyg. The slant-eyed Prince is mine." There was a pulsing triumph in his words.

Their mounts were tethered far beyond. The red-clad Escorpiun army of Vanand, their fine-tuned muscles steeled from years upon the Marin playing fields in competition with the men of Brise, climbed monkey-like into the spreading branches of the oaks.

And when the Caprans came stealing by below, the Escors leaped upon them like lightning bolts.

Polyg fell heavily with a grunt of surprise, Madimiel upon him, but soon the Capran chief had rallied and was wrestling with the second Escor; in an instant Polyg's dagger was at Madimiel's throat. But like a flash, a third Escor had driven his own knife through a seam in Polyg's mail, and with a dreadful cry the warrior chief fell prone upon Madimiel, his back a welter of red.

Madimiel rolled out from under his terrible burden and sprang to the defense of Vanand, who seemed in need of aid against the struggles of Monoceros.

But the great Escor, his power multiplied by rage akin to madness, abruptly flung the more slender Capran from him and, springing up, delivered Monoceros a savage kick with his hard-mailed foot. Vanand laughed maniacally.

Two other Escors lay dead, and many Caprans were dying, but the raging Escor Vanand saw nothing but the battered face of the hated Capran, the helpless chest below his mailed heel.

Still laughing, the great Escor unsheathed his wide-bladed sword and with it made a swishing pass at Monoceros' loins.

The Capran cried out in an agony of terror: Vanand thrust his falchion into the Capran's heart.

At the sound of the first terrible cry, the Mayor's broad gray stallion reared, threatening to unseat the Crabba.

"Desmos!" Chiton bellowed to his Peisun kinsman. "There was the cry of a man wounded . . . and that is the road from Erde."

"Let's go!" the Peisun called to the men of the train, and they began to gallop away, with daggers drawn, in the direction of the cry. "See to the women!" he cried to Chiton.

Dione the little Marin dismounted, shaking, from her gentle palfrey and crumpled into the dust of the crossing roads.

"My lady!" Volan ran to Dione. Earla was scrambling from the wagon, Chiton descending awkwardly from his horse.

It was then that a green-robed, hooded mendicant appeared in the shaded entrance arch of the star-temple opposite.

"My brother!" Volan shouted. "Please aid us with this lady."

Immediately, the mendicant came hurrying from the shadows and ran to the little group at the crossing of the roads.

"A Peisun." Chiton breathed a sigh of relief to meet a cousin-race. And a man, he thought, sufficiently set up to bear the Marin!

The mendicant in green came to Dione and gathered her up in his arms. "I will take her to the quarters of the women," he said to them in muffled latter-Marin. He kept his head slightly turned away from Chiton and the Bole.

Seeing that neither knew the monk, the minstrel broke out in a flood of easing sweat.

"I will go with you," said the Bole.

Volan's heart was fairly in his mouth.

"You need not, madam," said the stranger gently, "but as you please."

"Go, Earla, go," Chiton said crabbily. "And see to the child." Already his deepset eyes were straying longingly to the commotion in the thicket, and his petulant mouth trembled as if in memory of Desmos' unwitting offense to his manhood. "I must see how Desmos fares. Help me, Volan."

Reluctantly, the minstrel turned his blue eyes away from the departing figures of the Bole and the mendicant carrying the little Marin. Grunting, the Crabba was mounted, and without thanks galloped away down the road toward endlich-Erde.

With a soft exclamation of triumph, Volan took off after the Bole and the quickly striding mendicant. They were already disappearing into the shadow of the temple.

The minstrel began to run; he heard, from within the shadowy structure, a sharp cry and a woman scolding in erst-Erden. Earla has discovered them, it came to Volan; he could picture her face! And mingling with the beating pulse of fear within his narrow throat was a crazy bubble of incipient laughter.

He entered the Church of Stars, and despite his apprehension, he paused. He was struck with dazzlement to see this magical place that he had never seen before, with its vaulted darknesses and the gem-like flames of its star-glass windows ignited by the strengthening sun of afternoon.

The varicolored tapers of the star-races burned serenely over the central altar; above it, Volan's wondering eyes beheld the great golden disc of Helios in the center; surrounding it were the wheel of gods, the gods of the star-people of Erde and Mar, of Brise and Sabbia, symbolizing the long, sweet amity of nations.

For an instant the specter of conflict rose before the slender minstrel's gaze, obscuring like a scarlet cloud his anxiety for Dione and the sorcerer.

Then his upward glance took in the graceful jeweled forms of the star-gods—Ares, Mars, the god of war with his golden spear; Venus Aphrodite in her draperies of soft rose color symbolizing love and beauty; Hermes, or Mercury, the ruler of the Maeden and the Twisan, with his winged feet and laughing mouth.

Volan shook himself from his blinking reverie and turned his eyes from a contemplation of the gloomy god Chronos, ruler of the Capra and the Waetergyt. A mumbling sound nearby and the rustle of agitated draperies had caught his ear.

The sound issued from a shadow beyond a side altar to Vulkanos, another god of the Maeden. Cautiously, Volan crept over to investigate, glancing at the statue of the lame celestial aide to the laughing Hermes. Dimly, Volan made out a dark, substantial shape in the shadows.

It was Earla, loosely bound by hands that obviously desired no pain for her, and gagged with a long fragile handkerchief of the Lady Dione's. Volan knew its beloved pattern well.

Loosening the handkerchief, he drew back from the volley of Earla's words. "You!" she spat out. "You have conspired with them! Whatever shall I say to the Lord Mayor, and to the Crown Prince Monoceros?"

Volan made no reply.

"Loosen these bonds!" shrieked the Bole. And the minstrel leaned down to obey.

"Oh," she moaned, "the Prince's anger will be terrible."

"The Prince will know no anger." Startled, they turned in the direction of the somber voice. It was Chiton, and his face, by the jeweled light of the windows of stars, was an ugly blend of grief and ire.

"The Prince will know no anger," he repeated, "or indeed any vengeance or joy. Vanand has slain him."

Earla gasped, and Volan was stricken dumb.

"And you," Chiton said sternly to the minstrel, "will pay for your part in this little game."

The pale eyes of the Brisemarin met the deepset eyes of the Lord Mayor of Mar and saw in them his punishment.

Yet in his heart he wished them godspeed, the sorcerer and his beloved friend.

PART II

ARES AND APHRODITE

(Love and Discord)

CHAPTER 1

"Only a little way," Fahne had said, loosening her from the first desperate embrace. "My steed is hidden in the woods. Shall I carry you?"

The small Marin had shaken her head, and she clung to the sorcerer's firm hand as they raced among the slowly falling leaves of ruby and of gold into the thickening forest.

At last, in a clearing, she had seen the satiny flanks of a great roan stallion waiting without a tether in the amber light.

The sound of their approaching feet had caused the steed to turn its massive, narrow head and begin a nickering of joy.

"Merddyn," Fahne had said softly, and at once the great roan horse had been still. "Good lad." The sorcerer had put an affectionate hand on the creature's flank.

Fahne had turned to the Marin and folded her urgently in his arms. "My love." Her head had whirled anew in his nearness.

"We must go." He had lifted her with great care to the pillioned saddle of the roan and sprung up before her on the saddle, ordering softly that she hold him around the middle.

Now, as Fahne reined in, she glanced about the empty wood. Without a word, the sorcerer dismounted and stood looking up at her with tender eyes. His own dappled gaze held a hunger so deep and plain that Dione cried out to him.

He lifted her from the pillion and held her tightly as she came sliding down, so tightly that her body knew all of his, and knew the pounding of his urgency.

Slowly, her feet descended to the leaf-strewn forest floor.

"We are safe here for a little while," he said in a breathless fashion, like a man who had run a long race and gasped his words out now from bursting lungs.

The forest was so still that she could hear his every breath, and even the little hush of their meeting clothes were whispered voices.

He released her gently, laughing. "I have wooed you far too long in this woman's guise." He flung away the constricting robes of the mendicant and stood before her in his teal-blue hose and doublet of the Maeden.

The sweet male musk of him, quite suddenly, overcame her quivering senses. Swaying, she fell against him, close again, so very near that she met the seeking hardness of his flesh and felt her center's melting fire.

She shook from head to foot, too weak to say a word; his own broad frame was trembling, too, like the trunk of a mighty quercus tree in a gale that threatened to uproot each growing thing of earth.

The sorcerer bent his stately head to hers and their parting lips clung trembling to each other while his hands explored her softening, thin-clad curvings, and her fingers stroked his oaken torso and his steely limbs.

Fahne the sorcerer made a groaning sound, the sound of a man in pain beyond enduring, and he drew her downward to the leaf-rustling bed.

With quaking, tender hands he began to unfasten the neck of her garment; as it fell from her white flesh, revealing the glimmering star in the neck's hollow above her delicate breasts, he made an inchoate sound of wonder, for her skin was so white that it seemed to be lit from within, giving out almost an incandescence. He was powerless to speak.

Then, kneeling over her, the sorcerer whispered at last, "Do you remember your salute of my hands and arms in the garden?"

With half-closed eyes she nodded weakly.

"I shall so salute your body's loveliness." And leaning to her he began to caress her white and shadows with his tongue. The Marin, shuddering with delight, almost feared that she would rend, or that her pounding pulses would stop, so great was the power of ascending sense that flailed her body like the sea.

And through the mist of lowered lids, she saw him fling away his clothes, glorying in his smooth and tawny skin, his firmness, as half-heard murmurings of alien words and

strange small crying came; she could not discern whose
words they were, the sorcerer's or her own, and last came
the vision of a wand, a light gathering at its tip, transmuted
where it caught the sun into a tiny star; and her own
sweet cry of "Enter," bracing for the wound she knew
would be inevitable, but feeling with unbelief no pain at
all, only a heightened shuddering, a brightness flooding all
her dark; a long, laboring climb, an unbearable ascension
to a tall, thin place of strongly beating wings, high shrill-
nesses.

She came into the world again, looking dazed into the
branches of the overhanging quercus trees, bearing on her
white breasts now the sobbing Fahne.

Not three within the border country of Erdemar knew
that the dappled thicket far from the winding road was not
a thicket at all, but a house.

The man who had built the house, a long-dead Peisun
whose Maeden wife had yearned for mittel-Erde, had com-
promised his own sharp longing for the city of Mar by
erecting this water-green and earth-brown dwelling in the
sunny cloudiness between the two lands.

Enamored of aloneness, skilled at camouflage, the Peisun
had decreed that the house bear the likeness of the trees
around it. So magical was the blend of walls and branches
that no one glimpsing it from the road could know a house
stood there. And so for many circles had the Peisun and
his Maeden wife lived in the hidden house, in joyful isola-
tion among their books and lyres and flowers. The Peisun
would spend countless nights tending the beakers in his
laboratory, passing along his peculiar secrets to his son.

One drowsy afternoon, about a month after the events
at the Church of Stars, an ancient man with a protracted,
snow-white beard came toward the dappled house tapping
his gnarled stick. He wore the russet garment of a Bole.
Had anyone looked closely or considered deeply, he would
have judged the old man too tall and slender for a Bole
and found a quality in him that did not speak of years and
dying.

In fact, when the aged man had hobbled nearer to the
hidden house, he suddenly tucked his gnarled staff below
his russet-clad arm and began to stride along with the
fast, resilient steps of a far younger man.

Catching sight of the delicate boy emerging from the

house, the man began to run. Nearing, he could see the boy's small mouth break into a wide, peculiar smile, a smile almost like a grimace of pain—the greeting of the Peisun—though the slender figure was dressed in the water-green and earth-russet of the Erdemarin.

When the slender arms were flung around the neck of the tall robed man, the russet vest fell back to reveal the swelling breasts of a woman.

"My love, you have been gone so long," Dione said, bending back her head for the tall man's kiss. She clung to him, and her green cap slid away, releasing a waterfall of night-black hair. She laughed like a child, but the eyes of the man were serious.

"Your guise gives you more freedom than mine," he commented wryly, "except for this." He caressed her glittering fall of hair. "We must go cautiously, my darling."

"Yes." She nodded and obediently retrieved her soft green cap, stuffing her wealth of hair inside it again.

"How good it will be," she said brightly, almost prancing at his side, "to see the fair!"

"Have you felt confined?" he asked her softly, pausing.

"Confined!" she repeated with wonder. "My darling." And again she lifted her white face for his kiss. "I had not known that life could hold such happiness." Fahne smiled.

"I thought it wiser not to take the horses. Someone could recognize them. It is not far."

"I care not how far it is," she said, and as they neared the winding road, she slowed down her dancing step to match his hobbling one. He had resumed using his cane.

"You make a very pretty boy," he quavered in erst-Erden.

"I love you, my dear uncle," she replied, and the lightness in her tone broke into a solemnity that was almost anguish. "I love you so," she repeated.

Fahne examined the little Marin with loving eyes. In truth she made a handsome boy, with her slenderness and pallor emphasized by the green and russet clothes, the doublet, hose and open jerkin, and the soft cap concealing her glittering hair and fragile ears.

"How shall I keep from embracing you at the fair?"

Laughing, she took his arm and held it tightly. "That would be most unseemly, Uncle."

But looking up into his brindled eyes, she wondered how

she, too, could be restrained from taking his broad, long-fingered hand and rubbing it against her cheek.

These last few weeks, she mused, had held enchantment she had never dreamed to know, not even with the sorcerer. When Fahne had asked her anxiously whether she sickened for the silver Mar, she had answered in truth that she would gladly live forever as his parents had, in the masked house alone with him.

And yet there had come a morning when the sorcerer saw the faintest wistful look about her mouth, and he had said a little sadly but with great calm, "This has been a time of blessed sleep, you know, a resting. I have been to many lands and seen a thousand faces; to keep you here is to cage a creature with wings."

Though she had protested, and they had come together with a fullness they had never known before, Dione could hear the truth in what he spoke.

"We will have to face them all someday, I fear," he said as she lay in his arms that afternoon, caressing the bare skin of his tawny chest with her tender mouth. "The world still waits."

And so it was with wariness and care that the sorcerer had disguised himself and gone into Erdemar. Always over them brooded the shadow of Vanand and the threat of Chiton.

He looked at her again, this drowsy afternoon on the winding road to the center of Erdemar, and his love had an edge of fear, a poignancy that was new to him. Better not to mention, he thought, the rumors that were bruited about at the fair.

Gonu the high priest of lower Erde, riding in the train of the Princess Shira, felt a prickle of foreboding. He could not have told the reason, yet his trauminition—the intuition of his mystic dreams—had sent him visions of deceit. The old man had seen, quite clearly in his sleep, a flock of great dark birds of prey, and the prey on which they descended had no eyes. Surely it was an omen.

Gonu shuddered and glanced at the royal litter of the Princess. She lay back on her luxurious float with heavy-lidded, sensuous eyes, indifferent to the weariness of the eight muscular servants who had carried her all the way from lower Erde. Barbaric! the priest reflected, when all the other women of high estate went mounted or in closed wagons. But to the Princess Shira, the serfs were a form of lower animal, treated with far less care than the soldiers' steeds, those prancing beauties gotten from the sands of Sabbia.

He had hoped that, with the death of her brutal brother, the Princess' reign might be more benign. True, she had, in council with the priests, sworn an upholding of the faith, and greater leniency to the brotherhood.

His look turned again on Shira. There was a bored and sullen droop to her sensual red mouth, and her oblique, hot gaze was sleepy as she lay on her sumptuous pillows. She did not see at all the discomfort of her two-legged steeds, shivering now in the cooler air of Erdemar as the sweat of their toiling labor dried on their arms and brows.

Petulantly, she examined her jeweled arms and hands, gleaming with the dark wine-red of garnets and the blue-gray glow of the moonstone. Her fire-green gown was cut quite low over her full, shapely breasts; suddenly she felt the chill of the borderland, and she drew about her perfect shoulders a cloak bordered in dark fur.

On either side of the serf-borne litter, two comely Caprans rode. The Princess idly scrutinized their bodies with her black, slant eyes.

And then ahead, at a crossing of the winding roads, she saw the motley of the fair and heard the silvery tones of a countertenor's lay, the ripple of a gentle lyre.

"Hold!" she called out in her husky voice, and at once the train reined in. "Let us visit the fair. It will break the tedium of our way."

With pity, Gonu saw the tears of thankfulness sliding down the faces of the slaves. He could fairly feel the agony of their arms and the pained pull at the tendons of their calves.

One of the handsome, hard-eyed guards trotted smartly ahead to transmit her order to Buc, successor to Polyg and the leader of the train.

At last the serfs set down their seductive burden with quivering arms, gasping for relief.

"Will you walk, my lady?" Buc asked with reverence, but not before his flat, black eyes had flickered to her lush, half-covered breasts.

She nodded and said huskily, "Your arm."

Shira took his heavily muscled arm, moving closer to him. He could feel the swelling softness of her and colored.

Laughing, Shira walked with him into the babel of the fair. She caught the piercing glance of an impressive man, towering above the heads of the onlookers.

"Who is that Escor?" she inquired softly, leaning even nearer to her escort so the sweet weight of her breast crushed against his trembling bicep.

Dizzied with his lust, the Capran looked blankly in the direction of her nod and stammered, "He is no Escor. He wears the silver-green of the Crabba."

Shira answered, chiding, "A thround is still a thround, whatever his color."

Studying the man more closely, Buc exclaimed, "It is . . . Vanand, your brother's assassin!" His blunt hand went to his sword.

"Stay, my commandant," Shira said in a low, cajoling voice. "Do you wish to please me?"

Again he felt the softness of her against his body, and he almost swayed with the vision of her naked flesh. "You know I do, my lady. But the slayer of the Prince . . . my men have sought him everywhere! And you yourself have said . . ."

"Let them cease their seeking. I have another plan for him." Buc watched her studying the tall Escor.

He cursed the weathervane logic of women. And his body grew quickly cold: Vanand was a sightly fellow.

"Vanand!" The Escor turned his great head ever so slightly at the exclamation of Madimiel. "I think she knows who we are."

"Who knows?" Vanand's growling answer was indifferent, his mordant eyes still roving over the faces of the motley crowd.

"You fool, the Princess Shira."

Vanand looked then at the beautiful Capran and saw her restrain the gesture of the man at her side, who had reached for his sword.

Vanand smiled cynically. "And did you not see her action then?"

"Your obsession will have us slain," Madimiel insisted, though his green eyes returned with lust to the Capran woman. "Your Marin has no heat to equal that," he said.

"No one takes what belongs to me," Vanand answered coldly. "See you any friends of Chiton's?"

"None. I hope that wench will not change her mind."

Vanand laughed and glanced sidelong at Madimiel. "She hated him; I told you that. She will be the Queen." He sounded thoughtful. "And her armies are in her hands—I should say in her arms. There has never been such a one for bedding."

Madimiel's hard eyes glittered as he followed Vanand's returning gaze. "How is it in all these circles she has never been got with child?"

"Her ways of love are far too skilled and . . . peculiar for that. It is said she surpasses the famous empress who saw to a hundred centurions in one mad night." Vanand's voice was full of scorn.

Madimiel, however, felt an urgent drumming in his loins. "Do you think I might address her?" he asked Vanand.

"Your obsession will see us slain," the other retorted, resuming his scrutiny of the crowd.

Volan felt pain in his twisted fingers as he strummed his lyre and prayed that soon the time would come for him to rest. But the little mound of pewter and silver piled up at his feet. So he raised his silvery voice again, this time in the narrow phrases of *"Plasir d'Amur."*

Beyond him, in the crowd that obscured the minstrel from her sight, Dione of Mar took the sorcerer's arm and whispered urgently, "Volan! It is Volan! Oh, come!"

Fahne followed the slender girl in her boyish guise. And then, above the crowd that gathered about the minstrel, he saw the hated face above the tunic of the Crabba.

Vanand. Vanand and Madimiel. "Wait, Dione!" he called out softly.

But his cry was too late.

The next few nightmare moments were too swift for Dione to know all that had happened: she heard the sorcerer's warning cry, saw sudden recognition in the eyes of the minstrel, and felt hard hands upon her.

The sight of Vanand and Madimiel in the garments of the Crabba was too unreal to be believed; then she saw Fahne tear off his robe and leap for the great Escor. Vanand went down and Fahne tore her from his steely grasp, only to be attacked by still others who seemed Caprans. Volan mysteriously was near and then she felt below her the jouncing of a horse and heard dimly far-off bellows sounding like the shouts of Fahne and someone's curse in Marin before she drowned in blackness.

CHAPTER 2

Faintly, the sinuous music of distant flutes and savage, muffled drums came to the Marin. Her eyes felt very heavy. She opened them, and opening them appeared a mighty effort. There was an overpowering scent of honeysuckle. She saw between her shuttered lids, across the large black room in which she lay, a huge glass bowl; before it burned a line of ebon tapers. In its swirling waters were scores and scores of throunds, the deadly scorpion.

Dione screamed.

"Remove them." It was the whiplash tone of Vanand. Turning her weak head, she saw that he had addressed two heavy Boles posted by the door. They hurried to obey.

The slanted, flat green eyes, like those of a serpent, were smiling down at her.

"How do you feel?" The Escor's voice was tender.

"What is this place?"

"It is my castle. How do you feel?" he repeated.

She did not answer, but leaned into the pillows, which felt very smooth. They were of scarlet silk, she saw, and the enormous chamber, seeming windowless, was hung with ponderous tapestries. Their grounds of red were worked with a motif of lizards, serpents, eagles, phoenixes, and scorpions—the insignias of the Escors—in tarnished silver and in ebony.

"I hope the ride was not too hard." Vanand put his heavy hand on her shining hair.

Her clothes felt very thin. Looking down, she saw with horror that she was robed in fragile, almost transparent, black, the hue of death and evil. The bodice of her gown was broidered in shining crimson with the symbol of the middle-Marin, the sigil she had learned to fear. The star was gone!

On her nuptial finger was an intricate ring: it was fashioned of topaz, the gem of the Escors, and was gray-gold.

Arrogantly, the forked M of the Escors, like the tongue of a snake, overlaid the delicate sign of the Peisun.

"What does this mean?" she cried.

Vanand placed his great hairy hand on her thin white arm and smiled. "You belong to me, as you were meant to do. We have been wed."

"Wed!" Struggling, she sat up in the scarlet bed among the shining pillows.

"Yes." He caressed her pale shoulder. She felt a tremor of distaste. "I was pained to deceive you; you had been given a potion to ease your discomfort and make you sleep. But it was meant to be."

"What have you done with Fahne? Where is he?"

Ignoring her, Vanand said, "I have fulfilled the promise of the heavens . . . and the promise of your uncle, before he betrayed me. It is written that you belong to me. It has been spoken in the Tarot, reading after reading: where the seer sought the card of Yod, the drops of light"—the Marin's heart leaped at this reference to the birth-race of Fahne—"the indicator of the Maeden, again and again there rose the symbol of the scarab in the secret pool, the mystic sigil of the Peisun."

"The scarab in the secret pool is the symbol of the fusion of Peisun and Maeden," she said in a trembling voice.

Vanand's face hardened, but again he ignored her words. His large oval hand slid to her breast. "I know the ways of love," he said thickly, "and how to bring you the highest happiness." He drew down the glimmering coverlet. His breathing had quickened, and his oblique gaze raked her body, plain through the drifting, fragile fabric.

Sickened, she gasped out, "If you touch me I shall starve myself until I die. I swear it."

She delighted to see his face stiffen with pain, but as before he went on as if she had not spoken, his eyes filmed over with desire. She thought how similar they were to a snake's.

"I cannot enter you yet," he said, and then she remembered with a flood of relief the strange ceremony of the Escors—the rite of belonging. "In October," he went on, "we will hold the ceremonies of conception; you will lie naked, but robed in an open cloak of scarlet, like a queen." His breathing accelerated. "The incantations will be sung to bring our water child in the summer; and then, before I possess you, the curtains will be drawn around us in a circle, leaving us alone."

She shuddered and said sadly, "I would rather die."

He made an angry sound, and with one hard hand he pinned her, writhing, to the coverlet, and with the other he drew up the thin black gown. She felt his stiff-bearded face upon her breasts and his strong skilled tongue upon her skin, crawling slowly down her body. She struggled and cried out in angry loathing.

"I will take no food or drink if you do not release me." He heard the iron resolution in her tone and let her go, drawing the gown over her again.

He rose from the bed. "Rest now," he said tightly. Horrified, Dione saw that he had ripened with excitement.

She wept with joy when she heard the metal door clang shut.

When Dione awoke again the tapestries were gathered and now through the narrow windows she could see a thick forest of hemlocks and pines. An open pane let in the sound of the sea.

She still felt very weak, but strangely better. The chamber was less frightening in the light, not so much a nightmare chamber, but a room devised by children, garish and naïve. And with the darkness gone, she felt a stirring of rebellion, an anger that was almost hope.

Then she turned her head. Vanand, in a ruby-red chair close to the bed, smiled down at her. She stared back, unsmiling.

"The healer says you are progressing well." He sounded jubilant. Leaning to her, he delicately kissed her cheek.

Seeing her recoil, he frowned. "You need not shrink from me. I am your husband. I can bring you great power."

"Where is Fahne?" she cried.

Vanand's face was a blend of pain and anger.

"You will no longer be concerned with the sorcerer."

"Where is he?"

"You must eat," he evaded. He pulled the crimson bell cord by the bed. A plump Bole with an impassive face entered the chamber. She was carrying a tray of steaming silver bowls.

"I will eat nothing until you tell me of Fahne."

The Bole paused, transfixed.

"Set it there," Vanand ordered, indicating a heavy pewter table by the bed. The Bole placed the tray there and, after one quick look at the Marin, withdrew.

"Very well." Vanand sighed. "I had come to you with gladness, with news of riches and gifts, and all you can speak of is the gypsy."

Ignoring the word, which he had used like an epithet, Dione asked relentlessly, "Where is Fahne?"

Vanand rose and strode to the window, staring out toward the sea. "He is in a dungeon. You will never see him again."

Dione gave a piercing cry and in a rage approximating madness knocked the tray from the table, splashing the steaming contents of the silver bowls over the gun-metal-colored carpet, screaming and screaming.

Through the saffron light of her seizure, she saw Vanand yank at the red bell cord, and soon, coming through the massive door, was an aged Escor with the badge of the healer around his wrinkled neck on a pewter chain.

The old man came toward her, thrusting a goblet against her lips; she turned her head and the goblet struck against her teeth. But the healer persisted until the bitter stream of the calming potion was flowing down her unwilling throat, and soon she whirled again to nothingness.

"My lady, my lady." She heard the narrow, gentle words touched with the grace of the Brisen. Through the lifting mists came the thin, smiling face of Volan the minstrel.

"Wake up, my lady," said Volan. In his thin fingers he held a spoon of gleaming silver, filled with a brownish liquid.

"Volan! How came you here?" Dione cried in wonder.

"I followed you from the fair. And the Escor said to Madimiel, 'Let him come. He is privy to her mind.'" The last words were wry and sad. "But I am glad to be near you, my lady."

She saw then his twisted fingers that held the spoon. "Volan! Your hands!"

He shook his brindled head and sighed. "You will do anything to avoid the matter of eating," said Volan, and he began to chuckle. "You have not changed."

"But tell me." She sat up in the bed and stared into his face, putting a soft hand on his arm.

"Eat first," he insisted. "You have grown so pale and

thin." And he held out the spoon, as if to an intractable child.

"Very well. Give me the bowl." Smiling, Volan emptied the silver spoon into the bowl and handed both to her. Obediently, she took a sip of broth.

Then she said sadly, "Was that my uncle's work . . . or Vanand's?"

"Vanand's," the minstrel said. "Your uncle, whatever his other faults, could not have done it. Chiton meant to send me to a dungeon for a day or so . . . but the Escors are not so gentle." Bitterly, he looked down at his twisted fingers.

Dione set down the bowl and kissed the minstrel's hands. Hesitantly, she said, "But your playing . . . at the fair—it sounded like . . . the old days."

"When one is determined, my lady, everything is possible. But you are not eating your broth."

Impatiently, she took up the bowl again. "Where is he, Volan? Where is Fahne?"

A shadow fell across the minstrel's pallid face. "He is in a dungeon, my lady, in Mar."

"Then my Uncle Chiton has put him there," she said in a trembling voice. "But, how?"

"Oh, my lady, he put up a glorious fight!" Volan grinned, his eyes glowing at the memory of it. "He downed four men with his hands and feet alone, and it was only when the Caprans . . ."

"But why, Volan? The Caprans, when Vanand slew their Prince!"

"I know not, my lady. I think there is some plot afoot, some plot to . . ."

"Never mind," she broke in sharply. "Is he . . . well, Volan? Have you had word of him?"

"Yes, my lady, I have had word. I have many friends in Mar."

Dione asked quickly, "What sort of place is it . . . this dungeon? Can he not escape?"

"It is not so bad a place," Volan lied. "You know he will escape. And I have brought you this."

He held out his narrow hand; in the palm glittered her little star, the Star of Solomon.

"Oh, Volan!" She took it from him and burst into happy weeping. "I had thought it lost forever." She was about to clasp it about her neck when the minstrel hissed, "Quickly! Hide it. That is the step of Vanand."

Dione thrust the star under one of the scarlet pillows just as the massive doors parted, revealing the great Escor.

Busily, Dione began to spoon her broth.

"Well! This is much better." Vanand smiled. "You do well by her, minstrel," he said to Volan.

The effrontery of the man almost took her breath away. After what he had done . . . she could not meet his eyes, but she fought for control.

Volan withdrew.

"After your meal, I have a fine surprise," Vanand said to the Peisun. He sat on a large charcoal-colored ottoman below a mural of the Isle of the Thround.

"Yes," he said to her look of question. "First your broth, and then you shall come with me to see it."

When her bowl was empty, he brought her a voluminous robe of gray-green with a nap of silver, and he slipped small matching slippers on her feet. Embarrassed by these attentions, she wondered whether these Peisun clothes were an omen—a symbol, perhaps, that he was beginning to restore her to herself. She felt a little chill of hope: if he could be lulled by her apparent submission, then there might be a way to escape him. He turned as she slipped on the robe.

Dione was strengthened by her hope as he led her into the corridor, pointing to its extreme end to a shining moonstone door.

"My garden door!"

Smiling broadly, Vanand took her down the gray, red-carpeted hall and opened the glowing door. "The garden of the woman of Vanand," he announced. Trying to blot out his words, she entered through the moonstone door.

It was a perfect replica of her water garden in Mar—the shadowy grotto domed in glass the colors of Mar, thick with massy water vines, furnished with forms of the gods of the ocean. Even the coral bed, with its gem-like peisun, was there, and so was the bench of shells, and the chair of Celtic marble cast in the shape of the chariot of Ler.

"Is it not wondrous?" he asked proudly. His hard eyes swept the garden, naming it now as his own accomplishment, denying her grandfather's creation.

Dione could not reply; she saw his dark intent with clarity. He meant to keep her here forever, trying to distract her, as a child would be distracted, by these pitiful attempts to recreate her world.

And in his arrogance she felt the sinister resonance of their star-rulers, Proserpine and Kun—the Escor's, Proserpine, captured Princess of Hades, was reputed to overpower the benign, dreaming Kun. The evil omen almost overcame her spirit now, but, resolved to her course of escape by deception, she managed to reply at last, "It is wondrous, indeed."

Vanand, even at this small sign, seemed encouraged. And something obdurate in her, an Erden thing, buttressed her new resistance as she watched his reaction.

"Your mother," said Vanand, answering in his Escorpiun fashion her thought, "was a Bole. Your Venus is there: it draws my own Venus unendurably, being the opposition to my Escorpiun, and my fate."

Dione looked at the star-wheel on the breast of his tunic: it was true. Opposite the small circle topping a cross that was the sigil of Aphrodite, or Venus, the goddess of love, was still another red-arrowed M of the Escors.

Vanand strode to her, taking her awkwardly in his arms. He felt her stiffen.

"It is decreed in our star-wheels," he said stubbornly. "All the patterns of the stars have marked us for each other: my Sun in the Escorpiun is a fitting master to the Peisun; even your questioned rising star shines over the borders of the Bole, another magnet to my yearning Escorpiun." Vanand turned his glittering green eyes to the forms of ocean gods, then looked again into her face. "All the singing of the seas in you cries out that we are fated. Why do I arouse in you nothing but this unnatural distaste?"

He stared down into her dreamy eyes. But with a distant air, she turned away and wandered to the bench of shells where, at home, she had embraced the sorcerer of Erde.

Warlocked by his own peculiar stars, the Escor seemed to have read her thought. With a low curse, almost inaudible, he dropped his outspread arms.

Listlessly, he took from a recess in his tunic a small gray casket, handing it to her with a somber face.

"I forgot this," he said, then wheeling, strode away down the path of forms.

Dione heard the clang of the moonstone door. She sighed deeply with relief and set the little casket on the bench by her side.

She must begin a plan for her escape. Perhaps Volan

could tell her when the Escor would be abroad . . . there must be some pattern.

Idly, she then opened the small gray casket. Inside on a nest of lilac fabric was an exquisite pair of jewels for the ears: each was a web-like trident of white gold, the metal of Mar, studded with minuscule jewels of the Peisun—aquamarines like sunlit water, pink amethysts the shade of lilacs in May, and yellow-green peridots that were also the Maeden's gem of fortune.

Staring at the spring-like peridots, the little Marin suddenly breathed the odor of the trees of Erdemar—the trees that camouflaged the dappled walls of the hidden house of Fahne. And the sweet, lost weeks with him returned with painful clarity to tear her heart.

She clasped the small glittering star that had been hidden below her high-necked gown. The star! Even in her agitation and terror, how could she have forgotten its promised powers? Tightly, she held it in her fingers, closing her eyes, summoning Fahne.

And desolately she knew his dark, abiding place, and she breathed the blackness now of his cave-like dungeon, which admitted but a shaft of light.

Such a little light, she reflected sadly, for him who loved it with such passion. Dione began to weep with deep, tearing sobs until she thought she heard his bell-like voice.

And the voice said, "My beloved, never despair."

With new hope, she rose and left the garden, forgetting the small gray casket on the bench of shells.

CHAPTER 3

When he heard her bitter weeping, he sat up in his bed of straw, saying quietly, "My beloved, never despair." And then he seemed to walk with her down the path of forms in her water garden, his strong arm close around her small, soft body.

Her water garden! Now, that was strange. Could Vanand have returned her to her uncle's house? Impossible.

The sorcerer cursed. His mental wandering had lost her now, lost the softness of her and the water-lily fragrance of her hair.

"What a fool you are," he said aloud. His Hermes-ridden mind, trained ever to consider rather than feel, had overridden his delighted sense, and she was gone, the one for whose ghostly presence he had been waiting these long days and nights.

The Peisun, he reflected, were not so tainted with this fault of mind. "Bless them," he whispered aloud again for the comfort of the sound, remembering their exquisite differences of temper, as well as flesh. His center pained him, wanting her. Would to the stars tonight there could be a coming-together with her whiteness; his thought was as agonizing as a prayer.

And a prayer, from him, was miracle enough. The sorcerer smiled to himself wryly in the dimness of his cavern, and he looked about him again.

No use, for now: he had examined every sooty crevice with his sensitive, wise fingers and with the light from the narrow, window-like opening reflected by his star, which served as a minuscule torch. At best, it would take him, with a companion, even, three years to dig out a path.

And his attempt to hypnotize the warder had come to naught; the timid underPeisun never met his eyes.

So he would endure it, at least until his plan was fully formed. And then, he thought, fortune had smiled by delivering him to the nonviolent Peisun and Crabba!

Fahne almost laughed, remembering the stunned look on the mottled face of Chiton, summoned to the prison when the Escors had dumped him there, his head still ringing from their blows. He had come to consciousness to hear the Mayor splutter, "Impertinence! The impertinence of him," knowing that Chiton referred to Vanand.

Smiling, the sorcerer recalled the Mayor's confusion— the hated Vanand, slayer of his niece's promised husband, had had the gall to steal her from him, then to deliver Fahne into his keeping.

The sorcerer's hollowed face fell dark again: he had, through a mighty effort of will, locked out the images of Dione in the thrall of Vanand. He dared not think of it, and he turned his thoughts instead to the savage anticipation of killing the Escor. Fahne could feel the massive throat inside his hands at this moment.

Sweating, he turned the picture off. These images would so drain him that he might weaken physically. And his strength must be gathered now as it had never been before in all his days.

For distraction, he wandered toward the narrow shaft of light that pierced his dungeon: it looked like afternoon, perhaps the hour of one-light, the hour of the Kani, the strong and optimistic star-race ruled, like the Peisun, by Jove! He needed every beneficial omen. The answer could come to him before the hour ended.

Fahne sat down again upon his bed of straw and soothed himself with images of the little Marin and the memory of their first morning in the hidden house. And, miraculously, he felt the nearness of Dione once more; she was using her star now, he knew, and she was all right.

His heart pounded like a mallet. She was well . . . and still untouched by the hated Escor! Fahne's eyes filled with his joy, and the tears gushed down his cheeks.

"My love, my love," he heard her say, and it was as if they awakened together once more in the veiled marriage bed of the hidden house. Fahne saw again the small tousled head of the Marin on his shoulder; he had held her with such savage force that he had left, to his dismay, small bruises on her white flesh.

Heavy-lidded, her face flushed with desire, she had smiled and said, "The marks are beautiful to me; they are blue and lilac petals, like the shadows on the Brisen snow . . . like the blue rose broidered on the curtains that surround us." After a breathless instant, she had asked him softly what the blue rose signified.

"It is a symbol of the Maeden," he had whispered, noticing that her tender mouth shook even at the mention of his race. How sensitive she was! "The symbol of the center," he had continued when he could pull his mouth from hers, "the way from the labyrinth . . . the union of the lover and beloved."

And the symbol and his touch and words had so aroused her that the Marin moved to him with quick, sweet savagery, bestowing on his body a caress, she told him later, she had not known she knew.

"Blue," she murmured, "is the color of my sorcerer, darkness made visible."

And Fahne reflected that she herself for him was darkness visible, her body making plain all hidden mysteries that lived below the surface of the earth, the houses in the hollow of a wave. There had not been another hour for them quite like that until this moment.

He said to her now, in his cave, feeling that she heard and would respond, "Will it always be thus, this magic that grows and changes, hour together after hour?"

"Always," she said from far away.

So wound was he in her Peisun veil that the voice, although it was not harsh, seemed to bring a sound of tearing.

It was the voice of the underPeisun warder, calling out thickly at the oval opening of the cell's door.

"A visitor," the man was saying. Fahne shook his head as if to clear it, saying softly, "Farewell, beloved." But she was gone, and the warder with the fish-like stare was leading him to a chamber outside his cell.

Fahne's clear eyes took in his surroundings with the pace of lightning: no, no way out here . . . not yet.

The underPeisun led him through a heavy metal door, bowing with deep respect to the woman waiting there. The woman was Shira.

When the Princess saw Vanand the Escorpiun take hold of the Erdemarin boy and the ancient Bole fling off his robes, becoming Fahne, her sharp perception took it in at once. That little Dione was the one who had deprived her of the sorcerer! Shira saw the black waterfall of hair cascade, revealed, from the loose green cap, shaken out by the roughness of Vanand. And Vanand loved her, too!

"Aid the Escors!" she cried to Buc, commander of her armies. "Then take the Maeden!"

Buc gaped at her an instant, stunned with disbelief. Then he had sprung to obey. And Fahne, to her horror, had been spirited away by the companions of Vanand.

But now, she thought with rising triumph, he was here with her. Now she would do with him as she would! And Shira looked with hot eyes on the leanness of him as he came into the waiting room. He stared at her in wonder.

The Capran was at her best, blooming in the unseasonably warm air of the Bilance Circle, her white breasts almost bared by the square-cut neck of her garnet-colored gown. Its color made her skin seem petal-white, with the glazed whiteness of Brisen snow, and there was a high hue in her cheeks; her black eyes glittered.

"Good day," she said in a husky voice. Her slant gaze raked the body of Fahne with hunger.

"Good day," he said deliberately in Marin to symbolize his bonds with the Peisun. But he saw with contempt that the significance was lost on her; she merely looked puzzled. "To what do I owe this honor, Your Highness?" he asked coldly.

His coldness hit. But she answered calmly, "Your Majesty now, my friend. The King Icorn is dead."

"My condolences." He bowed his stately head with irony; she had hated her father, he knew, almost as much as she had loathed her brother.

Again his subtleties were lost, like arrows in the earth that felt no wound. Fahne could feel a bubble of hysterical laughter form.

Shira, bewildered at his strange expression, asked him crudely, "Do you want to get out of this place?"

"What a foolish question, Your . . . Majesty."

She felt a swift desire to claw his face with her sharp, garnet-red nails. How could she desire him so? How well he thought of himself, she raged in silence. But the melting heat of her limbs replied. I cannot look at him, even, she thought, without this raging of desire.

His nearness overpowered her for an instant; she could not speak at all.

"And what do I have to do to be released, my lady?" He uttered the last word with such sarcasm that even the Capran caught his meaning. Her angry color rose.

"You do not care to ingratiate yourself with benefactors," she retorted.

"I have not yet been informed that you are my benefactor," he said.

"Fahne, Fahne!" she cried, suddenly losing her iron control. She ran to him and flung herself against his lean, hard body. "Fahne," she repeated thickly, "be . . . kind to me, and I will see to your release."

The heavy musk of her scent filled him with nausea; it permeated her thick hair and assailed his nostrils now as she leaned against him, trembling. He kept his arms at his sides.

"Be kind," she said again, taking his hands to draw his strong arms around her body.

He withdrew his hands. "You try to unman me, Shira. Do not try that, for that is something that is not in your power to do. I do not savor acting like a ravaged maiden." His brutal words made her recoil.

"Do you not want to be freed?" she cried.

"On my terms."

She looked up at him beseechingly, but his face was immovable, and his far-seeing eyes stared over her head at something she could neither see nor comprehend.

"I think I know what they are," she answered coldly.

"I think you do."

"You are a fool, my friend!" She whirled away from him in ire and began to rattle the bars of the door. "Warder! Warder!" she shrieked, and her tone was as harsh as the cry of a raven.

With a lightning leap, Fahne was at her side, tearing from her belt the pouch she wore, ponderous with coins.

The underPeisun, opening the cage, cried out, "Felon! Unhand the lady's purse!"

He grabbed for the sorcerer, who took his forearm with a steely hand and threw the astonished warder over his own broad shoulder. The underPeisun crashed to the floor of stone and lay quite still.

The Queen of lower Erde had not regained her voice, but a guard, attracted by the warder's outcry, was racing down the stairs. Leaping aside, Fahne extended his long leg at the last possible instant, and the guard went tumbling. Bounding over him, the lean, swift prisoner was up the winding stairs on flying feet.

"Her Majesty the Queen," intoned the chamberlain.

Chiton, the Lord Mayor of Mar, with Desmos a step behind him, moved forward with ceremonious steps to Shira, flanked by Buc, her commandant, and his second in command, Hircinus.

"Your Majesty." The Crabba bowed deeply to the Queen. "Commander. Will you take refreshment, madam?"

The lovely Capra nodded, her gleaming glance on the handsome Peisun, Desmos.

"May I have the honor?" Chiton bowed again and offered her his stubby arm. She eyed his portly frame with distaste but accepted the proffered limb and moved sinuously at his side down the stairs to the sunken chamber.

Chiton led her to a high-backed carved chair, padded

in a gray-green velvet that had a subtle dusting of silver, like light upon the sea. She sat down, glancing at Desmos.

Buc and Hircinus dispersed themselves into neighboring seats, but Desmos, hypnotized, stood by Shira's chair. His large, dreamy eyes met the glaring flatness of Buc's in an absent fashion that incensed the Capra beyond measure.

The Queen, sensing the little duel of eyes, smiled upon the Mayor, Chiton.

The portly Crabba felt the magnetism of their opposition and fairly wriggled with delight, like a young, affection-seeking mastiff.

Clapping his hands together, the chamberlain summoned the quartet of footmen in the hall, who entered bearing heavy pewter trays of Chronan and Lunar and Jovian wines for the assembly.

The chamberlain handed massive square goblets of taxus, the potent wine of yew that only Caprans could take unscathed, to the alien officers; a delicate glass of violet was offered to the Queen.

Desmos intercepted the servant and took the goblet, handing it with a fervent respect to the beautiful Capran. She nodded, looking up into his gray-green eyes, feeling her earthiness draw his watery temper half against his will.

Shira smiled at the handsome Peisun and thought, I can use this comely fish. Desmos set his glass of cioufaria, untouched, upon a bloodstone table, still staring at the Queen.

Chiton took a sip of portulaca and declared, "Your Majesty greatly honors my house."

"It is a pleasure, though a sad one"—Shira's voice trembled skillfully—"to visit the promised kinsman of my brother." She closed her eyes a moment and dabbed at them with a silk handkerchief.

"My poor lady," Chiton murmured. "Could I place my hands upon the throat of that villain . . ." he said dramatically.

Shira smiled at him with seductive mock sadness. "I am aware that Mar is not a land of warriors; Erde's armies are renowned. I wish to offer you their services in vanquishing the slayer, Vanand, and to return your lovely niece to you unharmed."

Buc had almost to restrain a smile: the wily bitch was such a splendid liar. He cared not, so long as he was privy to her chamber. That Peisun—he glanced at Desmos, whose face was thoughtful—will do well to restrain his lust, thought Buc, or I will unman the bastard.

The sensitive Desmos had caught Buc's quick expression and wondered what it meant. But now the Capran soldier's hard face was smooth again, unfeeling and as smooth as a skinned egg.

The Peisun looked again upon the Queen: Poseidon, she drew at him, without a touch, as if he were a lapdog on a tether! His dual nature warred, his skin was on fire, and his fastidious spirit was rebelling.

But Chiton the Lord Mayor could see only the fascination in his nephew's stare. And the Crabba began to reflect on what a splendid match it might become, a splendor to reflect upon the house of Chiton.

He replied to the Queen, "My lady, all gratitude is mine. And if I could but offer you, and your retinue, the poor comforts of my house . . ." His soft, broad hand waved carelessly at the magnificent appointments of the chamber.

"You are too kind." Shira bent her handsome head. "But my commanders"—she shot a teasing glance at the offended Buc—"are quartered at the inn. I will myself with gladness accept your hospitality."

The Capran commandant intervened. "It is as my lady wishes. But our duties as the guardians of the Crown compel us to your side." His oblique black eyes locked for an instant with the Queen's.

"Her Majesty," said Desmos, stung, "is quite safe within these walls." His gentle voice had hardened and his slender hand went to the dagger sheathed upon his lean thigh.

"I assure you, sire, I meant no disrespect," Buc answered with cold, reluctant courtesy.

"Nonsense, Buc!" Shira snapped. "I rest in the confidence that Sir Desmos"—she let her hot eyes linger on the green ones of the Peisun—"will be diligent in his care of me."

Desmos colored, but he bowed to the Queen with perfect equanimity.

By Artemis, the Crabba thought, that was an invitation if I have ever heard one given. My nephew has no blood if he does not respond!

"You heap greater and greater honors on my humble dwelling," Chiton said aloud. "Perhaps the prime-woman could show Your Majesty her chambers."

"Excellent. I am a little weary and would rest." Shira rose, and the others quickly got to their feet. "Hircinus," she said imperiously to Buc's second in command, "you will send my maid to me from the inn."

Hircinus bowed to the Queen, and with the stone-faced Buc he strode from the sunken chamber. Half-turning at the massive door, the commandant sought out the lovely Capran's glance, but she was looking at Desmos.

With a light laugh, she said to Chiton, "Your women, I am sure, are skilled in serving . . . but only my maid is truly conversant with . . . my coiffure."

The Peisun, she was thinking, is too subtle for the usual procedures. This will call for all of Pendra's potions.

Desmos the Peisun felt excited sweat break out upon his chest and back and trickle down his body as the Capran took his arm and leaned, as if wearily, against him. Again that strong, half-willing heat assaulted him in every sense as he perceived her softnesses.

CHAPTER 4

The windows of Dione's chambers faced onto a promontory, she discovered, by the sea, offering no escape from the dark castle of Vanand. She had as yet been unable to discern, even with Voland's sly aid, any pattern in the comings and goings of the Escor.

As the Marin looked out upon the promontory's desolation, she sickened for the magic of Erdemar. In her secluded fashion, she had not been outside her chamber for long days; the simulated water garden was unvisited, despite Vanand's pleas that she do so, for it seemed a travesty of her own beloved garden. And to pain the great Escor brought her a savage pleasure.

A double Peisun, with both the sun and moon in the reclusive sigil of the Fish, Dione's interior life enriched her now, a mighty solace in her imprisonment. And the little star of Fahne had brought him near her spirit. Six times, now, six bewitching times that had been her sole salvation.

For she had intuited that he was well, although her heart had nearly ceased to beat for terror at his sudden silence in the dungeon's outer room. Yet she knew that he would soon be near in body.

It had to be, she reflected, for she could do nothing; more than ever in her days the Marin's impotence was clear to her. A triple mutable, with sun and moon in the dual, timid Peisun, Dione felt very frail. I am a child in the world of the real, she thought sadly.

And so to pass the declining days of the slow Bilance Circle, she had turned, with Volan, to the making of songs, and waiting, dreaming.

Vanand, to her wonder and delight, had not approached her intimately again. She puzzled over his inscrutable ways, asking herself uneasily what he planned in his red metallic chambers at night.

He visited her only in the early evenings and briefly after he had returned from some mysterious errand. Severe and bland, he would sink heavily into a scarlet chair while she and Volan ate their broth in a dining alcove, or he would listen with her as the minstrel softly strummed his bird-shaped cithara or worked at building hers. Volan was making her a lute in the form of a fish.

The Marin marveled at the minstrel's ease in the hated presence of the man who had maimed him; but somehow she was confident that Vanand would never harm him again. To do so, she intuited, would damage the Escor further in her estimation; and so she was quick to show her affection for the slender Volan.

In spite of her coldness, Vanand seemed to find a deep calm in their quiet presence, and he was pleased with the Marin's silent, secluded ways.

One evening he said, as she entered the room on sound-less feet, "You are like a little cat, so quiet and soft." Dione made no answer, not deigning to look at him, but she felt his sharp green glance upon her, looking perhaps for the jewels he had given her. Besides the trident earrings that she had carelessly left in the garden, there had been other sumptuous offerings of Peisun gems—amethyst, peridot, bloodstone, moonstone, and aquamarine.

But in her ears, below the wings of glistening black hair, she wore no gems at all. And she had removed the hated nuptial ring. Her star glittered openly in the little hollow of her throat. If Vanand was pained, his shut face never told her.

Sometimes she was almost lulled into the illusion that she and the minstrel shared their long-gone life, but then Vanand would appear and sit down, like a large, fierce animal momentarily tamed. And Dione would hear again the lonely soughing of the sea, and her heart would ache for Fahne and the hidden house. Then, full force, she would be struck again by her body's deprivation of the sorcerer and her unending imprisonment.

"What is he plotting?" she asked Volan when they were alone together.

"I know not, lady," the minstrel answered. "I have ever been bewildered by the shadowy temper of the Escors. But I am acquainted well with their sinister patience, their enduring obduracy."

Late in the nights she would sometimes awaken, hearing strange cries from somewhere far below the castle, carried upward by the chilling autumn wind—long, boar-like grunts and shrill screaming that filled her with apprehension, prefiguring somehow that dark All Hallows mentioned by the Escor, the ceremony he had said would be held under the moon of Proserpine in the time of the Escorpiun.

And Dione would pray to Kun that the sorcerer make haste.

She asked Volan about the sounds. The minstrel, who had become her greatest consolation, singing for her in the silver-throated fashion of the Brise, was searching for an air now to one of her poems.

"Do not concern yourself with the sounds," he said easily.

But Dione pressed him. He sighed. "It is a mournful thing, and I do not like to tell you mournful things. But you, with your obdurate traces of the Bole, in your Jove and Aphrodite, will never let me rest until I do." Volan smiled wryly. "It is the temple of barren women," he continued. "The Crabba and the Escorpiun, and certain Erden travelers to Mar, go there to relax themselves. It has never been a favorite of the Peisun or the Maeden."

She smiled, and her heart as always leaped at the mention of the star-race of Fahne. She put aside her fish-shaped lute and nodded at the minstrel to go on.

"Without love," he said, "like plundering Huns, the men go to the barren women for an orgiastic kyra in the temple."

"Kyra?"

"A budding rite of a strange sect," Volan explained.

"Oh, yes, the Kyrin." The little Marin nodded again. Fahne had told her of them. Some wandered in the deserts of far-off lands, eating husks, filled with impossible visions of happiness after death. Others had erected temples in imitation of the Church of Stars, preaching a sad mortification of the flesh; their underworld was full of fire, not shadowy like that of the star-races.

Dione recalled the sorcerer's words: "They build for the poor a pitiful delusion of an 'afterlife,' blinding the folk to any glories of the present, perpetuating the ills done to them by persuading them that their reward will follow life, not be found within it."

And with a quickly beating heart she remembered the circumstances surrounding their conversation on the subject—they had been lying naked in the rustling leaves of the woods of Erdemar, the sun dappling their appeased and peaceful flesh.

Dione recalled her comments to the sorcerer—that the aliens' leader had had a vision akin to the Other-Seeing of the Peisun, but differing from her own belief in that the Kyrin saw the soul and body as separate. The Peisun knew that each was a reflection of the other, inextricably mingled as the flesh and bone, the heart and brain, the reason with the marrow.

Fahne had smiled at this, caressing her. "Your watery knowledge is the quality we Erden seek so desperately; only the Marin are possessed of it, and, most of all, the Peisun. To most of us, the brain and body are . . . machines; the fiery Sabbians sing the body and the passions most; the airy Brisen, the mind, except for those of the warm Bilance, controlled by Aphrodite."

Volan's words broke into her reverie. "The rite in the temple of barrens," he was saying, "is a travesty of the aliens. Mar frowns on it, but it still goes on. The valley is a fearful place; even the trees are dead. It is a plain of blasted trunks and dry, gray branches. The wind cries through the bony woods like the damned crying in the time before time."

"You speak almost in singing," said Dione. "But I never heard you sing so darkly."

Volan smiled sadly. "There are dark things in the world, my lady, that the Peisun's glowing sight has shielded you from."

The Marin felt an arrow of pain, contemplating the sorrows she did not know. "Where did you learn of this . . . temple?"

"From a server here." Dione's soft voice had sounded with such a sickness that Volan hastened to speak of other things. "I have heard it said that a lady of very high degree is now in Mar.

Distracted, the Marin looked at him questioningly.

"Shira," the minstrel said, "the sister of Monoceros, now the Queen."

"Monoceros' sister! Do they come seeking vengeance of Vanand?"

"I know not. But only today I heard that Chiton attempts to wed her to your cousin Sir Desmos."

"My dear friend Desmos!" Her tone became ironic as she added, "My uncle is bent on allying Mar with Erde in any fashion, it seems." Then she asked, "Do you think that Vanand goes to the temple? And that is why he has . . . left me alone?" She flushed.

"Oddly enough, I do not think he does, as yet. He is too proud." And Volan took up his instrument and began to sing.

Dione listened, soothed, as he sang of the fatal order of things, of the wavering passions of flame and the air, and of the sea that makes fertile the land.

She was silent for a moment when he had done, then said teasingly, "That is a very religious song for a rebel of questioned birth."

There was a wordless interval as Volan strummed his instrument before Dione said awkwardly, "My friend, I am . . . with child. I feel it."

"Oh, my lady!" the minstrel cried out. "When Vanand learns, his rage will be terrible."

"No! Don't you see? It is the one thing he could never countenance—another man's 'leavings.' His pride will be so offended he will let me go—he will set me free!"

Volan shook his dark head touched with gold. "He will never let you go."

"He must. He will."

Dione rose and paced the chamber, small and fragile in her green and russet boy's attire that she had resumed wearing, scorning the many gowns offered by Vanand.

"Volan, I must be certain. Please, help me find a sayer. I cannot trust the healer of Vanand."

"My dearest lady." The minstrel sighed. Then he went to the little Marin and took her hand. "Very well. My friend the steward is permitted out on the morrow. He will find a sayer."

It was near full winter in the land of Brise. The Baron's guests from moyen-Brise were gathered this night near the roaring fire, their splendid cloaks befurred at neck and hem and sleeves, befitting those allowed to slay the higher beasts.

The delicate demoiselles of dernier-Brise and premier-Brise drew back from the flames. Their narrow nostrils quivered with distaste as the odor of roasting flesh filled the vast feasting chamber, a special dispensation to the moyen-Brise.

Shabatu, daughter of the Waetergyt who was the host, sat a little apart from the others, thinking of the glad day when the barbaric moyen-Brise would end their visit and return to their lower plateau. She was arrayed in an intricate gown of thinnest wool, a light blue of the winter morning, and encrusted with the amethysts of her February birth. Over the gown was a matching cloak of heavier wool. The pastel hues made a glory of her pallid hair, a gold so light it was almost silver. Her kindly, distant eyes were the color of the cloak and gown.

Putting the visitors from mind, Lady Shabatu applauded heartily as the whirling yellow figure with yellow hair wheeled through the air like a flake of snow and landed cat-like on his graceful feet.

Kaus the flame-haired Sabbian, leading his dancing dog to an alcove beyond the chamber, stared at Shabatu. "What a beauty she is!" he whispered to Gemelle.

Gemelle smiled and nodded, but he kept his narrow face cool. He took up his lute as Veris the Bole began to beat upon his tabor, and the Capran Bock put his panpipes to his full lips.

The three began an air, joined by the harmonies of the

castle's moyen-Brise, playing in one circle upon their viols, rebecs, gitterns, citoles, and micanons.

When the strains of the many-sided air had stilled, the Twisan Gemelle strummed softly upon his lute and began to sing a rondeau. The pale, remote glance of the Lady Shabatu met his, warming, but the narrow Gemelle seemed untouched by this sign of her favor. Kaus the Sabbian had returned to join the other music-makers. As he took up his Sabbian trumpet, he gave Gemelle a side glance of irritation. Would that Shabatu would look so upon him!

Prince Solidago of moyen-Brise fixed his large, violet-colored eyes, which seemed half-sleeping under their heavy lids, on Shabatu. The Baron Melik, it appeared, had not overmuch control over his lovely daughter. He moved his chair a little closer to the Waetergyt's, feeling her lean away from him.

"How do you, my lady?" he asked in his insinuating voice.

Shabatu's answer was as cool as the touch of snow, and higher, more silver than the tones of moyen-Brise. "The fire is far too warm; I must move my chair. You will pardon me."

And she gestured to a server to move her chair of yew farther from the blaze.

Solidago likewise moved his carved chair and settled near her again, shivering in the chillier air. The fragile Shabatu felt herself almost overpowered by his primrose scent—an odor of his ruler Aphrodite—mingled with the musky scent of the hated furs. She looked again at the yellow hair of Gemelle. He, she thought dreamily, would have the scent of the healing mandrake or the tart fruit of the cherry, clear as snow!

But fearing to reveal herself to Melik, Shabatu let her white lids veil her sky-blue stare, keeping her half-curtained look on the snowy hands in her lap. Their fingers were long and tapering, so narrow that they resembled the tips of wings.

Solidago longed to kiss the hands. The skin of Shabatu was in truth the texture of the falling snow, so delicate that the moyen-Brise had sometimes feared that if he kissed her she would disappear. Perhaps the Queen, his mother, was right. And yet . . . and yet . . . the indecisive nature of his Bilance race filled him with hesitation. She was so beautiful, so very beautiful!

Yet, now, he pondered gloomily, she had eyes for no one but the acrobat, no better than a server, with his nimbleness for hire.

The rondeau was done. In the pause the Baron Melik called out to Gemelle, "My friend! Where is that noted Maeden, the sorcerer Fahne? His fame has been noised among the Brisen for the last full wheeling of the year."

Gemelle hesitated. He thought of the Brisen amity with Sabbia and that of Sabbia and Erde. Then with calm mendacity he answered, "I know not, sire. His disappearance was most spectral; he has been transmuted, mayhap, into another form."

The Lady Shabatu looked sharply at Gemelle, but the Baron Melik heard nothing amiss. He laughed at the jest.

"I grieve to hear it," the Baron replied good-naturedly. "He was a man of many parts, a man of gifts."

His daughter, the frail young Waetergyt, studied Gemelle still; she could see a flash of pain in his dancing look.

And the dazzled Gemelle took in the wit, high and remote as a peak of the Brisen mountains, glimmering in her sky-colored eyes; the wanness of her Brisen beauty tickled his nerves.

Yet the question regarding Fahne had caught him unaware, filling him with pain and apprehension. For it seemed to him of late there had been rumors that Nobilis, powerful Prince of Sabbia, had been vying with the moyen-Brisen Solidago for the Lady Shabatu; that, moreover, Nobilis and Monoceros had met in frequent counsel before the Capran's death.

Was there something more in the question of the Baron? Even as his mercurial feelings leaped in homage to the snowy Waetergyt, Gemelle was haunted by doubt, feeling again the hollow in his life carved by the parting of the sorcerer.

Gemelle wondered for the thousandth time how the Maeden fared. How pleasant it would be to see his friend again! Bock and Veris, after all, were longing to return to the South before the flying of the final geese; and Kaus, Hermes knew, would bloom like a bright lizard again away from the blue-shadowed snow.

Yet here was the peerless Shabatu, Gemelle ruminated; few enough were the women who could melt the coolness of his veins, and he had dreamed of her so long!

CHAPTER 5

Eleven-dark, the hour of the Waetergyt, was chill this night in Mar as Fahne dodged into the shadows. The moon was ripening to perilous brightness, as it had that night in the water garden of Dione.

For an instant the sorcerer's memory lingered on that other sweet eleven-dark. Swiftly, however, he recalled himself to the grimmer task awaiting him—getting out of Mar unseen.

His tongue was furred with thirst and his lean belly was growling so from hunger that he almost feared it would give away his presence. Fahne's head, as well, was drumming from his exhaustion and its contact with the fist of the Crabba guardsman he had met at the top of the stairs.

Crawling through a narrow window that had nearly captured him, the sorcerer had dived into the dark canal, hiding below a barge until moonrise. Even now his doublet and hose clung damply, stinking of the water still unpurified of the drought-slain peisun. He shivered a trifle and peered from his hiding hole below an arching bridge.

I hope I meet a weaker polesman, he meditated wryly. His strength was not at its height at the end of such a day.

And his hope, it seemed, was soon to be fulfilled, for staggering down the escalade toward the waiting barge, he saw a bowed and tipsy Escor of advancing age. Behind him was an ancient man whose flowing beard of white was stranded with the black hair of the Marin; the old man wore a Peisun's gray-green robe with the H-like sigil on his chest. Apparently the old man was the Escor's passenger.

But the old Peisun came down the escalade on cautious feet, staring uneasily at the polesman, whose unsteady progress almost landed him in the canal.

"Thround," the old man quavered, "have a care! Are you fit to pole me to the castle of Vanand in upper Mar?"

Fahne could not believe his fortune. Every god in the wheel of heaven had conspired in this! he exulted silently.

"I think," the old man went on, in the wary, hesitant fashion of the Peisun, "that I will seek another polesman."

The sorcerer leaped from the bridge's shadow onto the deck of the barge. "May I be of service, sire?" he asked the aged Peisun.

The drunken Escor goggled at the sorcerer, and the old Peisun, whose eyes, Fahne saw now, were very deep and gentle, laughed in the whimsy-loving manner of his race.

"Are you, too, a seer, a spirit, to appear from out of nothing?" he asked Fahne softly.

"I am your polesman, sire, to bear you to the castle of Vanand."

Fuzzily, the Escor started to protest. The sorcerer put a soothing hand upon his shoulder. "Sleep, friend, sleep. I will do your task and you may have the pewter that I do the poling for. You may keep the mathale." All the while that he whispered to the polesman, praying that none of the guard would appear, Fahne looked deeply into the Escor's eyes.

The drunken man began to nod. In a moment he had fallen to the deck of the barge and was snoring soundly.

"Poseidon!" the bearded man swore almost inaudibly. "You, too, are a seer, my son."

Fahne nodded once and asked, "What is your mission, father, in the castle of Vanand?"

The Peisun hesitated, then replied, "I cannot tell you that."

"I have a proposition for you, sire."

"Proposition?" The Peisun's soft voice held his puzzlement.

"Let me go in your stead to the seat of Vanand." There was an urgency in the tall man's face that caught the pity of the Peisun. "I will repay you well."

"Why, my son?"

"It is an errand that is life and death."

The old man nodded. "I believe you. But I must know this, at the risk of revealing my mission—do you mean good or ill to the Lady Dione?"

Fahne's heart lurched in his breast. "The Lady Dione?" he cried. "What do you know of her?"

"Answer my question."

The sorcerer said in a thick voice, "She has my heart."

The old Peisun smiled. "Go, then, my friend." He shook his hooded head as the sorcerer offered silver. "No. No, I want no recompense. But I caution you: beware of Vanand. I will advise you of our trysting place." And he described the spot on the estate of Vanand. "I give you the water-gods' speed."

His pulse pounding in his ears, the sorcerer handed the ancient man up the escalade. "And I give you my eternal thanks."

Fahne pulled a voluminous red cloak from the shoulders of the sleeping Thround. What it lacked in length, it made up well in breadth and would cover him creditably. He threw a rug over the polesman and discovered to his delight a rough pouch of bread and cheese and a beaker of Hadean wine. Well, he would leave an extra silver piece for this.

Sniffing the beaker's mouth, lest it hold wormwood, Fahne scented hawthorn and quaffed it with relish. His chilled skin warmed. Then after wolfing down a hunk of cheese and bread, the sorcerer began with a singing in him to pole the barge upriver toward the castle of Vanand.

Desmos felt the great explosion of release and gave a cry muffled in the cedar-smell of Shira. He did not let go of her; an instant later he heard her answering cry, muffled like his on flesh, a small, hollow groaning.

When he was coming to himself, dreading already a little the aftertime, his widening eyes beheld first the smooth marble of her limbs; he kissed the satiny skin, feeling her residue of trembling, tasting clove and cedar.

But even now he could sense her incipient restlessness. Desmos stroked her, thinking with sadness that their aftermath would always hold this alienation—that primal strangeness between the minds of the Capran and the Fish.

His Peisun need for long, slow closeness of affection had never been quite met by this exquisite, slant-eyed witch he tried to capture now below his gentle hand. Shira's lust was fierce and sudden, quickly slaked, more swiftly than in any woman he had known; but afterward she retreated to aloofness—like a whoring man, he sometimes thought with distaste.

The Capran's ways shook Desmos still; yet he could not

deny the yearning of his flesh. It was as if she drew at him as a magnet drew metal to its breast. He recalled with a kind of ruefulness her ruler, Chronos, the sigil of permanent magnetism. For she always held an odor of sun and cedar, dark and green. How he longed to make her his forever!

He voiced these thoughts to her now. Turning, she lay a moment on the flame-green coverlet beside him—her maid had fitted out the guest chamber in Chiton's house in the hues of the Capran—and smiled. Her smile was the tolerant smile of an adult for a charming child.

He looked down at her smooth, self-contained face, with its oblique black brows like questing wings, and its full, rather sullen mouth. Desmos bent and kissed her with a kind of beseeching.

"You are very poetic," she said in her husky, harsh way. Her tone, like that of a woman appraising a gown, deflated him, and he felt his lyric words evaporate from his puzzled brain.

He sighed.

"What is it?" she asked a little more gently, running her small, blunt hand down his leg. Despite himself, he began to quiver again.

This time, with cold skill, she led him until at last he was so spent that there was silence for a slow and breathless time.

"I love you, I love you," he whispered. "We should be wed."

"And I you, my handsome one," she said lightly, brushing his shoulder with her lips. Pushing at him a little, she asked for her release. Reluctantly, he let her go and saw her move about the chamber, with that restlessness he had learned to dread and know. "But we cannot marry yet."

"Shira." She was standing naked at the curtained oval window staring down at the canal.

"What do you see so fascinating on the water?" he asked softly.

Without turning, she replied indifferently, "Nothing . . . only a ragged Escor poling a barge up the river. Tall for an Escor, however," she added with a peculiar intonation.

Desmos stared at her loveliness, admiring the perfect shape of her torso, the mark of the Capran, and the protracted fall of her straight black hair down her sweetly curving back. How mysterious, in their way, the Caprans are! he mused. Their origins, half-earth, half-ocean, made them alternately soft and dreamy, hard and practical.

Turning, Shira faced him unashamedly—he was always surprised, yet somehow titillated, by her lack of reticence— and asked him sharply, "What are you thinking of?"

He feasted his heavy eyes on her black-smudged whiteness and answered vaguely, "Dreaming—of marrying you."

Shira moved to a press, taking out a rustling, flamegreen robe, and slipped it over her.

"And what of your quarrel with Chiton in the matter of Vanand?"

Again the sensitive Peisun, for all his manly mask of strength, was jarred by the Capran's matter-of-factness. Desmos still could not grasp Shira's sudden reversals.

She was standing now before her tall oval glass, redding her face, blackening her eyes, as if she were alone in the chamber. She ran a square-shaped comb, aglitter with garnets, through a portion of her thick black hair. "Well?"

Desmos, covering himself, sat up in the wide bed and frowned. "It is not exactly a quarrel," he said with the slow, subtle precision of the Peisun, in the manner that the other races mistook for hesitance.

"Whatever," Shira said impatiently, taking up another lock of hair for her comb.

"He has charged me as headlong . . ." Her hard laugh intervened.

"Hardly," she commented. Stung, he resumed.

". . . headlong in my seeming eagerness to rescue my cousin Dione. I have told you I believe Vanand a villain. My uncle, in his merchant's fashion"—the Peisun's voice was scornful—"would now let her wed him, lacking the crown of Monoceros."

"Then why have you not done so?" she asked with impatience.

"I am not Hercules." His answer was wry and plaintive. "My uncle the Mayor has thwarted my efforts to raise an escorting guard."

She tossed her jeweled comb upon a table and came toward him. Sitting on the bed, she rubbed his bearded chin with both of her sensual hands. He stirred.

"What if I offered you an escort?" she asked in her husky tone.

"You? And your pact with my uncle, and with Mar?"

The Capran laughed, a low, husky laugh that always excited the Peisun beyond measure. "Must Mar be privy to all my woman's secrets?"

Desmos glanced at the star-wheel glittering on the breast of her nightrobe. In four sectors were the stormy topaz of the Escorpiun—magnet to the emerald-starred Bole in his own circle, the Escorpiun's fatal opposite. She was a match for anyone, he reflected.

And though he exulted in the knowledge that at last he would be able to save Dione, the thought of the Capran's lizard-like deceit still rankled. She had eluded him once more.

"Leave me, Ene." The calm Bole server wondered at the sickness in his master's demeanor. But obediently he withdrew from the chamber.

Vanand stared at the somber portrait above his massive ebon table. It was a likeness of Sclar, his father, the robber baron who had ridden down the neighboring demesnes before the people had risen to power in Mar.

"The people!" Vanand spat. He looked up again at the likeness of Sclar: the hawk-like face and the piercing eyes were identical to his own.

"I shall not fail you, sire." Vanand smiled strangely up at the painted face of Sclar, then fell into a dream.

As though from a very great distance, then, he seemed to hear the voice of Ene intone two alien names.

"Melik, the Baron of Brise," sang the Bole. "His Majesty Achir, the King of Sabbia."

And the iron portals to the echoing council hall were opened with a flourish, admitting the royal leaders and their trains.

Melik, the noble Waetergyt, wore upon his white-gold hair the dernier-Brisen's conic hat of wings, headgear of the titled men of air. He was very tall and slender as a reed in a blue-gray vernal robe of light wool, suited to the warmer clime of Mar. Around his narrow neck on a delicate silver chain hung the medallion of the Lion with Wings, symbolizing the amity of Brise and Sabbia, the wings for the country of the air, the beast-king for Sabbia, the country of the sun. The medallion glittered like the falling snow with pallid amethysts and crystal, garnets and the transparent snow-pearls of the Brisen.

Melik waved his blue-clad attendants back and paused to give precedence to the flame-haired retinue of Achir, the King of Sabbia.

Achir, stately and proud as the Leun-beast itself, came forward on soundless feet toward the great Escor, now risen from his chair.

The Leun monarch dazzled the Marin's dreaming sight: on his mass of mane-like fiery hair the King wore a crown of shining gold that rose in sharp points, like the points of flames. The crown was thick with rubies brighter than the monarch's crimson raiment, and on either side of him towered a noble-looking Leun officer. All of Achir's royal guard carried spears of gilt, and their daggers and trappings were also gilt.

"I bid you welcome, sire," said the High Escor; and his words, too, sounded distant to his own ears.

Vanand snapped his massive fingers at his chamberlain. The man in turn signaled to the six red-clad underEscors hovering by the doors, who disappeared in an instant and quickly returned, bearing great trays on which reposed the golden and flame-colored beakers of the wines of Sabbia, plus the beakers of blue and lilac that held the fragile liquors of Brise.

With great ceremony King Achir seated himself opposite the Escor, his shining guard around him. Melik, with the ironic look of the Waetergyt, sat down with less pomposity, accepting a lilac goblet of solanum.

"You honor my house, messires," said Vanand, sipping his wormwood wine. He could, even in his dreaming, taste it clearly.

Melik bowed his narrow head once. Achir, the flame-haired King, smiled broadly.

"We are pleased to inform you," said the Leun, "that the people of Sabbia and Brise will soon acclaim you as their highest King. Only the barbaric land of Erde remains to be captured."

Vanand seemed to hear a mighty singing, as of a titanic chorus of heavenly voices. His time at last was come! He was proud of his stately calm as he answered in a low voice, "And the coronation?"

Melik replied, after a glance at Achir, "The coronation, of course, will be held in Mar, with the armies of Sabbia in full panoply, and the attendants of Brise, as well."

Vanand felt himself nod without speaking.

"And, of course," Achir added genially, "my daughter, Princess Dafira, will offer you her hand, in concert with Melik's daughter Shabatu." The Leun smiled at the Waetergyt.

"Naturally," said Melik, "you will also retain Lady Dione, if you desire. And certainly some arrangement can be made with the Queen of endlich-Erde."

The soldiers guffawed at the reference to Shira.

"Splendid," Vanand replied. "Now, messires, if you will pardon me," he added negligently, "I have had a long and pressing day. I am sure my servants can see to your every need."

The Baron and the King rose at once, accepting their dismissal.

"My lord. My lord." The near words had a sound of having been repeated several times.

Vanand took his piercing gaze from the painted face of Sclar, his father, and turned in the direction of his accoster.

It was the puzzled Ene, his serving Bole. They were alone in the dim, oval chamber. Vanand's dream shattered.

The Bole restrained an exclamation of shock. The Escor's craggy face, below the iron eagle on the cresting of his father's chair, was unnaturally pallid and strained, his oblique eyes fixed in a wild, unseeing stare, like a man with a magnificent vision. He looked quite mad.

Vanand asked, "Have you seen to the Baron and the King?" He was in the dream once more.

Ene stared. "The Baron, sire? The King?" he repeated blankly.

"Are you a fool? I asked if you had seen to their needs." Vanand's lips were compressed and his green eyes were wild and bright.

The Bole replied softly, "Yes, sire, I have."

"Then why have you broken my privacy?" demanded Vanand.

"To inform you, sire, that Sir Madimiel and the others beg to be excused from dining."

Madimiel and Zur! He no longer required those petty burgomeisters, no better than Erden. He, Vanand, who was king of all!

"What matters that?" he growled at Ene. "Leave me."

The Bole, who had come at Vanand's urgent summons, felt a chill of unease. He bowed, withdrawing quickly from the chamber.

CHAPTER 6

When they had descended the plateaus of moyen-Brise, Gemelle had regretfully changed the airy *cheval de mont* —the mountain horse—for the sturdier Marin horse that would serve them until they reached the rim of Erde.

His companions, Kaus the Sabbian and the Erden Veris and Bock, seemed heartened at their southward progress. The somber geese were whistling overhead as they made their patterned journey down to Erde.

And tomorrow would bring the Circle of the Escorpiun.

Gemelle knew a deeper darkness of the spirit, an aggravation of the darkness falling when he parted from Shabatu. The Twisan glanced at Kaus; yes, the Sabbian felt it, too, for their temperaments of air and fire were oppressed by the sinister season of the Escorpiun, the Thround, the most inimical of the watery circles to their peculiar brightness.

Veris the Bole and Bock the Capran, cousined by the heavenly order to the water races, felt no such darkness. Indeed, the season of the Thround was warm in Erde, a gentle close to summer. Full winter in Erde would not arrive until the Circle of the Kani, a month following.

The wagon had descended now the last small rise that marked the borders of moyen-Brise and upper Mar. To Kaus the Kani of Sabbia and Veris and Bock, the small rain of the border air was a comparative blessing after the snowy wind of Brise; but Gemelle the Twisan smelled in the rain a sad dilution of the white, cold land he loved, a prefigurement of the arid warmth of Erde. Gemelle sighed, stroking Kaus' dancing dog.

Kaus the Sabbian, with unaccustomed softness—for his

temper was hard and loud and bright—touched the Twisan on his lean arm and said, "This parting from Brise was a double sadness."

Gemelle nodded his yellow head. His smooth-shaven cheeks looked very pale and hollow to Kaus.

The flame-haired Sabbian was not a man for meditation, but now as the wagon eased onto the more level ways of upper Mar, he thought of the last few weeks in the land of air. Gemelle the Twisan had been happier than Kaus had ever seen him, after that night when Shabatu first warmed to the man with yellow hair.

And what an imperious Queen she was! Kaus smiled.

In turn, Gemelle, who had once astounded the lusty Kaus by declaring that too much love injured his artistic equilibrium, had looked upon the lovely Shabatu like a sick gazelle. Therefore, it was with amazement that Kaus received the news of their journey South.

When Kaus had questioned the Twisan, Gemelle had replied evasively, saying only that the troupe had always returned to the more temperate climes for winter. Nevertheless, the Sabbian knew Gemelle was suffering, and his good-natured liking for the Twisan made Kaus uneasy now at Gemelle's agony.

Bock the Capran pushed aside the curtains of the wagon at this moment, putting a hard, blunt hand on Kaus' shoulder. "We had best skirt the city, had we not?" the Capran asked in his brassy voice.

Gemelle nodded. "The Marin may not welcome us with open arms. When we have reached the crossing ways, let us take the lower road to Erdemar, Kaus."

"Very well," the Sabbian replied.

The curtains closed again and there was silence. The gray, late light of upper Mar was closing in and a fog enveloped the road ahead.

"I don't like this," Kaus said to Gemelle.

"We will make slow progress," the Twisan answered easily, "but I have seen it worse. Have no fear."

The Sabbian, however, in his sun-loving manner, saw the graying cloud as an unlucky omen. He patted the dog's head.

The fog had grown so dense as he approached that Vanand could barely see the low-slung outlines of the Barren Temple—with its suggestion of barbaric lust, hint-ing in its patterns a supine female form with upthrust breasts.

The Escor was breathing hoarsely, for he had hastened to escape the puzzled scrutiny of his servers, running almost the entire distance from the castle.

Vanand entered the temple's vestibule, crowded with men.

A wave-like murmur lapped the gathering: "It is Vanand," the whispers came, "who was the Minister of Mar." For the Escor, too aloof and proud to frequent the public orgies in the past, was paying his first visit to the temple.

An ironic-looking Thround with sharp green eyes commented to a Capran beside him, "Apparently the little Fish is still elusive."

"Quiet," said the Capran, for one did not comment aloud upon Vanand. "He looks half-mad," the Capran whispered discreetly to the Escor, "like his mad father."

Indeed, Vanand's eagle eyes were strangely fixed, with an unnatural brightness, and his face was as white as the face of the dead.

"Is it almost time?" Vanand snapped at a russet-tunicked Bole. When the man nodded, the Escor strode into the preparatory baths.

His stay was brief in its steamy depths. Hurriedly, he scented his massive body with man-musk, and with a complacent glance at his strong, naked image in the glass, he stepped into the gray metallic mass-tunic of the Escorpiun.

The buxom Bole attendant, wearing only a russet loincloth, looked at him yearningly from her wide brown eyes, the attraction of their diametric races pulling.

Insidious flutes and savage, pounding drums sank down to silence when Vanand came into the tabernacle; his rigid flesh was snug in his silvery tunic.

He knelt with the others at the center of the temple upon kneeling benches padded with roseate silk; the backs of the wide, bed-like benches were covered with a shining, plush, napped fabric that suggested opulence.

The walls were bare of ornament; many low candles suggesting the curves of women lined the windows; they gave a rose-like flame and emitted a heavy, musk-like odor. A rose-red velvet bed lay crosswise upon the altar floor, and above the altar was an immense domed window of stained glass depicting the races of Mar and of Erde in

a wild confusion of naked limbs, wearing the heads of
bulls and goats, of fish and crabs and scorpions.

Vanand felt akin to bursting as the splendid barren
Veneris entered to altar-light from the shades beyond and
lay in a travesty of crucifixion on the rose-red velvet.

Her bare and tawny flesh glowed ripely in the dim light
above the altar; her great bovine eyes were shut, and her
rich golden-brown hair, with its hint of red, was spread
upon the floor and over the full, sprawling upper body.

On either side of her were rows of lovely acolytes to
the left and to the right. Each wore only a waistcloth of
glittering, thin fabric in the color of her race: the onyx-
haired Capra wore fiery-green; the Bole were in bright
russet; the Crabba wore the ocean-green of Artemis with
an overtone of silver; and the hot-eyed Escorpiun wore the
scarlet of the Thround. They began to sing in husky voices
a peculiar introit, a sensuous melody of subtle, titillating
plays on sacred words.

A deep excitement swept the great crowd of communicants, whose breathing quickened. Some began to moan,
and many were teasing their bodies against the curly
backs of the padded benches. "Chronos!" cried one. Another called on Aphrodite.

Now as the men began to move forward to the com-
munion, Vanand felt the massive pulsing of his loins; his
body ached and trembled. Now, he thought, Veneris will
have the great fortune to receive the king of all lands;
and the cool Peisun Dione will suffer, learning that I have
denied her!

Veneris lay writhing; the points of her bare breasts
blossomed. As the line of communicants approached her,
one by one, she saluted each with the flicked caress of a
famous queen, and yet she shook her shining head, moaning.

Each communicant then summoned an acolyte from the
gleaming row to the left or right and, leading her away,
proceeded to his particular delight.

The flutes and drums were heard again in mounting
volume, and among the kindred pounding on the floors and
the flute-like wails of women, Vanand approached Veneris.

Vast and rigid, he knelt above her. Her wide, bovine
brown eyes, the earthy eyes of the Bole, his fatal opposite,
stared up at him with overpowering lust: she gave a loud,

shrill cry and fiercely took him for the famous drawing
kiss.

The music stopped abruptly, and with half-closed, glaz-
ing eyes, some of the participants looked to see which fortunate the priestess had bestowed her favors on.

Then Veneris loosed Vanand from her particular, artful
touch and bade him play the man. Panting, he readied to
obey. But to his horror, at that very instant he saw the
shut face of Dione and felt his slackening, the draining of
his power.

Dazed, he fell on his elbows and knees, helpless and
stricken, crouching like a large, befuddled beast. He was
unable to move, the evidence of his shame shrunken above
Veneris, swaying in a lucid pendulum of impotence.

Groaning, Veneris turned like a maddened tigress to a
neighboring pair and threw aside the woman, demanding
of the partner that he do her bidding instantly.

With an exclamation of astonishment and pleasure, he
obeyed.

Vanand, shuddering with his ire and shame, rose slowly
and raced from the temple, sobbing.

In the heavy motions of a nightmare, the Escor had
snatched up a voluminous red cloak, whose property he
neither knew nor cared, and fastened it over his metallic
tunic. Unknowing, he stumbled from the vestibule and
through the entrance doors to the plain of dry and bony
vegetation.

Racing on and on, he reached at last the steep path to
the promontory. He toiled upward, sobbing, and at the top
fell prone on the cold grass.

"The devil!" he shouted. "She has removed my manhood's crown, and in the sight of all!"

Blindly, Vanand endured an interval of pain; how long
it was he could not know. When he awoke from it he
found himself staring at the inscrutable sea. It sounded to
him the placid obduracy, the elusiveness of the Peisun
Dione, who would always evade him like a shining sea
thing slipping from a net. It was as if, over the many
circles, Vanand had tossed a thousand spears into the sea
that sank into its ever-moving roll with impotence, never
connecting with their prey.

Impotence—the word struck at him like a blow.

He saw that the waves were white-capped now, and

roaring. Something in their angry rhythm soothed him, for this was not the music of the Peisun, but of the Escor!

He wiped his wet cheeks with his massive hand and knew that in this moment the sea at last was his—tumultuous, holding terror—no longer gentle, as it had been under the moon of the Bilance, when it murmured softly and returned unreadable to deep green calm.

For somewhere in the distance he heard the midnight ringing of the change of day, the bell of twelve-dark, Capra: Antares burned, and Aphrodite had handed the reins of the moon to Ares, god of war. It was the twenty-third of October, the first of Escorpiun.

This month, this circle of his own, he raged in wordless pain, was to have brought him the Peisun in the rite of belonging. Well, there were greater women now for his possession! And the Peisun was fit only to die.

Raising his massive arms so that his scarlet cloak spread out in fearful wings, the Escor began to laugh a wild, dreadful laugh. He shouted into the wind ascending from the sea, "Mark you, Ares, my god and my companion!" cried Vanand. "My sword and yours will rise again and never lower! There will be lively wars again to end your centuries of waiting! And we will destroy all those who bar our way!"

With a purposeful tread, Vanand descended the path from the desolate promontory toward the grotesque turrets of the castle. His slant, green eyes were as hard as emeralds.

The fog had thickened when the wagon of Gemelle took to the winding road above the sea. Bock and Veris stared nervously ahead, leaning from the parted curtain behind Gemelle and Kaus.

"I like it less and less," the Sabbian commented.

"Let me guide the beast," Gemelle replied, and leaping from the wagon, he prepared to change his place with Kaus.

But a sudden rent appearing in the veil of fog revealed a sight that gave him pause.

"Are you coming?" the Sabbian called.

"Not yet," Gemelle answered, his narrow Brisen tones ghostly in the muffling mist.

"Not yet!" Bock repeated angrily. "What can you be

about, Gemelle? Let us leave this at once and get to firmer ground!"

"Please, Bock. I see a most peculiar sight below."

"We'll see still a more peculiar vision when our wagon has tumbled from this cursed height in the fog," the Bole intervened in his firm erst-Erden, his customary calm deserting him.

"What is it, Gemelle?" Kaus leaped from the wagon and went to the Twisan's side, the dog trotting after.

"Down there . . . and there. Behold." And the narrow finger of Gemelle pointed first to two dim figures, far below, toiling upward in the fog, then to another, so far away it was almost imperceptible, a tall, strong figure in a scarlet cloak, gesticulating alone on a cliff above the water.

"Gods!" Kaus cried. "The one in red—is it Vanand?"

Gemelle nodded grimly. "And the others are Dione the Marin, if I mistake not, and the little minstrel. See, they enter now that small structure on the side of the rise."

Veris and Bock had joined the Brisen and the Sabbian. "Where, then, is Fahne?" Veris asked Gemelle tensely.

"Assuredly not in the castle of Vanand," Gemelle returned. He paused, then said, "I must remain."

There were irritated exclamations from Kaus and Bock; Veris was silent.

Gemelle held up his slender hand. He smiled. "I charge you, proceed and leave me."

Veris said sharply, "That I will not do."

"Nor I," Kaus said. Bock the Capran shook his night-black head with resignation.

"If all of you are mad, I must be mad, too," he commented dryly. "We cannot leave you here alone, Gemelle, to face the Escor, and who knows what number of assassins."

The Twisan smiled at his companions, clasping the hand of each in turn. "You have my gratitude. I do not judge we shall face danger. We shall stay well hidden in this fog that has become our ally." His whistle recalled the dog.

He turned to Kaus. "Come, let us move the wagon a little way. Stay within," he ordered the others. "I will reconnoiter."

Vanand the Escor, climbing the downward path, made a quick misstep and cursed. There was a shooting pain in his ankle. He had turned it, somehow, on the wretched fog-obscured path. The way would be long now, and slow. He started his hobbling progress cautiously down.

The garments of Fahne the sorcerer clung damply to him again; they had dried from his swim, he thought sourly, only to moisten again from his sweat. The trip upriver had been hard and long; he paused now for a moment to retrieve his breath.

The sodden Escor stirred below his rug on deck and muttered. Soon, flailing, he had sat upright and looked with puzzlement about him.

"Who are you?" he inquired of Fahne. His tongue was thick with the residue of sleep. "Where have we come?"

"Quiet, friend," the sorcerer said sharply. "Here is your mathale. I will pole myself a little farther on, and then you may hie yourself to Mar."

The polesman's mutters stilled when he saw the handful of silver. "Thankee, thankee, strange sire. You are most generous."

Without a reply, Fahne began to pole again to the bend of the stream that marked the landing place.

"Godspeed, strange sire," the Escor called thickly as the sorcerer leaped to land. Laboriously, he poled the barge around and started down the river.

Fahne the sorcerer moved slowly into the fog, sighting above him on the promontory the sinister castle of Vanand.

And then, not far away, well down the slope, Fahne saw the figures of the woman and the boy.

He made a sound of joy and triumph and began to run like a deer, sure-footed and renewed, up the steep slope toward them.

CHAPTER 7

The heavy sea mist swirled about them as Dione and the minstrel crept into the small stone structure that clung to the side of the hill.

Vanand, they had learned from his servant, had left in great haste, and the servant expected that he would be absent for several hours.

When they had climbed a little way down the precipitous path, Dione had looked up in wonder on the massive, sprawling shadow of the castle of Vanand, sinister against the chill October sky, half-cloaked in fog. She had not seen its startling exterior before.

Across the bottom of each narrow window of the facade were savage shapes like the brows of ruined skulls that formed small balconies. From the roofs sprouted perforated chimneys, imitating the fleshy maces growing from the bodies of men. The whole great brooding structure had an air of monstrous force, as if behind the red-lit windows dreadful acts of pain were meant to be performed in secret, without ruth.

"It is horrible," Dione whispered to the minstrel, drawing her borrowed cloak more tightly around her, for the night and her view of the castle had stricken her with profound cold.

"Come," said Volan, unheeding, and he urged her gently down the stony path.

When they were inside, he said, "This is better." Volan closed the pewter door; it gave off a desolate clang. "There must be some tapers here," he muttered. Fumbling in the dimness, his fingers met some phoenix-chased candlesticks. "Ah!" He held a taper wick to the flame of his lantern.

The center of the place appeared. "What is it?" Dione asked, startled by the sight of white forms with immobile faces and blind eyes.

"The temple of Sclar, erected for the mother of Vanand."
Now Dione could see a low, gleaming altar and the graceful forms in marble of the water gods and the gods.of the
Escorpiun—Kun, with her flowing hair and garments rhythmic in stone, like the waves of the sea; Ler, in his chariot;
Poseidon, bearded and smiling, bearing his trident proudly
like a scepter; and the glowering lords of war and the
shadowy underworld, the rulers of the Escorpiun. At the
sight of the last, the little Marin shuddered and whispered
to Volan, "Would that the sayer had made an earlier
tryst!"

"It was not in his power to arrive before," said Volan.
"Sit down here, upon this bench. It should not be long."

And he led her to a seat of marble wrought like the
chariot of Ler.

"I will stand," she answered nervously.

They heard the sound of firm steps upon the marble
stairway leading to the temple. Volan ran to one of the
arching oval windows. "It is the sayer," he whispered, then
hurried to the curving pewter door.

The sayer moved slowly, keeping his scarlet cloak wound
close around his tall, lean body. Its hood hid his face, but
Dione caught a glimpse of glinting eyes.

"He is a Thround!" she whispered anxiously to Volan,
hanging back.

"He is no Thround, my lady." At the moment that Dione
knew the beloved voice, the hood was thrown back, revealing the noble head of Fahne the sorcerer.

Dione's astonished joy had left her wordless: all that
she could do was stand rooted and trembling, devouring
with her wide gaze the smiling face and lean length of
Fahne as he threw off the alien scarlet cloak, striding toward her.

Fahne was too full of her to say a further word or greet
Volan.

The minstrel stammered, "I . . . I will keep watch," and
in an instant he was out the curving door, leaving Dione
and the sorcerer alone among the candle fires in the small
round temple of Sclar.

Still Dione was powerless to move, shaking with such
force she feared that she might fall. Her green eyes held
the hypnotic gaze of Fahne. She sensed in him, with his
terrible yearning, a wonder and a hesitance akin to her
own, for now it seemed they both feared they were dream-

ing; their apartness had been so dread and long! Was he
real? she wondered coldly, or would she awaken from this
magical vision to find herself alone in her chamber in the
awful castle of Vanand?

As if in answer, Fahne all in a moment found his voice
again, crying, "Oh, my love!" And in two long strides he
was near, his arms folded around her hard, drawing her so
tightly to him that she knew at once his body's urgent,
hesitant seeking as she sobbed out her incoherent words of
unbelieving happiness.

For a timeless time Fahne looked down into her eyes,
then slowly lowered his majestic head to kiss her mouth.
The kiss was at once so incredibly savage and gentle that
Dione was overwhelmed anew at the complexity of the tall,
passionate stranger who held her now.

When he raised his lips from her mouth, Dione voiced
her thought timidly: "I almost feel . . . as if you are the
hooded stranger in the garden."

She saw his smile by the candle fire, and his dappled
eyes were soft with understanding. "I know, I know," he
whispered. "Come, my beloved," he said softly, "let us sit
down." Fahne laughed a little. "Your excitement seems to
have made you weak, as if your knees could not support
you. And I am not much stronger."

Without replying, Dione leaned against him as he led
her to the bench formed like the chariot of Ler, one of the
sea-gods of the Marin. Still holding her, Fahne urged
Dione onto the bench and she lay against him, ecstatic in
his nearness. She knew then his hesitance did not match
hers; she felt the urgent pressure of his hand stroking her
arm.

"Oh, my love, forgive me," she whispered. "I am so . . .
shy."

Fahne murmured, kissing the top of her head. Then he
turned her face upward with a gentle hand and said in a
low voice, "Beloved, turn your face to the candle fire. I
have hungered for the sight of it for so long that to look
upon it is a very consummation."

She obeyed him, altering the angle of her white face so
he might gaze upon it, staring into his eyes. Those magic,
dappled eyes that held over her such power! Dione felt a
quickening in her pulse, a flooding heat over all her body.
His very eyes were so moving that to look into them was
to learn a new and more powerful desire than she had yet

known with him, even in the forest of Erdemar, or in the hidden house, whose walls seemed walls of leaves.

And as they looked at each other in the enchanted silence, broken only by their quiet breathing and now and then the faint sputter of the great candles, Fahne the sorcerer seemed to be possessing her with his steady, glittering look. Dione's wide green gaze began to drown in his, and to her amazement, she knew the touch of ghostly hands upon her, for all that Fahne the sorcerer's broad, long-fingered hands were still cupping her small face.

Breathlessly, she whispered, "You exercise a greater magic than before." Once more he bent to kiss her mouth.

And quite suddenly something new and wild in her, the thing that had awakened on the bed of red and golden leaves, and slept and hungered all the weeks without him, awoke to alien savagery. In a small, seductive voice that made Fahne's body tingle with delight, Dione whispered, "I have been wooed too long in this boyish guise." Hypnotized, Fahne watched her rise and snatch away her green boy's shirt with such ungentleness that it tore upon her pallid body, causing the exquisite lobes of her breasts to dance as they bared themselves in the candle flame; then she divested herself of the boyish hose.

Fahne could not speak. Breathing hoarsely with a moaning sound, he knelt before her, saluting her with the caress never forgotten that she had bestowed upon his hands and forearms in the water garden of Mar.

Dione shook like a delicate branch of the thinnest tree in an overpowering wind, all hesitation gone, all shyness forgotten. Strongly, Fahne held her with his broad, long-fingered hands, never slackening the tempo of his caress until she urged him: "Near, be near, be near!"

And he pulled her down, crying out an alien, guttural phrase she heard but dimly, rending his own garments to free his pounding flesh, to drown and rise and drown and rise again for an unceasing time when his mind and voice and eyes were quite gone, when only the drowning and rising and drowning remained and the time was not time, and nothing was in the world any longer except the softly warm sand of the beach that caressed him, the pulsing and satiny sheath that enclosed him in healing. Bewildered, he knew the wonder of strange new writhings and skills, reaping her knowledge of him, the drumming and pounding having become too aching and rending to bear; he knew a titanic impact and then an incredible peace.

Somewhere among his body's time of drums he had heard her shrilling cry. Now holding her closely at his side, he saw the dew of his sweat upon her softened, joy-distracted face, and the tears were splashing downward.

Fahne tasted her salty tears with his tongue and planted swift, small kisses on her nose and brow and chin, still holding her vise-like to his body's length.

They still had found no conscious words: he ran his strong hand down her curving side and felt her skin vibrating to his touch, like the belly of a cithara.

It was as if she could not be close enough; burrowing, burrowing into him, the little Marin seemed to be trying to enter his very side. Closer and closer he held her, knowing full well she must soon cry out with pain, and yet she did not, only moving ever closer to his body. With a stunned sense of disbelief, he felt the stir of newer lust, and realized, from the beseeching, cat-like sounds that issued from her, that the little Marin, too, had felt again the aching of desire.

This time, however, to his amazed delight, she fell upon him with a strong, relentless domination, and through half-lowered lids all silvered by the candle fire, he saw a white-ness and its precious shadow taking him, engulfing him again in narrow pillows of silk, to let him swim and swim in sun-warmed streams, instead of drowning down and down to set him leaping up into the silken sun, with the flight of porpoises that leap, reversing from the sky into the waves that are above them. This leaping was a dance more narrowing, and an excruciation of delight his days and nights had never shown the sorcerer. He led her leading of him, and again no time was ever time, no world existed but the leaping dance of him above himself into the blinding, silken sun.

Their outcry now was a primeval thing, their shuddering bodies meeting deep and meeting, meeting in an ache of feeling that she feared would end them, quite; they slowly rode a swaying sea of waves that rocked them slowly, diminishing; diminishing, they lay against each other, washed up at last upon the beach of consciousness that received them with tenderness.

Upon his breast, the Marin lay spent, feeling the edges of sleep. Drenched, he circled her still in his massive arms.

Her silky black hair curtained either side of his hollow-cheeked face, and his peace-heavy eyes could dimly see slivers of candle fire through her veil of hair. He caught a glimmering strand of it with his tongue and tasted its salt of their bodies' moisture, its sweet acrid savor of her water-lily scent.

She made another sleepy, cat-like sound, moving as if to free him of the little burden of her. But his arms protested and she remained, limp with approaching sleep.

"I would not," he whispered at last, "return from this spell to reason for anything on earth but you, for you are going to be chilled."

Dione murmured a soft dissent, yet very gently he moved her from him, and reaching over her, he took up her borrowed cloak and wrapped it around her.

Laughing at his own raddled clothes, he found the red cloak of the polesman and covered himself.

"I have showered the gods with praises for their benisons," she whispered sleepily, smiling. "And it is a glory to see you in any form at all. But how came you to be garbed like a Thround?"

He told her all of it then, making light of his discomforts and pains—the escape from the dungeon, his journey on the barge from Mar in the sayer's stead.

They were sitting close together now on the bench formed like the chariot of Ler, her head upon his chest. She raised herself and kissed his neck.

He softly placed his great hand on the top of her small, shining head. "Your touch upon my head," she said in a trembling voice, "is also like the benison of Jove."

Sliding his hand down her silken head, he caressed her ear, and bending his own head, he kissed her again deeply, again and again.

After a time he asked teasingly, "And you? For what purpose did you seek a sayer?"

Dione looked up at him with glowing eyes. "I felt that I was with child, but strangely, now, I do not know."

Fahne's large, caressing hand moved from her neck to her shoulder and her breast. "No, my beloved, you are not, not yet."

She was still, waiting interrogatively for him to go on.

"Our child," he said, "will be a winter child, not a child of summer."

"You know this," she answered, and it was not a question. Her small hand stroked his hard, lean leg.

"Yes." And his fingers went on their downward path to know her subtle curvings and her softnesses.

But when she looked up at his face again, his expression made her ask, "What is it?"

"We cannot stay here long." His reply was gentle, but dark. "Where is . . . Vanand?"

A shadow crossed her mouth. "His server told me that he was going to the Barren Temple."

"Ah, yes, the temple." Fahne's voice was contemptuous.

"You have been to it?" she asked in surprise.

He held her close against him. "Not since I have come to manhood. Since then I have had . . . fastidious tastes," he concluded dryly. And he raised her white arm to savor it with his mouth.

Dione trembled at the touch and drew his golden-brown head to her breast. "I was afraid that . . ."

"Yes?" The word was muffled against her as his opened lips probed her cloaked breasts.

"That you would think it . . . strange that I loved you as I did . . . and wonder how I . . ."

Fahne kissed her bare skin between the borders of her cloak and answered, "I know how. I have learned such lusting by being so long alone."

Holding his head to her, she kissed his hair and saw the glitter of her own tears dropping on its golden-brown fullness.

At the sighing sound of her breath, he sat up and saw the wetness on her face. He gave her a long kiss on the mouth that took her breath again.

"It came to me in our frenzy," she said softly, "that in you, the piercing of the sword of earth transmutes itself into the wand of air, your temper being the airiest of the Erden . . . into a wand of air and light, for I feel there is light within me while you are—a strong, warm light that drives away all cold and darkness."

He held her tightly once more, pressing her small head so close against his broad chest with his hand that she seemed to wear his touch, becoming his skin.

"Volan has been teaching me his minstrelsy," she said then, "and I have made songs of your wonders." His hand responded.

"Oh!" she exclaimed.

He feared to have pained her. "What is it?"

"Volan! Poor Volan is shivering in the fog out there somewhere."

Fahne said, "Then I will summon him, and soon. But, oh, my darling, give me another moment with you alone. It has been so long, so long."

She raised her mouth for his repeating kiss and then lay against him weakly. "His hands . . ." she began impulsively, then at once was silent.

"Hands? Volan's?" The sorcerer turned his stately head in question, staring down at her.

Reluctantly, Dione told him of the maiming of Volan by the High Escor.

With a low curse, the sorcerer rose, striding back and forth along the marble floor. "I have never killed, in all my strange and varied days. But now I burn to slay Vanand, to feel his cursed throat between my hands. I will welcome it with pleasure."

Dismayed, Dione stood up and went to him, taking his arm. "No, Fahne. Let us go. At least he has not . . . harmed me."

Fahne clasped her. "Your blessed star has told me that. If he had . . ."

She looked up into his lucid eyes, which held the hues and lore of distant places. And Dione saw a terrible anger in the sorcerer's look that she had never before beheld, a stare that made him a stranger.

"Let us go," she repeated, apprehensive.

Shuttering his grim expression, Fahne smiled down at her with tenderness and was himself again. "But a moment more," he answered. "Sit by me one more moment and let us speak of what the stars brought us when we were parted from each other."

He led her to the bench of Ler. They sat down, this time not even touching, letting only their eyes take joy in touching each other's face and limbs and body.

Dione clasped the glittering small star in the hollow of her neck, and she glanced at his own star, shining brightly by the candle flame in the center of his caduceus medallion.

"It must have been when you were in the dungeon," she said, "that my star led us back to the bed of the blue rose in the hidden house."

He nodded, smiling, and his heart began to quicken as she told him of their ghostly bodies' meeting—how, afterward, the small six-sided light had let her know a glimpse of his flight, the feel of water on her own body as he sank into the canal to hide himself below the barge.

Fahne moved closer to her on the bench, and as though reiterating an old rite, she leaned down and kissed his hands as she had at an earlier time.

"Once more, my love, please, only once more before we go out into the night." His tone was so urgent that at once she let her borrowed cloak fall back from her rounded whiteness and lay down.

Their meeting bodies then were desperate with haste and their increasing peril; he feared that in his hurry he would wound her tenderness. And yet, miraculously, the very desperation of their plight endowed the meeting with an excruciating edge of excitement neither had known before. Her quickening body replied immediately to his, and her senses leaped to match his almost instant easement. She felt a sharper paining, a sooner, almost unendurable ache than any former joys of him, narrowing, narrowing to a tortured fire that melted to a warmth so excellent and sweet that she could not still the little scream that came from her, hearing it as she would hear another cry, not coming from her own constricted throat. The warming flood became a gentler warming, throbbing, throbbing still at last.

Looking up at him, she saw that the sorcerer's eyes were blank with his profound appeasement; for a moment, they were not themselves, but only their flesh in simple gratitude. But soon again she knew his eyes. "I thank thee, lady, for thy benison," he said, and for a timeless moment he kissed her mouth.

With hesitant arms he raised himself, saying sadly, "My dear love, we must be gone from here." He raised her gently, handing her her boy's clothes. "It is, as always, like a tearing off of my skin to let go of you."

He began to dress her as if she were a child, and he wrapped her in the borrowed russet cloak.

"My little Bole," he said, teasing. He held her for an instant.

"Let us seek Volan now and start to Erdemar."

"To Erdemar," she repeated, her face alight.

"You will both await me in a safer place. I will steal us some steeds from the stable of Vanand. We gypsies, you know, are famous for that."

Her laughter answered his.

"I was so befuddled by my ardor, like a green boy, that I dismissed the polesman. The vision of you quite undid my reason."

He gave her one more lingering kiss before he led her toward the pewter door. "Now, cautiously, my love," he whispered. "Not a sound or breath. Be guided by the rein of my hand, little seahorse."

She nodded obediently and followed.

Quietly, Fahne pushed open the pewter door. In the mist there was no sign of Volan, but on the temple stairs, dimly seen by the pallid light of the still-burning tapers, swayed Vanand the High Escor.

CHAPTER 8

"Go back, my love!" Fahne ordered the Marin, and with thankfulness he heard the door clang shut behind him. He never took his hard, clear eyes from the Escor.

"The gypsy and his whore!" Vanand cried in a demented voice. "The gypsy's whore has sullied my mother's gods!"

He started up the stairs toward the sorcerer, and Fahne saw then that he was favoring one foot. For a breathless instant, the sorcerer had almost fallen into his own pity's trap: Vanand looked like a great, mad, wounded animal, snarling with hunger and pain. But in a flash the sorcerer regained his ecstasy of anger. The good, hot, welcome hatred powered him to leap, disdainful of the Escor's gleaming dagger, upon the massive body of Vanand and send him sprawling down the temple stairs. From far off came the barking of a dog.

Fahne's tempestuous rage renewed him, lending his arms and legs a mightiness he had not realized they owned. He was fighting blindly, without sight or breath, grappling the Escor with steely fingers that wrested the dagger from him and tossed it down the precipitous hill into the frozen grass.

The sorcerer's quick motion had left him a moment unguarded, and Vanand was swift to use it. He kicked at Fahne with his uninjured foot, but the sorcerer, with the parrying grace he had learned from Gemelle, dodged him as quick as a snake and, rolling over, grabbed his injured ankle. He gave it all the pressure he could muster in his steely arm.

The Escor screamed out in pain but relentlessly was trying to lean forward, reaching for the sorcerer's throat. Fahne jerked Vanand by the leg and whirled him over, leaping upon him to press his long fingers against the vital spots that would render the Escor unconscious. But Vanand's red madness drove him like an infernal engine, and he struggled out from under Fahne, somehow maneuvering to knee the sorcerer in the stomach with his uninjured limb.

Fahne grunted. Vanand had the moment's advantage and, rolling swiftly down the side of the hill, grabbed up his dagger with a triumphant cry. Fahne leaped upon him again, feeling a prick of agony where the steel had entered his shoulder, but the sorcerer, almost drunk now with the heat of his raging hate, did not pause, but butted Vanand like a goat and sent him tumbling down the hill.

The Escor, surprised by the unexpected blow, stood blinking stupidly, looking up at the sorcerer. Then Fahne grabbed up the dagger from the grass and leaped with it again for the Escor, sending him down with the steel point poised above the hated back.

"Mercy! Mercy!" the big Escor sobbed out, his words sounding thick and bestial as he burrowed into the frozen grass.

The sorcerer bent his lean, hard leg and pinned the Escor to the ground with his knee. "What mercy did you show to Volan, or to Dione of Mar?" he asked in a stony voice.

Vanand repeated his muffled plea.

All at once the sorcerer knew that this was not enough; to kill the bastard now, he thought, was too quick, too easy, too insufficient to his dreamed revenge.

"Get up," he said coldly. "Get up."

Amazed, the Escor got painfully to his feet, keeping his balance with difficulty on the steep brow of the hill. His equilibrium was so undone that he dared not lunge for

Fahne; he kept his weight upon one sturdy leg. Fahne thought he heard a man's voice call his name.

"Start climbing," said Fahne.

Vanand stared at him and began to sob. Not since his boyhood had he felt so powerless! And now his father was going to beat him.

"Father," he said piteously.

Sickened, the sorcerer knew at once that the cowering Escor had fallen into a deeper madness than he had ever known. Again, Fahne's compassion threatened to unseat his hot lust of vengeance. Once more he seemed to hear his own name called.

But he said to Vanand again, "Start climbing." He brandished the wide dagger.

Trembling, the Escor turned dizzily, almost losing his footing, and began, with the plodding steps of an old, sick creature, to climb up the slanting hill.

The sorcerer's disgust and hatred warred with his pity as he followed, holding the dagger point to the broad back of the Escor.

"I am in pain!" Vanand cried out.

The sorcerer, silent, kept the dagger at the Escor's back, forcing him relentlessly up the rise. All his compassion had fled, and he burned again to reach the level ground where he could administer the proper blow he had so long craved, ever since the afternoon on the canal when he had seen Vanand take up the little Marin in his arms. And Volan must share in it.

While Kaus slowly guided the wagon into a concealing thicket, Gemelle the Twisan had called out to the Sabbian's dancing dog, "Come, Arr. Let us keep watch together."

Responsively, the great black cur had raised its enormous ears, trotting after Gemelle, who squatted in the shelter of some rocks to look down on the temple.

He saw the little Marin and Volan disappearing into the small round structure, and not long after candle flame began to shed its feeble light through one of the oval windows. What were they doing? he wondered. And where was the villainous Escor?

Gemelle exclaimed. Arr gave a low growl in sympathy. "Quiet, Arr," the Brisen said, then caught the black cur by its collar, soothing the animal. A tall, red-clad man was running up the slope. Was that Vanand? No, it could not

be, for there was a grace and swiftness in the figure that
belied the heaviness of the High Escor. Could it be . . . ?

"Fahne!" Gemelle said aloud, and the black dog Arr
made a strange mourning sound deep in its throat, the
prelude Gemelle had come to know to joyful barking. It
was Fahne; it had to be! The Brisen was full of delight,
but as Arr's bark escaped, Gemelle said sternly, "Quiet! Be
still!" At once the trained beast's happy bark was smoth-
ered, and it sat down at the feet of Gemelle, awaiting
further orders.

"Thank the gods!" the Brisen whispered to Arr. "Good
boy, good boy," he added absently, stroking the dog's wide
head as he kept his pale eyes fixed on the temple below
them.

He squatted down behind the rocks. In a very short time,
he saw a narrow figure slipping through the dark, metallic
door. Volan, that must be. The Brisen smiled broadly;
there would be no room for three in that house now, he
reflected.

Gemelle watched the slender minstrel—his dancing walk
revealed him clearly now—slip into a nearby grove of
trees, thinking of the joys his friend must now be tasting.

After a long look around him, the Brisen sat down on
the cold ground and leaned against a large round stone.
Arr curled near him for warmth, looking up inquisitively
at the man with yellow hair.

Caressing the big dog's dark flank, Gemelle remembered
his parting from the sorcerer and his puzzlement over
Fahne's unswerving passion for the little Marin. That had
been, he thought with a stab of longing, before the days
of Shabatu.

The Brisen peered into the mist above the dimly lighted
temple and dreamed of the shining daughter of the Waetergyt.

Only to Fahne could he have told his heart—he who, in
his cool, lighthearted fashion, had always seemed to like
the chase more than the capture! Now he, like Fahne, was
pierced with that inevitable dart, seeing again in this sea
fog over upper Mar the moon-like hair of Shabatu, smelling
her fair skin, which had the scent of the vanilla flower,
reliving her flying gestures.

The morning after their concert for the guests of the
Baron Melik, Gemelle remembered, he had risen early to
tune his agile limbs, climbing to the castle's parapet with

a strange inner singing in him, and full of the delicate witchery of Shabatu.

The brilliant, pallid sun of dernier-Brise glittered on the gray-white stones as Gemelle climbed into the light that magic morning; the lilac wings of the birds of upper air were fragile on the brilliant sky. The Twisan began his wheeling turns, a whirligig of yellow in the morning stillness. And then, some demon of exhilaration made him leap onto the very parapet, dancing along its periled way, and daring death, he cartwheeled on the same small path at a dizzying height above the pure, wing-shadowed snow.

But his foot gave a sudden slide, and he was hanging by his steel-strong hands in the midst of nowhere. Calmly, he wondered if he were about to die. No, he resolved, I have not yet embraced the shining Shabatu! My time is not yet.

And skillfully he summoned all his tensile power, ordering his disciplined muscle for the incredible feat. Saying a silent prayer to Hermes, god of the fleet, Gemelle pulled himself with painful care upward, upward ever so slowly by his sinewy arms and, with one titanic effort, brought his lower body up and whirled over the ledge with a trout-like leap, landing in safety.

His head rang with the might of his relief, and he thought for an instant he would fall, collapsing on the frosty stone. But the sound of a great explosive sigh, the joyful cry of a woman, came to him. And turning, he beheld the Lady Shabatu, far whiter than the snow, frozen with terror, beginning to weep.

And he had gone to her and held her in his arms, turning up her fair face for his kiss. Her skin, in the dazzling light, was as poreless as the snow, and her eyes of silver-blue looked into his with such love that he knelt down at her feet and saluted the hem of her blue woolen robe, with its path of amethysts, repeatedly with his shuddering lips that had, for the moment, no more laughter.

Gemelle stroked the heavy back of Arr again and smiled. That magical lady, who had seen him climbing to the parapet and followed, had had the exquisite wit to save his skin! She had not expelled a breath until his feet were standing on the solid stone.

The days that followed so inflamed their delicate desires that the Twisan knew she would never give herself to Solidago. And the inflaming of their bodies, its blue heat leaping from their eyes, ignited Melik's nervous ire to such a height that Kaus and Veris cautioned him. Not that he had ever taken heed!

Gemelle's rueful laughter stilled. There was someone else approaching the temple now—the hobbling, hated figure of Vanand the High Escor. Unsheathing his dagger, Gemelle leaped up and began to run down the foggy slope, snapping to Arr, "To Kaus!"

The large black dancing dog raced in the direction of the wagon, barking wildly.

Gemelle could no longer see the sorcerer and the Escor.

Desmos, riding next to Hircinus along the path beside the promontory, heard the Capran's brassy, low-toned oath. "The night is like wool!" he said to the Peisun. "How can we maneuver in this?"

"Let me go ahead," said Desmos. "My Marin eyes are certain in the fog."

Glad enough for Desmos' guidance, Hircinus drew back to let the Peisun lead his graceful Marin steed ahead on the narrow road. The gleaming gray stallion moved with the rhythm of slow waves, surefooted and bland in the tall mists of upper Mar.

Hircinus' own heavier steed lay back its ebon ears and rolled its great eyes nervously. "Easy, fellow," the Capran said softly. "My steed likes not the scent of the night," Hircinus remarked to the soldier beside him.

"Nor do I, Hircinus," the soldier answered. "I think we have come on a fool's errand, for a whore."

"Quiet," Hircinus snapped. "Her . . . consort will hear you. And he is no mean adversary, my friend."

"You speak truth." They both remembered well the night that the Peisun, seemingly so mild, had laid the jealous passions of Shira's commander Buc to rest.

Suddenly near them in the mist they heard the deep-throated barking of a dog. Hircinus' black mount started at the sound, but the Capran sawed at the beast's mouth, bringing it to calm.

"Listen," said Hircinus' neighbor, "I hear the sound of feet below the path."

Ahead the Peisun Desmos held up his oval, gauntleted hand. "Hold," he called quietly to Hircinus, and in turn the Capran held up his blunt, club-fingered hand, signaling the riders behind him. The gestures were barely discernible

in the swirling mist, but Hircinus could make out now a
gesture from Desmos asking his advance.

Walking his black mount cautiously, the Capran rode
to Desmos.

"I see a scarlet cloak . . . there, do you see?"

Hircinus assented. "That could be our prey."

"Yes. The mist is clearing here a little. Wait for my
signal. Remember, I know this terrain. I do not think we
have long to tarry."

"Tranquillea!" Kaus ordered Arr, and the big dog came
silently to his heel.

"Gods," the Sabbian whispered to Veris, "this is worse
than being blinded by the snow."

"Be easy, Kaus," the Bole said in his calm, low tone. "It
thickens and clears with the inconstancy of a Twisan."

"Where *is* Gemelle?" asked Bock the Capran.

"He has plunged into the fog and been swallowed up,"
Kaus answered, his anxiety apparent.

"Wait!" said Veris, grasping the Sabbian's arm. "I think
I see them now, emerging there."

The slender Capran soldier at the end of Desmos' train
looked very young, the captain thought. Why had Hircinus
brought this unseasoned boy on such an expedition?

Surely he had not been with them when they left from
Mar. The captain began to count the horses. No; there was
something amiss. . . .

The voice of Hircinus broke in upon his reverie, however, and he thrust the matter from his mind, spurring his
reluctant steed up the rise after the others in the heavy
mist that swirled about the promontory from the sea.

"Volan! Volan!" The minstrel, shivering in the underbrush, heard Fahne calling his name and crashed out
through the boughs onto the open hill.

Astounded, he saw the swaying form of Vanand, then
the sorcerer behind him with the Escor's own dagger
pointed at his back.

"Messire!" He ran to the sorcerer. "What do you wish
of me?"

"I give you the gift of choosing his manner of death.
Here, have you a bond of any kind?"

"I have my sash, messire." The minstrel untied his narrow green sash and handed it to Fahne. Fahne shook his head.

"No, Volan. He is yours. Tie his bonds yourself, with the hands that he has maimed."

The minstrel's eyes gleamed as he did the sorcerer's bidding.

"Come, then," said Fahne. "We have a little way to go."

And they continued up the rise, the minstrel almost mourning the peculiar tractability of their captive, the Escor.

"I see them now," Desmos whispered to Hircinus. "There are two of them, two Escors, and yet another behind. The first two, do you see, in scarlet? I cannot make out the raiment of the third."

"Then is it time?"

"Not yet," said Desmos, his gentle voice pulsing with excitement, tightly reined. "I will give you the word."

"Look!" said Kaus. "It is the Escor. And behind him . . ."

"Fahne and Volan the minstrel," said Gemelle.

Veris the Bole cried out the Twisan's name. "We thought to have lost you, my friend."

"All is well now," Gemelle said softly. "Let us join them now and aid him in his rite of sweetest vengeance."

"It is fitting," Fahne said coldly, "that an Escor so high enjoy his execution in the highest place."

The sweetness of his hatred soured a little as he looked upon the sickly face of Vanand, pallid in the moonlight that had knifed the swirling fog along the promontory. But Fahne steeled himself to the deed he had been lusting for, spurred on by the sight of the twisted hands of Volan.

They were standing upon the very edge of the cliff, and the sorcerer said to Volan, "The choice of death is yours. Name it, my friend."

Vanand the Escor gave a terrible pleading cry and the minstrel wavered.

"Speak, Volan," said the sorcerer.

But at once there was a babel of voices, a confusion of sounds; they heard the drumming of hoofs along the narrow road, and hazily Fahne saw a line of mounted Caprans emerging over the brow of the rise. He recognized the face of Desmos, who was leading the Caprans; then somehow

Gemelle was there, and Fahne heard the far-off barking of the black dog Arr.

Suddenly a Capran was riding toward Fahne, shouting, "Take the Escors!"

Fahne heard Desmos call out, "Hold! Hold! It is Volan the minstrel!"

Tearing at the mounted Capran with Vanand's dagger, Fahne heard a ghastly scream. Vanand the High Escor had tumbled over the precipice.

A dynasty was ended, Fahne thought; the accursed Vanand was dead! But now, as the Capran moved upon him again, Fahne knew he had no moment for pity or for pause: the slant-eyed soldier's falchion was raised.

Before Fahne could leap aside, the Capran's sword had torn a great rent in his doublet, slicing at the skin of Fahne's chest.

Fahne's sight was red with pain. The last sound he remembered was the frantic barking of Arr, the dancing dog of Kaus, before a jolting blow upon his head sent the sorcerer down and down to utter blackness.

CHAPTER 9

"How does he fare, Veris?" Kaus the Sabbian asked softly of the Bole, whose competent, broad hands were probing the wound of Gemelle.

"He is better than I feared," Veris the Bole replied. "But the other needs a healer." His wide brown Erden eyes went to the white face of Volan.

"What is he saying?" Bock inquired of Kaus. "You know the Brisen tongue."

The Sabbian bent his ear to the young minstrel's bloodless lips and listened intently. "Something," he said, "about 'the lady.'"

"The Lady Dione, it must be," said Veris. "She must be in that little temple down below."

"Would that Gemelle had come to sense!" Kaus' brassy Sabbian voice was high with his tension.

"It is as well," Veris answered sadly. "I relish not giving him the news of Fahne."

Kaus was silent a moment. The minstrel suddenly cried out, "My lady!"

The Sabbian leaned to him and asked gently, "Where is she, Volan? Where is your lady? In the temple down there?"

After an excruciating pause, when the others feared the boy would lose consciousness, the minstrel gasped out, "Yes . . . must go . . . to her."

"Tranquillea, tranquillea. She shall be found."

Volan's tight face relaxed at this, and then he fell into a deeper senselessness.

"We had best not tarry," Bock the Capran said curtly. "They are gone now, Veris?"

"They are gone," said the Bole. "I will go for her, Bock. It is best you and Kaus attend the others."

"And a healer?" the Sabbian asked with anxiety. "We cannot set foot in Mar, you know."

"We will pray that the boy will last to Brise," Veris said grimly. "It is our only nearby refuge now."

"But what of Melik's ire against Gemelle?"

Veris the Bole frowned at the Sabbian. "We will have to risk it. I will go now. And should Gemelle awaken, I pray you keep from him the news of Fahne for the nonce."

"I will," said Bock the Capran gloomily. Before his slanted eyes there lingered still the picture of the lifeless sorcerer surrounded by the ring of Capran soldiers.

Dione of Mar rose weakly from the kneeling bench before the image of the goddess Kun. Her constant tears were chill upon her face. The temple now was very cold.

She wandered to the bench of Ler and sank down disconsolately, leaning her small head back. Her weariness was overpowering, her exhaustion so deep that at last it had become greater than her fear.

For what seemed hours she had stood with her face pressed to a window, attempting desperately to penetrate the fog with her terror-widened eyes, so stretched with panic that the eyeballs pained her, but there had been nothing—nothing, not even shadows, and the heavy stone walls admitted almost no sound.

There was no help now, no action but the waiting, and to wait among the dying candles, not knowing whether he was among the living or the dead. . . .

Dione took a deep, sobbing breath and felt her limbs, leaden with the weight of spent love and of fear, resign themselves to sleep.

She dreamed—at first that she clasped the little crystal star, knowing an enormous terror. She was Fahne leap upon the Escor, feeling what the sorcerer felt as he struggled with Vanand. Dione gave a cry of pain, and it was the pain of Fahne. After a long, red interval there was nothing, nothing at all in the night but silence and the sputter of the dying candle flames.

Dione called out Fahne's name, but he gave no mystic answer, as he always did when she called him with the star.

She cried out in her sleep.

After a time, then, Dione dreamed that she was sitting in a small, square space before a narrow opened door admitting green-gold light.

The space was hardly larger than a server's room, yet there was a sense of richness and of luster, warm and welcoming. And where Dione looked out through the rectangle of greenish-golden light, there was a spacious golden-brownness that might have been a meadow.

In another corner of the small sun-flooded space, there was a shadowed semicircle gleaming with peculiar implements; she could not quite discern them. The colors of the nearer space surrounding her were brown and green, and green tinged with bronze, like a woodland stream or the sea bronzed by the sun, and a circular splash of sapphire color, the Maeden color of heavenly reward. Fahne's hue!

Through the mists, with her hands, Dione felt the smoothness and shape of an apple and acanthus flowers. And Dione was filled with puzzlement.

Now in the dream she saw approaching her two tall, slender men; their faces were in shadow, but their raiment was clear. One was wearing the teal-blue tunic of the Maeden, the other the sea-green vestment of the Peisun.

Somehow, then, the men were in the room, and Dione was pouring them goblets of wine. She seemed to recognize the scent of valley-lily potion, pouring it into a glass of brown for the tall stranger in teal-blue. For the green-clad Peisun, Dione poured out the scarlet strawberry liquor into a goblet of gray. And distantly she heard someone playing on a cithara, singing a silver song.

Dione cried out to flee the dream's captivity; yet she could not be free of it, for it still wound her deep within itself.

She felt the aura of the man in blue contained the magic that would settle her body's fires—the passion of the Sabbian Kani, the horseman from the quicksand country full of magic lore; the Capran earthiness that made an ancient serpent of desire coil low within her being; the Seeing Escor, with his enchanted silences; and, most of all, the magnetism of the gentle Maeden, her opposition and her fate. Surely the man in teal-blue was the sorcerer . . . and yet he did not seem to know her!

Dione felt a hunger in the man in blue, then heard him say, from a great distance, the word *"temenos,"* repeating the word *"temenos."* And she cried out to him, but her cry was in silence.

Then she saw the stranger holding in his hands a gilt-chased, heavy volume; she felt him speak, rather than heard, for all was still that puzzling silence, as she tried, almost weeping with the effort, to voice an answer. But her answer also was unheard.

But now she knew the man in blue was Fahne, the man in green her cousin Desmos, who seemed to be saying silently to Dione that she should not speak out, but preserve this bewildering silence among them.

Then in the puzzling dream Dione saw the man in blue hold out the book to her, and his hands were very clear; they were the broad, long-fingered hands of Fahne the sorcerer.

She saw the hands put down the book upon the round, vivid splash of sapphire-blue, and then they took her own hands. The man raised her small hands to his shadowed mouth. She felt his kiss upon her fingers.

The man in green, she knew with clarity, was Desmos, for the old familiar warmth of kindness was in him. She felt her own mouth sadly smiling, widened into the Peisun smile that seemed almost a grimace of pain, and she knew her own body's trembling.

Vaguely, then, the Peisun Desmos, her cousin, could be heard speaking the name of Volan the minstrel, and Dione heard in her dream the minstrel's narrow tenor raised in song. Dione could hear the melody, but the words were dim and random, some of them unclear, as if snatched away by the wind, yet she recognized the sound of "quicksand" and "Hermes' light" and "Erden horning."

In the dream Dione heard herself cry out an agonizing protest, her voice freed at last. Desmos and the sorcerer were melting quite away, as if they were wraiths fleeing with the sun, and Dione found herself alone with the one who apparently was the minstrel. She burst into wild, desolate weeping.

Weeping, Dione awoke to the dying tapers of the temple of Sclar above the grotesque castle of Vanand, examining the mysterious dream that had come to her.

Hearing the pewter door behind her opening, she leapt up with a cry of joy, running toward the entrance to the temple.

"Fahne!" she screamed, and the echo of the word was eerie in the empty chamber, reverberating on the forms of the blind marble gods of water. "Fahne!"

"It is Veris the Bole, my lady," the man at the door said sadly. And he came toward her, holding out a supportive hand.

"Fahne is dead," said Veris, and when she fell, he caught her in his massive arms and carried her from the empty temple.

CHAPTER 10

Passing the long-barred entrance to the water garden, Chiton the Lord Mayor of Mar paused in surprise. His mottled jowls worked like gills with his indignation.

"Impossible!" he said aloud. That wild girl's garden had been sealed up, he thought. He had certainly ordered so, for the Lord Mayor had no desire to wander in its moist discomforts. Yet now the entrance stood ajar, and he heard the unmistakable sound of heavy feet. He started to cry,

"Who goes there?" But he abruptly stopped. It might be a wandering cutpurse . . . an assassin!

Cautiously, Chiton called out to the underPeisun on the stairs, "Crantif! Melan! Come hither!"

The underPeisun came hurrying down, a look of apprehension in their fish-like eyes.

"There is someone in the water garden. Quickly!"

On slow, unwilling feet the green-clad footmen pushed back the metallic gate and entered. Chiton heard a startled cry, the exclamation of a woman who spoke Marin with the accent of Erde.

"Earla! Is that you?" Receiving her affirmative, the Crabba pushed past the relieved underPeisun and blundered along the path of forms, shivering in the chill of the month of Escorpiun, for that autumnal circle had an edge in Mar.

"Go, then, go!" he snapped at the footmen. And he irritably inquired of the Bole, "What in the name of Artemis are you doing here now?"

Earla answered with asperity, straightening from the coral bed, "I feed the lady's creatures. And I take a paining in my bones."

"Serves you well." The Lord Mayor sank puffing onto the bench of shells. "Have you been tending them all these circles?"

"Yes, my lord." The Bole grasped at her hip and grunted. "Aphrodite! My back is shattering." Then she added, "I could not let the creatures die; my lady always doted so upon their colors."

She sat carefully on the bench formed like the chariot of Ler.

"Your lady," Chiton retorted, "is no longer our concern. She made her bed with the gypsy, ignoring all my pleas."

"And ended on the evil couch of Vanand," Earla returned with spirit.

Really, thought Chiton, the old fool was becoming quite intractable; it was time she was pensioned off to Erde. And yet no one could turn such a dish as the old bitch could, he reflected, or keep a rein upon the foolish underPeisun! Therefore, he supposed, he must choose between her impudence or a mad, untrammeled house unwarmed by her comestibles.

"Would you have had her marry a dead man?" the Bole demanded.

"Better a dead king than a live wanderer," the old man said querulously.

"And you say," Earla went on with heat, "that she is no more our concern! Fie, my lord! Do you rest content that she is captive to the Thround, the slayer of Monoceros? When will my lord come to his senses and allow the Caprans to retrieve her?"

"And what would I do with her here?" he countered. "She is no longer pure for the bed of any proper husband."

Earla snorted. "Few enough husbands are 'proper.' 'Proper,' forsooth."

"Earla, what do you say, woman?" Chiton sounded scandalized. "You take my meaning very well." After an uneasy pause, he said, "She is well enough where she is. Vanand will not do her ill."

"Vanand," said the Bole, rising, "is a madman and a murderer. You cannot know he will not do her ill." And she burst into tears. "Would that I had not betrayed her!"

" 'Betrayed her'?" Chiton cried. "What do you mean, you bellowing fool?"

"She trusted me," Earla sobbed, "and I betrayed my lady."

Holding her broad apron to her sodden face, the Bole hurried down the path toward the inner gate.

"You are not to enter this garden again!" Chiton called after her irascibly. "I order it!"

"A fig for your orders!" he heard her snap, amazed. "I shall care for my lady's creatures against the day of her return."

The metal gate slammed shut.

"Oh, name of Artemis," the Crabba sighed in exasperation. The cursed old cow had been given far too much dominion in this house ,and now he was paying for it, paying dearly!

Shivering, the Lord Mayor of Mar felt his own bones start to ache, and heavily he rose and lumbered down the path of shells toward the warmth of his cozy chambers. His flushed eyes shone at the prospect of his wines of poppy, wintergreen, and saxifrage.

A curse upon the healers who had tried to limit him to water!

But where, he wondered then, had the lovely Shira been this night . . . and his nephew Desmos? They customarily waited to dine, he thought wryly, before slaking their lust.

With a sigh of envy for Desmos, Chiton labored up the winding stairs.

The flame-green leather vest was large and awkward on Shira's narrow body, and the ponderous shortsword's weight chafed at the tender hip as she guided her black steed from the thicket and joined the end of Desmos' train. The heavy fog that muffled her horse's hoofbeats also filled her with panic; accustomed to the clarity of Erde, the Capran looked upon the fog as a sinister foe. Somehow it seemed to elude her as Fahne had, ever; and it had the maddening qualities of Desmos and his breastless cousin, the cursed Dione.

Shira's hatred for a moment warmed her sensual body, chasing fear. The sword and dagger were no longer burdensome, but sweet, for when she rode alone to the castle of Vanand and found the Marin, with what pleasure she would pierce her thinness with the steel!

In the last days Shira the Capran had seen the death of her elaborate plotting in Desmos' increasing determination. Her hope of saving Vanand, and thereby ensuring the continued thrall of Dione, died. For Desmos' will was steeled to the slaying of Vanand the Escor, and there was no means of stopping him without revealing her eternal lust for Fahne.

But this, she thought, peering through the thickening fog, was better still! To slay the bitch, to take her once and for all from the sorcerer's reach! And surely, at last, Fahne would be hers to teach the truths of pleasure as only Shira could.

Again she blessed the mist, and the concealing cap she wore with its leathern wings that shadowed from the soldiers her woman's face. She heard the captain ahead remark to his companion, "It will be a little way before we reach the seat of Vanand."

And secure in the knowledge of revenge, Shira let herself begin to dream again of Fahne.

Her memory drifted back the seven years to that enchanted summer night in Erde, when she had first beheld the face of Fahne the gypsy sorcerer.

It had been during the month called the Circle of the Ram; spring, they said, was coming to the Marin and the northern country of Erdemar, yet in the land of the Caprans, the air was hot betimes, and the shrilling of the

insects in the long brown fields had teased the Princess
with her own perpetual singing of desire.

So constant was the lusting that she feared she would
turn mad; for all the multitudinous caressings of her brother and his companions, of the serfs and soldiers, Shira had
not yet found the one supreme release. Therefore, it was
with a sullen face that she received the news from her foolish father of the minstrels' coming.

The old man had looked at her with such anxiety, she
remembered, taking her lovesick air for a wasting sickness
of the flesh.

"I would that you would wed," he said for the hundredth time.

And she had answered sharply, "There is none that I
would marry, none."

She had been wearing, she recalled, her favorite gown of
rustling silk as green as fire, cut so low upon her full white
breasts that they threatened, with each breath, to escape
confinement. Her glittering black hair was ornately dressed,
and upon her head was a tiara of moonstone and onyx that
matched the bracelets, necklets, and rings of the same gems
on her soft white neck and arms and fingers.

She moved sinuously into the feasting hall that evening,
holding her hesitant father's arm, and she looked indifferently about the company of men whose bodies she had
long known, who had given little joy to her, or failed to
ease her at all.

The sensual Capran horns and lutes made of ibex gut
that gave a deep and throaty twang merely aggravated her
senses' itching heat. She sank into the high-backed carved
chair of yew pulled out respectfully for her and took a sip
of violet wine, hardly tasting it.

But then the traveling minstrels had come in. She looked
with momentary interest on the lean, equine form of a Sabbian, flame-haired, who led a dancing dog, and the whirling
yellow brightness of a thin young Brisen, his clothes as
yellow as his hair.

The Sabbian, she thought, was just possible. She yawned
and watched their performance with heavy-lidded eyes until
the entrance of one who almost stilled the beating of her
heart. He was a very tall Maeden in the teal-blue of his
race. His slenderness was powerful, and there was something in his face that spoke of sleeping lust as great as hers,
perhaps greater. His mouth was full and generous, his

hawk-like nose fairly quivering with the promise of titanic feeling. And his eyes! His deep, compelling eyes drew hers as no man's had ever done in all the circles of her days. They were dappled and strange, clear and many-colored all at once, and they seemed to hold the knowledge of the ages.

All throughout the evening, then, Shira did not take her eyes from the sorcerer, regardless of the sneering glance of the eunuch Mahar, the ironic looks of her brother Monoceros, and the worried gaze of her gentle father the King.

The Sabbian called Kaus came boldly to her with his dancing dog, despite the glaring of the Prince her brother, and her father the King. Yet she hardly saw him, for all her mighty passion had been aroused by the one cool man who regarded her only with respectful indifference.

Her head whirled with him, and her belly was sick; yet the sorcerer, whose name, they said, was Fahne, looked at her as if she were no more than the dancing dog—indeed, less, for he caressed the beast with affection.

Irritably, Shira noted that the dancing dog, like the stewards' hounds, cowered back from her; unlike the hounds of the stewards, the black dog was too well trained to snarl, yet the sorcerer in his all-seeing way had seen the dog draw back. Shira wanted desperately to beat the creature, for it had somehow given her smaller value in the Maeden's sight.

She felt her chilled face color with shame, remembering what came after, when she had almost thrown herself at his feet, and he had responded with courteous indifference. How she had hated him then, and thinking to punish him she had taken to bed time and again with the willing Kaus.

But the sorcerer's face was bland and unchanging when she challenged him with Kaus. He had looked at her a little sadly with his brindled eyes and turned to stroke the dancing dog and the stewards' hounds. And so her sweet revenge had been turned against herself in the end; seeking to arouse his ire, she had only succeeded in arousing his contempt and cooling him more.

Now, however, now she would have her vengeance! Guiding her steed up the rise, unheeding of the peril of the precipice below her, Shira's heart began to beat with high excitement and her limbs were warm with stimulating malice. Soon the silly Marin Dione would be dead, and somehow, somehow the sorcerer Fahne would be hers. As yet she knew not how, but of a certainty she would never be defeated.

Suddenly she saw the line of horsemen pause and reined in her own slender beast. It was almost time to secrete herself: if Desmos discovered her—in a plot to slay his cousin . . . !

Now was the opportune time. As they approached a clump of massed trees discernible but dimly in the shifting mist, the Capran drew at the reins of her gentle mount, directing him toward the thicket.

But she was arrested by a bladed order from the nearby captain. "Ho, boy! What are you about? He is soon to give the signal for the charge!" And the captain waved her sternly back into the line, studying her demeanor with a kind of puzzlement.

Dear gods, she thought, turning cold with panic, he has caught me out. She led her mount into the double line of hard-faced men. But, no, the captain had turned his stony gaze ahead again. Shira felt the dew of relief clammy upon her body under the awkward leather vest.

She saw then the oval, gauntleted hand of Desmos rising, and the riders, urging their steeds beyond with a touch of metal-clad knees, started to advance.

And Desmos and Hircinus, riding at the head, knew with chagrin that there were no massed Throunds to charge; there were only two tall, red-robed men. The tightly clasped hood of one concealed his visage; oddly, he was holding an open dagger to the back of the other Thround, a heavier man whose hood, falling back, revealed the maddened face of Vanand.

In the din and confusion that followed, Shira saw the still-hooded Thround grab at the leg of Hircinus and jerk the astounded Capran from his mount as Desmos jumped upon the pale Vanand, driving his dagger through the heart of the Thround. Desmos did not hear the second man cry out.

Shira was in an agony of fear. Somehow she leaped to the frozen ground, the impact of her fall stunning her momentarily before she gathered her courage and rolled down a short incline to the shelter of a rock.

Lying an instant in its protective shadow, Shira the Capran sobbed aloud with her relief. But hearing the cries of the Capran soldiers and the Peisun Desmos, Shira rose shakily to her knees and peered over the rock at the scene of the battle before her.

The veil of mist was lifting now a little, and by the dim illumination of the Thround's moon, she saw five other men appearing, without warning, daggers drawn.

Astonished, Shira recognized the yellow-clad figure of the tumbling Brisen, the companion of Fahne; the flame-haired Kaus, the Sabbian, in his purple tunic. With them were two she but dimly knew and a narrow boy she had never seen.

Suddenly, she was sick with apprehension. To see the friends of Fahne must mean that he was near, and in great peril. And what almighty fools they were to rush in on a troop of Capran soldiers, wearing only their soft clothes, and bearing only daggers! But where was Fahne?

The Capran shook so that her limbs could hardly support her and she leaned weakly against the rock, not able to remain upright, yet not daring to take her gaze from the scene before her. For at any instant he might appear, like his cohorts, from the farther mists—the tall man who was the center of her world.

And she saw that the battle so gallantly joined was pitifully in favor of the soldiers. Vanand the High Escor had looked bloodless from the start, unfit for combat of any kind, and now the Peisun's thrust had quite undone him. Vanand crumpled under Desmos' blow and rolled over into the blackness of the precipice, his dread scream echoing as he plummeted.

The other lone Escor appeared to be weakened from a prior injury, though he gave Hircinus pause. The Capran soldiers, recovering from their amazement at the sudden sight of the strangers, rode upon them now and began to thrash at them with their unsheathed swords.

But before he was downed by the captain, the yellow-clad Brisen shouted, "Fahne! They have slain him!"

Shira's heart fluttered to her very mouth as she heard the Brisen's words.

It could not be! And yet . . . there had been a way about the second Thround . . . Struggling upright now, careless of discovery, Shira looked upon the ring of soldiers surrounding the still form of the remaining man in scarlet.

Blind to all else, she could not see that there were wounded Caprans, torn by the dagger of Kaus when he had sprung upon them like a tiger, that one of the dark-clad men was restraining the bleeding Gemelle as he reached

out his slender hands toward Fahne. Nor did she see the
strangers drag Gemelle the Brisen and the narrow boy off
the narrow path beside the precipice, or hear Desmos calling, to the captain's growling protest, "Let them go! They
are no allies of Vanand!"

She could see only the small, green-clad ring of Capran
soldiers surrounding the still form of a lean man in a scarlet robe whose torn blue hose and tunic revealed patches of
his tawny flesh.

His hood had fallen back in his titanic resisting struggle;
he lay in the stillness of the slain. The bright blood trickled
from a wound upon his brow down the unaccustomed pallor of his face.

It was Fahne the sorcerer, and surely he was dead.

In her fever of grief, the Capran vaguely heard the voice
of Desmos: "It is Fahne!"

And screaming, screaming, she scrambled from the shelter of the rock and ran toward the circle of men, who
turned with astounded faces to see the young soldier moving with the motions of a woman, to hear the scream that
was a woman's scream.

Wordless, Hircinus stared from among the gaping men,
but Desmos looked at her with unseeing eyes, not pausing
to question her presence or examine her motives.

"Take him back to Mar at once," the Peisun snapped at
the captain and indicated the lifeless form of the sorcerer.
"He may yet be alive. Take him not to the house of Chiton;
get a healer. He is my friend."

"But, Sir Desmos . . ." the bewildered captain began.

"Do as he says." It was the voice of Hircinus.

"Come," Desmos said to the commander, "we must ride
now to the castle of Vanand, where the Lady Dione is
captive."

"You had best return with me, Your Majesty," the captain said.

Shira nodded miserably, watching the soldiers lay the
body of Fahne across a horse before the saddle and secure
it.

Without a backward glance, Desmos had mounted and
was riding down the slope toward the castle of Vanand.

PART III

THE STAR
OF CHRONOS

(Hardship and Limitation)

The Policeman leaned back wearily against the slick padded flap of the back seat chair, and began to sense the impending fate he would not Clinton on his uncle's awakening... Why reveal now he realized that the place was dead and

CHAPTER 1

It was with mixed emotions that Desmos regarded the gross face of Chiton on the pillows of silver-green.

For more years than he could remember, Desmos had drawn back from the coarse and foolish man who was his uncle, sharing this alienation with Dione. Yet now as the Peisun stood by his uncle's sickbed, his pity overcame his long distaste, even though the Crabba's very greed had placed him there.

The gentle Peisun healer straightened from his scrutiny of the Crabba's flabby chest and exchanged a gloomy glance with Desmos. "The potion," the healer said gently to Earla the Bole, who stood watchfully at the other side of the vast green bed. She took up a gray-green goblet of dark fluid and held it to Chiton's lips.

The old man drank and soon began to nod with sleep.

Gesturing to Desmos, the healer led him to the far side of the chamber and whispered, "I regret to say his time will not be long; he will not tarry for another circle. The pumping of his heart is insufficient to bear the abuse he has heaped upon his body. He was warned, many times."

Desmos the Peisun nodded. "I know. Do not reproach yourself."

The healer showed his gratitude, saying, "I shall return tomorrow." He withdrew.

"I shall keep watch for a time, Earla." Desmos seated himself by his uncle's bed in a walnut chair with a high, carved back like a shell.

"Very well," the Bole sighed and left the chamber.

The Peisun leaned back wearily against the silvery padding of the high-backed chair and began to weave the fanciful tales he would tell Chiton on his uncle's awakening. Why reveal now, he reflected, that the Escor was dead and Dione gone, like a leaf on the wind, beyond their aiding?

At least, thought Desmos, the news of his marriage with the Queen would cheer the old Crabba.

And marry her he would, the Peisun repeated to himself with silent stubbornness, despite the tales and snickering and the warnings of Fomalhaut and all the others. In spite of her appearance in a soldier's guise that night on the precipice of Vanand—perhaps because of it! he reflected, amused at his own Peisun love of masquerade.

For even in his anxiety for Dione, Desmos had seen, that night, Shira's womanly magic intensified in the boyish gear, the magnetism that held him so in thrall that he could no longer imagine a night without her.

To think that all his uncle's ambitions, and the growing peace between the states of Erde and Mar, depended on that bud. Desmos smiled with the Peisun's deep enjoyment of this irony—vastness ruled by the minute and in essence almost bodiless thing. Well, conquerors of worlds had done no less.

Desmos saw the flushed lids of Chiton the Crabba stir, and then he saw his hard green eyes, set in his great mottled face like cruel little emeralds, focus themselves on the vaulted ceiling and his gaze wander about the luxurious chamber. The eyes at last rested on Desmos, and Chiton made a rasping sound.

The Peisun leaned forward, compassionately touching the old man's oval hand, the soft hand of the dissolute Crabba.

"Desmos." Chiton formed the name with difficulty.

"Yes, Uncle." Desmos rose from the chair and bent to the figure on the bed, leaning with his ear close to Chiton's sensual lips.

"Dione . . . is well?"

"She is well," Desmos replied with soft mendacity. "And she will come to see you ere long."

"Then she has forgiven me?"

"I am certain so," Desmos lied again. "And I will wed Her Majesty this circle," he added, relieved at the freedom of truth.

"They say she is a whore." The Peisun's skin crawled at the old man's matter-of-factness. He flushed.

"They will not say it to me." Desmos' reply was cold and firm.

Chiton began to chuckle, but his laughter caught in a debilitating coughing fit that left him lying weaker on his pillows. Desmos offered him a goblet of water from the glazed ewer on the table.

Sipping, Chiton protested, "Not this swill!" Even in his weakness, he was as irascible as ever, his nephew noted. "Give me a little saxifrage. What does it matter now?"

"What do you mean?" Desmos countered weakly, dismayed at the steady knowledge in the old man's hard green eyes. "The healer forbids it."

"Come, boy," Chiton said sadly. "What does it matter now?"

But the Peisun, knowing that to surrender would be also to surrender to Chiton the truth of his imminent dark, shook his handsome head. He smiled to soften the refusal.

"Very well." The old man sighed. "You do the wisest thing to wed the lovely Shira. Gods, how I envy you her bed! That is a sweet field for your plow to turn."

Again Desmos reddened, his Peisun sense of privacy offended.

Chiton laughed weakly again. "Tell me," he whispered, and his dry tongue snaked out to moisten his sensual lips, "is it true that she bestows the drawing kiss of that ancient queen?"

The Peisun was filled with wonder and disgust, and yet as well with a kind of admiration for the old Crabba's everhungry senses, even in the shadow of his death.

"It is," he answered, feeling his loins begin to stir at the memory of Shira's caress.

"Gods!" the Crabba sighed, licking his lips again. "And you will be her husband." The Peisun felt close to weeping, but he sternly controlled his melting grief.

"There will be peace between the lands of Erde and Mar," Desmos said then to distract his lusty kinsman, to turn his own thoughts away from the remembered fires that threatened to undo his calm.

Apparently he succeeded, for a beatific smile lit the gross mouth of the Crabba and he reiterated softly, "Peace."

With an easier rhythm Chiton slept.

The first thing that he saw was the creature with the pointed, furry ears and evil grin; the creature's feet were hooves.

It was a picture—a picture on the cloth at the foot of the bed where he lay. And surrounding the creature were others resembling him, hooved and grinning, only their loins concealed in narrow pelts of beasts. And the other beings with the pointed ears were pursuing frightened women with flying hair.

Pan. With dreadful strain, as if he were lifting a stone of impossible heaviness, the man on the bed drew up the half-remembered word from the blackness in his mind.

He looked down at the cover over him. It was checkered in a shiny cloth of bright green and ebony. The hues of the race of . . . there was a name he had forgotten. The man regarded his own body's length below the coverlet.

I am very tall, he said silently, beginning to examine the puzzle. But what of the rest of me? He held up his hands. They were the broad, long-fingered hands of the race he could not name; yet he knew that it was a race other than that of the creatures in the picture of cloth.

My face, he said to himself, and turning his head, he looked about the chamber. Yes, there was a glass, on the near left wall by the bed.

He pulled down the vivid coverlet with his long-fingered hands, regarding his naked legs. I have strong legs, he judged. But when he had swung his legs to the floor and summoned them to stand him up, they were not very strong. He swayed a little, then leaned on the square black table by the bed.

A square means something. What does it mean? But first to see his face.

Again he stood, and this time his legs consented to support him. Slowly he began to walk across the wide space between the bed and wall, and it was very strange, for it seemed that this, too, was a new action to be learned.

But he reached the glass and looked at the face staring back at him: he saw a man with thick, golden-brown hair and an unruly beard that had not been cut for some time. The cheeks above the beard were very hollow, and the mouth was full but looked sad. I have a large beak for a nose, the starer reflected, tracing its shape with his long fingers. What is it they are called? Another piece remained unfilled in the blank hole of his mind.

But what kind of eyes were these? he wondered. Dimly, he recalled the hues that he had learned—it must have been a long time ago, for he could not remember them at all. But he saw something in these eyes that was awry, a dappled mingling that was colored like a place he had once known but also could not see, at this moment, clearly.

Something was wrong, the man decided. Or was it thus with all of them, all the others? Still, he did not know who the others were. The hooved men in the picture were not all, for there he was! His own eyes had seen the difference in the pictured creatures and his own face in the glass.

Suddenly the man felt very tired. He stumbled back to the bed and lay down. He must try to find the answer! Perhaps the answer was in this room.

With effort he looked about with heavy-lidded eyes. Below the cloth picture of the men with hooves was a large, heavy-looking chest; carved on its doors was the image of an ancient bearded man in a chariot, brandishing a . . . scythe.

That was better—he knew the word "scythe." Tasting its white sound, the man recalled seeing such an instrument in the hand of a brown man in a field of waving grain. And the air was very hot, humming with constant insect sounds. As his recollected words became more complex, the man realized something else, that he was a lettered man. And his brindled eyes gleamed as he examined the rest of the chamber.

The square black table by the bed contained a goblet half-filled with liquid. The goblet was gray-blue, a color not in keeping, he noted sensitively, with the rest of the chamber. He picked up the glass and started to drink. No. Obviously he had been ill, and the liquid might be a soothing potion that would put him back to sleep. And he had slept long enough. Who knew how long?

So he replaced the goblet on the table of fine-grained wood and continued his inventory of the room. It was square-shaped—again that symbolic form that teased at his memory—and, he saw now, hung with other hangings than the one before his bed. These were large, luxurious cloths that bore what seemed to be a crest of royalty. On a flame-green ground that glowed like jewels was worked a black figure of a goat with a fish's tail; the goat was crowned in gold.

The image plucked at the edge of his recall—the Kap . . . Cap . . . Capran! This was the house of a Capran, the race of lower endlich-Erde. Endlich-Erde—the words had the curve of the sea goat's very form. And this must be a castle, to judge from the richness of the room and its appointments.

But how came he here, when he was not of these people?

The man on the bed felt weak with his effort to remember.

He was hungry, very hungry! And he saw the vivid green tasseled cord by his bed. He pulled it.

A door by the hanging of Pan opened immediately. A woman dressed in a gown of coarse gray stuff and with very slanting eyes of deepest black stared in at him, cried out as if in amazement, and disappeared, closing the door.

Puzzled, the long man lay back in the bed.

In an incredibly short time, a handsome woman dressed in a shining gown the color of a dark red gem came rushing into the chamber. Her oblique eyes, like hot onyx, gleamed with a strange excitement in her smooth white face, and on her full, rather sullen red mouth was a trembling smile.

She hurried toward him and knelt beside the bed. His nostrils were assailed by a strong odor of violets, and something in her manner reminded him unpleasantly of a falcon.

"Fahne!" she cried, then reached out to touch his hand.

His hand lay passively under hers; the touch of her fingers was very warm.

"So my name is Fahne," he said, hearing his voice aloud for the first time with a kind of wonder.

"Do you not know me?" the woman in red asked urgently.

"My lady, I hardly know myself," said the man on the bed.

And Shira saw Fahne's eyes stare back into hers, quite blankly, with no recognition.

Then she saw his eyes move to the tapestry that faced his bed. She followed his stare.

He was looking at one of the dark-haired, naked women, the satyrs' prey. And she resembled the Capran's bitter foe, the fragile Marin Dione.

Mahar, the ironic friend of the late Prince Monoceros, reined in his glossy horse and lazily descended to the dusty road between the fields.

"Ho, there! Ho, friend!" He called to the bent figure binding the sheaf.

Aspel the serf looked up in amazement at the sleek lord addressing him. Obediently, he ceased his labor and hurried toward the road.

"Messire?" Aspel tugged at the forelock of his head, his

weary eyes devouring the splendor of the stranger's raiment. The lord was tall and well made, but with a peculiar womanness in him, Aspel thought. On his chest was a starwheel made entirely of gems—black ones and red, and a kind of sad yellow. His doublet and hose were of the finest stuff, and his vivid green cloak was pinned with the greatest stone that Aspel had ever seen, even on the passing King.

"Messire?" he repeated.

"I wish to have a word with you and some of the other men," said the lord. How kindly he spoke! "If you will meet with me this Chronosday upon this spot, at ten-dark, I will bring you a suitable reward."

Aspel looked at him stupidly, not knowing what to say. "Reward?" he repeated.

The lord smiled with his mouth alone, the serf saw, and not with his slanted eyes. "Reward," he said. "How many of the men can you assemble?"

"As many as you desire, my lord," the serf gasped out with eagerness.

"Splendid. Ten-dark, then, on the Chronosday that comes." The elegantly attired nobleman began to walk away.

"Messire, messire!" Aspel cried out. The man paused.

"What will be . . . what will be the reward?" the serf inquired in a timid voice.

"A piece of silver each for a hundred men," the lord replied.

Speechless, Aspel watched the man depart, thinking with joy about the silver. Slowly he returned to the binding of the sheaves, looking forward to the dusk, when he could quit and take the news to Beta.

Then a peculiar thing occurred to him: once in the men's workroom he had heard the steward Dabih, who knew many things, discourse on the strange sect they called the Kyrin. The chief of the Kyrin's evil spirits had looked, according to Dabih, just like the lord in green who had brought the tidings to Aspel.

Shira, kneeling by the couch of Fahne, reflected in a rage of despair that even in the blackness of his mind, the sorcerer clung to Dione the Marin.

But she repressed an exclamation of ire that was springing to her lips and repeated, "You do not know me."

This time it was not an eager question, but a dark declaration.

"No, my lady, I do not. And neither do I know my origins or how I came to be in this, your house. It is your house?"

Shira rose and sat down in a yew-wood chair. "It is my castle," she said calmly. "I am Shira, the Queen of endlich-Erde."

Again only blankness from him met her words.

"You are Fahne the sorcerer," she went on quietly. "You met with . . . an accident, and we brought you here to heal."

"A sorcerer," he said with a detached interest. "I know nothing of sorcery."

"Look at the medallion on your neck," she said.

He felt then the weight upon him of which he had previously been unaware, and he took up the medallion on a heavy chain around his sinewy neck. It was a caduceus —the name came back to him in a flood of recall; it was the emblem of the god Hermes, the fleet, the magical! And in the center of the emblem was a six-pointed crystal star that glittered like the light on a descending flake of snow.

"A sorcerer," he said again and looked at Shira. She was a beautiful woman, he reflected, and yet she did not draw the eye like the woman in the picture. It was all most strange.

The Capran's slanted eyes of shining black caressed the sick man's face and hair, sweeping down his long, lean body outlined by the silken coverlet.

She hungered for him so! But this must be maneuvered carefully, reflected Shira. Therefore, she forced a smoothness to her face and asked in a low, husky voice, "Do you know the name of Desmos?" He shook his head. "Monoceros?" Again he made the negating gesture. "And . . . Dione?"

She watched him keenly, and with great delight she saw nothing move in his eyes. He shook his head.

"I remember nothing," he said calmly, "nothing before I came into this room."

A faint hope flickered in her hot black eyes. Perhaps they could begin again, she thought, exulting; perhaps he would never remember her abasement before him, and his own rejection of her! Shira's heart pounded and her soft body sickened with the old desire.

"You have been very kind, Your . . . Majesty," he said then. "I hope I can repay you in some manner soon."

Smiling, she replied, "Do not think of it. But you must have great hunger now. I will have the servants attend you." And she moved to the green tasseled cord.

"My lady," he said.

"Yes?" Eagerly Shira turned at the sound of his address. "How did you know my name?"

Confounded, Shira replied evasively, "You are weary now; the healer says that you must rest longer. We will speak of this again."

And with reluctance dragging at her relief to be gone, the Capran left the chamber. What, indeed, could she tell the sorcerer that would not reveal all that she wanted dark?

CHAPTER 2

Half-waking, Dione the Marin felt a sensation of brightness and extreme cold. She pulled the wagon rug up to her neck. A bladed sharpness pressed against her closed eyelids.

She had lost all reality of time. Somewhere in the wretched hours past she remembered her impotent struggles with Veris, the calm, strong Bole who had told her Fahne was dead, unwilling until she had seen his body with her eyes to come with them in the wagon. And there had been the horror of looking on Volan, as pale as death in the back of the gypsy wagon. And there was her own collapse, when she was nearly comatose with weeping and exhaustion, into an endless-seeming sleep.

And somewhere in that sleep she heard, or dreamed she heard, an animated exchange in Brisen, a tongue she recognized from her reading, catching only random words, for a high, sudden wind carried the sounds away.

But she heard someone say in surprise, *"Chatu"*— Brisen for "castle"—and pronounce the names "Melik" and "Shabatu." It had been the slow, deep voice of Veris the Bole, speaking the narrow Brisen with the heaviness of Erde.

No tears were left to weep, nothing before her that mattered, so she heard the voices with indifference and lay back in her aching stupor.

Now she felt a more intense sharpness on her shuttered lids and raised them a little.

There was a stabbing brightness through the wagon curtains. She raised her head and looked out from their kindly shade.

The wagon had paused in a windswept mountain clearing of light so strong it was unbearable. The snow seemed brighter than the naked sun. Dione saw an arch of gray-white stone, like the ingress to a courtyard.

She closed her burning eyes again and felt their copious tearing. She reached out her hand to touch the brow of Volan, who lay next to her. He was less feverish, she noted with thankfulness, cooled by the potions of the flame-haired Kaus. Feeling Volan's chest, Dione perceived that his breathing was easier.

The forecurtains were drawn back and Kaus said kindly, in thick-accented Marin, "We have arrived."

Dione sat up and tried to open her eyes, but the light was too painful.

"I cannot see," she said in a sad, dull voice.

"Come," the Sabbian said. "I will guide you."

"She is unused to the brightness." It was the deep tone of Veris the Bole. "The Peisun have very sensitive eyes."

She felt muscular arms raising her, and then her feet met the snowy ground. The air was very sharp and dry. Dione gasped and choked.

"Jove!" the Sabbian said. "Is she always this fragile?"

"She has been through a great ordeal." Veris reproached him. "And the Marin need a wider air of more shadow."

Dione heard then a man's voice greeting the others in Brisen. *"Merce,"* the brassy voice said, "thanks. Let us get them inside."

And there was another voice, a woman's, crying out in silvery-thin Brisen, trembling and apprehensive. "Gemelle!" the woman cried. And there were soothing murmurs in Brisen from the man.

It seemed to Dione that they walked an endless distance,

over snow and stone. At last they were climbing winding stairs.

Veris said, "We are here. Can you open your eyes?"

She made a great effort. "No," she answered dully. The quality of the air had altered; they must be inside, in a room. The weight on her eyelids lifted ever so slightly.

"Welcome." Dione heard an amiable male voice, thin, like all Brisen voices, but richer in timbre than that of Gemelle the Twisan. "I am Uras, the brother of the Lady Shabatu."

After a pause, he asked, "Is the little Marin sightless, or is it our unaccustomed light?"

"It is your light," said Veris, and Dione felt him guiding her to a chair. She sat down gratefully. "She has always lived," Veris added, "in the shadowy light of Mar."

"I shall draw the curtains closed."

Suddenly the great pressure on Dione's lids was eased and she could open her eyes. She saw, standing by the circular window, a very tall, thin man with hair so pale yellow that it looked almost silver. He had a long, amiable face, and his ugly smile reached his pallid eyes, the color of the winter sky.

The chamber was full of hyacinthine shadows; the color was so articulate of Fahne—his gem, the sapphire, and the hangings of their blue-rose marriage bed in Erdemar—that Dione's numbness was pierced. She felt completely the desolation of her loss. And she began to weep in dreadful, tearing sobs that shook her slender body.

"She has suffered greatly," Veris the Bole said softly to Uras.

Uras the Waetergyt gestured to the servants by the door. "Take her to her chamber," he said gently. "And send to her the calmer of moyen-Brise."

When the servants had led the Marin up the curving stairway of pristine glass, Uras turned back to the three men.

"Please sit down," he said amiably, "and take the refreshment of your race." He indicated the Erden and Sabbian wines on a silver table in the center of the chamber.

The room was brilliant with tiles that seemed fashioned not of stone, but glass, and along the curving walls at intervals were fragile shapes of flying creatures in shining silver. The curving stairway seemed almost to float to the high reaches of the floor above. The roof was domed and transparent to the cold November sky.

"My sister, the Lady Shabatu," said Uras, after the men were seated and had taken up their goblets, "is with Gemelle. He will be afforded the finest healers; so, of course, will the little Marin lady and the brindled boy. What is his name?"

"Volan," said Kaus.

"Ah, yes, Volan. The Lady Shabatu," said Uras, smiling, "enjoys great freedom, even by the standards of our country, dernier-Brise. But when my father Melik returns from Sabbia . . ." He paused delicately, his long face somber.

"We had hoped, messire," said Bock the Capran in his blunt way, "that the . . . connection of Gemelle and the Lady Shabatu might be broken, for her sake as well as his own."

"You see the difficulty, then. The royal sons of moyen-Brise and Sabbia are vying for her hand. My father means to press the suit of Nobilis, Prince of Sabbia, to warm the amity of our nations." Again Uras smiled his ironic smile. "But the Lady Shabatu is willful and intractable, with the fixed mind of the Waetergyt, and she has not received the news with joy. The Baron Melik will return by rise of Kani Circle with the Crown Prince Nobilis."

"He will not find us within the palace," said Kaus. "When Gemelle is fit to travel . . ."

Uras nodded. "Then you understand that what appears to be my coldness is indeed concern for your well-being."

"Of course." Veris nodded, then said, "My companion Bock and I desire in any case to return to Erde. As to the minstrel and the little Marin . . ."

"They are free to stay as long as they like," said Uras. "My sister," he smiled, "can weave a likely tale for our father, as she is wont to do. But now you must be weary. The servants of my sister learned from friends in upper Mar the terrors you endured. And surely now you want to rest yourselves."

The men murmured their gratitude.

"I will have some supper sent to your chambers," Uras said as the three began to ascend the curving stairs.

For a long moment the tall man with light hair stood still in the gleaming room, with its hyacinthine shadows like pools of blue water on the glimmering forms of wings.

Uras had seen on the star-wheel of the little Marin the

mark of her questioned birth, the star ascending on the border of the Twisan, the mark that cousined them. And the blood of his race of the magical will, beating, recalled her beauty and turned him toward the tomorrow of change.

In his eccentric eyes, which were the color of the winter sky, there were points of warm and alien light.

The Lady Shabatu had arranged makeshift quarters for the refugees; she had sought the senses of the Bilance, authorities in Brise on the palpable, in a benign attempt to simulate the natural habitats of the strangers.

But with all their delicate imagination, the Bilance of moyen-Brise could but approximate, considering the materials at hand: there was no green in Brise, where even the vegetation was bluish-gray; no gold or orange for Sabbians. Kaus was glad enough for the pallid yellow of the Twisan to warm him. The brown and russet of Erde were translated into the rosy colors of the moyen-Brise.

Dione the Marin noticed none of this; she lay on her pale blue bed without expression, neither moving nor speaking.

And when the calming healer Ven entered her chamber the following morning, he concluded that she probably had not slept, as well, for she lay in the same position as the night before, with wide, unmoving eyes.

"Good morning," Ven said gently, smiling, but the Marin did not respond.

There was a slight sound behind him, and he heard the door opening. On the threshold stood a boy, quite thin and pale, so thin the calmer feared his legs could not support him. His hair was dark, like the hair of the Marin, but it had peculiar gold highlights that spoke of Brise.

"You are the Marin's friend," said the calmer. "Enter."

Volan nodded and moved to the bed. His face was stricken by the sight of Dione's unmoving stare. "Has she taken food?" he asked.

"No," Ven replied soberly. "She neither moves nor speaks nor drinks nor eats. She only lies and stares. I have never encountered such an illness."

The boy began to weep, putting his thin face into his twisted hands. "I fear that she will die."

Ven said quietly, touching the boy's shoulder, "We will not let her die."

Volan noted at once his gentle confidence, and he looked

at him face-to-face for the first time. The calmer was a pleasant man of middle age with the cherubic face of moyen-Brise. He wore the rosy tunic of the Bilance, and his chin was deeply cleft, like those of most children of the Scales, but his violet eyes had a penetrating quality uncommon to moyen-Brise.

He said to the minstrel, "The little star she wears—what does it signify?"

Volan told the calmer.

"I see." Ven nodded. "Speak to her of it, my friend. I think this will be the key to unlock her cold embrace with death."

The minstrel stared at the man from moyen-Brise and leaned over the unmoving Dione. He began to say again and again the name of the sorcerer, and he touched the glimmering star that rested in the hollow of the Marin's throat.

Staring at the star, Volan cried out in amazed delight, "Look! Look at it!"

And with a trembling finger he pointed to the star. Although the light in the chamber had been constant—the curtains had been tightly shut to shield the Marin's eyes—whereas before the crystal had been blank as ice, there moved now a single, peculiar shadow.

And Volan said urgently to Dione, "My lady, my lady! He is alive! Fahne is alive, for the star has spoken!"

For the first time the wide green eyes of the Marin moved to touch the familiar face of Volan. And there was a trace of a smile in them, a kind of recognition.

Gemelle the Twisan dreamed of a field of snow; but the snow was warm, and upon it were two small pink roses. He wandered down the field, his mouth discovering a patch of gold, like a lily's heart, and he drank from it, tasting the musk and spice deep in the flower's throat.

He felt a trembling in the warm expanse of white. The snow had turned to silk, and he heard a high, singing cry, like the far singing of the lilac birds of Brise's highest air.

A small mouth touched his skin, and narrow arms enveloped him. Gemelle the Twisan opened his pallid eyes. Overhead were stars, the roof was transparent to the night, and there were glimmering blue walls with lilac shadows on them from the dancing of a fire.

He breathed a scent of musk and violets, and a spicy

sweetness from a web of gold drifted to him. He explored the web with his tongue. It was a woman's hair. Focusing at last, his sight took in the pristine face near his.

"Shabatu!" His seeking mouth covered her lucid face with kisses, and he felt her fragile hands upon him, bold and quickly stroking.

"Shabatu, Shabatu," he whispered hoarsely, and the shape of her name was the form of her body and the rhythm of their moving as he entered through the narrow golden door on the house of silken snow, climbing and climbing to tread the taut silver wires of the tallest air and to hear the pale birds singing.

The Circle of the Escor ascended to the Circle of the Kani. Late November was chill in Mar, so Veris and Bock were grateful to enter the smoky tavern.

"It seems another age when we sat here before," said Bock, rubbing his blunt hands together.

Veris merely nodded, with a shadow in his brown, sleepy eyes. But they brightened when he saw the voluptuous Crabba approach them, the same one, he noted, who had been so pert to Fahne that other evening in Maedentime.

Leaning to them, the Crabba's heavy breasts exposed themselves almost to their tips, and Bock the Capran stared at her with longing.

She met his gaze with her deepset green eyes, asking, "What are your desires?"

Repressing an obscene retort, Bock ordered a wine of his race and for Veris requested a liquor of Aphrodite.

The Crabba started to go away, but she suddenly paused and turned back to the Erden, an expression of bright curiosity in her deepset eyes. "I remember," she said in her thick Marin. "You are friends of the sorcerer."

The Erden exchanged a wary glance. Were the Lord Mayor's spies still seeking them?

"Why do you ask?" Veris inquired with caution.

The Crabba shrugged her soft shoulders, half-bared by her low-cut green gown. She showed the resentment of the hypersensitive to rebuff. "Yonder Capran spoke of him just now," she answered sullenly, nodding toward a nearby table. She started again for the alcove of wine and mead.

Veris' wide eyes were alight. "Wait, my lovely one," he

said softly, catching her by the arm. "What did yonder Capran say?" He showed her a piece of silver.

Mollified, the Crabba smiled at the pleasant Bole and replied, "That he is in Erde in the castle of Queen Shira." She took the silver.

After she had left them, Bock said urgently, "We must send word to Brise at once."

"Come," said Veris. "We must find an early traveler to the land of snows."

Dione's blossoming hopes had begun to fade. The star, for all her seeking, brought no answer from the sorcerer; if he lived, she feared, then he had forsaken her. For there had been no sweet and ghostly meetings, as there had been in circles past, when his mind so clearly answered hers that it seemed his very body was near.

This evening in the smaller festivity hall that the family of Melik frequented when alone, Dione sat a little apart with the minstrel from Kaus and Uras, Gemelle and Shabatu.

A slight shadow hovered over them all, for this was the last evening they would have together before the return of the Baron Melik.

The Marin glanced at Shabatu; each day and night she had seemed more blooming than those before. Dione knew that this was the doing of Gemelle, and her own heart ached, remembering her own time with Fahne in their few golden days.

Volan the minstrel softly strummed his cithara, and Gemelle called out, "Please sing for us, my friend."

At once the unmanned minstrel raised his bird-like tenor, with its glimmers of silver and gold rooted in his questioned birth. He began to sing one of the wistful airs of the Lady Dione.

The Marin was so lost in her reveries that she did not see the winter-blue eyes of Uras fixed upon her. She sat quite still, the firelight gleaming on her borrowed lilac gown; she and the Lady Shabatu, who had been generous with her raiment, were almost the same size. The friendship of the two frail women, whose birth stars neighbored them on heaven's wheel, had grown warm. Even now, in the Marin's small ears and on her arms and bosom were handsome trinkets of aquamarine, a birth gem of the Peisun and a stone beloved of the Waetergyt.

As Volan ended the haunting air and began to sing another, Uras rose from his yew-wood chair and went to Dione, standing next to her chair and gazing down at her.

The Marin glanced at Gemelle and Shabatu; their faces were already dark with their imminent farewell, for, with the coming of Melik, the departure of Gemelle was inevitable. And Melik was bringing with him Prince Nobilis of Sabbia. Dione's heart ached for her friend.

"It will be a sad thing to see Gemelle go," said Uras to Dione. "I am consoled by the thought that you and the minstrel will remain."

"Volan and I must go, as well," Dione replied. "I can no longer presume on your courtesies."

"Presume!" Uras said sadly. Dione felt a prickle of uneasiness. "Why must you leave at all, Dione?" he asked softly.

And although his voice was gentle and his pale eyes kind, Dione could hear in the words of Uras an eerie echo of the declarations of Vanand.

She knew then that even if Fahne had forsaken her, there could not be another, that she must go on the morrow with the others from the castle of Shabatu.

CHAPTER 3

The Baron Melik would arrive at twelve-light; therefore, Kaus had urged Gemelle to be gone in the young day from the castle.

The white sun of early morning caught the looking glass of Shabatu the Waetergyt, reflecting its brightness on the lovers' white, shut lids.

Gemelle awoke first, and seeing the gleam on the face of Shabatu, he held her more closely, whispering, "You are like the morning on the snow."

Trembling, she moved nearer to the Twisan, enclosing with her wing-like hands his head of bright yellow hair, a deeper yellow than her own, which was so pale it was almost silver. She kissed him deeply, and he could taste the acrid tears in her kiss.

He held her even closer, so close that their bodies kissed, too, and with such savagery that there was a pain in their meeting. "I cannot let you go," he said, "I cannot let you go."

"Stay but a moment longer." Her narrow voice was distorted by her urgency; he hardly knew it. And Gemelle kissed her again, on her soft, rose-colored mouth, all over her clear white face, and his mouth tasted the ineffable savor of her pale hair, with its smell of the vanilla flower.

"How can I leave you?" he murmured. "It has never been so for me, not in all my days. I have been . . ."

"A true Twisan?" He moved back a little way and looked into her remote, soft eyes, the color of the sky of Brise in winter.

"Yes." He moved back close to her again, saying, "I fear I cannot make myself part from you."

"Then let me go with you," she whispered urgently.

"I cannot take you into that gypsy life, you who have always lain on silken beds, with women to attend you, placing jewels in your hair."

"What can that matter," she cried, "when all my life before I have waited like a captive in a crystal cage? Only now have I begun to breathe, and live, to know the blood that courses through my veins."

Gemelle drew her head onto his lean chest and stroked the pallid gold web of her hair. She was weeping.

"Oh, do not weep," he said softly, kissing her head and stroking with his powerful fingers her silken back.

"Take me with you," she said again, her voice muffled in his lean flesh.

"Oh, Shabatu!" He raised her head from his chest and kissed her. "Do you not know how I long to take you away with us this day? My bed will be a bed of ice and stone without you. You must know that. But I have seen what wounds the love of a wanderer can tear a woman with."

"The tragedy of Dione and the sorcerer need not be ours," she said stubbornly. With rueful affection he heard the fixity of the Waetergyt. For all her frail appearance, Shabatu was as obdurate as the other fixed races of the Escorpiun, Leun, and Bole.

"I cannot now," he repeated.

"Perhaps you are still a true Twisan," she answered coldly.

"Please, my love, let us not part in enmity." With great gentleness and pleading, Gemelle touched her fragile face.

"Forgive me," she said, and she came into his arms again, and they moved closer, ever closer, while the young sun grew more yellow, unknowing of the hour or their parting or of anything beyond the warming of the other's flesh.

Gasping, Gemelle raised himself from her throbbing slenderness and lay back on the ice-blue pillows. They were wrapped in silence. Shabatu saw a flock of lilac snow geese wave above them through the transparent ceiling of the chamber.

A soft, sharp knock dismayed them.

"Kaus," said the Twisan softly, and his pale eyes said good-bye to Shabatu's.

Dione had risen betimes. Not waiting for the servant, she smoothed down the pale blue bed and hung the glimmering lilac gown and the fragile nightrobes in the carved press against the silvery wall.

Then with a kind of sadness she took up the green and russet clothes of a boy that she had worn from upper Mar; they were clean and mended, brushed and quite renewed, yet to don them again was to relive the horrors of the night upon the precipice, and the joys as well that had come before, the joys that would never return.

As she fastened the russet weskit around her slender form, noting its looseness, Dione the Marin said aloud with regret, "How I shall miss Shabatu."

The gentle white Shabatu, star-cousin to the Peisun, had delighted Dione with the freedom of her ways and with the wide-ranging brilliance of her mind. Even in the land of Brise, where women were given a higher value than in Erde or Mar, Shabatu's learning was unique. And they had planned to pursue together certain studies smiled upon by Melik, but encouraged by Uras—the Lady Shabatu was versed in alchemy, and she had already imparted some of her lore to Dione.

Remembering the peculiar dream of Desmos and of Fahne in the strange small space, with its peculiar instruments that might have been those of alchemy, the Marin felt a deeper pain of loss. Perhaps, she reflected, brushing her lustrous hair, she had been meant to remain.

But that was foolish, she resolved, replacing the jeweled brush on the fine-grained table. Her place was with the minstrel and the friends of Fahne, her fate to wander where the sorcerer had gone—even though he had forsaken her, she added bitterly, feeling her green eyes moisten.

"Madame, madame." The soft voice startled her; she must not have heard the servant knocking. The little under-Twisan in her narrow yellow gown stood waiting respectfully for Dione to reply.

Apologizing for her inattention, the Marin smiled. "The Lady Shabatu," said the servant in her narrow premier-Brisen, "begs that you remain. She wishes to converse with you."

Surprised, the Marin nodded and sank onto the pale blue bed. Dione had thought she had wished to spend these last few minutes with Gemelle and had planned to leave without saying good-bye to her friend.

The underTwisan quietly withdrew, and in a moment or two the door opened again, and the Lady Shabatu entered.

The Marin repressed an exclamation of concern: the pallid face of the Waetergyt looked bloodless, and the snowy skin below her distant eyes was lavender with shadows, puckered from her weeping. The hollows of her cheeks were prominent.

"My friend," she said, moving with her floating motion toward Dione, her fragile nightrobe wafted out behind her like a blue pillar of smoke.

"Oh, leave me not bereft!" cried Shabatu, sitting on the broad bed by the Marin and taking Dione in her arms. She burst into bitter weeping.

"My lady, my lady," Dione said in a low, soothing voice. "Please do not weep so. You will be ill."

"I cannot bear it all alone!" Shabatu was sobbing.

"But my dear friend, I cannot remain any longer."

"But why not? Oh, why?" the Waetergyt demanded, wiping her pallid cheeks with her trailing sleeve.

Dione put a gentle hand on Shabatu's arm. "Because of your brother," she said in a low voice.

"Uras?" Shabatu stared. "What has he done?"

The Marin colored painfully. "He has done nothing that has not been kind," she said. "But I feel that he . . ."

"I see. He wishes to woo you. And your heart is still Fahne's."

"Yes. Otherwise, dear friend, I would never desert you now."

Shabatu took the Marin's hand. "Never mind. I will see to Uras," she declared with the charming imperiousness that Dione had come to know so well in this last circle.

The Marin smiled and her smile was rueful. "I do not think it will be so easy," she protested.

The Waetergyt retorted, "I will make his days most unpleasant if he persists." And Dione heard the obduracy that had been so plain a little while before to Gemelle.

"But I . . ."

"Please, my friend, oh, please." Shabatu looked at her, beseeching, and Dione was touched by the sadness in the thin face. "Do not desert me now . . . and deprive the little minstrel of his comforts," she added slyly, knowing that the Marin's love for Volan would sway her.

Reading the Waetergyt's intent, Dione laughed aloud. Why, indeed, she thought, should they go now, to live with Gemelle and Kaus, perhaps to be a burden on them? What other life was there for her?

"Very well," she said to Shabatu, touching her hand with affection. "If you will make things clear to Uras . . . and if you can justify me to your father. . . ."

"Oh, my father!" Shabatu made a careless gesture. "Even here in Brise, the presence of another woman will almost go unnoticed. And as for poor Volan . . ." Delicately, the Waetergyt paused.

"Yes." Dione nodded, smiling a little sadly. "Volan has never been a threat to anyone."

"Then it is decided!" Shabatu rose, and her whole demeanor now was one of hope. "Do take off those ugly clothes and put on the gray dress, the one with the silver. I have some lovely things to give you, as well."

"You are most kind." Dione smiled and obediently began to unfasten the boy's jerkin.

"Now," said Shabatu, and the sadness had returned to her, "I must send word to Gemelle that you will remain. And I will say my last good-bye to him."

At twelve-light, noon of Capra, Prince Nobilis of Sabbia stared up at the curving battlements of the castle of the Baron Melik. The yellow sun glittered on its glassy, transparent domes, and it looked like a castle from a fairy tale. At one of the innumerable windows the flame-haired Prince fancied he saw a white, snowy face between wings of pale gold hair, and his massive loins warmed with the image of Shabatu.

The Leun Prince Nobilis bore a strong resemblance to his father, the King Achir. On his mass of mane-like, fiery hair he wore a crown of gold that rose in sharp points, like the points of flames. The crown was encrusted with rubies, the star-gem of the king of beasts, and his raiment was crimson and gold. He sat upon his chestnut steed with pride, his broad shoulders tapering to a waist of incredible leanness, like the body of the lion itself, and his strong legs controlled his mount with immense power.

Riding next to him on a graceful gray was the Waetergyt Baron Melik, a very thin, ironic-looking old man arrayed in robes of cold blue-gray, but the robes were paved in many glittering amethysts, star-gem of the dernier-Brise. And his seat, though less pompous than the Leun's, was that of a man not a bit less stubborn and royal, for the Waetergyt, like the Leun of Sabbia and the Escor and Bole of Mar and Erde, was a fixed race of the heaven's wheel.

Catching the young Sabbian's ardent glances at the battlements, the Baron Melik felt a deeper satisfaction. This marriage would forever seal the amity of Brise and Sabbia . . . and this intractable young man would surely be the one to tame the intractable Shabatu!

Those in Mar too impecunious to maintain a staff of servants and those merchants who preferred to entrust their treasures to professionals were among the patrons of the couriers' stable. It was but a step away, the landlord of The Cup and Crescent had advised Veris and Bock.

The Erden entered its whinnying warmth, breathing the aroma of horses and hay. The Capran, who, like the Kani and the Multuns of Sabbia, had been born of the lighter-hooved gods, was stirred by the sight of the beautiful beasts—the patient *Erdenpferd* who would bear the riders to the South, the sensitive grays of Mar that moved with the grace of sea waves, maintained for the journeys to upper Mar, where they would be exchanged for the snow-treading *cheval* of Brise.

Veris looked about for the proprietor. Just then a heavy Crabba approached from one of the stalls.

"A good evening, sires. I am Granchio, the master of the stables. How may I assist you?"

Veris told him, holding out the sealed missive he had penned in the tavern.

"Alar's the one you want," said Granchio. "He is called the 'son of lightning,' a Twisan who travels constantly to the land of snows."

"Where is this Alar?" Bock asked.

"At the moment, he is in The Wheel, having a cup before his journey starts. If you go now you can just detain him. He has taken with him his traveling steed."

Receiving Granchio's directions to the inn, the Erden hurried away.

The Wheel apparently was so named for its custom—all the races of the stars—for emerging from its brightness the Erden saw men of varied dress with every color of hair. The dark heads of Erde and Mar mingled with the golden ones of Brise and the flaming ones of Sabbia, and the cloaks of the patrons were green and russet, purple and turquoise, scarlet and gold and yellow.

"I think that is Alar. We are in luck," said Veris, pointing to a reckless-looking young Twisan in a yellow doublet and hose. His short cloak was trimmed heavily in pearls, impudent, Bock thought, for a man who was to travel the lonely roads to Brise. Alar, however, had a tensile strength in his leanness that would serve him well, the Capran reflected.

Veris greeted him.

"Yes," the Twisan said, his dancing eyes studying the Erden keenly, showing his interested surprise. The Bole had greeted him in Brisen; it was uncommon for the Erden to be conversant with the courtly tongue. "I am Alar. I start soon for the snows of Brise. What is your commission, gentlemen?"

The Bole held out the sealed missive addressed to Gemelle.

"A pewter piece," Alar said carelessly. "It will be no burden, and my way is past the castle of the Baron Melik."

"Splendid."

"But wait," the Twisan said, "I know the name Gemelle.

He is the acrobat of no little fame." He smiled at the Erden.

"Yes," Veris replied, "he is our close companion and our friend. And this missive," he added, "is of great import."

"It shall be delivered safely, I promise you," Alar responded. "I have never failed in a commission yet."

"Veris," Bock said to the Bole in a lowered voice, "perhaps the missive should be addressed to the Lady Shabatu, in the event that Melik returns before it is in Gemelle's hands . . . or perhaps it could be addressed to the Lady Dione."

"You say true," the Bole answered.

"Well, gentle sires?" Alar's silvery words had an edge of impatience. "I must soon be gone."

"I would have the missive delivered not to Gemelle," said Veris, "but instead to the Lady Shabatu, daughter of the Baron Melik."

"As you will," said Alar. And Bock handed him a piece of pewter. "The missive will rest safely among . . . other items in my sack." And he placed the letter in his heavy woolen pouch, which he then secured to his saddle. With an agile leap he was on the back of his swift, nervous steed. "I bid you farewell, gentlemen."

"A moment, messire," Bock called, and Alar detained his gray mount gently.

"Yes?"

"Do you not fear to travel the unfrequented roads in your . . . jeweled raiment?"

Alar laughed, and his light laughter lit his dancing, pale blue eyes. "Both the Council of Mar and the Baron Melik of Brise take active measures against highwaymen, and surely you know that the Church of Stars punishes them with the angers of the gods. No, messires, I have traveled these roads in the blackest dark with untold treasures, never coming to harm. Have no fear."

And he spoke to his graceful steed, urging it onto the crossing road that led from Mar to upper Mar and on to the snowy land of Brise, the country of the air. He waved at the Erden lightly as he cantered off, the lanterns gleaming on his pearl-encrusted yellow garments.

The Erden made their way into the bright and smoky depths of the tavern of all the stars.

As the landlord found a servant to show them to their chambers, Veris whispered to Bock, "Look there."

A sinister-looking group of Escors was departing. One of them said something in a low voice to his companion, and the second Escor gave an evil laugh.

The Bole thought he had caught the name "Alar."

"Come, Veris," the Capran repeated. "I am tired enough to drop. We cannot start at the sight of every Thround in Mar."

Veris, subdued, followed the Capran and the servant up the stairs to their lodging place.

But long after Bock was snoring, Veris the Bole lay wakeful in the cramped chamber of The Wheel, trying to shut out the sounds of the carousing below them and picturing the lean Alar beset by the evil-looking band of red-clad Throunds on the lonely highway from Mar to the land of snow.

CHAPTER 4

Gonu the Pfarrer, high priest of lower Erde, did not take drink, even at the marriage feast of the Queen. Therefore, he could look with clearer eyes on the foolish, flushed faces about him and hear with sad clarity the slurred pronouncements of the guests.

An ancient man with long, coarse hair in ragged curls the color of trodden snow, the Pfarrer was clothed in a voluminous robe made of the skins of hooved creatures. In his gray face his night-black eyes, more profound than those of the Erden around him, held a look of perpetual sorrow.

Sickened, Gonu heard the ironic tones of Mahar, the confidant of the late Prince Monoceros, brother to the Queen. Whereas most of the other carousers had the look of arrogant stallions, Mahar had the more delicate air of a gazelle. But there was a sullen droop to his thin mouth, and his words were barbed.

"If the guests," he was saying now to his companion, "numbered all those she has bedded, this festal hall would not contain them." He had spoken very audibly, though he seemed less drunk than the general company.

"Hush," his companion said sternly. "The priest is near you. And you know she countenances you with little patience, now that Monoceros is dead."

"A curse on the bitch," Mahar retorted, but Gonu noted that he had lowered his voice a little.

The Pfarrer sighed and looked about the festal hall, a riot of vivid color where the noble Caprans from the other great houses of lower Erde whirled, dancing in their clothes of fiery green and blazing claret-color, gemmed in enormous garnets and onyx and moonstone. Among them were many Marin, the fated mates of the Erden, made doubly welcome now with the symbolic wedding of Shira to Desmos of Mar. There were Escors in scarlet and topaz; many Crabba, the magnetic opposite to the Capra, were arrayed in silver-green and pearls, glowing with the moonstone shared by the Crabba, the Peisun, and the Capra since the earliest time of stars; and there were a few quiet Peisun, who seemed to have attended out of amity with Desmos, for the Peisun were the Marin least attuned to the Capra.

Gonu had always liked the Peisun, for their dreamy intelligence comprehended the trauminitions—the dream-intuitions—of the mystic Pfarren. And the priest liked Desmos, consort to the Queen; and he pitied him.

The priest's sad eyes sought out the Peisun consort; he was dancing with the Queen, in her voluminous, gleaming gown of ivory-white, whose virginal color, Gonu reflected with distaste, had caused a snicker among the women, especially the sharp-tongued Throunds. She did not look like a bride; her white face was smooth and emotionless, though glowing with its accustomed loveliness. Her thick black hair was alight with scores of moonstones strung on a delicate web of white-gold, and her magnificent breasts, far whiter than the gown, were covered only at the nipples.

Gonu the Pfarrer studied Shira, and he saw her hot black gaze attach itself to the lean person of the Maeden —the man with no remembrance—they called Fahne. Gonu had grown very fond of the mysterious Maeden, for even in the present blankness of his mind, Fahne had comprehended instantly the concepts of the Pfarren. And Gonu, with great excitement, had seen at times a glimmering in Fahne of magical lore remembered. He had come to love the man.

And some old connection, still unknown, had made the man named Fahne beloved of Desmos the Peisun, whose wife continually cast her hot, yearning eyes on the Maeden! No good could come of this tangled web, Gonu reflected.

Desmos, consort of the Queen Shira, looked down on the shut face of his voluptuous wife as they whirled in the Capran dance, his Marin emotions stirring to the sound of the lutes and horns.

The sensual melodies of the genial Bole, the musical folk of Erde, titillated Desmos' nerves, and he burned to lean down in the sight of the entire assembly and taste with his trembling mouth the richness of the breasts revealed so boldly.

He drew Shira close, feeling her thinly clad body on his, pressing the weight of her soft breasts to his heart that beat so hard he could not at the moment speak.

Shira made a little sound of protest and struggled in his arms. "I cannot dance if you hold me so tightly." Her voice was cool, as cool as if he were a stranger, and not the man Gonu had made her husband.

And unbidden, all the memories of their empty after-times flooded the Peisun—her instant lust, its quick, almost male, appeasement; then, always, the vacancy.

But studying her delicious, sullen mouth, which bestowed on him that treasured and remarkable caress, Desmos knew his senses' fire, and his aching heart's inevitable defeat. She beats me with her body, he thought sadly; I cringe before her nakedness like the lowliest serf of her fields.

And his inflamed desire, which never seemed to cool no matter how many times he lay with her, blotted out all other images, erased his discontent.

When he could speak at last, he whispered, smiling, "This feast has been forever, and we have danced around this floor for years. When do you think we might escape the company?" He could feel the pressure; his clothes constricted him horribly.

"Not yet," she answered carelessly. "I must give some consideration to my guests."

The Peisun thought darkly that she was not accustomed

to consider other than her own desires, and he wondered uneasily at her answer. Nevertheless, he nodded with an amiable submissiveness, and he whirled her in a wider circle.

But this time he did not heed her injunction to hold her loosely, and he drew her closer in his arms, his gentle face pressed to her own, inhaling the sleep-bringing violet scent of her hair. The fragrance so dizzied the Peisun that he closed his eyes and did not see Shira's slanted gaze seeking out the face of the sorcerer.

He was awakened rudely from his sensual trance by her cool voice, abrupt in his ear: "I am weary of dancing. Let us sit down."

"But we shall interrupt the other dancers," he said gently.

Shira, who had looked with anger upon the Peisun with whom Fahne was dancing, smiled cat-like up at her husband.

"Let us sit down," she repeated.

And as the royal couple left the dance floor, the other dancers perforce followed after.

Desmos, glancing sideways at his wife, saw a sly expression on her face that he had seen before and dreaded. His Peisun intuition read her as if she were a child. Shira was plotting something.

Fahne saw with relief the departure of Shira and Desmos from the ring of dancers. The little Peisun, a distant in-law of the Queen's, was pleasant enough, but the sorcerer had never cared for dancing or the light conversation accompanying it. And the blankness of his own remembrance made his answers to the Peisun tedious.

Nevertheless, his growing regard for Desmos obliged him to be as civil as possible, and nothing would have wrung from him his deep dislike of Desmos' wife, the lovely Queen Shira.

Fahne had looked with pity on the Peisun's face while they were dancing. The crystal Maeden sight remaining despite the mists of his recall gave Fahne a lucid picture of their love—Desmos, patiently profound and open; Shira, with an indifferent lustiness that would, Fahne thought dryly, be easily aroused by any man.

With courteous indifference, Fahne poured out a goblet of strawberry wine for the little Peisun. Leaning to her, he was struck for an instant by some nostalgic scent, and he felt a faint warmth in himself. What was it? Water lily, he supposed, for he had relearned laboriously in the past weeks, with the gentle tutelage of Desmos, many of the symbolic star lessons of his youth. And the water lily, he repeated to himself, was a flower of Peisun.

But why had the odor made him warm all of a sudden and filled him with a haunting sense of something lost? His head began to ache and he tried to dismiss the matter from his mind. How much, he reflected sadly, there was left to learn! And how mysterious, above all, had been his strong reaction to the fleeing nymph in the tapestry. There was something in the face. . . .

But about them guests were rising to their feet, and his friend Desmos was saying genially, "A toast!"

Fahne imagined he saw the Queen giving the server a significant look; the bottles from which the others' wine was poured were separate from his. And the server paused before him, lifting another beaker that strangely gleamed, decanting a dark liquor into Fahne's goblet.

Fahne was reluctant to drink. But when Desmos said, "A toast to the beauty of the Queen!" and drained his glass, Fahne followed suit. A path of fire ran down his throat, along his veins and vitals. He felt himself begin to warm peculiarly toward the alien company, and for the first time in many moons his body was burning with desire, an undifferentiated lust that had no specific object.

Something glimmered at the edges of his memory, a small white body on a bed of red and golden leaves . . . a house. But Fahne shook himself free of the gray strands webbing his brain, for the breasts of Shira shone now before his fevered eyes; she bared herself, he thought, as no other woman dared. She had caught his look; deliberately bending, she let him look on the twin globes in all their glory. He could see the rosy shadows of their tips, and all at once his lust was overpowering.

Fahne blinked his brindled eyes, dazed at his own reaction. He had never liked the woman, never looked upon her in this fashion. And now, when she had become the wife of his friend . . .

But Desmos was looking at him now. Quickly Fahne looked away and fixed his bewildered eyes, as if absently, on the passing server. The man felt his stare, and all unwillingly he returned it.

For no reason he could name, Fahne took his caduceus medallion, with its central crystal star, in his fingers and began to dangle it to and fro.

The server paused and stared into the depths of Fahne's strange and dappled eyes. The decanter fell from the server's hand, and he tumbled from the dais to the floor below and lay there senseless.

"The *Vau!*" cried Gonu. "The *Vau* of the sorcerer!" An uneasy murmur swept the marriage guests.

And Fahne remembered then the Escor in the tavern of Mar, and words he had murmured above a still, small figure, the same white figure on the bed of leaves.

It was true, then, as Gonu had told him—he was a sorcerer. But whence had he come, and from whom had he learned his mystic lore? How came he here to the castle of Shira, looking with desire on the wife of his friend—he who could not even remember desire, nor his last experience of it?

And overcome with confusion and despair, Fahne rose and rushed headlong from the festal hall of Shira, blindly seeking the stairs to his alien chamber.

Rushing down the gloomy corridor, he heard the desolate echo of his own steps in the cold silence. There was no one near, for all the servants were below attending to the festivities, and Fahne breathed a sigh of relief for the sweet aloneness. He felt he might be going mad, to look upon her so, the wife of Desmos!

He reached the haven of his room and slammed the heavy door. Without undressing, he flung himself upon the bed of checkered green and ebon, recalling the weeks that had gone before, since his birth in this chamber.

Fahne's body was still beating with that cold, impersonal desire that had overcome him in the festal hall. A name occurred to him, flaring in his mind: basil. Basil! Of course! The witch had given him that, the aphrodisiac essence of Mars that inflamed the senses and clouded the mind. And yet his eyes' strength had rendered the server senseless. No, he was not as weak as he had thought.

Suddenly, with a confusion of images whirling in the eye of his brain, Fahne leaped up from the bed and lit a taper. He moved with it to the tapestry before the bed and held it near the image of the fleeing nymph with the delicate face and night-black hair. Who was she, who was she? his sickened brain demanded, but he found no reply, only blankness.

Setting the taper in a cresset by the arras, Fahne the man without a past lay down again upon the green and ebon bed, his body aching with need, and began to weep.

He must have slept, he knew not how long, but he felt that many hours had elapsed since he heard his own desolate crying. He opened his eyes. By the gods, his flesh was still burning! The witch must have dosed him well, he reflected sourly.

Then he was arrested by the creaking sound of the opened door.

By the taper's light his astonished eyes took in the naked form of the Queen Shira: her thick black hair fell like a gleaming shawl over her bare arms, half-veiling her magnificent breasts, reaching almost to her perfect, curving thighs.

Despite himself, the sorcerer could not cease his staring. She was perfection, from the oblique glimmer of her black, black eyes and the moist red mouth, parted with her eagerness, to the great globes of her breasts, the shadowy triangle of Aphrodite, and her shapely legs and naked feet.

As she came forward in the candlelight, Fahne lay back, hypnotized, trying to summon up the wistful face of Desmos to halt the pulsing in his fiery blood. But it was useless; the holocaust of demoniac feeling devoured him, and he lay passive as she ripped away his clothes and began with slow, excruciating skill to taste his body, thrusting her mouth upon his flesh.

And he gave himself up to her caress, blindly, no longer knowing her face or her name; she had become a nymph of the forests, belonging to no man, owing fealty to none, or mercy. Her caresses were brutal in their eagerness and urgency, and he could feel the breaking of his skin where her sharp teeth sank into his flesh, and he heard her bestial grunts and squealing cries.

He knew then he must have begun to take the action of the man, for he was looking down on her sprawling, leaping body and the flood of night-black hair spread out on the dazzling black and ebon of the coverlet, and her cries were like the beasts of the field; she was covered with his blood.

Something exploded in his brain, and half-relieved, the sorcerer came to his senses. Withdrawing from her, where she lay sobbing and appeased, Fahne knew a terrible anger and a vast disgust. He had emptied himself into the grossness of her lovely flesh; it was as if a demon had come to him.

Shira raised herself and crawled to him over the bed. Making small, mewling sounds like a newborn animal, she licked at his chilling feet.

"My god, my god!" she gasped out, her sharp tongue still lapping at his skin.

Gently, Fahne pushed her away and sat with his head in his hands. He could see the trusting face of Desmos the Peisun, who had become his friend and brother in these desolate days of his new beginning.

"Please," he said softly, "please go now."

"Go!" she spat out. "Go from you now!"

He turned and looked at her without speaking, and she was chilled by his eyes.

"I will never let you go," she retorted, and her tone was calm and cold.

Then shielding her perfect body with her arms, she moved with a slow, deliberate walk toward the heavy door.

At its closing sound, the sorcerer expelled a sighing breath. The small wounds on his skin were smarting badly, and he shook with chill. He stumbled to a basin on a nearby table and began to bathe his wounds, still trembling as if with a dread ague.

Seeking the warmth of the bed, he lay for a moment staring into the dimness. The taper sputtered and went out.

The mild, autumnal winter of lower Erde was soft at morning. The castle's inhabitants, wearied from the celebration, slept as Fahne the sorcerer moved softly down the granite stairs and across the entranceway.

The faded teal-blue doublet and hose stuck to the drying blood of his minuscule wounds and stung abominably. He cursed his own exhausted lack of foresight; the moat door, of course, was shut, and the strength of four men was required to open it. He would have to find another way.

Stealing back across the entrance hall, he sought the stairs to the lower levels. He dove into the moat.

"The Circle of the Kani is a gentle month in your land," Veris said drowsily to Bock, and then he spoke to the patient horse drawing their wagon. The light of early morning played over the long brown fields where the grain was still being harvested.

The Capran murmured in agreement, too sleepy yet for much conversation, for the hour was young.

"This looks like the road to the castle," Veris said then as they bumped along the dry and rutted way.

"It is," said Bock tersely, closing his slanted eyes.

It was then that a peculiar hue caught Veris' attention: a patch of teal-blue, the color of the Maeden, broke the endless monotony of brown beyond them in a field.

"Bock, what's that?"

The Capran blinked awake and said irritably, "What's what?"

"That," responded Veris, pointing. "That patch of blue in yonder field."

"I think it is a man," Bock said slowly.

Veris reined in the heavy horse and leaped from the wagon, Bock on his heels.

In the stubbled grain they came upon a tall, lean man in the teal-blue of the Maeden, lying on his face. There was something very familiar about him, Bock thought. He looked excitedly at Veris.

"Is he dead?"

"No. No, he is breathing—look. He is asleep." The Capran bent down and cautiously began to turn him over.

The man, still deeply asleep in the sleep of great exhaustion, had small dark smears of dried blood on his clothes where his tunic stuck to his body.

And the man was Fahne the sorcerer.

CHAPTER 5

Dione was standing in her water garden, but the dome, instead of rose and green and blue and lavender, was transparent to the starry sky. And instead of the perpetual murmur of the Marin river-streets, she heard the long, unchanging chirr of insects, like the sounds of Erde. The night sky through the dome was very clear, unlike the shadowy nights of Mar, and thousands of glimmering stars in alien formations, constellations that the Babylonians had never seen, were lucid above her. It was as if the wheel of heaven whirled before her very eyes.

Dione felt a dreadful vertigo, looking up at the glittering chaos that violated all of heaven's laws, and she was afraid.

And then she knew that she was not alone in the garden. There in the shade of the massed vines was a tall, lean figure.

It was a man in the cloak of a Maeden. His long arm was stretched out to her, as if pleading, and she could hear his words but dimly. Dione could not move; she was rooted to the path of shells.

But at last she understood his words. "Wait," he was calling. "Wait for me. And help me from the dark where I am bound."

The tall man began to move toward her in long strides, his blue cloak flying backward in a sudden, mysterious wind. Dione moved toward the entrance to her chambers, and to safety. The approach of the tall man filled her with apprehension. But now he was calling, "You cannot escape me; your flesh is dyed with me, your blood."

The whirling stars above were slowing, and as Dione looked upward, unbelieving, she saw that all the planets and lights and stars except for three were fading to blackness.

One was the bright immensity of Jove, and the second, the greenish light of Poseidon that the ancients had only dreamed but never witnessed, both the rulers of the Peisun; and in the line of polarity whirled the tiny body of Hermes, as swift as the winged creatures of air, ruler of Fahne the sorcerer.

"My lady, my lady!" Dione the Marin awoke to the soft greeting of the minstrel and saw that she was not in the water garden. The man in blue was gone, and the night above the domed ceiling of her chamber glimmered not with whirling constellations, but with a random, quiet star.

"I was dreaming," she said, still thick with sleep, and she felt again the weight of lone reality. She was, of course, in her delicate room in the castle of Shabatu . . . and not quite alone, she chided herself, smiling at Volan.

"I would have waited," he said gently, "for you to awaken, but you cried out so in your sleep."

"It comforts me that you are here, my friend," she said, consoling him. "My dream was very strange and sad." Dione sat up in the bed and leaned back against her lavender pillows.

Volan reached down beside his chair and picked up his beloved bird-shaped cithara. He began to touch the strings with gentleness. "You dreamed of Fahne?"

"I do not know. I dreamed of a man in blue with a hooded face." And she told Volan the rest of her dream.

"It is a sign, my lady, a true sign," he said eagerly, "an omen of a bondage, but his unchanging love." The minstrel's fingers had stilled upon the strings.

Dione shook her head and sighed. "I fear he has forsaken me, Volan. My star has given me no answer; he comes not, still."

"You must have faith, my lady." The minstrel's voice was firm. "He comes not because he cannot."

"Have faith and keep away from Uras' path," she commented dryly. "Shabatu has been most clever in helping me avoid him."

"And you have greatly aided her," Volan replied, his eyes twinkling. "You have not made it easy for the Prince Nobilis."

The Marin grinned. "It is not easy to woo two women who are ever twinned together. But I fear that the Baron Melik grows suspicious," she added. "I will not long be welcome in his house when the truth is out."

"I would miss it," said Volan with frankness, examining the luxurious chamber. The Brisen temper of his wheel of stars bloomed, the Marin knew, in the fragile splendor of the castle; he loved the pallid, shining appointments of blue and lilac, white and silver. "It is like a garden of coolness," he said softly, "and what a glory it is, with the windows and the looking glasses and the plates in the form of unique flakes of snow!"

His delight was like a child's, and the Marin realized, with an emotion of guilt, that this was the first such splendor he had ever known.

"Do not fear," she said to soothe him. "I do not imagine that we will be banished so soon."

Yet she turned her white face from him so that he might not read its sorrow and mourn in her behalf. She would have exchanged greater splendor than Shabatu's for an hour with Fahne on the simple bed of leaves.

The Circle of the Kani was rising to heaven's zenith, nearing the time of Capra, and the impatient Nobilis had not received the answer of Shabatu.

This night in the family festal hall he sat close to the roaring fire, wrapped in the bright-furred cloak of Sabbia, and glared at the sleepy-eyed Prince of moyen-Brise.

The Bilance Prince and Uras, brother of Shabatu, applauded heartily as Dione and Shabatu ended their impudent *sirvente*, a satiric litle air that ridiculed the lowly state of women.

Uras' pale, eccentric eyes twinkled with delight, and the cherubic face of the Prince Solidago was wreathed in a tolerant smile.

But the Baron Melik, noting the scandalized look of the conservative Sabbian, applauded with less vigor and reproached the women. "I think a song of love might be more pleasing to our royal guests."

With an ironic glance at Nobilis, Shabatu struck her lyre with her wing-like fingers and began to sing one of the artificial airs of courtly love acceptable to Melik. So subtle was her derision in the rendering that it was not apparent to her father and the Sabbian, but Uras and Dione had to contain their laughter. The Marin met Volan's eyes with amusement.

The star-wheel of Melik, unlike those of his children, was quite untouched by the Twisan's winged spite; his stars had taken much from the leisured Bilance and its preoccupation with patterned courtesy.

Both women looked peculiarly untouchable tonight, reflected Uras.

Shabatu's increasing thinness gave her a wraith-like loveliness. She was arrayed in a voluminous gown of smoky-blue. Down the long, tight-fitting sleeves and bordering the hem in the scalloped motif symbolizing air gleamed hundreds of rose amethysts and aerolites, gems related to the celestial sphere that the ancients called the house of a descended god.

When Shabatu put down her cloud-shaped lyre, she took up a fragile feather fan, an emblem of unfolding air; it was made of the plumes of a molting bird, for the inhabitants of dernier-Brise frowned on slaying. It was only because of the presence of Solidago and Nobilis, for whom special dispensations had been made, that the air was fetid with the smell of roasting flesh.

Shabatu and Dione, well back from the hearth, employed their fragile fans to wave away the unpleasant odor.

Dione the Marin carried a silver folding fan for the phases of the Moon that was exalted in the Peisun, and her dress of silver cloth reflected the blue leaping flames and the purple shadows of the corner where she sat.

Uras meditated on the women's recent maneuvers and inwardly smiled. His sister was trying to keep them apart. But he could wait; with the patient fixity of the Waetergyt, he would win out.

Though air, he thought, was a medium more subtle than water—and he had always found the Marin amiable but ponderous—the Peisun was the closest kin to Brise, and Dione, with her questioned stars that shone on the Twisan's rim, enchanted him even more.

To Melik's great annoyance, Uras had encouraged the women in the composition of the pert *sirvente*—satire was a time-honored weapon of the male. But Uras exulted in the sharpness of the little Marin's mind, and he had observed with pleasure her gradual mastery of the cithara, the harp, and the lute, and also her progress in the arts of the ballade, rondeau, and virelay, the poetic forms of Brise he loved so well.

Yes, he would win out!

Of Nobilis, he was not so certain. He glanced at the red-haired Prince, sitting closest to the flames, muttering to Solidago.

When the women's songs were over and they had relinquished their instruments for their fans, the little orchestra of Melik began a sensuous air of Sabbia, featuring the krumhorn, trumpet, cymbals—for brass was the blazing of fire—and a savage little drum, for the passions of the desert people.

The Leun's tawny eyes were alight and he smiled at the distant Shabatu as the wily drummer beat with emphasis upon his drum. It was significant, Uras knew, for the drum was the symbol of the union of upper and lower worlds, the high peaks of the Brisen with the flat, gold desert of the Sabbians.

My father is strong for this union, Uras thought, to have

troubled himself in all these minute details; no doubt he had instructed the members of the orchestra in everything, with the slyness of the Bilance that so deeply colored him.

Uras the Waetergyt sighed; the omens, it seemed, were not in favor of Gemelle. And he knew his stubborn sister!

Under the cover of the music, while his feline look remained on Shabatu, Nobilis the Prince of Sabbia said, smiling, to Solidago, "I shall slay you if you press your suit. You may choose any sport at all; I can best you at any."

The Bilance studied the Leun with deceptively sleepy eyes that held the violet mendacity of Aphrodite. "I will be pleased," he said with a calm that almost maddened the fiery Sabbian.

Solidago did not deign to look at Nobilis again. He rose and with a general bow to the room, he said gently, "The hour is late. I must return to moyen-Brise. My thanks, my lords and my ladies, for your courtesies."

Melik rose in polite protest, seconded by Uras, but the Bilance saw with a sinking sensation that Shabatu barely acknowledged his departure. She gave a slight nod of her pale gold head, her eyes blank.

Dione and the minstrel rose also and made their good nights. At once Shabatu was at the little Marin's side, paying her cool respects to the company. Quickly the women and Volan were gone.

"Well, messire," said Melik with uneasy brightness, not looking Nobilis directly in the eye, "will you have a glass of sundew or tormentil . . . perhaps a beaker of poppy to send you well to sleep?"

"Only Shabatu can send me well to sleep," the Prince said bluntly.

Melik's Bilance-colored temper, Uras saw, was quite offended. But restraining his ire, Melik answered quietly, "The Lady Shabatu cannot be hurried."

"The women of Brise," thundered the Leun, "are allowed to run wild! My sister the Princess Dafira would not be allowed to dally so."

Uras felt his anger rise. Affairs of state or no, this barbarian could not be permitted to press his sister. "You exceed the bounds of courtesy," he said coldly to Nobilis.

Placatingly, Melik said, "The Crown Prince Nobilis is unacquainted with our ways."

"Then let him become acquainted!" Uras retorted. "I

have not approved this arrangement from the first, as you well know."

The proud Leun was almost speechless with his anger. Then he managed to say, "Your ways apparently do not secure the peace and order of your house."

All the dominant nature of the king of beasts was in his hot reply. Uras reflected that for all their fated magnetism, the stubborn Leun and the fixed Waetergyt were not the calmest mating.

"I think," said Melik diplomatically, "that we are all a little weary and overwrought, that this had best be discussed tomorrow."

"There is nothing to discuss," said Nobilis with arrogance. "I have challenged that other popinjay who hangs about to fight me any way he chooses."

Melik's astonishment was plain on his narrow face. "You have *challenged* . . . Solidago?"

Nobilis nodded.

Uras said solemnly, "You are aware that slaying is anathema to dernier-Brise."

The Leun snorted. "I am indeed aware. But I, my lord, am a Sabbian, and my honor is offended."

He turned on his heel and left them in a swirl of gold and scarlet draperies.

Uras and Melik stared at each other for a moment. Then the latter said, in a weary voice, "Sit down, my son. Let us speak of this. You must help me unlock the mystery of Shabatu."

When the two women and the minstrel reached the door of Shabatu, Dione said an affectionate good night.

"Please," said the Waetergyt, "tarry a while." Her soft blue eyes, the color of the winter sky, were beseeching.

Dione smiled. "Very well."

"Come with us, Volan," Shabatu said warmly, for the young minstrel had become a welcome friend in the lonely weeks past. He entered the fragile chamber with the women and took his favorite seat upon a white silk hassock formed like a flake of snow.

Volan, who had become privy to the secrets of Shabatu as he had to Dione's, barely listened as the women, murmuring, sought out a crystal alcove to sit down. Softly, he touched the strings of his bird-shaped cithara, enjoying their indifferent presence and the softness of his surroundings with the complacency of a cat.

Shabatu watched the lilac forms of night birds swimming by the crystal wall, and she said to the Marin, "I know not what to do: Nobilis importunes me day and night, and my father's patience grows thin."

"Will Uras be of aid?"

"I do not know," Shabatu said sadly. "He twits Gemelle for not carrying me off."

"As well he should." Dione was stern, remembering the urgency of Fahne and their quick escape.

But the shadow of her loss must have shown upon her pallid face, for Shabatu took her hand and said quietly, "You still think of him, always."

Dione nodded.

"And I of Gemelle. By day I envision him, and by night I dream of his whirling grace. To see him move is to see a circle of the falling snow, but he is a flake of gold, with his yellow hair and garments! And he smells of the tart fruit of the cherry and of the freshness of the lemon flower of Sabbia!"

"He has your heart, indeed," Dione the Marin said, and she squeezed the Waetergyt's slender hand. "I think that you must wait . . . and believe," she added, smiling at Volan with a melancholy little smile.

"As you should believe, my lady," he returned.

"Yes, as I should believe." Dione was solemn, a new glimmer of hope arising in her.

After a time, she murmured, "It is very late, my friend. I feel that we should leave you; you look weary."

Shabatu sighed. "I am. I am weary of Nobilis and Solidago and my father—weary of waiting!"

"It will come right," Dione consoled her, kissing her thin cheek.

When the gentle Marin and the minstrel had withdrawn, Shabatu began to undress herself. Somehow at this moment she could not face the clinging attendance of her woman, choosing instead to unfasten with difficulty the billowing, gem-encrusted gown and toss it upon a chair.

Removing the gems from her neck and arms and ears, the Lady Shabatu took up an oval brush encrusted with amethysts and began to brush her long, glowing mane of silvery-gold hair.

The soothing rhythm of the rasping stroke was almost

sending her to sleep. How tired she was, how tired! The strain of these weeks in the overpowering company of Nobilis was telling. She could not endure it much longer.

Her frail arms ached with the protracted brushing, and suddenly her body began to shake with a nameless apprehension. She would never see Gemelle again; her father would win out. And she would be forever exiled to the heat and noise of Sabbia, enslaved by Nobilis.

There was a way—a way to face none of it any longer. Calmly, she rose from the table and wrapped herself in a nightrobe of dull gray. In the festal hall had been a scarlet beaker of poppy wine, placed there for the soothing of the Sabbian Nobilis, never touched by the Brisen. For where it calmed the thick, hot blood of the Leun, it froze the cool, slow blood of a Brisen into eternal sleep. And Shabatu knew only that it would still her perpetual ache of longing and her fears.

She crept into the dimly lit corridor: the castle was very still; the lilac taper's flame flickered in a sudden draft. How desolate it was . . . how final her mission! There could have been such glory with Gemelle.

But resolutely she continued down the corridor toward the winding, glassy stairs that seemed to float downward to the glittering entrance hall.

She heard her whispered name and whirled. There, a little distance away, near the stone stairs descending from the parapets, was a familiar figure. He had such grace that even in stillness he seemed about to dance. It was the yellow-clad figure of the Twisan Gemelle.

Their first embrace was a timeless silence. Then he whispered, "I have come to take you away."

She looked up into his blue eyes, which no longer danced, but were as dark as a stormy sky with his long loneliness and gnawing passion. The skin below his eyes, like hers, was shaded with strangeness to sleep.

"I will go with you now," she said.

He heard her at first as one who is dazed. "I cannot believe it, I cannot believe it." Then he came to himself and said softly, "We must go soon, but we cannot go out the way I came in." He grinned. "I ascended hanging to a rope like the Hanged Man of the Tarot, appropriate to my longing and expectation. Hurry, let us go to your chamber and gather your belongings."

"I need only a cloak," she said, smiling.

And when she had snatched up a heavy cloak and dressed herself in a simple woolen gown, they stole almost soundlessly down the shining stairs and out of the castle of Melik.

CHAPTER 6

"Attend to it, will you, Desmos?" the Queen said sleepily when the servant announced Dabih. Her lazy flesh still throbbed with the memory of Fahne; what cared she for the dreary business of the estate this morning! For if there had been one night, there would be another. She would devise it somehow.

Glancing at her with surprise, for she was not quick to relinquish any posture of command, Desmos the Peisun said to the waiting footman, "I will see him in the council room."

And giving the Queen a light kiss on the top of her gleaming head, Desmos pushed back his fine-grained carved chair and followed the footman into the echoing corridor.

It was bright for the December time of Kani, he reflected; the strong sun cast its light from the square, high windows of the vaulted ceiling, and shone on the polished granite of the floor. But, then, it was still autumn in Erde, whereas full winter had come to Mar. The warmth was coursing through his body from the blessed night with Shira. After the endless feast, it had been such a heaven to drown in her that he had slept long and deeply, so deeply that his Marin temper lingered yet in dreams.

Desmos hoped that the business would not take long; Shira had remarked languidly that she felt tired, and she would likely return to her chamber for a time. The Peisun's pulse quickened. He would join her there.

The sigil of the Capran, in the council room, was everywhere, from the tapestries of ebony and flame-green to the ponderous, square tables, formed in the shape of the earth-symbol, and the heavy, darkly cushioned chairs. The somber mail of the ancestors of Shira gleamed at intervals along the gray stone walls.

Dabih, the chief steward of the estate, was standing nervously by the great central table. At the sight of Desmos, he brushed at his neat brown clothes.

The Peisun greeted the steward courteously and said, "Sit down."

"Oh, sire, I could not do that." The man's oblique eyes stared at Desmos in surprise.

"Nonsense, Dabih," the Peisun replied, pulling out a ponderous chair for the steward. "We do not abide by such customs in Mar."

Dabih gave him a questioning look that seemed to say "We are not in Mar." Nevertheless, he sat down opposite the Peisun at the table.

"What business have you with me?" Desmos asked easily.

"Sire . . . I think it is the matter of a serfs' rebellion." The steward's answer was reluctant.

Desmos raised his black, graceful brows, but his face was calm, with the detached sympathy of the latter-Marin. "Why do you say this, Dabih?"

"I saw a group of the field men, sire, long after curfew, meeting in the southmost acre. And there was a man addressing them."

"Who was he?"

"I know not, sire, for the moon had fled behind a cloud, obscuring his face. But, although his raiment was plain and dark, he had the demeanor of a lord."

"A lord, Dabih? Of what race?"

"Undoubtedly he was a Capran, messire. His movements and his body told me that."

Desmos looked thoughtful. "And what did he say to the men?"

"I could not hear it all, for fear of revealing my presence. But he was . . ."—the steward paused painfully, then went on—". . . inciting the men to . . . rise."

"This is very interesting, Dabih," the Peisun said softly, and the steward wondered at his calm. A Capran, even the old King, would have raged and sworn dark vengeance. How strange were the Marin, Dabih thought. But he waited respectfully for Desmos to resume. "Perhaps we shall watch together on another night. Did you hear of another trysting time?"

Dabih nodded eagerly. "Yes, my lord. They plan to meet again the night that follows tomorrow."

"Good, my friend. Then we shall watch together and see what we can see."

Dabih was nonplussed. "But, messire . . . if I may be so bold . . ."

"Yes?"

"Do you not plan to carry out reprisals?"

"Reprisals, Dabih? For what—for meeting peaceably in the fields beyond curfew?"

The Marin, Dabih thought, must all be mad. "Of course, messire. We can nip the trouble in the bud before it blooms to unmanageable proportions."

Desmos smiled. "And what reprisals would you suggest, Dabih, if you were in charge?"

The steward said indignantly, "Why, beating, sire, or an hour or so at the wheel. That would straighten them out."

The Peisun shook his handsome head and replied coldly, "There will be no such punishment while I am in this castle."

The steward stared at him, bewildered and shaken. "But, messire . . ."

Desmos rose and said dismissively, "That will be all, Dabih. Thank you for your confidence. A little while before the time of the next assembly in the fields, you will come to me and we will plan our observation. Good morning."

The steward stammered a reply, then bowed, backing out from the chamber. The old King, he reflected, would be turning in his tomb had he known that such a one was now in command of lower Erde.

Bock the Capran and Veris the Bole, standing behind Fahne, who was surrounded by a ring of gaping Erden, heard him say in his deep, gentle voice, "Tell me, madam, how your afflictions take you."

Veris smiled at Bock. "His healing," he said softly, "makes our elixirs seem as foolish as the 'tabarmaq of Khorassan.'"

The Capran nodded, grinning at the Bole's reference to

the ancient charlatan of the Oriens who had hoodwinked a King with his mythical concoction.

"In truth," Bock said, "it is a good thing to have him with us again." They had turned from music to healing: the pewter and the silver in their pouch had been increasing as the people flocked to Fahne. "I cannot comprehend that he still does not know us."

Veris looked somber. "Bock, come," he said, "come aside with me a little way. I wish to speak with you apart from this."

They walked together a little distance from the ring of seekers.

"What is it?" the Capran asked.

"How long are we to let this go on?" Veris asked earnestly. "You have allowed me to tell him nothing to help him remember. How long are we to let him continue like a man half-alive, with no memory of Dione the little Marin, or his father, or his former days?"

Bock sighed. "I have told you repeatedly, and I still believe as the Pfarren do, that to press him to recall may be to lead him to madness. These things cannot be hurried. It is a strange posture," he added, smiling, "for a man of Aphrodite to recommend a course so precipitate. Usually we are at odds in such affairs."

The Bole good-naturedly accepted Bock's reference to his race's leisured deliberation. What the Capran said was true: it was the custom of the sons of Chronos to take comparatively decisive action, twitting the slower Boles for their hesitation. Nevertheless, he repeated, "I think he should be told."

"I think that he should not," Bock retorted stubbornly. "If she were loyal still, why, then, did she not speedily reply to our missive?"

"Perhaps it never reached her," Veris said with the obdurate persistence of his race.

"Let us rejoin him now," Bock answered. "You know he likes not to handle coin," he added dryly.

Veris nodded and they moved back toward the opened end of the wagon, which served as a platform for the sorcerer in his consultations, in time to hear him saying gently, "Thuja will relieve your eyes, and slippery elm must be taken for your limbs' continual aching."

Bock, busy with the preparation of the elixirs, did not at once look up when the Bole exclaimed.

"Bock!" Veris repeated. "Look you there!"

The Capran's oblique eyes turned a moment from his task and beheld a lathered steed being reined in by its Capran rider.

"Good gentles!" he called in his brassy Erden to Veris and to Bock.

The Bole went forward and greeted the man as he dismounted. "Can I aid you, sir?"

The lean, quick Capran retrieved his swift breath and answered, "Yes. Have you a remedy for beasts, as well as men?"

Bock the Capran handed the elixirs to Fahne and came forward curiously to the Bole and the horseman. He nodded. "We have, sir," he said. "What ails your beast?"

The man told him. "Let the sorcerer Fahne put his hands upon your mount," said Veris the Bole.

"Fahne?" the rider repeated. "I have heard his name."

"I doubt not that you have," Bock retorted. "He is known in Mar and Brise and Sabbia, as well as Erde." Then he turned and called out to Fahne.

Excusing himself to the company around him, Fahne the sorcerer leaped lightly down from his wooden platform and came to the beast.

He put a soothing hand on the horse's muzzle and at once the trembling creature seemed to calm. "Your steed must be rubbed down well with cloths," he said gently to the rider, "first of all. We have them in our wagon." Already Veris the Bole was departing for the cloths. "Now, let me have a look here."

The horse's rolling eyes had ceased their frightened rolling, and the beast was rubbing its head against the shoulder of the sorcerer like a large, friendly dog.

"Good boy, good boy," said Fahne caressingly in the tongue of lower Erde. "I know what balms you need."

And he led the tractable beast to the wagon.

"He is a sorcerer, indeed," said the Capran rider.

"You are a courier," Veris remarked. "Is your journey long?"

"Only to Erdemar, I thank Chronos. The roads from Mar to Brise in these days are very perilous."

Bock raised his black brows. "The Escors?" he asked.

The rider looked gloomy. "The Escors; they have slain even the fleet Alar."

Bock the Capran cried out, and Veris asked quickly, "When? When was Alar slain?"

"On his last journey to Brise; he carried a heavy pouch of gold and gems, and I doubt not numerous missives."

Veris and Bock exchanged a look.

"May I seek the boon of some water, friends?" the rider asked. "It is dry work galloping the dusty ways to Erdemar."

The Bole gestured him to the wagon. "There is a water pouch there, by the elixirs."

As the rider walked away, the Bole said to the Capran, "Then our letter was lost, and she does not know of Fahne."

"You think we should send another missive, then."

"There is no question! Whatever the mist that shrouds the mind of Fahne, we owe Dione the intelligence," said Veris. "We can send a missive by this man to Erdemar, and a courier there can proceed from Mar to Brise."

"You are right, Veris. And this time, I pray to Chronos that she receives it."

They went to meet the courier.

Fahne, who was applying a soothing balm to the legs of the weary horse, heard himself murmur, "There, now, good fellow, Merddyn, good fellow, Merddyn." And he suddenly realized with a deep excitement that another small point of light had pierced his recollection's darkness.

When the twilight descended and the wagon tongue was shut again for the night, the people having returned to their houses, Fahne the sorcerer sought a time of quiet.

The other Erden noted that he still lived on an island of self-created silence, despite his sharp awareness and compassion, and they had become accustomed to his stealing away at dusk-hour.

Fahne had found a favorite hiding place that was still unknown, he imagined, to the others—a still spot inside a ring of trees beside a murmuring stream populous with the squat, ugly brown fish of endlich-Erde.

Fahne, less dedicated than the other Erden to the eating of flesh, often spoke to the ugly little peisun, congratulating them on their good fortune. For the lower Erden never ate fish; their flesh was considered too alien to the Capran body's temper, and the slant-eyed people preferred to feast on mammals.

This quiet evening the sorcerer watched the peisun sinking to the depths of the water as night approached and bade them farewell until the morning.

"How warm it is for *Teveth*," he said aloud. Again, he felt the stabbing brightness, as of light against closed eyelids. He had remembered another word! His head ached a little as he examined the phenomenon: *Teveth*, the ancients' term for this month, the Circle of Capra.

Fahne pondered, too, his affection for the peisun and the calming effect of the murmuring stream. This he was able to understand, for with the aid of the gentle Pfarrer Gonu of the household of Shira, he had been able to discern his lost star-wheel, with its prominent Escorpiun aspects. Therefore, he knew that water was compatible with his temper.

And patiently Gonu, a highly lettered man, had led Fahne to rediscover much of the star-knowledge of his youth: the sorcerer was awake again to the implications of his star-race, the Maeden, and the Maeden's symbolic love for the little peisun, badge of the latter-Marin, who were his fated opposites on heaven's wheel.

There had been many nights when Fahne was prey to variegated, haunting dreams, always of symbols and a faceless woman with a sweet, low voice whose touch was gentler than a feather stroke, the light touch of the Peisun.

And when Fahne brought his dreams to the priest Gonu, the old man had heard him with a calm, impassive face, offering none of his own interpretation, always merely guiding. Had he remained in the castle, thought Fahne, perhaps Gonu could have brought him back to full remembrance. But after the mad, drugged night with the faithless Shira, it had been impossible to remain.

The sorcerer sighed and leaned to the stream, dipping his long fingers into the lucid water. He would have liked to bid farewell to Desmos, whose kindness was the first he had met on his mind's birth in the Capran chamber. But to look into the Peisun's trusting eyes, after his own unbridled passions had led him into such treachery . . . no, no, it was impossible.

Late darkness was gathering when the sorcerer rose and made his way again to the wagon. *In any case,* he reflected grimly, *I have regained my knowledge that will earn my bread. The rest will have to wait, if ever, indeed, it comes at all.*

Meanwhile, he meditated, *I once had a horse, and the horse's name was Merddyn for the greatest sorcerer of Erde. Not much, but it was something! A knowledge a little closer and more personal than the names of herbs and seasons, and the recipes for elixirs!*

And the strange thought comforted Fahne the sorcerer, lifting some the shadow on his heart.

It had long been the custom of the royal father of Shira to welcome Capran couriers to rest their steeds in the castle's stables.

And secure in his welcome, the courier whose steed Fahne had soothed sighted the ponderous castle with relief. His mount, though improved, must pause and rest throughout the night if it were to come unscathed to Erdemar.

The courier knew well the way to the stables, and his horse, scenting journey's end, gave a joyous nicker as it took the path.

"Good evening, courier." A genial-looking Bole was emerging from the stable as the Capran rode in. The Bole, like the Capra, were the star-races of hooved creatures, and they were as skilled as the hostlers and herdsmen of Erde.

The hostler began to rub down the tired animal as the courier dismounted, speaking softly to the steed with the way of a man who knew the creatures with affection.

"Come, then," the Bole said calmly to the steed, and he led the animal into the stable for unsaddling. The courier followed.

He unsaddled the beast and hung the saddle on an iron hook, then led the steed into one of the stalls.

"Its legs have been a problem," said the Bole, and it was not a question, but a statement.

"Yah." The courier nodded. "Had it not been for the sorcerer Fahne, who balmed my horse well . . ."

"Fahne!" the Bole broke in. "Sir Desmos, the consort of the Queen, is about to seek him. He disappeared from the castle not two weeks gone."

The courier, in the cool manner of a Capran, did not reply, but his oblique black eyes were bright with interest.

"Where did you encounter this Fahne?" inquired the Bole.

The courier gave him the location of the wagon.

"Let us go to Dabih's house," said the Bole. "He will quarter you for the night, and I will give him this intelligence for Sir Desmos, the consort of the Queen."

The Capran nodded. After a glance at his contented steed, he followed the Bole to the steward's house.

CHAPTER 7

The morning in Brise, land of snow and light, came early, but Mentha the admiring Bilance, who attended the Lady Shabatu, never woke up the Waetergyt until the day was advancing.

Therefore, it was ten-light, the hour of the Peisun, when Mentha came quietly into the chamber and drew back the curtains to admit the light.

Clucking with annoyance at the disarray, the Bilance hardly glanced at the great bed, with its diaphanous curtains still drawn. She began to gather up the shining garments scattered on the delicate hassocks and chairs, then took an armful of them to a crystalline press for hanging.

Then in the leisured, soft-fingered way of the Bilance, the servant tidied her noble lady's table and straightened the looking glass that was in the shape of a wing.

At last she took up the lilac tray with its steaming teas of sage and violet and approached the curtained bed. The sage had been carefully chosen for its appetite-arousing character, for Mentha had been anxious at her lady's thinness, and the violet for its calming effect.

Astonished, Mentha saw then that the great bed, with its shining coverlet of silver-blue and its hangings as fragile as smoke, was empty. She set down the tray on a small table formed like a snowflake and went to the dressing closet.

Shabatu was not there, and the little table, with its long

looking glass, was as smooth and empty as ice. Uneasy now, Mentha began to look among the multitudinous gowns behind the shining curtain: all were there.

She returned to the great crystalline press in the main chamber and counted off the gowns. A heavy woolen gown, one that Shabatu was about to discard and give to Mentha, was missing, and so was a heavy cloak of sober color and plain design.

How very strange, reflected Mentha. She does not often rise so early . . . and to array herself so plainly when the Prince of Sabbia was in residence!

Increasingly disturbed, the Bilance sought out a footman in the corridor. "Have you seen my lady this morning?" she cried.

"My lady?" The young underTwisan's surprise was plain. "No, madam, never at this hour."

"Hold your impudent tongue," she snapped at the boy, and she bustled down the hall to the chambers of Uras, the brother of Shabatu.

The valet of Uras opened to her knock. "Good morrow." He greeted her in a puzzled fashion. It was not the custom of Shabatu's woman to approach the chamber of Uras.

"Come into the corridor," she whispered urgently.

The valet, like herself a violet-eyed Bilance under the rule of the leisured Aphrodite, merely blinked.

"Come!" she said in a louder, more agitated whisper.

At last he closed the door and joined her in the drafty corridor.

"Have you seen my lady this morning?" she asked quickly.

Again the man blinked his heavy-lidded eyes. "She never rises at this hour, to my knowledge," he said slowly.

Mentha cried, "I know that, you calf-eyed varlet! But she is not in her chamber, or her dressing closet."

"Perhaps she has gone for a walk," he suggested calmly. "You should inquire of the lower servers before you rouse her brother."

"I have no intention of rousing her brother!" Mentha said irascibly. Her ascending star, the flaming Ramm of Sabbia, made her sometimes quick of temper.

And she flounced away and down the glassy stairs that seemed to float to the floor below.

Amused, the valet watched her from the floor above, but

when she apparently received a negative from the servers there, his smile faded. And he saw her approach the shining stairs and slowly ascend them again.

"This is a dainty dish," she said sourly, "to set before the Baron."

Thus thou wilt possess, Uras read with pleasure, *the glory of the brightness of the whole world, and all obscurity will fly far from thee.*

This thing is the strong fortitude of all strength. . . .

A soft, annoying sound nibbled at his concentration. Curse it! He looked up frowning from his delighted perusal of the *Tabula Smaragdina,* ancient Emerald Table of the alchemists. His valet, Ervum, was hovering above him.

"Pray, do not hover, Ervum," the Waetergyt said irritably.

The Bilance, in the hypersensitive way of moyen-Brise, looked deeply injured but replied, "My lord, I have a sinister intelligence to present you."

Uras laughed. "A 'sinister intelligence'? Chronos, Ervum, who has schooled you in such language? Surely not I!"

Ervum restrained his expression of disapproval and said, "My lord, it is of great import."

The Waetergyt countered, "It will no longer have any import if you don't soon tell me."

The Bilance said in an aggrieved tone, "The Lady Shabatu, my lord, is missing from the castle."

Uras slammed down his volume with a curse. "Missing? Nonsense! Who told you so?"

"My lady's woman, Mentha, has inquired of all the servers; else, my lord, I should not have so advised you," Ervum said severely.

"I am properly subdued," said Uras. "I humble myself before your thoroughness."

"Oh, my lord," said Ervum, shocked.

"Very well." The Waetergyt made a sound of exasperation, and placing the book on the table by his bed, he threw back the coverlet and rose. "I shall look into this myself, Ervum. Get me something to wear, would you?"

The Bilance, his sense of elegance and fitness upset, withdrew to the press. There he chose a suit proper to the hour and the season and arrayed the Lord Uras in it.

" 'Something to wear,' forsooth," the valet repeated silently. His Aphrodisian sensibilities that were soothed by ordered beauty were rasped by the Waetergyt's indifference to raiment.

"There, my lord," he said with satisfaction, regarding his intractable charge.

"Thank you, Ervum." Without a glance in the glass, Uras strode out of the chamber.

"Gone! Dear Ouranos!" The Baron Melik set down his goblet of sage so hard that the delicate glass rang. "Impossible!" He glared up at his lean blue-clad son.

"I fear not, sire. She is nowhere in the castle, nor has she been seen on the grounds. And assuredly she is not out shooting with Nobilis," he added with distaste.

Melik colored. This was not the first reference his son had made to Melik's inordinate permissiveness. Slaying of the birds was anathema to Brise, yet the Baron had winked again and again at the Sabbian's sport.

"That is probably one of the reasons she is gone," Uras said brutally.

"How can you speak so foolishly?" Melik spluttered. "She has run away because I have given her too much liberty. Thanks be to Chronos that Nobilis *is* out shooting; the Sabbians are very early risers. Else I should have this to justify to him. I will die with shame." He paused, then with a brighter look, said, "I will tell the Prince Nobilis that she is indisposed."

"I will tell Nobilis she is indisposed to *marry*," said Uras harshly.

"I will have no more of that!" cried Melik. "Have you sent out searching parties? Your sister may be lying ravished, or wounded, or dead in the snow!"

"And meanwhile your concern is a tale for Nobilis!" Uras shouted, trembling with anger. "There will be no searching parties, for I think I know where she has gone, and that she is quite well and in no peril."

"Explain yourself!" bellowed the Baron.

"She has found a way to be happy," said Uras. "So tell your tales to the Sabbian, with my blessing." He turned on his heel and started to go away.

With a rasping sound, the Baron Melik pushed back his carved chair and rose, overtaking his son. He grasped Uras by the arm and shouted, "You will tell me what you mean! Where is my daughter?"

"My *sister*," Uras retorted meaningly, "is happy now. She was not abducted; there was no sign in her chamber of struggle or harm. She has left of her own will, and I admire her for her action."

"How dare you!" screamed Melik. "Has she eloped with some low-born varlet, like a whore?"

"Don't be a fool, Father, more than you can help. And give my best regards to Nobilis."

Shaking with ire, the old man sank down into his high-backed chair and took up his goblet of sage. The tea was cold, very cold.

As Uras left the dining chamber and retraced his long steps through the glittering entrance hall, a young under-Twisan clad in yellow approached him shyly. The footman held a tawny missive in his slender hand.

"It is a message, sire, from Erde, for the Lady Dione of Mar."

Uras' silvery brows rose in surprise. "From Erde," he repeated thoughtfully. "Give it to me," he said. "I will place it in her hands."

"Oh, sire," the footman said painfully, "the messenger . . . the messenger . . ."

"Said that it should be delivered only to her?" Uras smiled. "And it will, I assure you, by me."

Submissive, the underTwisan handed the missive to Uras.

With a bland face but a quickly beating heart, Uras the Waetergyt took the gleaming stairs to the level of bedchambers. On the landing he glanced back; the footman had disappeared. No use, he reflected, risking the gossip of the servers; it would surely reach the ears of Dione.

He resumed his upward climb and on the second floor sought out an alcove with a crystalline form of Ouranos, a table, and a silver chair. He sat down by the table and broke the missive's seal.

Uras' long, lean face grew somber as he read the letter of Veris the Bole. So the man lived, after all. He folded up the letter and thrust it into his tunic—none too soon, he saw, for the Lady Dione and the minstrel Volan were approaching from the wing of women.

The little Marin's eyes were brighter than he had seen them in many days; they gleamed greenly in her heart-shaped face, and the face itself was not so pale as he was used to beholding it, but was flushed with a faint rose color, like the inside of a seashell or the neck feathers of a young dove.

"Good morrow," he said, smiling, and bent to kiss her hand.

She received his salute absently and asked with excitement, "Is it true, as the servers say, that a courier has come from Erde?"

Uras' heart sank; Volan must be her spy. The boy knew everything the servers did, and Chronos knew that nothing could be kept from the servers! "You have an amazing system of report," he said, smiling, to the minstrel.

Volan colored. "The . . . servers of your lovely house are very friendly," he replied.

"Never mind." The Waetergyt's answer was good-natured. Then to Dione he said, "I fear not, my lady. The courier came from Mar with a message for my father." He emphasized the last delicately.

Dione blushed a rosy-red. "I fear you think me very intrusive," she said.

"Not at all. The presence of a courier from another nation is always something of an event in any house. And, my lady, how could you intrude on any matter affecting us?"

The Marin looked uneasy at his intimate tone, and she nodded good morning, proceeding with the minstrel to the stairs.

"Where is Shabatu this morning?" She turned and questioned Uras.

"The Lady Shabatu has gone from the castle."

"Gone!" Dione's amazement raised her voice to an uncharacteristic shrillness. "Then he did . . ." She stopped abruptly, covering her small pink mouth with her oval hand. Volan was frowning darkly.

"Yes, I think he did," Uras answered easily. Laughing, he moved away toward his chambers, leaving the Marin and Volan staring after him with widened eyes.

Morning in Brise, the land of snow and crystal light, came early, and the day fled as soon. At four-light, the hour of the Maeden, the lilac shadows deepened on the milk-white drifts around the castle of Melik. The crystalline towers assumed the wonderful hues of the departing sun—a rosy-mauve succeeded a golden-rose and would quickly turn to lavender and purple-gray with the coming on of darkness.

Uras, returning to the castle from the stables, where he had been arranging to send the men for word of Shabatu, looked up at the fairy-like towers. A lifetime in Brise had not dulled the edge of his excitement on beholding its loveliness. There was something in the shifting, gentle hues that recalled the temper of the little Marin, whose own race was dyed with the changing colors of the ocean waves in varied lights; the shining scales of the peisun, indeed, shared the magic of the Brisen towers.

And now he saw, high on the topmost parapets, a familiar dark-haired figure in a cloak of silvery stuff. It was Dione the Marin.

The Maeden-hour four, which was blue in Mar, had always held enchantment for the little Marin, even before the coming of Fahne. Now, more than ever, it had become her hour for a still withdrawal from the house of Melik, a time when she would steal away, glad even for the absence of Volan and Shabatu.

This Maeden-hour the winds of Kani whistled about the lonely towers, but, undaunted, the Marin was keeping her customary vigil on the parapet. She had found a sheltered place to stand that still caught a welcome ray or two of sinking sun. She held out her crystal star to watch its glitter and exclaimed.

Even in the brilliance of the Brisen light, she could see within the star a tiny, moving shadow. Testing her own senses, she moved the star again in the ray of sun and found the shadow remained. Again it moved, mysteriously. Surely this was a sign from Fahne! She knew he lived. And whatever the reasons for his silent absence, she must persevere.

Dione heard again the words of the hooded figure in her dream: "Your flesh is dyed with me, your blood." And suddenly she suspected the explanation of Uras. What if the message had been word of Fahne?

She sickened for Shabatu: how good had been their

times together, how sweet to talk to her of Fahne. She hoped indeed that Shabatu's escape had been with Gemelle, fervently wishing joy to the Waetergyt.

But with her departure, Dione thought, her own position in the castle was ambiguous; there was no longer any reason to remain, more than ever reason to depart, in the face of Uras' attentions.

She heard approaching footsteps on the frosty stone, and she turned to meet Uras. So bemused had she been that she had not seen his light approach across the drifts below her.

"Good Maeden." She greeted him with nervous civility.

He controlled his annoyance at her greeting; even the hour, he thought, conspired against him to remind her of the sorcerer. Disdaining to return the salutation so, he replied "Good evening" in Brisen. But he smiled warmly as he came near her.

"You have the secluded ways of my sister," he said gently. "But do you not find the air of Kani chill?"

She shook her head, confused by his fencing manner. "Has there been word of Shabatu?" she asked evasively.

"You can be at ease," he said. "I am aware that my sister loves the Twisan, and I doubt not that it was he who took her off."

Again she avoided a direct answer, saying only, "Your father the Baron Melik would frown on such a match."

Uras laughed. " 'Frown,' indeed! He will do all in his power to bring her back for Nobilis the Sabbian. My men are seeking her out, however, and I shall do all within *my* power to ensure her safety with Gemelle."

Dione looked at him with renewed warmth. "Do you mean it? If so, I am very glad." After a moment, she said, "My visit must end, however. It was only for the sake of Shabatu that Volan and I have lingered. I must," she added a little wistfully, "find a new haven."

"Must you, Dione?" Uras asked. Coming nearer, he put a slender hand on her narrow shoulder. "Your presence has been as great a joy to me as it was to my sister. I have so delighted in the riches of your mind, in your burgeoning arts. And I had hoped to pursue with you the newfound pleasure in the art of alchemy."

"Uras," she replied with gentleness, "my pleasure in your company is great, and my gratitude to you is profound. But my feelings for you are only those of Shabatu."

"I beg of you, Dione, to give me time. I have been delving into a certain alchemical magic that is very wondrous and strange, a magic that I believe will strengthen the Twisan temper in your wheel of stars and make us admirably suited for each other."

In spite of her reluctance to listen, Dione's interest was caught.

Encouraged by her expression, Uras went on. "I have been conducting experiments with certain potions that contain a high concentration of the herbs of Hermes, ruler of the Twisan. I have taken them myself and have found my own Twisan temper ever emerging. Have you not noted that my eyes have changed and my motions have become more cousined to the dancing motions of the Twisan?"

"I have," she admitted.

"So you see," he went on with great eagerness, "if you partook of them, your own Twisan stars would shine ever brighter, and soon you would be suited to me for the Ceremony of Belonging."

"Uras, my heart has been given."

"Your *heart*, my dear!" Uras cried. "I seek a union with your mind."

"But that is unnatural."

"You will see that the love of the mind is all that endures, Dione. You will see how trivial is the passing fever of the body. As to that"—he made a careless gesture—"there are skilled Bilances to quiet your sense."

She made a sound of shocked protest. Then she said quietly, "I am pledged forever to the memory of Fahne."

"A memory that will send you away homeless, or to Mar, where your uncle will mate you to some ponderous Crabba or Escor who will never comprehend your sensibilities!"

"Whatever fortune sends I will bear," she said darkly. "But I will never belong to anyone but Fahne. And whoever keeps me from him condemns me forever to wandering and to aloneness."

She had said the last words with only a slender hope that Uras would reveal to her the truth of the message, but she saw now that the shot had gone home; his pallid face colored and he could not meet her eyes.

He turned from her a moment and looked out over the twilight-darkened snow. Then he turned to her again and said, resigned, "You must know the truth. The message was from Erde. And the sorcerer lives. He has no memory."

Her soft face was transformed and glowed with an almost unearthly light as she cried out her joy and exultation.

"Oh, Uras, Uras, I give you my thanks," Dione said. Taking up his slender hands, she kissed them.

Sadly he watched her swift, graceful departure from the frosty place where dark was falling.

CHAPTER 8

The Queen Shira watched Desmos' train depart down the winding road from the castle and reach the crossing road that led on to Erdemar. The Peisun reined in and turned back with a hungry look at the lovely Capran, perched upon her night-black mare in her boyish hunting clothes. She knew he was asking her once more with his gesture to accompany him to Mar.

But the impassive Queen made no response except a careless wave before she spurred her eager steed into the wood. Desmos, with a somber face, gestured to his men and rode away.

Galloping into the thick wood behind the hunting train, Shira almost shouted aloud for joy, inhaling the crisp winter air of December Capran Circle, a time that always filled her with elation, but especially today.

It had seemed weeks since the night the servant had brought the news, although she knew quite well it had been only days. An eternity before her freedom had been won!

That night she had been in her dressing closet, where her maid was arraying her for the night, anointing her perfect breasts and her white skin with the scent of violet for Desmos' pleasure. The maid had just slipped over her naked body the filmy gown of vivid green that displayed so clearly all the sweet shadows and darknesses, and she was brushing out her glittering hair.

Shira heard the opening of the outer door and the low voices of Desmos and a servant. She caught the name of Fahne and noted that her husband's voice had risen with surprise, that he was exclaiming with delight. Then she had listened to Desmos' steps approach the dressing closet.

"Leave me," she said curtly to her woman, and the maid withdrew through the other door as Desmos entered.

His face was alight. "My love," he said, "there is splendid news!" And he knelt before her, kissing her breasts. He heard her accelerated heartbeat and caressed her, saying softly, "Is all this excitement for me?"

"Of course," she lied, touching him with a careless stroke that started him trembling. "What is the news?" she asked with painful casualness.

He kissed her knees through the thin cloth. "They have discovered the whereabouts of Fahne." His hands sought her breasts again. Her heart gave such a sickening lurch that she feared it would leap from her body.

Misinterpreting her strong response, he said thickly, "We will speak of it tomorrow," and he began to kiss her wildly, bestowing upon her a pleasing caress that kept her rooted to her stool. She had been afraid to speak further then of the sorcerer, lest she arouse the Peisun's suspicion, and gave herself up to him as he lifted her in his arms, continuing all the while his urgent, rhythmic caress until he laid her on the bed, resuming it again.

She closed her eyes and allowed him to do as he would, pretending that his touch was the touch of Fahne. But long after he had fallen asleep, she lay wide-eyed in the dark in a fever of impatience for the coming of morning, when she might question him about the sorcerer.

Customarily, Desmos, in the dream-wound manner of the Peisun, was very slow to awaken, but Shira had found that he awoke very quickly indeed at the proper touch. Therefore, she applied her most skilled arts to rouse him; it was barely dawn, yet at once his green eyes opened and he cried out with delight at her touch. With great swiftness she drew him to his final gasping cry and felt him shudder under her hands before he lay back again with a blissful smile and observed her below his half-shut lids.

"My love, my dear love," he murmured and made as if

to rise to caress her in turn. But she stopped him with a
sleepy hand on his limp flesh, and he stayed quite still,
content at the gentler stroke that seemed to prolong the
earlier ecstasy.

Then she said in a deceptively careless tone, "And so
they have found your friend." Her belly was heating at the
thought of Fahne.

"Yes," he said happily. And he told her in great detail
what the messenger had said, and of the whereabouts of
the sorcerer's wagon.

In the days that followed she had burned with impatience, fuming for the hour when she might go to him,
seek him out on the dusty roads of endlich-Erde. But the
hour never came; the Peisun barely let her out of his sight,
and to be absent for an afternoon, even, seemed a hope
beyond all possibility.

Then at last she had been liberated by the news from
Mar: Chiton, the old Lord Mayor, the uncle of Desmos,
was sinking fast, and Desmos' presence was urgently necessary.

"You will come with me, of course, my love," Desmos
had said to her.

"I fear I cannot."

"Cannot? But surely . . . why can you not?"

Shira smiled. "The hunt takes place tomorrow. I have
absented myself from it, in your honor, ever since last
Capra. I can no longer deny myself, Desmos."

"The hunt?" The Peisun's face was sickened. "You
know I cannot endure for you to engage in that barbarian
. . . murder. And to say that the hunt is more vital than
my uncle. I cannot believe you, Shira."

"My dear, what will my presence serve? The old man
will die as quickly with me as without me."

Desmos stared at the beautiful Capran. Her white face
was as smooth as silk; no line of compassion or concern
marred its perfection, and her oblique black eyes were
cool.

How in the name of Kun, he asked himself, have I ever
come to love her? And again, his enslaved body replied to
him coldly, for even at this moment, when he hated her,
his flesh was drawn inevitably to her sweet flesh, and he
could not take his stricken eyes from her bosom's swell

and the heart-stopping curve outward from her narrow waist. Defeated, he gave it up.

And so it had come to pass that now she was galloping like a faun through the thickening wood, her inner eyes inflamed with the image of the lean, naked body of Fahne the sorcerer.

Fahne looked up from the child's hand, meeting the slant black eyes with a stunned amazement. He had been so intent upon the drawing out of the sick humor from the child's infected thumb, and speaking soothingly to her, that he had not noticed at all the sound of drumming hooves or the sharp exclamation from Veris.

"It is the Queen," the Bole said in a low voice to the sorcerer, and Fahne nodded indifferently, turning back to his task.

When the child had been led away, he could avoid her no longer. Coolly, he met her hot black gaze with his dappled eyes; she stared so long into them, drowning in their shadows of blue and brown and green, that she felt herself swaying on her feet like a wind-blown reed.

His distant, gentle look took in her costume, and his face hardened: she was wearing the hunting clothes of endlich-Erde, the boyish, tight-fitting hose of fire-green, with a matching doublet cut in a deep V that exposed the cleft of her full, white breasts and a jaunty hunting cap on her shining hair, falling loose to her waist. Her full red lips were moistly parted and her sensual eyes beseeched him.

She watched his gaze move to the costly, carved crossbow of horn, with its goat's-foot lever, slung from her saddle, and smiled a rueful smile. "You are an Erden, yet you frown on slaying the deer?"

"Slaying sickens me," he said bluntly.

"And healing?" she asked dryly. "Do you restrict your healing powers to all but me?"

"I do not take your meaning, my lady," he said deliberately. "What do you wish of me?"

"You take my meaning perfectly."

"What do you wish of me?" he repeated coldly.

"I have a message from my consort Desmos."

He held out his hand. "Then, by all means, deliver it."

She smiled, and her hot look dropped to his mouth. "I wish to deliver it in private."

"Very well." He would have it out with the bitch for good and all, thought Fahne. Else they would linger here till darkness in this foolish jousting.

He gestured her to a clump of trees a little distant from the wagon, indifferent to the staring eyes of Bock and Veris and the gaping peasants, who looked with wonder on the sensuous woman in her boyish raiment. She wandered farther into the shadow of the little forest, and when the wagon and the people were lost to sight, she took hold of the deep neckline of her tunic and ripped at it, offering him her white, rose-tipped breasts.

He looked on her unmoved and said quietly, "Yes, you are very beautiful. But I have little desire to make the beast with two backs again with the wife of my friend. I am not drugged now, Shira; my flesh is quite calm."

She was speechless with shock. Then her proud anger overcame her senses and she leaped upon him, beating at him with her fists, reaching up to lash at his face with her nails.

He grasped her by the wrists. "I would be called a fool by any man," he said softly. "But the wonder is, you move me not in all your splendor. Why must you humiliate yourself like this?"

Her face suffused with rage, the Capran struggled in his hold for another moment; then she ceased to struggle and looked up at him. The only emotion on his mysterious face was sadness, and his dappled eyes were staring above her head into the wood at something she would never understand.

Finally he looked down at her, as if seeing her for the first time. "Go back, Shira," he said as if she were an unruly child. "I will bring you your steed and something to cover yourself. I would have no woman made sport of."

"A curse on you and your pity!" she shrieked. "I care not if the entire countryside looks on my flesh."

And she ran from the wood, careless that her freed breasts were exposed to the gaping people around the wagon and to the astonished Veris and Bock.

With the agility of the Capran, the race of the hoofed gods akin to all creatures with cloven feet, she resumed her saddle and galloped away.

And down the dusty road she urged the steed on to greater effort, cursing and sobbing. At last, fearing that the beast's heart would burst, she drew in the reins a little and paused.

A lone serf was laboring in the field nearby. He shaded his dazzled eyes from the sun, convinced he was dreaming, for the beautiful lady on the lathered steed was touching her bare breasts and smiling, smiling at him. And she seemed to be quite alone.

The serf went slowly forward to meet the white vision.

After the close air of Chiton's sickroom, the air of Dione's water garden was more than ever sweet to breathe, and Desmos entered gratefully with his old friend Fomalhaut the councilman.

A narrow moon could be seen through the dome of water-colored glass, giving little light, so that the hues of rose and blue and green and lavender were very dim. Fomalhaut followed the direction of Desmos' eyes and left his thought unspoken: The new moon that saps the strength and takes away the dying.

Indeed, the old Crabba did not have long; the wonder was that he had lived beyond Kani. But stubbornly, with the deep earth-love of the Crabba, he had clung to life beyond the expectations of the healer.

With his death, Fomalhaut reflected, the awesome task of governing Mar would descend on Desmos, whose ties with Erde pleased some and discomfited many. There were those who looked on the alliance as a surety of peace; others feared the corruption of the feudal Shira.

"When my uncle dies," said Desmos, as if in answer to his friend's thought, "I wish to delegate you, my old friend, as Council head." The younger Peisun sank down on the bench of Ler.

"I had no idea of such a wish," said Fomalhaut in surprise. "I have not even considered such a thing. Ever since you were a child, it has been thought you would succeed your uncle. The people still would set aside an election. You are greatly loved in Mar."

Desmos smiled. "And I love Mar greatly. I long for it, perpetually. But the kingdom of my wife is in Erde. And there is much in that land I would help to alter." A shadow fell upon his face.

"The serfs?"

Desmos nodded.

"That is a large and sweeping change," said Fomalhaut dryly. "You would upset the traditions of centuries."

"I am not intimidated by difficulty."

No, Fomalhaut agreed silently, nor indeed impossibility! His young friend had never been quailed by either. He glanced at the star-wheel on Desmos' breast, dimly discernible by the pale moon and the random blue lanterns of the water garden. Among the aquamarines of the Peisun, there were many pearls of the retentive Crabba and emeralds of the immutable Bole.

"And what is your wife's view of these matters?" he asked Desmos.

His young friend colored. "We have not yet . . . gone into these matters deeply."

Or at all, Fomalhaut thought, preferring in common with many Peisun to leave some comments unexpressed, for thus was peace so often made and kept.

"The matter of the Escors disturbs me greatly," Desmos said abruptly.

"Yes, they have increasingly turned to crime and malice since the rift with Vanand."

"It is not so much the fact of their ways that disturbs me as the underlying cause."

Fomalhaut snorted. "It is not the underlying cause that sheds blood, but the 'fact' itself, as you so delicately put it."

Desmos raised his hand. "That goes without saying, but until the Escors are restored to a place on the Council, the resentment of the race will deepen and deepen until we are confronted with a civil conflict."

"Surely you exaggerate."

"No, Fomalhaut. I see great difficulty to come." Again the older Peisun examined Desmos' star-wheel; yes, by the form of Hermes, the god of knowing, there appeared again the symbol of the Peisun outlined in glittering aquamarines. Desmos' intuitive sight was strong.

"And you wish me to guide in your stead, with all our differences?" Fomalhaut smiled.

"Because of our differences," Desmos retorted. "You are a man who thinks for himself. And you will come to see the justice of my opinions." He grinned impudently, and Fomalhaut laughed aloud.

"You are very sure of yourself," said Fomalhaut.

"Sure of my *course*, my friend, and what I know to be right."

They were silent for a time, and then the older Peisun asked, "And the Lady Dione? You have still not found her?"

"No. But I heard only yesternight that a courier has returned from the castle of Melik in Brise, where he delivered a missive to her. I had made some inquiries before in the land of snow, for it appeared that since Gemelle had left the others, he might have taken my cousin and her friend Volan under his wing. I hope to know her whereabouts within a day or two."

"And the sorcerer?" asked Fomalhaut.

Desmos told him of the blackness of Fahne's mind and of his precipitate departure from the castle. "He now plies his trade again, I am told, with his friends Bock and Veris." The Peisun was silent, then added, "What a joy it will be to have my little cousin back again! She will be safe now," he said sadly, "from the importunities of our uncle. It is a dark thing that his death will bring her freedom . . . and the restored amity of Mar."

"Think you that the Lady Dione still loves the sorcerer?"

"I would wager all upon it," Desmos replied. "Their love was so immediate and deep that even death could not extinguish it. I felt at times in Erde, though he knew me not at all, that Fahne preserved somewhere in his mind's darkness the image of my cousin."

"And she? I wonder what she will do when he confronts her as a stranger."

"She will persevere. I know my stubborn little cousin. Her rising star, you know, shines on the rim of the changeless Bole. Nothing can deter her from her goals." Desmos smiled.

They heard the heavy step of a woman on the path of shells, and Earla the Bole stood before them, wiping her wet cheeks with the corner of her russet apron.

"Come, good gentles," she said. "Milord Chiton is soon to part."

Desmos put his lean arm around her shoulders and walked with Earla down the path toward the stairway to the bedchambers, Fomalhaut behind them.

"Poor old man," he said softly to the Bole. "He so loves the earth, it seems a pity he must leave it now."

Earla began to sob. "Oh, Sir Desmos!" she cried. "Sir Desmos! Who will I have to quarrel with when he is gone?"

The Peisun led her with affection from the garden and toward the chamber of the Lord Mayor of Mar.

CHAPTER 9

"I demand," said Nobilis the Prince of Sabbia, "to see the Lady Shabatu. She has been closeted this week or more. What is her ailment? What is her condition? As her chosen husband surely I have the right to know!"

The Leun's very flaming hair seemed stiff with indignation, Uras noted wtih bitter amusement, and he watched his father's poor attempt to smile.

"It is a minor indisposition, Your Highness," said the Baron Melik, "that will soon be cured and she will be among us again."

"I have pressing business in Sabbia," protested Nobilis, "that must be attended to when my business in moyen-Brise is done."

"Moyen-Brise?" Melik inquired.

"Have you forgotten that the Prince Solidago has made such business necessary?" Nobilis' dark face was grim.

"It appeared to me at the time"—Uras' voice was an insolent drawl—"that it was you who made the tryst, and Solidago's manhood bound him to reply."

The Leun's big hand went to the golden dagger in his belt. "If you were not the brother of Shabatu . . ."

"Let not that deter you," Uras snapped. "I will need no weapon." The dernier-Brisen, like the Maeden and the men of Mar, were skilled in the martial arts, fighting only with their hands and feet and their agile bodies. And Uras, for all his lean and scholarly appearance, had a tensile strength akin to the acrobat Gemelle's.

"Uras!" Melik cried. "Nobilis! I will not have this brawling in my house!" Uras was heartened at the commanding tone that seemed to herald the return of his old power, the power that had been weakened in his pursuit of Nobilis as a son-in-law. "Is it not enough," Melik said sternly to Nobilis, "that you mean to battle my neighbor? Now you dare to challenge my son!"

The quick Sabbian temper of Nobilis the Leun took fire. "I will no longer presume upon your house! I will quarter my train at the inn. But before I depart, once more I demand to bid farewell to the Lady Shabatu."

Melik and Uras exchanged glances.

Uras said quietly, "How long are we to play out this poor comedy, Father?"

The Baron sighed.

Uras said to Nobilis, "She is not in the castle. She has fled."

Nobilis stared at the two Brisen in stricken silence. He repeated stupidly then, "She has fled?"

Melik nodded.

"But where?" Nobilis cried. "Where has she gone?"

"We do not know," Uras replied. "Our men have scoured Brise, from the land of the Twisan to the land of the Bilance. And she is nowhere to be found. She may have gone to Mar, or Sabbia."

"Sabbia," Nobilis said thoughtfully. "If she is in the land of fire, you may be certain she will be discovered. We have more efficient methods in my country that you of Brise do not know."

"I am sure of that," Uras commented dryly.

"And what do you mean to do?" asked Nobilis. "Do you not mean to pursue her?"

"Inquiries are being made," said Melik, "in Mar and Sabbia."

"Therefore," Nobilis said with contempt, "I am to return to my father the King and advise him that you have let my promised bride escape from me?"

"Advise him what you will," Melik replied with asperity, stung by the Leun's tone. "In any case, your murderous tryst with Solidago need not be kept. There is no longer any reason for you to battle him."

"No reason!" cried Nobilis. "My honor has been offended and must be avenged, no matter where the Lady Shabatu has gone."

"I beg you to reconsider," Melik beseeched Nobilis.

"It is done. I will leave your house today and put up my train at the inn on the border of dernier- and moyen-Brise. The Prince Solidago will meet me in combat, as planned. As to the rift between your land and mine, I will leave that to you and my father the King."

Nobilis bowed stiffly to the Brisen and withdrew from the chamber, his spurred boots making an eerie jingling sound in the crystal stillness, the echo of his threatening words ringing in the ears of Uras and Melik.

As he watched the flaming hair and garments of the Leun disappear into the shadowy corridor, the Baron Melik sighed and said to his son, "We must stop him, Uras. Shabatu is lost to me, but I have no desire to see my neighbor Solidago, who is like another son, go to his death."

"We will try to stop him, Father," Uras said consolingly.

The old man went wearily to the window and stared out over the snow. "Where is she, Uras? Somewhere in the deserts of Sabbia, or in the shadowy, green land of Mar? Do you think she is well?"

Uneasily, Uras answered, "I am sure she is. Were she ill, or in peril, my men would have been advised."

Melik did not reply. His son was thinking with a stab of guilt that it was a cruel thing not to let the old man know. And yet only in this deception lay her safety! For Uras' men had found the Waetergyt in company with Gemelle in the city of Alioure in premier-Brise.

"What ails our friend?" Bock asked Veris coarsely. "That is a sweet steed to ride; I would have gladly climbed into the saddle. He might have left her to me."

"Quietly," said the Bole. "He is near."

Fahne the sorcerer heard without shame or resentment his companions' low-voiced remarks and sought out his customary twilight place in the ring of trees by the stream of peisun.

All that day, following the departure of the lovely Shira, the sorcerer had moved and spoken with an indifferent calm that wholly mystified the Bole and Capran, who were still shaken by the vision of the distracted Queen in disarray racing from the thicket to her gleaming horse and galloping away into the afternoon. Women had hidden their children's eyes from the shocking sight, and nearly an hour had been required to calm the gathering. Veris, in his deep, mendacious voice, had murmured of the lady's "madness." In desperation, Bock had given out vials of free potions, and all the while the sorcerer had stood by, bland and a little sad, with unseeing eyes.

It happened that the night before Fahne had entered into such a dream of love, lost and unreachable, that it froze him to all other lust, so locked him in its embrace that even the sight of the exquisite Queen could move him not at all.

He had lain wakeful that night before for long hours, bedded in the wagon with the others, listening to the peaceful snores of Bock and Veris. Wide-eyed, the sorcerer had suddenly grasped the medallion around his sinewy neck and had seen in the black night the star begin to glow with strange colors, the colors of the Marin.

This sudden reawakening of the star had seemed to Fahne an omen. When at last he fell asleep, it was to visit places unremembered in the company of a frail white woman he did not know.

It seemed he rode an hour on the canals of Mar, watching its golden lanterns stretch out like a necklace of small moons on the dark, unmoving water, hearing the voice of a minstrel, thin as a silver bird, sing of the green sleeves of a lady who was lost.

Then it seemed he walked with her, this white woman, and her body and her voice, her scent and her hair, were lucid to his senses, while her face was misted over with a kind of white shadowiness, like a veil of snow. She smelled of water-lily flowers, and her glowing hair, black as a night bird's wing, glittered in the alien overcast that was at once, and either, sun and cloudiness. And she was small, so small that the top of her gleaming head reached but to his breast, and her voice was as gentle as the evening wind in the leaves of his twilight hiding place or the murmuring of the little stream where the brown peisun lived.

They moved together beneath the sunny cloudiness over a field of green-gold grass, of bluebells and lavender, of the clove-scented gillyflowers. She was laughing, and she led him to a dappled thicket of gold and green and russet that might have been a wall of leaves or a close-marshaled fortress of branches. But as they drew nearer, he saw amazed that the wall of leaves was the wall of a hidden house, for she led him through its door—it was a house so like the hue and texture of the trees it could not be told from them if one beheld it from the road beyond the field.

And the small white woman led him through the hidden door into an ancient house that was all quietness and glimmering. It, too, had the fragrance of the pink, clove-smelling gillyflower, and of roses and lilies, and lilacs and lavender. He saw as through a golden mist the vague outlines of massed harebells and other sweet blossoms everywhere, but he could discern nothing clearly. All of the appointments of the house were quite familiar, but vague and shadowy, veiled in a mist that was not white and cool, but golden and heated, as if each object had been dazzlingly splattered with sun, and each blinded him to their lines and true proportions.

Like to the other features of the still house were the polished stairs where she led him upward, laughing, and through a veiled door to a chamber where the ever-present, half-clouded sun of the strange afternoon, with its gilded dazzle, blinded him to the minute details, showing him only her now-naked silhouette, throwing a jagged, golden aura about her gleaming hair, which covered her upper body, changing its raven blackness to a dark of riddled silver.

In the center of the chamber was a massive bed, curtained in stuff as filmy as the wings of a dragonfly and as light as the touch of her fingers; the stuff was broidered in roses of blue, the emblem of the impossible, symbol of the Maeden and the center, the union of the lover and the beloved.

And the woman with the face of mist entered with him through the golden fog beyond the curtains, knowing no moment longer any impediment of the world beyond the chamber, no words that must be said, no perils to guard themselves from, no faintest whisper of the passing hour.

Fahne could not hear his breath, nor hers, and only in his flesh cried out when he felt her multitudinous, quick, moist kisses upon his hands and wrists, his arms and shoulders; there were a hundred small kisses like the wings of moths or the variegated touch of summer rain upon him everywhere.

He only felt his moaning as he leaned to her whiteness, powdered golden by the sun, saluting her with his caresses as she trembled like a drop of crystal water before its descent from the leaf that lets it go reluctantly, never pausing in the rhythm of his kisses as she leaned back limply in the silken bed, her black hair streaming like satin in the dazzled light as his flesh listened to her sweet outcries.

Then from a dim blue distance he could hear her urging him, "Be near, my love, be near." And their bodies clove together while he heard, for the first time now, their corporeal voices uttering strange, guttural phrases and thin, small cries, like wounded animals. The golden light was shut out to blackness full of lightning-flash of purple and of crimson, where gentleness was not, but only hunger feeding, feeding. And for the black, unceasing time there were drums only, and the pounding, the pounding of the fearful horses through the air of the country of the bellowing blind, and the body's dancing and the drums.

And he knew the wonder of a strange, small serpent's writhing below him, a creature that sang sweetly an insinuating song and closed him tightly in a skin of molten, silken writhing, and his skin heard the narrow, writhing song, of such an aching ecstasy he feared his hour to die was now upon him, that his vitals would be scattered from his frame in the titanic impact when his loins let go.

There were no words between them; they drew near to sleep.

A time beyond a time he awoke within his sleep to drown again in her, diving dolphin-like into her tropical seas, leaping and diving again and again with a magical repetition that grew sweeter with each repeating, until all the world above him was forever fled, and there was nothing to his senses but the warm, clove-scented breakers of his play wherein he was the merman who would never willingly again come back to shore, but on and on until eternity would go on diving down into the slow green waves of watery enchantment, never to see a light except for the light of the self-illuminating creatures of the deep in the coral forests of the ocean floor, the axis and abyss.

Fahne had awakened drained and shuddering, with an ache so poignant that he knew in his flesh an answer he had not been given before in all his nights and days.

And it seemed to him in his vision he had both acted and observed, a knife-like edge of brightness in the dark of his recall informing him that this hour had been lived in other times with a woman who was flesh and bone and not a wraith of golden mist or a thing of his imagining.

Therefore, when the beautiful Queen had bared herself to him in the harsher light of morning, her flesh had merely been the ghost of other flesh, her words an insect echo of the one voice that could arouse him. And his drained loins could find no more response to her lesser fires than the flesh of a man dying.

"I am coming ever nearer," he said thoughtfully to the brown peisun, which were seeking their watery depths for the night, even as he had drowned in the woman of his dream. "I am coming ever nearer from the dark into the light."

And consoled by the unseen company he kept, the sorcerer looked again at his medallion. He saw with a wondering delight that the star was still glowing in the twilight with the colors of the peisun in the sea, bluebells and pink gillyflowers, the green of leaves and lavender, and the silver of the sun on the woman's black hair. The omen was alive and would continue to guide him.

Dione the Marin saw, through the softly drifting snow, the long-legged ice birds teeter over the frozen surface of the pond and pause to peck at the shining ice. They were very comical, with their fat lilac bodies and their long purple legs; but suddenly they turned ruthless with greed and speared the ice with their beaks, bringing forth the narrow silver fish.

The Marin shivered and looked away. The pursuit of the fish by the birds was like the pursuit of Uras. But tomorrow . . . tomorrow she would be away . . . and on the road to Fahne.

She looked beyond the frozen pool, upward over the drifts of frozen white, to the fairy-like pile of the castle of Melik. The late sun of four, the Maeden-hour, her time for solitary dreaming, glittered on the crystalline towers, turning them rose and gold.

The colors were a signal that she still had time before Volan came seeking her. Dione raised her face to the kiss of snow, thinking how strange it was that in Brise the snowfall never dimmed the sun.

And she saw again, as she had all the day, the sun of her dream of the night past, when she had been given once more, like a miracle, the nearness of Fahne and the blessed knowledge that even in his black forgetting, his passion for her was unchanging, never dying.

In the dream he did not know her name and could not see her face, yet she saw him breathe with pleasure her water-lily scent, and she felt his broad hand smooth her hair as they seemed to float together over the sunny grass and the pastel meadow flowers and garden flowers of the hidden house in Erdemar.

This time it was she who led him through the cleverly fashioned door, and she had polished the house throughout until it shone and had filled it everywhere with harebells and roses, with lavender and gillyflowers, all for his delight. And he had been tall and lean beside her; she looked up at him with worship, on the well-loved, long-remembered features of his stately face—his deep, dappled eyes with their piercing gaze, his hawk-like nose, and full, tender mouth below its drooping, golden-brown moustache.

And somehow she knew he did not know her face. He seemed to be peering at her as through a thin but concealing veil; yet he knew so well her touch and her body as she led him into the chamber of the blue-rose bed, where they lay together naked in the dazzling sun that made a golden halo of his tawny head and ignited the pale hairs on his arms and the rest of his body.

And she had leaned to him, bestowing the hot caresses learned in her agony of starved loneliness, remembering his words about the tutelage of hunger, while he in turn had fired her body with his lips and at long last closed the endless distance of their parting with his seeking flesh.

For Dione it had been the filling of all emptiness, the warming of all cold; she who had lived an eternity in a cavern of wind, all desolate, felt the entrance of the sun in fullness and a flood of fire and there had been, in their time together, a time of black and crimson when the witches danced and sang, when they had left themselves to become the primal beasts of all lost innocence, and they were other than their names and only one desire.

Dione had known such a purity of lust appeased that it left her with a new consciousness of her womanly power, so that in their next hot, breathless meeting she had learned the motions of an alien dance whose gyrations wrung from him ever deeper cries of savage, wild delight.

And awakening, she had known exhausted joy, knowing also that after this encounter, his flesh was hers as hers had so long been possessed by him.

Her body singing with the remembered delight, Dione the Marin had gone lightly through the tasks of the day, preparing herself for the morrow's journey, and seeking at Maeden-hour this quiet place by the pond to dream of the sorcerer.

Now through a veil of snow she could see a slender figure in a heavy blue cloak plodding downward toward her through the milky drifts.

"My lady!" It was the silvery voice of the unmanned minstrel Volan.

She smiled and beckoned him to her, feeling now the bite of the twilight's chill and noting that the towers were changing from golden-rose to lavender.

"You have been here so long!" the minstrel cried as he came softly, crushing the snow.

She did not answer, only smiled as she rose and drew her borrowed cloak of gray more closely around her slender form, fastening the hood.

Dione took Volan's arm and gave it an affectionate squeeze, starting to move around the pond.

But the minstrel stood still, staring upward at the dreamlike towers of the castle of Melik. "We leave tomorrow," he said softly, and with a hint of wistfulness.

"You need not go with me," she said in a quiet voice. "You know you are welcome to stay. You may join the Baron's little orchestra."

"Oh, no, my lady." He shook his narrow head with its dark hair so peculiarly dappled with gold. It was bare today, and he wore a cap of snow. "Where you go, I will go, too, for no one else has been so good a friend to me."

"But will you not yearn for the splendors of the castle—all the little stools and plates shaped like flakes of snow?" she asked with teasing affection.

"There are splendors in your water garden that are greater than Melik's."

Eerily, she heard an echo of her words to her Uncle Chiton on that night so long ago, and she answered sadly, "We may not be able to stay there, either, you know. No doubt my uncle has found another suitor for me to reject. You make yourself a fugitive, Volan, by remaining my companion."

The minstrel took her small gloved hand. "Your fortunes will be mine, my lady. Never mind. We will come to journey's end."

And gently he led her up the white rise toward the castle of Melik.

CHAPTER 10

The glittering metropolis of Alioure was situated at the foot of the highest peaks in premier-Brise, homeland of Gemelle the Twisan; it was literally a city of ice. Long ago, before the city was, great rivers had roared at the mountains' feet, but in all the time remembered, they were always frozen over. So the streets were gleaming ice and commerce upon them possible only on metal-bladed shoes or horse-drawn carts that had not wheels, but bladed runners to withstand the ways of glass.

The bladed shoes were easy for the fleet, agile Twisan, the city a perpetual whirl of varicolored, gleaming motion. The changeable Twisan, ruled by Hermes, swift messenger of the gods, wore every conceivable color that was pale of hue—yellows of narcissi and winter sun, green of spring leaves and peridot, pale purple of early lilac, the small rose's tinge, celestial-blue and silver-gray of evening snow.

The structures of Alioure, with oval towers symbolizing air, were ornamented everywhere with Hermes-glass, the stuff of mirrors. Therefore, the metropolis was dazzling, no brighter in the pallid sun than in the evening time, when the shadows of dusk transformed the palaces and star-cathedrals and the justice halls and merchants' arcades into a vast and throbbing looking glass of blue and purple. Night was never black in Alioure, always a hyacinthine-blue, and the night lanterns gave the city a look of fairy-land.

The most brilliant of the palaces in the city of Alioure was that of the Duke Cylenius and his Duchess Menita, Brisen of riches almost incalculable whose pleasure it was to hold elaborate fetes. One such was being held this night in the immense central hall of the palace.

The Duke had engaged an orchestra of forty pieces and a band of strolling players and acrobats from the theater of Alioure to entertain their noble guests.

The host and hostess were seated at an endless crystal table on a raised dais of carpeted Hermes-glass. He was a reedy Twisan of middle years with a dancing, lustful eye. In him reigned supreme the ironic coldness of his race. To his left sat his lady the Duchess, a Waetergyt of excruciating plainness who was dedicated to the scholarly pleasures. Nonetheless, she arrayed herself as if she were a beauty. Her headdress was of indescribable intricacy and her silvery gown was so encrusted with frost pearls and amethysts, so voluminous of sleeve and train that it was difficult for her to move, impossible for her to lift a goblet from the table without sweeping several other goblets to the floor.

As the Duchess took a number of glasses of wine, and the sweeping sleeves demolished other goblets, one servant was engaged in sweeping up the Hermes-glass on the floor by her place.

The women and the friends of the players and musicians sat at tables far removed from the royal dais. One of these women, a fragile Waetergyt of exquisite loveliness, regarded the Duchess' sleeves and her noble companions, most of whom were the worse for wine, with a quizzical expression.

The Duke Cylenius, whose dancing eyes were very sharp, caught the amused expression on the lovely young woman's face and took in her slender beauty. She had the look of good birth, he thought, examining her small, well-chiseled features and her remote, proud eyes. She was wearing the simplest gown of lilac-blue say, cut in a modest oval above her white breasts, with sleeves of a delicate flow like a ripple of air. Her hair of silver gilt, like the winter morning's sun, was simply dressed, and her only jewels were a string of frost pearls and a band of crystal on her wedding finger.

What a pity, thought the Duke, that she is wed—not, however, that it made much matter, either in the raffish society of the players or the equally raffish circle of the Brisen nobles. The color of her gown reminded the unsentimental Duke, quite strangely, of a gown his old nurse used to wear, and by extension of a fragrant little folk air she was wont to sing to him.

All of a sudden he saw the lovely young Waetergyt's pale face color, like the newest summer blossom, and her eyes ignite. The drums gave forth a hollow roll, and the lights blazed on a whirling yellow form, like a whirling flake of golden snow—the prime acrobat, Gemelle, was twirling into the immensity of the glass-bubbled, mirrored hall to perform his most daring feats of perilous skill.

Ah! thought the Duke a little sadly, so that is the one who has her heart. And with the rest he watched the yellow-clad Twisan land cat-like on his feet with a brilliant smile. He bowed so smoothly that he seemed to have no bones, and with a dance-like motion he leaped to the first rung of a silver ladder strung from a perilous point near the very top of the mirrored dome of the festal hall; the bibulous guests, who had not noticed it before, beheld a little path of gleaming rope, high in the air, and gasped.

The Duke glanced back at the lovely Waetergyt. Her face had paled and she watched with anxious eyes each tensile step of the boneless man in yellow as he took the upward flight. The Duke could fairly see the beating of her heart below the lilac-blue breast of the simple, clinging gown.

The drums stopped abruptly, and a single flute took up a most ethereal air, an air so piping and narrow that it seemed to be the cry of a newborn bird, and the watchers were so still they could hear every breath of the melody. The Duke fancied he could almost discern the swish of the acrobat's yellow-stockinged feet as they placed themselves with care and grace upon the high and narrow silver path.

Now the flute song stilled, as well, and the great hall was as silent as the new-laid snow in the hush of morning before a single bird has set its star-foot down. And the Duke saw the lovely Waetergyt place a wing-like hand upon her slender throat, her face more white than the frost pearls she wore.

And the yellow-clad boneless man, with ineffable grace, began to walk across the silver rope as easily as if he were skating the ice-streets of Alioure. He reached the end of the silver path and turned, with incredible skill, to make the repeat journey across the gleaming rope in the highest air. More slowly this time, extremely slowly, the agile Twisan made his dancing way, his yellow raiment glowing in the mirrored dome, reflecting in the moving globes of Hermes-glass around him, until there were a score of lean Gemelles defying death above the noble guests of Cylenius.

Halfway along the perilous route, the acrobat appeared to slip; there was a great gasp from below as the yellow-clad bird of a man slipped from his perch and fell. But, astonished, they saw then that he was laughing as he caught with arrogant ease the silver rope with one tensile hand and whirled himself around and around, like a golden flake of light, to the very end of the path of silver rope. Righting himself with one enormous flip, Gemelle landed cat-like on the glossy platform at the gleaming rope's end.

He bowed insouciantly and waved to those below as the drums began to roll again, and the orchestra of many tones broke out into a triumphant air.

Swiftly the man named Gemelle descended the silvery rope ladder as another man would run down a flight of stairs, and he gave the noble guests of the Duke and Duchess another elaborate bow. He then bowed more deeply, and for a longer time, to the table of the frail young Waetergyt.

Cylenius watched him go to her and kiss her hands. Around the Duke there were loud murmurs of astounded praise. The Duchess belched softly and swept another goblet from the crystal table with her massive sleeve.

"Magnificent," she drawled, then gestured for an additional glass of yew.

Gemelle pulled the white woolen coverlet around them in the closed sleigh, feeling the sweet weight of Shabatu's head in the pit of his arm. For a moment or two they were contentedly silent. The crystalline jingle of the horse's bells was pleasant and dim in the late-night quiet.

The Waetergyt watched the few remaining lanterns glimmer on the passing facades of Hermes-glass, their pallid golden orbs like little moons on the hyacinthine ground of fallen sky. Then she began to giggle like a child. "The Duchess!" she cried. "Her sleeves! She was like a great belching ice bird, with that fat body and long, thin arms!"

Gemelle's laughter answered hers. "No doubt her legs are just as thin. I waited for her to pull a peisun from the table with her beak."

Their bubbling laughter rose and overcame them. Shabatu wiped her eyes with her gray-blue glove and sniffled. "And, oh, my love, her exquisite condescension when she was playing the commoner among us."

Gemelle gave a great guffaw of laughter again. "When you quoted her that alchemical law, she looked as though a spear had pierced her."

Shabatu gave a final gasp of mirth, and leaning to her husband, she kissed him below the ear. Gemelle lifted her white face and gave her a deep, lingering kiss on the mouth.

And he said solemnly, "It is not so funny as that, I think. It saddens me to see you go about in say while that grotesque creature wears cloth of silver and gems enough to sink a galley."

The Waetergyt looked at him in surprise. "What nonsense," she answered softly, taking his hand. "You are jesting."

But his profile, in the pallid light, was grim, and he said with great seriousness, "No. No, it is not nonsense. I could not bear to see Cylenius look on you with such desire. Were you openly, still, the Lady Shabatu, he would have been obliged to show you greater courtesy."

"He showed me no offense," she said gently, stroking the Twisan's hard, lean arm.

"He showed you little courtesy," retorted Gemelle. "Oh, Shabatu, Shabatu, I ponder so often, late in the nights, the injuries I have done you by taking you from Melik's house."

"Injuries!" she repeated, aghast. "Gemelle, look at me."

Swiftly, he obeyed, turning to gaze upon her fine-skinned face, as white as milk, upraised to his. There was a tender light in her remote blue eyes, and her small, rose-like mouth trembled with passion. "Do I look," she asked tenderly, "like an injured woman?"

He kissed her for answer, again and again, and for another long moment they were still, listening to the narrow crystal bells of the steed that bore their sleigh to the inn.

At last she broke the silence. In a tone half-jocular, she said, "Sometimes I think I cannot bear to see you again in peril of your limbs, in the high air, where only the birds should live."

He grinned at this, then returned, "What would you have? Shall I be a merchant, or a slave? Or perhaps a duke, so that you may sit beside me in state, belching fumes of yew and demolishing the crystal with your sleeve?"

"It is never in your temper to be serious," she said with mock reproof, but there was an edge of apprehension in her reply. "Do you not know my constant fear?"

He drew her nearer and kissed her hair where the heavy hood had fallen back to reveal its gilded gleam. "That saddens me, my love. But it brings us much silver," he added dryly, "and much silver buys gowns and gems and the passage to lands of anonymous freedom."

A slight shadow fell upon them, and Shabatu wondered about something she had kept from Gemelle—the encounter with a man one afternoon on the streets of ice who resembled a servant of Melik's. Why had he not approached her? Why had Melik not come after them?

She shivered, and Gemelle asked, "Are you chill?"

"No," she answered softly, moving closer to him, "I am not chill. A Chronos shadow moved across the moon, that is all." She used the private jest about her darker character, hoping to distract him.

With fine illogic the name moyen-Brise was not geographically descriptive. It referred to the posture of the

Bilance on heaven's wheel, between the Twisan and the Waetergyt. The land of moyen-Brise was situated below the countries of the other two, on low plateaus bordering the gentler cool of upper Mar, and sharing with the Bole of Erde the rule of Aphrodite.

Such rule had cousined the Bilance with the Bole in many ways: they were slow of speech and leisurely, great worshippers of beauty, and both were fighters of men and slayers of beasts, unlike the less physical men of premier- and dernier-Brise, who ate no meat and who, if they fought at all except in debate, employed their fine-trained hands and feet and bodies.

There had always been, since the time before time awoke, a certain code of honor among the nations: only the weapon-skilled men of moyen-Brise made war on Erde or Sabbia, where similar customs were observed; in turn, those of Sabbia and Erde could make no war on Mar or the upper lands of Brise or mittel-Erde.

So it was that Melik frowned on and Uras ridiculed the projected joust between the young Princes of moyen-Brise and Sabbia, but Solidago and Nobilis rose to it this day in the consciousness of right, with light, exulting hearts.

When the deceptively sleepy-eyed young Prince of moyen-Brise had said so casually to Nobilis that he would be pleased to fight, he spoke no less than the truth, for the young Solidago, for all his cherubic face and violet stare, was a deadly opponent; he had not deigned to practice with the quintain, the pivoted arm set on top of a pole, the knight's barometer of skill. He had offered it, however, to the Sabbian with heavy courtliness, and Nobilis, with stung pride, had hotly declined.

However, goaded on by his determined equerry, Ayil the Ramm, the Sabbian had sullenly made use of the quintain thereafter.

It was a fine day for the match, meditated Solidago. The sky was overcast, in the very temper of Aphrodite, and this would give him an added edge, for he knew that to the sun-loving Sabbians the clouds were a heavy omen.

He smiled easily at Zaban, his own equerry, a massive young Bilance with a Saturnian physique, arrayed like him in the colors of brown and rose. But whereas the equerry wore only a padded gambeson and carelessly displayed the shield of Aphrodite, above his short sword and matching dagger, Solidago was wearing his tilting armor of bronze with the great semicircular vamplate, giving full protection to the right side of the body. This was another invention of Erde. Easily in his right arm Solidago cradled the sharp lance to be used for the running tilt, and from his saddle hung his splendid helm, lengthened by gorget plates and sprouting rich, rose-colored plumes.

The two Bilance had reached the tilting place and saw that already the Sabbian Nobilis, on his nervous chestnut stallion, was waiting with his flame-haired equerry Ayil. The Sabbian, too, wore bronze borrowed armor and carried a lance of moyen-Brise; but his plumes were the hue of flames, and his shield bore the emblem of a raging lion of gold with ruby eyes.

The four, unhelmeted, approached each other with a slow pomposity, and Solidago, smiling, said, "I hereby say to you, my lord, that our quarrel may be mended. How say you?"

Glowering, Nobilis cried out, "Our quarrel but flames hotter in my heart! Lay on, my lord!"

Solidago's smile died on his lips. He bowed coldly from the saddle to Nobilis, and their equerries followed suit. Then the four rode back to their starting places, the equerries drawing aside.

And Solidago and Nobilis put on their helms, each disdaining the help of his aide. The men in the helmets nodded. And Ayil cried, "Lay on!"

Their lances atilt, the noblemen galloped toward each other, Solidago with a posture of cool ease, the Sabbian displaying tense anger in all his demeanor. With an almost arrogant touch, the Bilance's lance clanged against the armor of the Sabbian. It was obviously an action meant to irritate and not to wound. Enraged, Nobilis bellowed a curse at Solidago; his brassy voice was terrible and hollow from the cavern of his helm.

Still cool, the Bilance maneuvered away from a strong thrust of the Sabbian's, and Zaban shouted, "Splendid, sire!"

So stone-like was he now with ire that the Sabbian looked rigid upon his mount, even in the comparatively soft chain mail he wore in common with Solidago on his lower legs and on his left arm below the heavier plate. Ayil's face was anxious: such a posture, he had learned, was catastrophic in this deadly game.

The Sabbian galloped back again, the courteous Bilance allowing him the advantage, and, gathering all his angry power, he began to gallop in again on Solidago.

But in the flashing of an eye, the swiftest gray that any of the men had ever seen came streaking down the hill and headed to the place between the tilting men. On its back was a slender Waetergyt of many years, completely unarmed, and wearing only tunic and hose and a cloak against the chill. Behind him and his steed there rode another man, on a white steed whose swiftness equaled that of the pounding gray.

Now the chestnut stallion of Nobilis was bearing in on the old man mounted on the gray, and there was an awful bellow from the man on the white horse behind. With desperation, Nobilis tried to swerve his steed, but the excited horse, sniffing the thrill of imminent battle, was beyond control.

And the sharp, tilted lance of the Sabbian drove itself through the body of the man on the gray. The old man's scream rose above the shouts of the others and echoed and re-echoed in the valley as he fell, a welter of blood, on the frozen ground.

"Ouranos! Ouranos!" cried the man on the swift white steed. Jerking his mount to a stop, he leaped from his saddle and ran to the old bleeding man.

The helmeted men in armor and their stunned companions seemed incapable of speech or motion.

Then Solidago cried out to Zaban, "Help me get down!" And the equerry galloped to him and assisted him heavily from his mount. Slowly, dragging his armor's weight, he managed to reach the body of the dying man.

"Melik, Melik," he sobbed, his face exposed now through its opened helm, "why, why?"

Uras, who was leaning with his ear close to the old man's mouth, listened to his whisper, then looked up stonily at the Bilance. "He says, you barbarian fool, that he was trying to shame you into life."

Laboriously, the young Solidago turned to the still-mounted Sabbians and snapped at Nobilis, "Has there been enough, then? Or shall we continue?"

"There has been," said Nobilis in a barely audible voice, "enough."

And Zaban and Uras slung the old man's body over the

graceful gray. Then Zaban and Solidago mounted their horses, and with Uras in the lead on his white beast, holding the rein of the gray, the five men rode from the site of courtly battle.

PART IV

THE STAR
OF JOVE

(Good Fortune and Expansion)

CHAPTER 1

To Uras' regret and to the relief of Dione, the Waetergyt said that he would not be able to accompany her to upper Mar, but he had been generous in fitting out their conveyance. And he had pressed upon her and the minstrel a heavy bag of silver, sending with them two sturdy servers from the country of moyen-Brise; each man wore the curved bronze daggers of the Bilance as surety against the Escors still threatening the highways.

As they took the steep road now above the precipice, Dione recognized the spot and turned quite pale. They would soon be approaching the overlook upon the castle of Vanand, the scene of a nightmare that the Marin, try as she would, could never blot out.

Volan, seeing her expression, took her hand and said quietly, "Have no fear, my lady. Vanand is gone forever, and, indeed, the house of his mad father Sclar is in rack and ruin. Look at the sea, how lovely it is today."

Dione turned to him in surprise, deaf to distraction. "But what of his Uncle Sinapis?"

"The old man went wholly mad."

They could see the sinister castle now: truly in the latening light of afternoon, it looked hollow and gray, nowhere illuminated as it should have been in the early dusk of upper Mar. "How dreadful it appears," Dione said.

"But the terrible line of the mad Sclar has been cut off," the minstrel replied, "except for the ghosts they say that walk the windy corridors." The soughing waves below echoed his somber words.

Then to cheer the Marin, Volan said brightly, "We are in good time. We shall reach The Flying Fish inn well before dark. It is a clean and pleasant place, most suitable to quarter ladies."

Dione smiled. "It has a pleasant name—The Flying Fish."

Volan grinned back. "It might have been called for us," he said, "with its marriage of water and air." His tone turned practical. "In the morning the servers will go betimes to Mar and seek out your cousin Desmos. He will be able to tell us what to do."

The Marin nodded, loosening her borrowed lilac cloak in the warmer air. Already the heavy servers, Volan noted, were sweating. But his heart was filled with joy when he saw that the Lady Dioné was losing her apprehension, relaxing in the suave, moist air, with its silver hint of the sea, the sea that rolled below them now in calm as their conveyance took the untroubled road to the inn.

There were twelve dark barges in the funeral train of Chiton the Lord Mayor of Mar, one for each month of the year, one for each star-circle in heaven's wheel. Only those of high degree were accorded such a burial, and the people of Mar lined the canals to watch the stately procession pass.

Each barge was draped in the shining sorrow hue of the Crabba, star-race of Chiton, a dim gray-green with a verdigris of silver, like the twilit sea, and every polesman had been chosen for the dignity of his mien.

The prow of every barge was carved with a particular symbol for the stages of the life of man: the boat at the head, where the body of Chiton lay in state, was ornamented with the double Peisun and the H-like glyph of that race to mark the House of Dissolution, where the body faded into spirit as the year dissolved in Peisun Circle from winter into spring.

Each barge that followed was lovelier than the one before: in the Boat of the Profession stood the high officials of the Council, the Crabba in the verdigrised mourning green of their race, the Peisun in silver-gray. And the people along the embankments remarked, in the Marin's quiet fashion, on the presence of several Escors wearing their dark maroon of sadness.

The rift, the people murmured, must be healing.

"It was the doing of Desmos," someone said. And the faces of some observing Escorpiun became a bit less grim.

In the fifth barge, emblem of the Family House, the Peisun Desmos stood solemnly by the polesman at the prow. The nephew of Chiton wore a splendid suit of silver-gray encrusted with aquamarines, his star-wheel glimmer-

ing in the overcast. The Marin people gave thanks that the
sun was invisible, for brightness was a sign of unforgive-
ness of the dead at Marin funerals.

Behind Desmos sat the Queen, sallow in her dark green
Capran mourning. She shivered in the chill, her furred
cloak fastened high around her throat, garnets and moonstones looking dull in her crow-black hair.

Dione of Mar, with Volan behind her on the right, and
Earla on the left, sat beside the Capran Queen. The Bole
had arrayed Dione hastily in an old mourning garment of
her mother's, but its tarnished silver could not dim her
poignant beauty, serving only to make her white face more
phosphorescent in its clarity, her soft green eyes more
gentle and profound.

Unlike the earthy Capran Queen, the Marin bloomed in
the cool overcast, the chill bringing a faint rose tinge to
her pallor. Over her mourning robes she wore the elaborate
star-wheel wrought for occasions of state: its exquisite fil-
igree circle, studded with moonstones, peridots, sapphires,
and aquamarines for the positions of her stars, hung from
a delicate gray-gold chain thick with the same gems and
with pale pink amethysts, like the breasts of Marin doves.
In her hair was a trident-shaped tiara of the same jewels.

Now from the music barge rose the keen of six-and-
thirty flutes, horn of the sea, the number marking the six-
and-thirty divisions of the races of stars.

In the midst of the flutists stood Anunitum the high
priest of Mar. On his noble head was a wide headdress in
the form of the crescent moon, symbol of Artemis, who
ruled the race of Chiton. The priest was flanked by two
small Crabba acolytes in silver robes, one bearing a branch
of carved abalone, the second a volume covered in mother-
of-pearl from which Anunitum would read the final rites.

Dione of Mar, consoled by the presence of the beloved
Desmos and of Volan and Earla the Bole, sat in an aching
mist of bewilderment and exhaustion. It had all happened
so quickly—she had been whirled without warning back
into the past, yet into a present wholly new and strange.

That morning when the genial servers had returned from
Mar with the intelligence that Desmos' house was shut,
and that her Uncle Chiton was dead, the half-awake Marin
had been rushed from the quiet of the inn, jostled in the
conveyance to the house in Mar.

Succeeding each other with the flash of passing birds were pictures of the somber face of Desmos, greeting her with open arms at the door, the wide brown eyes of Earla the Bole beseeching her forgiveness, and the brief sight of her old chamber, where the Bole removed with wonder the strange Brisen garments and arrayed her in the mourning robes and gems of state.

There had been no time for talk or rest, no moment to attune herself to all the differences—Desmos' married state and the hostile face of his bride, the Queen; the new respect accorded her by Earla; the dim realization that now, as heir with Desmos to her uncle's fortune, she was her own mistress at last.

Most of all there had been no quiet time to grasp the fact of her uncle's death. At first with shame she knew a kind of happiness in her release; now there was only a sad vacancy, a deep exhaustion.

Uneasy, she felt the malevolent stare of her cousin-in-law, the beautiful Shira, and she wondered why the Capran seemed to hate her.

But there was no more time for inner questioning, for the line of barges was nearing the harbor. The polesmen ceased their plowing motion and the barges came to stillness upon the flat, green water.

The six-and-thirty flutists trilled their final cry and then trilled no more. There was little sound except for the soft slapping of water against the boats and the rolling of the sea beyond the harbor.

Anunitum the high priest of Mar took from the acolyte's small oval hands the splendid book and, opening it, began to sing in his graceful Marin the burial service for the Crabba dead.

The words were musical but brief, for the compassionate Marin had no desire to burden the living with protracted expressions of mourning. And when Anunitum's chanting had ended, the Boat of Dissolution, crafted strong to meet the waters of the harbor, moved past the other barges into the bay. The tall towers of Mar, sharp as auger shells and gleaming abalone in the overcast, rose up behind the merchant ships riding at anchor, a small wind billowing their sails of gold and scarlet, of purple and blue and green for the races of the stars. They set no sail this hour in honor of Chiton's farewell. Their silent crews were watchful on their decks.

And the Boat of Dissolution bore the stilled Lord Mayor toward the sea, where twelve strong Crabba gave him to the ever-moving tide.

Ten-dark, the hour of the Peisun, was late for the exhausted little Marin, Desmos thought as he sought out Dione in her water garden.

How like her was the magical enclosure, Desmos reflected, looking upward at its grotto, domed in glass the hues of Mar and thick with massy water vines.

Shira his wife had disdained the garden, remarking sharply that Capra was too chill in Mar to linger out of doors. In any case, he reflected, it was just as well, for the two women did not seem easy together. It was an unhappy thought.

But the Peisun's handsome face broke into a smile when he caught sight of his small cousin, seated on a chair of Celtic marble made like the chariot of Ler, the rounding moon casting soft refractions of pastel color through the water-hued dome.

Volan the minstrel sat near her, strumming his bird-shaped lyre, singing *"Plasir d'Amur"* in the courtly tongue of Brise.

Desmos waited until the last haunting strains of the air had died away, then moved toward Dione, his hands outstretched.

She rose and said, "Oh, Desmos, how good it is to be with you again!" She took his hands.

They sat together on a bench ornamented with shapes of shells. The minstrel, in unobtrusive silence, had sought another part of the garden, thinking to leave them in privacy, and they could hear from the small distance his murmuring instrument blending with the gurgle of blue water in the many ponds.

"Earla," said Dione with tenderness, "has nurtured my creatures with care." Her soft eyes lingered on the grottoes of gem-like peisun.

Desmos squeezed her hand. "How many enchanted days we spent together here in the old years," he responded. "So much has changed."

A wistfulness in his tone caught her delicate inner ear, the other-hearing of the Peisun, and she asked, "Are you happy now, my dear friend?"

"Happy?" He seemed to examine the word, as if it were

strange. "Oh, yes," he said at last with a kind of evasion. "Of course. Does it not seem sad, however, that our uncle has had to die to give us freedom? Now you are free from the shadow of a loveless union . . . and I am free to govern here, as I choose, or to abdicate and go to Erde."

She nodded, distracted from her concern for him by this new train of thought. "But, my dear," she said eagerly, "tell me of Fahne."

And her cousin related all that he knew of the sorcerer—his stay in the castle of Shira, the blackness of his mind, which still, according to his Erden companion, had apparently not lifted, and his life with Bock and Veris.

"And what of you?" he inquired, smiling. "Will you go with us to Erde to meet with Fahne?"

"Yes. Oh, yes. For it matters not whether he knows me at all; the only thing in life that weighs with me now is to see his face, to speak with him, even as . . ."—her voice shook—". . . a friend," she concluded more firmly.

"The cloud will not lie on him forever," Desmos said consolingly. "I felt in him the brightness of a memory of you."

"You did?" Her eyes were alive with hope.

"Yes, I did, truly." And Desmos told Dione of the sorcerer's reaction to the pictured nymph in the tapestry who so resembled her. "You must never cease to hope," he added.

"I shall not, I shall not, no matter what comes." And the little Marin looked at the small peisun flashing in the pools, blue-green and rose and orange and pearl-white by the lantern light.

"We will go, then, the day after tomorrow," said Desmos. "Will that allow you time to see to your feminine concerns?"

She smiled at the affectionate teasing in his voice. "Quite enough time. I cannot rest until I look again on Fahne."

"And what of the son of Melik?"

"How did you know that?" she asked, surprised. "I have told you nothing."

"I guessed, with my brilliant Peisun-colored knowledge," he retorted lightly.

So the Marin told him of Brise, and of the escape of Shabatu, which Desmos lauded. Then he sobered, and he began to say gently, "Dione . . . about Shira . . ."

"Yes?"

"I love her very much," he replied solemnly. "And it will be very sad if you do not love her, as well."

Dione grasped her cousin's hand. "I promise you, my dear, I shall love her."

But, discomfited, the Marin only hoped she could comply, for there had been in the Capran an obscure malice she felt would never be vanquished.

Shira the sensuous Capran hated Mar. The Escors were attractive enough, but the others, with their dreamy eyes and almost womanish gentleness, irritated her beyond endurance. Worst of all, it was agony to be in the presence of the bony little Marin.

That one—the beloved of Fahne! She flamed with indignation and leaned her shining head back against the silver-green nap of the chair in the sunken chamber. And the two of them, skulking in that frozen garden! She would never understand the Marin. Shira stretched out a dainty foot to warm it at the fire.

Except the Escors, she amended, and a sensual smile curved her sullen mouth. They had a fiery look, indeed. And it was said, she ruminated, that they were the only Marin of sufficient steel to drink the wormwood wine, as the Caprans drank their hemlock and yew! There was a certain kinship between the children of the sea goat and the Escors.

She reached to the bloodstone table at the elbow of her chair and picked up her own goblet of yew, tasting its tartness with relish.

For some reason her oblique gaze strayed then to the heavily carved chest fitted to the curving wall and to the beakers and bottles gleaming there. There was quite a selection, she had noted, of the wines and liquors of Erde and Mar—the lunar wines of the Crabba and the weak brews of the Peisun, she thought with contempt; all of the wines of Erde. And there were the scarlet beakers of Escorpiun wormwood.

Thoughtfully, the beautiful Capran rose from her chair, gently placing her goblet on the bloodstone table. With her flame-green velvet gown trailing behind her, she walked slowly to the chest against the wall and examined the scarlet beakers. On each was a small oval tag of pewter, engraved in block letters with the legend WORMWOOD, ONLY FOR ESCORS.

Shira's smile widened. How easy it was, then, to dispose of the damned little interloper, the foolish and fleshless creature that was the subject of his obsession!

Stealthily, the Capran took up a gray beaker of dandelion wine, the Jovian essence that was a favorite of Dione, but which, Shira knew, Desmos did not drink, and poured it into the fire. She looked with blazing eyes into the hissing flames that leaped up, ignited by the wine, and she laughed softly. Then she returned to the chest with the gray beaker and set it down. She was about to take up one of the scarlet decanters when she was startled by the entrance of the broad Bole Earla.

Moving her blunt hand swiftly to a green beaker of yew, Shira heard the Bole cry out, "Oh, Your Majesty!" And she saw the Erden hurrying toward her.

"Touch not the wormwood!" the Bole cried. "It is deadly poison to all but the Escors. I know not why it still remains, in any case," she grumbled. "There has not been an Escor in this house for circles and circles."

She took up the red beakers in her broad hands and bore them from the room. "If Your Majesty requires anything, I shall return at once," she said over her shoulder.

Fuming, the Capran poured herself another glass of yew and returned to the silver-dusted chair.

She had planned to pour the Marin a glass with such a sisterly affection, and now the officious old fool had ruined it all.

But she was not done yet; she was not done with Dione the Marin. For on the day after tomorrow, she would be returning with them to endlich-Erde. And the opportunities would be far greater in the castle.

Earla returned, inquired with deep respect if she wished anything. She shook her head with a mendacious smile that froze on her face when the doors parted again, admitting Desmos and Dione.

"I hope you will be friends," her husband was saying, and Shira submitted to the Marin's kiss on her cheek.

But as Dione's lips touched the Capran's warm white face, she caught sight of Shira's eyes, and her blood turned cold within her.

CHAPTER 2

"Take that!" Sebba the kitchen maid cried with satisfaction as the whisk flattened the offending fly.

"The creatures know that spring is coming," she grumbled to Cife, the castle's chief cook. "The Circle of the Waetergyt always brings them out in droves."

"Here." The broad-faced Cife handed her a piece of string. "Soak this in honey and hang it in the pantry." Then with a gimlet gaze she peered over the shoulders of the kitchen women busy at plucking the birds for the rosée.

"I have told you the chickens must be scalded twice for plucking!" Cife shrieked at an anxious-looking woman, then glared at another who was cutting bacon lard into small squares. "Not small enough!" she snapped.

Cife was the terror of the kitchen women, for every dish that reached the table of Shira the Queen was scrutinized first by her exacting little eyes, set in her broad face with the obliqueness of wings and as hard as onyx.

"Here"—she addressed a third—"peel these almonds and wet them with beef broth. Then you run it through the strainer."

Cife rubbed her blunt hands on her apron and thought: Thank Chronos the Lady Dione is not dining with them tonight! The one fish course would suffice for Sir Desmos.

"Ho, Sebba," she called to the chief kitchen maid, "kindly bring me a glass of cooled sage. My vitals are griping, and it will bring me much relief."

She wiped her moist forehead with a corner of her apron and sank down at a wooden table set apart from the busy women. The table was pallid from long scrubbing; Cife rested her elbows on its smooth wood, sighing.

She nodded her thanks to Sebba when the girl set the glass of sage tea before her and said gruffly, "Sit down a moment."

"You are full of cares this day," Sebba remarked in her softer tone.

Cife nodded her gray-threaded head. "Indeed, I am. Some of these field women are very hard to train. Their hands, forsooth, are like feet."

"It is a heavy task," said Sebba to appease her, "to oversee a repast of thirty-one dishes and to see it served well."

Soothed by the younger woman's sympathy, Cife smiled. "At least Sir Desmos is easy to satisfy, and quick to praise. I think he hardly knows what he eats. I suppose that is the way of the Peisun."

"But, mercy, the Lady Dione! Why, at the dinner a night or two gone, the serving footman said she hardly touched her dish; she only had a pair of chastelettes, and she only picked at the bream."

Cife agreed explosively. "Indeed, indeed! And the care I took over that broth of eels!"

"How the Peisun bear such meats . . ." Sebba's smooth brow wrinkled in her disgust. "Only Chronos knows what the creatures eat themselves, there in the depths of the water."

"She is a kindly lady, though," Cife said more quietly, "not like some others I could name."

Uneasily, the younger woman looked over her shoulder; the chamberlain was passing on his way to the cellars of wine.

Lowering her voice, Sebba leaned to the cook. "Did you hear what the men are saying in the fields?"

Cife shook her black, gray-threaded head and bent her ear to Sebba's mouth with a gleam of anticipation.

Sebba whispered something.

"Nyn!" The older woman's full, shriveled lips remained in an astonished stretched position, holding the syllable.

"Yah," Sebba said with triumph, grinning.

"I must say I am not surprised," Cife commented, belying her recent amazement. "And all above the waist, you say?" she whispered.

"Yah!"

Cife shook her head again with a look of wonder. One of the kitchen women was lingering at her elbow. "Yes, yes, what is it?" Cife asked irascibly.

"Oh, please, madam, please . . ."

"Yah, yah?"

"We have no clove for the rosée."

"Then take the red cedar," Cife answered patiently. "It will serve as well."

The woman withdrew to the cupboards.

"It is said," Cife remarked in a stage whisper, "that the high one abominates the gentle little lady."

"Oh, yes, I had it from the boy of the chamberlain," Sebba replied in an authoritative manner.

"Well, she had better have a care," Cife commented dryly, "when she takes her wine. I would not put it past that one . . ."

Sebba looked shocked. "Do you mean it?"

The cook declared, "Yah, yah, I do, my girl. Now I myself must see to the parboiling of the larks and to the glazed spices. The Queen is very particular about the larks."

Sniffing, her young assistant returned to the straining of her gravy.

"Come," Desmos appealed to the sorcerer, "let us go into the inn for a moment." He was bewildered by Fahne's expression. The Maeden's face showed a mingling of distaste, restraint, and some obscure agony that the Peisun could not comprehend. "You must tell me how I have wronged you, my friend."

Again the Peisun saw that peculiar look of pain on the sorcerer's mouth and wondered at it. Fahne replied, and his words were choked out from deep in his throat, as if they hurt. "Wronged me? You have in no way wronged me. It is I who have wronged you."

"But how?" Desmos cried. "Come in, my friend," he repeated. "This is nothing to be discussed on the public road."

With great unwillingness Fahne followed the Peisun into the smoky depths of the Inn of Bacchus. Desmos looked about him with distaste.

The place was not designed to please either man: the Peisun and the Maeden thrived on peace, and the Bacchus, frequented by the hoof-marked Bole and Capra, was brightly lit and rough with loud voices.

Nevertheless, the Peisun and the sorcerer found a table of comparative quiet, a little apart from the others. Ferum, the landlord of the Bacchus, received them with deep respect but some surprise; unlike the freewheeling society of

Mar, the land of lower Erde was not accustomed to the sight of lords drinking with the workers.

Therefore, it was the landlord himself who served the Peisun and the sorcerer, alive to the strangeness of the situation. When the sturdy Ferum returned to the alcove of meads and wines, he cut short the mumbled question of the server.

"It is not for us to question the ways of the gentry," said Ferum severely.

An ironic-looking Capran at a nearby table overheard. He was leaner and more delicate than most children of the sea goat, and he cocked a satiric black eye in the direction of the sorcerer and Desmos, consort to the Queen.

"Now, my friend," said Desmos when the servile Ferum had set their glasses before them and withdrawn, "can you not tell me why you fled from the castle without a word?"

Fahne took a great gulp of his mandragora and colored. Slowly he framed his reply. "I . . . beg your forgiveness for my precipitate behavior. And I want to give my thanks for all that you have done. But I found it impossible to stay longer in the castle. I am . . . accustomed to the wandering life. It is as simple as that." He smiled miserably. The speech in his own ears sounded very thin and hollow.

He is lying, thought Desmos. But why?

"Very well, my dear friend. You need not ask for my pardon, and gratitude is superfluous for the little I have done."

"We will soon be leaving lower Erde," Fahne said quietly.

"Leaving!" Desmos' apprehension made him cold. Jove! If he left without meeting Dione . . . "You cannot!" he blurted out.

The sorcerer examined the Peisun curiously with his dappled gaze. "Cannot?" he repeated softly, and Desmos head the subtle obduracy of his Escor ascendant, about to assert itself.

Desmos laughed nervously. "Forgive me," he replied. "I meant to say, I beg you not to leave for a little while."

"There is something you wish of me," said Fahne, and it was not a question.

Desmos nodded. "It would sadden me for you to feel that I am laying on you any . . . obligation . . ." he began with discomfort.

"There is nothing you may not ask of me," the sorcerer cut in, and again his disproportionate emotion and his peculiar look of agony and shame mystified the Peisun.

"You are most kind." Desmos paused and looked about him. Then he said softly to Fahne, "There is a foment stirring among the serfs of the estate." And he told the sorcerer all he had learned of it, about his observation of the gathering of men in the fields.

"I am in agreement with their aims, you see." He smiled his crooked Peisun smile that almost seemed a grimace of sorrow, and a dim memory glimmered in the mind of Fahne. "But not with their methods," Desmos went on in his gentle voice. "Their present course will doubtless end in the shedding of blood. I want to find a better way, and find it soon. My wife, of course," he smiled wryly, "will not be easy to convince."

He glanced at Fahne; the sorcerer's face was shut. Suddenly a dim reflection of the truth shone in Desmos' consciousness. Was it possible? he thought, and his limbs chilled and weakened with his suspicion.

Fahne, in his turn, was reliving in full the horror of his betrayal. He could see again quite clearly the seductive form of Shira in her boyish hunting clothes, and then another image, ignited perhaps by the color of her raiment, imposed itself upon that of the Queen: a slender little form in a green, boyish shirt, a weskit, and hose.

The sorcerer's head began to pound and his eyesight blurred. He rested his head in his broad, long-fingered hands.

"What is it?" Desmos inquired gently. "Have you remembered something?"

Fahne did not reply. The pain in his brow was so overwhelming that he was almost paralyzed with it.

Desmos put a sympathetic hand on his forearm and said in a low voice, "The pain." Gonu the Pfarrer had told the Peisun that the onset of such pain was a sign of imminent recall. Desmos, during his circles in Erde, had delved like Fahne into Pfarrer lore and held it in respect.

Fahne made an almost imperceptible gesture of assent. In a moment his face cleared and the Peisun knew that the pain had eased. He said encouragingly, "You know what Gonu said of this."

The sorcerer nodded, but his expression was somber. "Yes. But there is the terrible gray mist still in my mind.

When will it end? I feel that the answer lies away from lower Erde."

Desmos smiled. "Oh, no, my dear friend, the answer lies most surely here in lower Erde." His gentle voice had an almost teasing quality that titillated the Maeden. "But I have no right," Desmos continued, "to burden you with the affairs of the estate."

"On the contrary," said Fahne softly, "you have every right."

And at last Desmos saw it clear: he knew now the reason for the sorcerer's puzzling withdrawal, his pain and shame. And the Peisun's heart ached with pity, for he knew somehow that it had been Shira's doing, that Fahne for all his strength had been a kind of victim.

Fahne, looking back into the Peisun's sad, far-seeing eyes, perceived with his own crystal sight the knowledge of Desmos. And as they parted, Fahne knew that it would never be spoken between them at all. He watched with a kind of weary sadness as the Peisun mounted his graceful gray and took the ascending path to the castle of Shira the Queen. There was a sickness in his very posture. He would never sit upon his mount, thought Fahne, with quite the same familiar pride again.

The weakness of the man was so severe that his limbs could not support him. They had brought him to the sorcerer upon a pallet, and he bade them place the pallet on the tongue of the wagon. Fahne felt the slow-beating wings of the man's pulse at his wrists and throat, examining his eyes and tongue and the color of his skin.

The sorcerer gave him potions made from camomile and melilot. Then he asked Veris and Bock to make a charcoal fire the length of the sufferer. In the fire he placed many herbs, and when the coals had cooled a little, he caused the man to lie upon the warm coals until he began to sweat heavily.

In a while they wrapped him again in a cloth of clean linen and lay him back on his pallet. Already the motions of the man's limbs were easier, and strong.

"By the morrow he will be upright," said Fahne to the invalid's grateful daughter. "I can see no more folk for a time," he said then quietly to Veris, "unless there is great pain or illness."

The Bole nodded, for indeed the sorcerer's skin was

pallid with exhaustion, and from time to time he put his long-fingered hand to his own brow as if he suffered.

"Shall I bring you some marjoram?" Veris asked.

"I have taken it. I must be still for an interval. I shall return before the hour is gone."

"Do not make haste," said the Bole gently. "Bock and I can no doubt care for them."

"I will be a little way into the woods if I am needed," Fahne said.

It was with a sense of deep relief that he found the quiet pond inside the circle of trees. He had never visited the spot so early in the day. The sun was high, and its warm rays misted the air above the murmuring pool with gold, catching the iridescent wings of the dragonflies that hovered over the water. The color of them, a brilliant blue-green that the peacocks wore, reminded Fahne so forcibly of something that his head began to pound again. The terrible ache of remembering was upon him, soothed no more by the balm of the marjoram.

He threw himself down full-length in the warming sun by the pool of ugly little peisun, almost welcoming the agony hammering at his broad temples; in these haunted, solitary days such pain was almost sweetness, for it heralded sometimes the ghostly visit of the woman in his dream.

Fahne's eyes pained him, too, but he opened them with effort to look down at the crystal star in the center of his caduceus medallion. Yes! Yes, even now, in the brilliant noon sun of the Erden Waetergyt, the star gave forth not a diamantine glitter, but a variegated glow of colors like the wings of the dragonflies.

He closed his eyes again, cradling the star between his finger and his thumb, reflecting. She must be a Marin, then, for although he had not seen her face, he could clearly remember that particular night-like sheen of her hair, with its highlights of rose and purple, like the wings; the color of the Marin's hair. And her little hands, he recalled, had had that unmistakable oval shape with the padded softness below the thumb that bespoke the exaltation of Aphrodite.

And Aphrodite was exalted in the Peisun.

The sorcerer felt a tiny, whirring weight upon his outstretched arm. He lay quite still, not expelling even a breath, and opened his eyes again: a dragonfly had settled upon his teal-blue sleeve. He smiled, thinking, I am a dry pool, a shriveled leaf for such a lovely friend to land upon. Again he was pleased by the beauty of its glozed, transparent wings.

A dress! The memory came so sharply that he made an involuntary movement and the dragonfly whirred away. The flaming blue-green color of a dress, he mused . . . and a bed of red and golden leaves that he could almost hear crackling beneath him.

Crackling: the colored leaves made such a sound only in the autumn circles . . . in Erde. Or Erdemar!

The colors of the crystal star seemed to whirl, and dizzily Fahne closed his eyes and saw her, above him, on a chestnut colored horse. But he still could not discern her face; the sun was behind her in a great golden aura whose jagged rays reflected outward from her shining head.

And he was lifting her down from the steed, very gently, feeling his hard flesh seek the melting softness of her below the softness of the peacock-colored gown. Her neck above the high-cowled collar was very white, made even whiter by the vivid hue of the gown. When she slid down from the mount into his embrace, he held her hard, her down-soft breasts crushing into his chest.

His lips met first the top of her shining head and tasted her sun-warmed hair, which smelled of water lilies and the gillyflower. He kissed its satin, sun-bright darkness, and then she turned up her face so that he might kiss her on the mouth. He closed his eyes and savored deeply her tender mouth with his opened lips for a long, still interval.

Then he cried out some beseeching word that even he did not recognize, and still with half-shuttered eyes he began to unfasten the neck of the dragonfly gown. And she was a blinding, phosphorescent whiteness against the gold and scarlet leaves.

From that moment Fahne saw no more; his lids were shuttered, but the iris of his fingers and his flesh and tongue discerned the present magic. He felt the color of the autumn sun upon his body, knew the fragrance of her lights and shadows, and tasted her fragility.

Now in the lucid magic of his body's vision, the hungry sorcerer once more was nourished; his distance from her narrowed, narrowed, and was closed. He gave himself to the enormity of his release, hearing her share in it, feeling her exquisitely near.

He fell asleep to the sound of the dragonflies over the murmuring water, his breath so light he could barely hear, with the earth-hearing of the mittel-Erden, the tiny popping sound of the insect-seeking peisun on the surface of the pool.

The voice of Veris awoke him from the black depths of his dreamless slumber.

"A message," the Bole was saying quietly into his ear, "a message from Desmos, the consort of the Queen."

Blinking, the sorcerer took the Peisun-sealed missive from Veris and read it with an impassive face.

"We plan to go on to upper Erde tomorrow," said the Bole. "Will you be going?"

"Not yet," Fahne replied.

"The message, then, prevents you."

"No. No, this is of no great moment. It is only a request to visit the Lady Dione."

The Bole restrained his expression.

"There is a matter in which Desmos requires my help," Fahne continued. "I will stay at the inn for a while."

"Of no great moment!" Veris repeated silently as they left the woods, remembering the sorcerer's words in the tavern of Mar. How much had changed, he meditated with sadness.

CHAPTER 3

One-light in the city of Alioure on a certain day of declining winter, the birthday of Shabatu, was a brilliant hour. The round-domed towers wrought of Hermes-glass reflected the snow-bearing clouds of the Circle of the Waetergyt and the lilac birds of highest air. In the clarity of the risen day, the ice-streets flashed and hummed with a multitude of fleet, pale-raimented Twisan, and the few travelers—the silver-haired Waetergyt from dernier-Brise, and a random Sabbian whose flaming hair was a startling cry of color in the pale glow of Alioure. It was generally the

equinoctial Ramm, or the active Kani, fated opposite to
the fleet Twisan, who came to the glittering place. The
Bilance of moyen-Brise found the pace too swift, and the
proud, stately Leun of Sabbia did not enjoy the perilous
means of transport in the streets; the bladed shoes upset
their sense of dignity.

Therefore, there were none of these on the glassy streets
this gleaming hour as Shabatu and Gemelle skated lightly
toward the house of the seller of gems. And yet, although
their coloring was very like those about them, and their
raiment was extraordinary in no way, the people stared at
the slender couple flashing by: the pure white gown and
cloak of Shabatu and the clear yellow clothes of the
Twisan that matched exactly the yellow of his hair lent
them such a brightness that they seemed to the passersby a
prince and princess from a fairy tale.

Gemelle's bladed shoes were of silver-gilt, and Shabatu's
of Hermes-glass. They both were gliding with such grace
and their clothes had such a flowing freshness that it was
not extravagant to compare them with wind-driven birds
or great clear flowers detached from their stems and
carried along in the breeze. They skated impudently in the
street.

The Twisan took his wife's gloved hand and steered her
skillfully around a horse-drawn sleigh; she laughed mer-
rily at the shocked expression of the lady passenger. It was
the Duchess.

When Gemelle saw who it was, his loud laughter joined
Shabatu's, and he turned with her to glide onto the skating-way that led to the gem seller's house.

But he was arrested by a low cry from the lovely Waetergyt. Gemelle turned his head with inquiring sharpness
and saw in his wife's remote blue eyes a look of fear. She
was staring down the skating-way at the figure of an approaching man. He was wearing the gray-blue garments of
dernier-Brise, and on his breast was the crest of Melik.

"It is one of my father's men!" said Shabatu to Gemelle
in a stricken voice. The Twisan held her hand more tightly
and replied with urgency, "Let us make haste."

But it was too late, for the server had sighted them and
was gliding swiftly toward them with the competent but
awkward glide of the stranger to Alioure.

"My lady!" the man cried.

The Twisan and Shabatu waited with a desolate air for

the man to draw near. "You have come to fetch me back," said the Waetergyt coldly. "Well, you may tell my father I will not come."

The man's face was somber. "My lady, your father the Baron Melik is dead. I have come at the request of Lord Uras to summon you to the Baron's farewell and to give you this letter." With a nod of respect, the man handed her the gray letter with its silver seal of the eagle, the signature of Uras. And he glided away.

The Waetergyt was trembling so that she let the missive fall from her gloved hands onto the shining ice. Without letting go of her hand, Gemelle bent down with his customary ease and retrieved it.

"Come," he said tenderly, noting her stunned, helpless posture. Gemelle tucked the missive into a recess of his yellow cloak and urged her on with a gentle pressure of the hand. "Are you cold?" he asked softly.

She shook her hooded head without expression.

Receiving her reply, Gemelle led her more slowly down the skating-way into a little wooded park furnished with benches of crystal and Hermes-glass under trees leaved in vegetation that resembled white, feathery fronds.

Choosing one in an isolated spot, Gemelle guided Shabatu to the bench and said, "Sit down, my dear."

Limply, the Waetergyt obeyed. Her expression was still blank, her remote eyes staring before her, unseeing.

"I have slain my father," she said in a cool, monotonous tone that brought bumps to the Twisan's flesh.

"Nonsense," he said, purposely offhand and brusque with a desire to restore her balance. Then, with more gentleness, he added, "You have not read Uras' letter."

With a tremble in her voice that reassured Gemelle as a sign of returning emotion, she said, "Read it to me, please, my beloved."

The Twisan held tightly to her hand with one of his; with the other, he adroitly worked open the flap of the missive and snapped out the page to its full length.

Hesitating over the narrow hand of Uras, the Twisan began to read in silver, unaccented dernier-Brisen:

My dearest sister,
Our father the Baron Melik is dead at the hands of Nobilis . . .

Shabatu gasped. Gemelle tightened his hold on her hand, and said softly, "No, wait, wait."

He read on:

. . . but not through purpose. Our father attempted to intervene at the tilting meet of Nobilis and Solidago; riding between them, he was pierced with the lance of the Sabbian. His death, however, was caused by me. Riding behind him, I was not swift enough to stop him before he was slain by Nobilis' accidental thrust. The Sabbian was truly grieved by the dreadful act, and the battle between him and Solidago ceased forever.

If there be any comfort in it, let your comfort be that our father's death appears to have ensured the peace between the lands of Brise and Sabbia. For the old King Achir, who will journey to the castle for the final rites, advises me that his son's monstrous error has greatly subdued him. Solidago likewise bears a heavy burden of guilt for his part in the affair.

The ceremony of farewell is being planned for a week hence to allow you sufficient time to return from Alioure. I have known, my dear, for some time of your marriage to Gemelle and approve it thoroughly. I fear that it was my deception that kept your father from knowing where you were; I am still of the mind that it was the right course. When your husband returns with you, I will make him aware that the castle is also his home.

My dear sister, I hope that my bluntness has not offended your delicate nerves. But I have always believed that plain speaking in matters of such import is far kinder than the vulgar circumlocutions of those such as the moyen-Brise, whose hesitancy to reach the point cruelly prolongs suspense.

I pray you are well, and I send you my love.

The letter was signed simply "Uras" in a bold, eccentric hand. Gemelle took his hand away from Shabatu's for a moment, and folding the letter, he thrust it into his cloak. Then he enfolded the frail Waetergyt in his arms. "Shall we return to the inn and begin to prepare for our journey?"

She nodded. He helped her rise, and they glided slowly

from the small park of feathery trees back onto the gleaming ice-streets of Alioure.

Glancing at Gemelle, Shabatu saw him gazing at its mirror brightness with regret.

"We shall return," she said gently, but he only smiled at her without an answer.

Dabih the chief steward of the estate crossed the gleaming checkerboard of the entranceway, his soft shoes soundless on the flame-green and black of the tiles. Annoyed and puzzled, he wondered at this summons.

Shira the Queen, and Monoceros and Icorn before her, had always given the steward a free hand with the slaves, and Dabih had done well. He saw no reason why there should be a change in this late year.

He followed the announcing footman down the vaulted corridor. The bright morning of the Circle of the Waetergyt blazed through the high, square windows, brilliant on the green marble and the black granite of the floor. The footman opened the massive doors of the council room and bade him enter.

Desmos the Peisun was seated at the great central table. "Good morrow." He smiled, greeting Dabih with easy friendliness.

That was another thing, the Capran reflected; it was not seemly for the consort of the Queen to accept him so familiarly! Nevertheless, Dabih replied with warmth to the Peisun's address, standing before him.

"Sit down, sit down," Desmos said a little brusquely. The man's stubborn servility half-annoyed, half-amused him. "I have several things of import to discuss with you."

With awkwardness the steward pulled out a high-backed chair opposite the Peisun and sat down in it.

Desmos took up a long sheet from a sheaf upon the table and thrust it at Dabih. "You will have this, and others like it, posted around the estate," he said.

The steward, proud of his status as a lettered man, began to read the notice.

The Peisun laughed, observing his expression of shock, and his black brows raised so high they almost reached his thatch of night-black hair. "Read it, Dabih," said Desmos. "Read it aloud."

And Dabih obeyed, but haltingly, for he was unaccustomed to such an exercise.

"It is hereby proclaimed, by the order of the Queen, that the laboring day of each man and each woman upon these lands shall be shorter by six lights, or hours; that the egg- and chicken-rent due to the castle shall be no more required."

"Why, my lord," Dabih blurted out, "this is madness! This is by the order of the Queen?"

Desmos frowned darkly. "The Queen has delegated me to conduct the business of the estate," he said with severity. "Do you call it 'madness,' Dabih, to show compassion and justice to your fellow creatures, and to allow them to enjoy some of their labor's fruits?"

The steward colored. "I beg your pardon, sire, for my outburst. But this proclamation is . . . is most unreasonable."

Desmos asked curtly, ignoring Dabih's comment, "Is it true, what I have been told—that there are lettered men enough upon the lands to read this paper and to spread its fame among the men?"

"Yes, sire, there are. There are six lettered understewards, and the . . . friend of the late Prince Monoceros, a man called Sir Mahar, who has been appointed royal chamberlain."

"I know the man Mahar," said Desmos with distaste. "This afternoon please bring them all to me, so we may plan the dissemination of this news to the people."

"Sire, I . . ."

"What is it, Dabih?" the Peisun asked impatiently. "If the task is abhorrent to you, perhaps one of the understewards would be willing to relieve you of your duties." Desmos felt his irritation rising.

Subdued, the Capran steward nodded, then replied, "Very well, my lord."

"At two-light, then," said Desmos, "the hour of the Escorpiun."

Dabih bowed his head and left the chamber, raging silently. How generous he is, the steward thought, with the tributes that belong to me!

In the dark of lower Erde the Waetergyt's near-spring was somewhat chill. The twelve men in the cave muttered impatiently among themselves and some of them stretched out their blunt hands to the lantern flames for warmth.

Therefore, they started eagerly when they heard the light footsteps at the cavern's mouth. "It is Mahar," one said, and the men rose.

A slender, sly-faced Capran in the soft green clothes of a lord, with the motions of a gazelle, was picking his way among the rocks.

"I wish you good dark," he called softly, "and I crave your pardon for my lateness, but I have brought you news of some import." He came into the light and withdrew from his cloak a long ivory-colored scroll. "But first," he said smiling, "I bid you take some drink." And from another recess of his cloak he drew out a leather-covered bottle and passed it to one of the men.

The man uncorked the bottle and drank from it, tasting the welcome tartness of hemlock.

Mollified by the unprecedented courtesies, the other men drank in their turn and settled down to listen to Mahar.

The man with the ironic face drew nearer to one of the lanterns and unrolled the ivory-colored paper. None of the men around him was a lettered man, and they watched with respect as he held the paper closer to the light and began to read in his brassy voice.

When he had concluded and looked up with an expression of triumph, there was an angry muttering among the others.

"So you see, it is as I promised," said Mahar. "The whore has appointed an even greater tyrant in her place, the Peisun Desmos, who wishes to take from you even greater rents, and orders that you labor even beyond the dark, robbing you of the little rest you now can snatch from the endless days. And in his villainy he has caused these proclamations of deceit to be shown around the estate, with their lying words for the lettered stewards to read to you as truth."

Again there was a growling murmur from the listeners.

"Are we to allow this whore to bleed you and your faithful wives, to take from your children what little they have now? This jade who has made the two-backed beast with Rikku in the fields, for the whole land to know, and who lies on silk while your chaste, faithful women are the property of any lord, and who labor with their sweat from five-light until the dark, and past it, to be rewarded with beds so harsh that their skins are chafed by them?"

The eloquence of the sly young lord had heated a feverish ire in his hearers. One cried out, "The whore must be driven out . . . and the Peisun tyrant with her!"

"Yah!" another shouted, then another.

"We are together, then!" cried Mahar. "She shall be driven out of endlich-Erde—before the end of the Waetergyt!"

"Before the ending of the Waetergyt!" The shouting of the twelve, the serfs who had been made Mahar's Committee of the People, rang out in the flickering dim of the isolated cavern.

And as they dispersed, Mahar thought with triumph: And at the rising of the Peisun, I will occupy the castle of the whore.

On the wall above the old man's poplar table, the fire's refractions glimmered on an image of a sea goat sprouting wings.

Orn the second Pfarrer, seated beside Gonu at the table, watched the old man's busy quill race across the vellum.

Orn's face was alight. He was many years younger than the other man, but he wore the same voluminous robes sewn of the coats of hoofed creatures, and around his neck on a lusterless chain was a replica of the winged sea goat on the wall. On his head was the crown of the Pfarren, fashioned also of skins, in the shape of a square, the symbol of earth. His long, coarse hair, hanging in ragged curls, was dark, whereas the hair of the other man was the color of trodden snow.

Suddenly Gonu's quill paused and he said, "It is done."

Orn was silent, his heart beating with high excitement.

"It is fitting," said Gonu, "that this historic proclamation will be made as the year's dying night gives way to the morning of renewal. This is the summation of all our dreams and hopes, of the centuries of our trauminition.

"You have seen the young Peisun from Mar, with the green gaze and the compassionate face, so gently wresting from the Queen her cruel power. And you have seen him learning our beliefs, so cousined to the other-seeing of the Peisun."

Gonu smiled at Orn. "And now this proclamation will bring new hope and freedom to the people."

The younger man returned the high priest's smile, but there was a question in his oblique black eyes, like Gonu's, more profound than those of the other Caprans.

"But, Your Grace," he asked softly, "what of Shira's armies and their power?"

"You may well ask, my *zahne,* my son. But the number of the slaves is even greater than the number of the soldiers; the very greatness of their number can withstand the forces of Shira. Besides, the soldiers grow slack and drunken, fat with idleness." The old man smiled. "The marriage of the Queen to Desmos has diverted Erde from war upon that nation; and now the bruited peace of Sabbia and moyen-Brise leaves the Erden with no partners to aggression. The army sleeps," Gonu concluded with satisfaction.

"And the people," said Orn, "are toughened from their labor in the fields."

Gonu nodded. "And driven by the fires of their passion for freedom."

"I pray, Your Grace, that you are right," said Orn, sighing.

The old man closed his eyes an instant.

"You must rest," Orn said sternly.

"I shall rest far longer soon," the old man returned sadly. "And you will rule the Pfarren in my stead. For now we must use guile with the Queen. We must pretend that we no longer resist the ancient injustices of endlich-Erde. We will swear our fealty. And all the while we will press our holy aims.

"Remember, Orn, the goat has the tail of a fish, and the fish has wings: the shining scales are the sigil of evasion, joined with the goat of earthly endurance, and wings for our aspiration to ascend."

The old man looked very weary. Again Orn protested that he should rest.

"Not yet," said Gonu. "Bring me my book, Orn. I want to hold it for you to vow upon."

Orn went to a table by the high priest's bed and took up a massive kid-bound book, worn thin through years of loving touch, and handed it to Gonu.

"Vow," the old man said to Orn. "Should my end come, I ask you to vow to carry on the purpose of the Pfarren and of the liberator Desmos."

Orn laid his square, blunt-fingered hand on the ancient book. "I vow," he said softly, "I vow to you, Father Gonu."

Gonu sighed with relief and said, "Now go to your bed, and sweet fortune."

When the younger man had withdrawn from the chamber, Gonu the highest Pfarrer read again the words he had written with great satisfaction, the proclamation freeing the bound people of lower Erde.

CHAPTER 4

"Why, it is hardly bigger than a servant's house," Earla the Bole had said indignantly.

Dione of Mar, smiling, had replied, "Surely it is at least as big as a burgomeister's." The little house that Desmos had found for them had been vacated by just such an official, and it would easily accommodate the Marin, Earla, Volan, the little maid, and the two stout ushers, a Crabba and a Bole, retained for their protection.

The Marin gloried in the little house; its dark beams were rich and lustrous, its appointments warm and welcoming. Earla the Bole went about with an air of dignity offended and status lost; she was used to the multitudinous servers in the palace of Chiton, and she constantly bemoaned its imminent decay without her supervision.

"If it pains you," said Dione with mischief, "to be so long from Mar, I give you leave to return."

The Bole threw up her broad hands in a gesture of horror. "And leave you unattended in a house of three men! What would the Queen ever say?"

Volan thought dryly that the Queen would like nothing better than a household of men, but he refrained from saying so. He grinned at the Marin, and she happily went about her tasks of arranging the little house and supervising the renewal of the garden with the aid of servers from the castle.

Very quickly she familiarized herself with the flowers and herbs that grew in the modest garden and in the surrounding meadows. With delight, she filled the rooms with the blossoms alien to Mar, some of which she had discovered during the brief golden time that she and Fahne had lived in the borderland—the clove-scented gillyflower and the bluebells, whose color sang to her of the Maeden, the amaranth and black poppy, the latter of an incredible dark scarlet and native only to lower Erde.

This afternoon in the drowsy warmth of the rising spring of February Waetergyt, Dione was sitting with the minstrel in the small, square main chamber, before the open door, looking out on the long brown fields and greening meadows when she saw the visitor so long awaited.

She saw the sorcerer approaching, followed by her cousin Desmos. And in a flash of remembrance she knew she was living again the dream of the temple, the night she had awakened to the news that Fahne was gone.

The men were passing now through her little garden; in its center was a fountain, and in the middle of the rushing water was a small column, whole and firm, the perfect structure, rising above a dolphin's form—emblems of love and the sea.

And she saw the sorcerer's glance pause on the dolphined column and the singing fountain, and a singing rose in her that she had made the garden and the little house for him, although she was still to him a mist within his mind.

Dione heard the Peisun's gentle voice say her name and replied with calm as she nourished her starved eyes on the tall, lean figure of Fahne.

And in the beloved face, as Desmos had warned, she saw no hint of recognition, no fire in the dappled eyes that once had been so full of her, only the blank warmth of a companion's companion.

Desmos was saying, "The Lady Dione, my cousin and my friend."

And all the while the Marin felt her pulse beating in her ears like the pulsing of the fountain. Fahne still did not know her.

Amazed that her speech was so serene, Dione greeted them and asked them to be seated, moving to a chest along the wall that held the beakers of Erden and Marin wines.

The sorcerer moved forward with an absent air that she had never seen in him, and there was in him a blankness and a seeking, as if he were a man half-blinded by the sun that gilded the little room.

Hardly knowing what she did, Dione poured out the valley-lily for the sorcerer in a glass of blue, strawberry for Desmos and dandelion for herself in green goblets, and a blue glass of lavender for Volan.

Then somehow Volan was seated on a small stool at her feet, and the time was very like her dream: Fahne looked about the chamber, which was a subtle blend of the symbols and hues of Erde and Mar—the browns had a tinge of green, the greens of bronze, like a woodland stream or the sea bronzed by the sun—that she had devised to signify their bonds. And it seemed to Dione that the faintest glimmer of recognition touched his eyes.

Their blended star-wheels hung like a talisman over the low entrance door. On a small table at her elbow, covered with a sapphire-hued cloth, was an arrangement of acanthus, symbol of the mittel-Erden's tenderness for lowly things, and glowing apples, for the savor of earthly desires.

And Volan began to play his cithara, singing in his silver tenor an air she had made for Fahne in some far interval of solitude, comparing the sorcerer's eyes with the dappled ones of a cat, looking at her from "the same Egyptian irises."

Fahne seemed to listen with care to the delicate words, and then she saw that he was staring with pity on the maimed hands of Volan. Her heart leaped at this familiar dearness of his temper, and she blessed the quiet bond of their companionship. The Peisun and the Maeden both looked with distaste upon those who chattered during music, and the interval gave her the leisure to feel the sorcerer's unchanged air. In him and still strong—despite his mind's darkness—were the qualities that always soothed her body's fires—the passion of the Kani, the Sabbian horseman of quicksand and magic; the Capran earth that ever coiled in her the ancient serpent of desire; the enchanted stillness of the Escor that saw; and greatest of all, the magnet of the Maeden, her opposition and her fate. Withal, he did not know her!

At the conclusion of the song, Dione remarked in a shy way on his friendship with her cousin. It seemed to her heated fancy that she caressed Fahne with her speech, and that he felt it, too; his dappled eyes took on a glow. But with the glow she saw a look of deeper puzzlement that tore at her heart.

"You must be very close to him," said Fahne.

Dione heard his words with surprise and she trembled in the profoundness of his stare, recalling similar words she had said to him in her garden during Maeden Circle last.

"Why must I be?" she asked him gently.

He hesitated a moment, then blurted out, "Because I am cousined to you both."

"Cousined?" she repeated, and she glanced at Desmos. His green eyes were alight, yet he made an almost imperceptible warning motion with his head. And she remembered the warnings of Gonu: to press the sorcerer to remembrance could unseat his reason.

She moved nervously and in doing so pulled awry the collar of her peacock-colored gown, revealing the glittering little star resting on its delicate chain in the hollow of her throat.

The sorcerer exclaimed, staring at the medallion.

And Dione knew then that the star would be the key to unlocking their distance.

Desmos began a desultory conversation with the sorcerer, and the Marin was free to feed her long-starved sight. She felt that the very breast of her gown must be leaping with her leaping heart. And she fought for calm, staring at Fahne's familiar, hollow-cheeked face, at the hawk-like nose, above his full mouth, with its long golden-brown moustache. She trembled to remember the magic of that mouth.

And his eyes! She had not seen them so hungry or so deep, not even in the quiet wood of Erdemar, when he had looked up at her, perched on the back of Merddyn, waiting to be lifted down.

Then she came back to the moment, for Fahne, turning from the view of the little garden, was addressing her. ". . . the land of infancy," he was saying, " 'the fountain in the center of the garden of the self.' "

Dione made a vague reply, regretting her absence of mind, but she had been so bemused by the sound of his loved voice that she had ceased to listen to the sense.

"Your garden is 'temenos,' " he said, "the ancients' name for the hallowed place that gives you strength."

And dizzy, the Marin heard the dream within the dream, the selfsame phrases he had used in the water garden on the night of their first fatal tryst.

"Desmos has told you my secrets," she said and smiled.

Fahne nodded and smiled in reply, but his eyes still looked at her through the mist that separated them. And she felt again, weakly, the almost palpable magnet of him, and she leaned in his direction as if he pulled her on a fragile tether.

Her eyes studied the firm, hard splendor of his arms, his torso, his mighty leanness, thinking for the hundredth time: He is like the quercus tree.

A faint brightness lit Fahne's eyes. His glance fell on a corner of the sun-flooded room, in which there was a peculiar alcove with the tools of the alchemist—the beakers and pans, cucurbits and other occult objects. Dione had arranged it so to remind herself of his cellar room in the hidden house.

The sorcerer's glance moved to the table at her elbow covered in sapphire-blue, the Maeden color of heavenly reward, with its bowl of acanthus and scarlet apples.

Her heart lurched within her. Would he understand the symbolism of the little display? But he had picked up a gilt-chased book lying by the bowl of apples and was caressing its ancient leather with his long-fingered healer's hands.

He asked with eagerness, "My lady has an interest in alchemy . . . or is it the pursuit of another in your house?"

Blessing Uras and Shabatu, Dione replied with joy, "The interest is mine."

"It is an uncommon taste for a lady."

"My cousin is an uncommon lady," Desmos returned with a conspiratorial look of affection at Dione.

The book that Fahne held was a translation of the celebrated *Tabula Smaragdina,* the *Emerald Table* of alchemical dogma ascribed to the ancients' Thoth, the great god Hermes who ruled the race of Fahne.

And the Marin was deeply stirred by the connection. The myrrh and samphire of his blood smoldered to her excited sense; she caressed the silk and ivories of the Oriens, and she heard again the small gold bells of swarthy places. She remembered when he had called himself a "gypsy," and her body heated with the memory. And the Marin knew that always and forever, if he never knew her face again, he would burn within her like a flame of green, burning away her lust for any other. And she spoke in her silence the very phrase he had spoken in the dreamed water garden on the autumn night, the words she had held to herself so long in her loneliness.

"It is exquisite," he said, "that you possess this table of Thoth."

She looked up at him, towering above her, his craggy face joyful in the golden hour of the Waetergyt, almost as warm as Marin summer. She saw his pulse beat below his ear, and she remembered kissing him there.

The hour that struck was the twelve-of-day, the time of Capra that no longer filled her with dread. And the sunny light gilded the sorcerer's tawny hair and magnified the dappled colors of his eyes, which blended the hues of Mar and Erde, of Sabbia and Brise.

He opened the ancient book and read while the minstrel's cithara rippled like the water of the fountain. " 'Thus thou wilt possess the glory of the brightness of the whole world, and all obscurity shall fly far from thee.' "

Fahne looked up from the page and exchanged a bright glance with Desmos, repeating, " 'and all obscurity shall fly far from thee.' "

There was such hope in his tone that the Marin felt a glow of wild hope in her own breast.

Then Fahne said to her with a strange urgency, "Thank you, my lady, thank you for having this book." And he laid the volume on the table. This time his eyes lingered on the blue cloth, noting the significant bowl of apples and acanthus.

He took her small hand in his and raised it to his lips.

Dione felt her vitals stir and fought for calm, not daring to look into the eyes of Fahne. But she saw that Desmos' gentle face was full of compassion, and she knew that he dreamed, as she did, that the cold spell would soon be lifted and all would be what it had been so long ago.

"Have I my lady's leave," Fahne asked, and she could not help smiling at his eager air, "to examine the alcove?"

"Please," she replied softly. "I would be glad if you would practice there yourself." Catching his puzzled look, she added quickly, "Desmos tells me you are familiar with the art."

The tall man said, "You are very kind."

And he wandered to the alcove, taking delicately into his hands in turn a flask, an alembic, and a double pelican, examining them and setting them down again with little sound.

"These have the look of Brise," he said to Desmos, and the Peisun marveled at the riches of his knowledge.

"They are from dernier-Brise," Dione replied, exchanging a glance with her cousin. She knew that Desmos was thinking as she was, that perhaps the mention of Brise would ring a memory of Gemelle.

But the sorcerer did not pursue the matter, saying instead to the Marin, "I trust that you have heard that books, though splendid, are inadequate—that the rest in alchemy is oral teaching. One must be especially blessed. You were born under a very suitable star."

He smiled a little, as if to mock his pedantic tone, and looked up at the entwined star-wheels above the door.

Suddenly Desmos said sharply, "Fahne! Do you know what you have said?"

The sorcerer, bewildered, stared at Desmos.

"How did you learn these things? From whom?" Desmos cried eagerly.

"I do not know," Fahne replied sadly, and an incipient fire in his eyes was quenched. But he looked again at the entwined star-wheels and Dione's heart began to hammer.

"The Peisun wheel is yours, of course . . . and the Maeden?"

He did not know, then, his own star-wheel! Fahne, mistaking her pain for offense, begged her pardon for his intrusive question.

The Marin feared that soon her calm would shatter, that she would tear from her face this bland mask that Desmos had bidden her to wear, and cry out to Fahne who was the center of her world.

Yet this was the only way, so she answered quietly, "No friend of Desmos could intrude in any way. The Maeden wheel is that of someone . . . most beloved."

Desmos sought to rescue her, for he saw that her sadly smiling mouth, widened into the Peisun smile that was almost a grimace of pain, was trembling perilously.

"Volan," Desmos said hurriedly, "sing us one of Dione's airs."

But the minstrel was of no aid, for he had been dreaming and was taken by surprise. By ill fortune he raised his narrow tenor in another song to Fahne:

"When first your quicksand drew my body down,
And Hermes' light lay silver on the sea,
The hues of Mar were pallid on my gown,
And Erden horning summoned you to me."

Dione heard her own soft outcry of pain and put her white oval hand to her mouth.

The sorcerer, torn between the patterns of courtesy and his desire to take her in his arms, stared helplessly upon her without speaking.

At last he said, "I fear we have wearied you," but his dappled eyes, locking with hers, said more. And in her soft green look the sorcerer saw a fatal greeting.

In great confusion he rose and went to the little Marin. He looked down for a long moment on her glowing black hair and her white face, with its open, childlike look, its pallor in stark contrast to the peacock-colored gown. He took her hand, and something in its silken texture, in the look of her eyes and the vivid color of the gown, reminded him very strongly of another hour.

He felt the warning arrow of pain in his brow: they must hasten their departure, he reflected, for he did not want to appear ill and wan before this lady. He looked appealingly at Desmos.

The Peisun rose, too, and Dione to her dismay heard herself crying out, "No! No, do not go!" Shamed, she elided her tone into a social protest, "Do not go so soon," she said more quietly.

But the sorcerer's crystal sight had caught her air of disproportionate emotion. He felt his breast warm with a peculiar, excited tenderness.

At last, with her voice in control, Dione rose and went with them to the open door. "I hope," she said blandly to the sorcerer, "that you and my cousin will soon return." Then with more warmth, she added, "It would please me for you to make free with the little laboratory."

Fahne, who had not been deceived by her earlier inflection, leaned and kissed her small hand, looking deeply once more into her eyes.

She swayed, as if dizzy from entering their depths, and managed to smile as she watched them leave the little house and depart through the garden.

Dione saw the sorcerer look away for an instant from

Desmos at the form of the dolphin and the fountain, and she heard him murmur something to her cousin.

When they reached the end of the path, the two men turned and Desmos waved to his cousin. When he looked at Fahne, the sorcerer was staring at the little figure in the doorway with an expression that embodied many warring feelings—Desmos saw bewilderment and joy, conflict and peace, and something the color of hope.

"What do you think of my cousin?" asked Desmos casually.

Fahne replied with a kind of slow care, "She is the most beautiful lady I have ever seen. And there is a quality in her . . ." He paused and threw up his hands, finding it impossible to express.

As they walked down the long path toward the meadow, the sorcerer asked with painful shyness, "How is it that . . . such a lady is alone?"

Desmos paused, choosing his words with extreme caution. "She is . . . waiting."

"For whom?"

"For a . . . moment of revelation." How difficult it was! Desmos thought.

But he realized that his answer had been the happy one, for Fahne's brow cleared; it was as if a burden of apprehension had been lifted from him. However, his puzzlement remained, and the sensitive Peisun saw it clearly: the sorcerer's loyalties were in conflict, between the woman of his dreaming, whose presence he had shared with Desmos, and the lovely white lady in the little house, the soft lady in the peacock-colored gown.

CHAPTER 5

Fomalhaut the acting Lord Mayor of Mar looked up at the slaty sky and felt the small rain of February Waetergyt, the gentling of winter, and he smiled. Peace was in the air: this day would mark the welcoming of the Escorpiun. Like all the cloud-loving Marin, the Peisun Fomalhaut reacted with brighter spirits to the mist that veiled the auger-sharp towers of the gleaming city and nourished the calm waters that bore the omnipresent barges.

He pondered for a moment the missive from Desmos in endlich-Erde. How quixotic of his friend, thought Fomalhaut, to be plotting such revolutionary change! But all would be well, he consoled himself; Desmos would come to sense and the calm of their lands would continue unabated. For he knew his friend. Fomalhaut smiled. It would not be long before Desmos would be seduced by the Marin need of him back to his rightful place, and his dream of a rebellion would be abandoned.

Fomalhaut's compassionate eyes turned to the oval arch above him; he was entering the city palace of Mar.

He was heartened by the sight of it, gleaming there since he could remember, a symbol of the beauty that would be eternal: in the center were the forms of the sea's gods, Varuna, Ea, Poseidon, Kun; on the westward column were the badges of the Sabbian—Multuns, Leun, and Kani. To the East were the eagle and angels, the double columnar sign of Twisan, the Bilance's scales, and the figure with its water urn, symbolizing the races of Brise. Below the arch, set in the square upon the green marble floor, were the Erden's images, the Maeden, the Capra, the Bole. These images, reflected Fomalhaut with pleasure, had always sustained him, for they meant that all the races mingled in peace within the silver city of Mar.

A Crabba guard saluted Fomalhaut with reverence.

The usual petitioners lined the verdigrised benches along the inner corridors. Fomalhaut saw many Peisun, with their

pronged trident hats like his, their doublet and hose of
ocean-green, and the shadow-eyed Crabba in their head-
dresses formed like the crescent moon. And he was elated
to see that the red-clad Escors looked peaceable. Perhaps
Desmos had been right; the cause of civil peace was better
served by appeasement rather than punishment.

He reached the pewter doors of the Council chamber.
The guards bowed low and tapped the ornate metal with
their spears, then opened the doors with respect.

Eleven men were already seated at the Council table.
The Prime Chair of the Sea, with its pewter emblems of
the water gods, glimmered in the rain-dimmed light. And
Fomalhaut saw that its upholstery had been subtly adapted
in color and design to fit his Peisun race.

"Good gentles," he said in his musical voice, "I crave
your pardon for my lateness."

The faces of the seven men in silver-green were friendly;
those of the four in scarlet were tentative but bland.

There were four men representing each race of Mar—
Twipeisun, Crabba, and now the Throunds, or Escorpiun.
Their dress differed in subtle ways from that of the petitioners in the halls. These Peisun wore fabrics of great
softness with a patina of active silver that looked like moving water in moonlight; their racial symbols were not merely broidered, but outlined in aquamarines, bloodstones,
moonstones, and amethysts. The Crabba, dressed similarly
to the Peisun, but with hats in the form of the crescent
moon, were decorated in moonstones and in pearls, and the
patina of their garments was woven to give a gleam of
stillness, like the lunar globe that moved more slowly than
water. The Escors were decked out splendidly in a more
vivid scarlet than that of the petitioners, and their gems
were opals and topaz. There was no longer any evidence
of the golden scorpion, for the death of Vanand and the
madness of his uncle had put an end to the line of Sclar.

Fomalhaut seated himself in the Prime Chair and faced
the Council genially. He tapped the table of green marble
with his silver gavel. "And now, my lords," he said easily,
"what is the first order of business in this Council session?"

Mollis the Crabba and the Escors displayed their surprise. The old Lord Mayor Chiton had ruled with an iron
hand and set the agenda himself; yet here was Fomalhaut
taking the agenda from the oval hand of the Peisun Fixas!

Fomalhaut's quick green eyes scanned the vellum, and

then he announced, "There is first the matter of the Escorpiun."

The Escors were forthwith restored to the council's favor. And after a brief debate on the treatment of the malfeasant Throunds, agreement was reached in amity. Fomalhaut was elated.

But when the Crabba Mollis asked for recognition, the other-seeing Peisun knew an intuitive apprehension. And confirming Fomalhaut's feeling, the Crabba Mollis said darkly, "There is a matter of grave import to be brought before you. It is the unprecedented action of our former colleague, Sir Desmos, the consort of Shira the Queen."

Anxiety stirred in Fomalhaut. "Present your specific declaration," he said with some asperity to the Crabba.

"I have been advised on sound authority," said Mollis, "that Sir Desmos plans to wrest the power of endlich-Erde from the Queen and, as the head of her armies, conquer Mar."

"Arrant nonsense!" Fomalhaut cried. Then he added more quietly, "I beg your pardon, Lord Mollis. But that is a wild allegation. Sir Desmos has handed the reins of Mar to me, and he has no designs," he added ambiguously, "on the throne of endlich-Erde." For certainly that was so—Desmos' desire was to liberate the people, and not to rule. As he spoke, Fomalhaut wondered uneasily how the Crabba had received his information. Did he have a spy in Fomalhaut's own house?

The Peisun inquired sharply, "What is the source of your advisement?"

Mollis answered, "I am not at liberty to divulge it."

The other Peisun and Crabba exchanged glances of great unease, and with dismay, Fomalhaut saw on the faces of the Throunds that obdurate expression he knew so well—the determination to pursue a matter to its bitter end, to unravel a puzzle even if it meant shredding the whole cloth.

For whatever the threat, real or imagined, to Mar's supremacy, the Escors, thought Fomalhaut, would opt to meet it in the most warlike fashion. And as the new debate raged on, Fomalhaut began to question the certainty of the civil peace.

The Baron Uras of dernier-Brise said to his young equerry, "Please leave me a moment. Wait for me in the sleigh."

The equerry bowed, restraining his look of disapproval, and withdrew from the shining circular room. A large and prominent party was awaiting the Baron at the castle. And it was very strange that he chose to stay behind, seated at the crystal table on the dais in the People's Chamber of dernier-Brise.

Around the slender Waetergyt the circular seats of amethyst-hued crystal were empty, where not long before sat the august company, the nobles of dernier-Brise and their fragile ladies, raimented in colors as pale as the frost birds of the air and shadows upon the snow. Uras could still hear the echo of the flutes and the chorus of countertenors, the chorus of Twisan summoned for the rites.

There was nothing now but brilliant silence, a silence so great that Uras could hear the shush of his father's velvet mantle when he moved his shoulder, the minute rasp of his gilded hair against the constricting silver crown with its path of amethysts.

Through the transparent walls and ceiling of the lucid hall, the Waetergyt could see the passage of the fleecy, snow-bringing clouds and the austere shapes of the frosted mountains. They were shedding now the winter whiteness from their lower elevations. Soon the lighter snow of early spring would fall, and the frost flowers would bloom in the valleys. The Circle of the Peisun neared.

And the newly crowned Baron Uras sighed, longing for the little Marin. A flock of lilac birds swam by the transparent wall, their wings so pale against the brightness that they were almost invisible. Uras recalled a morning on the parapets when the Marin had held her white hand up to the light, and the sun had rendered it so fragile he could almost see through it, or felt that he could! Dione the Marin, with her magic blend of Brise.

So deep was Uras in his dream that he did not hear the soft approaching feet. But when he raised his gilded head from his long hands, he saw Shabatu before him, smiling her rueful, ironic little smile.

"My dear Shabatu!" he said with gentle reproach. "You should be in the castle with our guests."

A kindly light in her remote blue eyes belied her sharp retort. "You are the guest of honor, my dear brother."

"How did you know I would still be here?"

Sinking down beside him in the crystalline chair of the Second Lord, his sister replied softly, "Because I know your feeling of . . . desolation that makes you tarry where you are."

"Desolation?" He stared at her questioningly. How lovely she was today! he reflected. She was arrayed in a gown of state that was the hue of dusk-shadow; the entire bodice, like a small jerkin, was sewn with rose-de-France amethysts and frost pearls, and over it her matching cloak's enormous collar, also gem-encrusted, rose up behind the glory of her pallid hair. "You have felt desolation with . . . Gemelle?" he asked anxiously.

"Never!" she cried, her face alight at the mention of the Twisan's name. "I meant the desolation of high estate."

He nodded, relieved. Only the Peisun, generally, could understand such a dilemma. He felt a twinge at the silent pronunciation of Dione's race. The others—the elegance-loving Bilance, the conservative Erden, and the mighty Leun of Sabbia—so loved power and estate! We should have been the children of some obscure merchant, he thought wryly, free to ply our chosen trades of student or player.

Shabatu leaned to her brother and touched his thinning hair above the crown. Then she kissed his lean and smile-lined cheek and, gently bending down his head, his thought-furrowed brow.

"The crown, though light, is heavy," she said softly.

"Yes," he said, removing it and placing it before him on the crystal table. "I cannot help remembering the famous queen who said that she always did not what she wished, but what she must, that such a life was greatness and not joy."

"Forgive me," she said suddenly.

And he looked at her again, with her glimmering skin the texture of the falling snow, her remote eyes like the winter sky. "For what, my dear?" he asked.

"For sheltering the Marin from your addresses. Perhaps it was wrong of me."

Uras touched her hand. "It was very right, my dear. Her heart could never be touched by anyone but Fahne. And now, in any case, it is too late."

Shabatu's porcelain lids were shuttering her sky-blue eyes. Then she looked up and said to Uras, "I, too, feel the weight of the castle upon me . . . and upon Gemelle. We cannot stay, you know."

"He longs for the player's life, and Alioure?"

"We both long for it, unendurably. Now that the ceremonies are ended . . ."

"I understand," he said with false cheer, but she heard
his deeper desolation and it tore her heart. "Would that I
could flee, as well. But there is no one else, Shabatu."

"I know." She could not bear his look of loneliness.

He was rising, however, with a determined air and she
helped him settle the silver crown again upon his narrow
head. He arranged his mantle and offered her his arm.

"Let us go, then, my lady, to the festivities." Slowly
they descended the crystal stairs to join the equerry in the
sleigh. No one but Shabatu could have heard the reluctance
in his step.

The brown country of lower Erde was turning green as
the Circle of the Peisun neared, and it would remain so
only until the Circle of the Bole. Then the long summer
would return to darken the vegetation; the leaves would
not be dead, however, only brown.

Desmos saw the change with deep relief. He sickened
more than ever for the silver-green of Mar and its refresh-
ing, cool small rain that fell most of the year. The greening
of endlich-Erde was a nostalgic reminder of the city of
canals, and seeing it, he could fairly smell the sea beyond
the sail-bright harbor.

Returning to the castle from his stroll this morning near
the end of February Waetergyt, the Peisun felt heart-heavy
with the changes in himself. There had been a time when
the magic of Shira's body had blinded him to his surroundings; touching her flesh had glorified the land and made a
shining fantasy of his world.

But now, since he had read the message in the eyes of
Fahne, all the stories to which he had shut his ears were
shouted to him at once in a dread cacophony. And the
Peisun was assaulted by the real on every side—the heavy
ugliness of the land, with its dry, dun colors, its harsh
voices, and its ponderous horses, with their great haunches
and wide, awkward feet. The factual blare oppressed him
so that he felt that he would sicken bodily.

Therefore, it was with a sense of reprieve that he took
from a servant's hand the missive from Fomalhaut informing him that he was urgently needed in Mar.

To see it again! he exulted. To be soothed and healed by

its silver gentleness, its infinite change and variety! Perhaps through some miracle Shira could be induced to come.

Desmos recalled with a flash of hope their early times together in the city of Mar, when she was a guest of his Uncle Chiton. Something in the air—or had he merely imagined it?—appeared to gentle her a little, render her more soft and pliable. Desmos meditated upon this with the dreamy optimism of the Peisun. Could it be that the watery roots of her Capran temper, half-goat, half-fish, were nourished in the atmosphere of Mar?

But no, he concluded with dry bitterness. His very desperation was making him see a truth in every chimera. So it was with a precognition of despair that he took his news to Shira.

He found her breakfasting in her wide goat-footed bed, with its rustling coverlet of flame-green, its crested hangings drawn aside for the morning, glittering with onyxes.

Desmos noted that the cup on her silver tray contained not moss, as she customarily took, but nightshade, an anodyne. After greeting her, he remarked, "That is a peculiar drink for morning."

"My nerves are quite on edge," she replied sharply, and he noticed the darkness of the white skin below her oblique, hot eyes.

"What is it?" he asked gently, seating himself on the edge of the bed.

Irritably, she righted the angle of the tray, unsettled by the pressure of his body on the coverlet, and said, "It is nothing of great concern." The sullen indifference of her eyes would have wounded him deeply a few days before, but now he sadly knew his own indifference.

Nevertheless he said, "If you are unwell, it is naturally of concern to me."

"I have no wish to discuss it."

Her reply cut, but Desmos repressed his annoyance and said, "I have been summoned urgently to Mar."

"How long will you be gone?" Her question was negligent.

I thought as much, he said to himself with coldness.

"Would you not like to come with me?" he asked as if by rote.

"You know that the climate of Mar is bad for me," she said irritably. "I always take a chill, and the amusements there . . ."

"Yes, there is little drinking, and no hunting at all." His sour reply, for the first time, brought a smile to her sullen face. It was as if she were glad to bring their conflict into the open.

"You will be far more comfortable without me," she said coolly.

Though he knew it was so, the sight of her seductive body, plain through the transparent fabric of her gown, caught his senses unaware. With a despairing groan, he leaned forward to her, upsetting the silver tray. The night-shade spilled upon the coverlet, leaving a dark, ugly stain, and some of it splashed into the white valley of her breasts.

She cried out angrily, "You stupid fool! Is there no end to your cringing lust? You remind me of a beaten dog."

A flash of overpowering rage, like a jagged ray of crimson lightning, fired the brain of the Peisun. Taking up the tray, he hurled it, with the dishes, across the room. The metal rang against the gray stone wall, and the fragile glass shattered into a hundred pieces.

Ignoring Shira's astonished outcry, Desmos snatched the coverlet away from her, and taking the shoulder of her gown in one firm hand, he tore it off her body. Fastening her to the bed with his hands, he took her fast and brutally, his red rage crying soundlessly to him: There is no end to my cringing lust, no end—the bitch will know when there is an end! And when she cried out again, begging him to cease from paining her, he did not listen, only continued the hard and rhythmic thrust that seemed incapable of slowing or stilling ever, on and on until he no longer knew how long, until he knew the climbing to the peak and there was a loud white bursting in his whole self and he came to a kind of reason.

Shira lay back with cold eyes on the flame-green bed, her face a study in dreary resignation.

When he saw her look, the Peisun drew his rent garments around himself and went quickly away.

Shira the Queen of lower Erde made a sound of disgust when she heard the closing door and opened her hard black eyes. Her body's ache and sting filled her with fury.

So the romantic fool was going to Mar, and she would not have to endure him, for a little while at least. Not that there was any purpose in it, when he had given over all his powers to Fomalhaut. They could have controlled both Mar and Erde, had he listened.

And then, she thought, there was the unrest among the serfs. But a smile, at last, curved her sullen mouth, for with Desmos away, she could pay a visit to Dione the Marin.

CHAPTER 6

With an almost satiric air, the athletic Shira hooked her knee over the pommel and spread the folds of her voluminous riding skirt in a graceful pattern. Her puzzled steed, feeling the weight of velvet rubbing its side, flicked its glossy tail and snorted.

Shira gave the horse a cut with her elaborate whip and the beast subsided. I will be damned, thought the Queen, if that little bag of bones will outdo me in womanliness. Indeed, the Capran was too splendidly arrayed for a morning visit. Her velvet outfit was a blazing green, befurred at the neck and wrists and hem with the pelts of the silvery fox, and she wore a number of onyxes.

Although the distance to the little house of Dione was not great, the Queen rode in panoply, with four green-clad attendants, two before and two behind, as if she were riding to a tournament.

When the minstrel Volan caught sight of the small pompous train approaching over the fields, he exclaimed, blessing the chance that had sent the Marin out to gather flowers.

Earla the Bole, however, gave the irreverent minstrel a repressive glance and bustled about the little chamber, patting cushions and blowing imaginary dust from surfaces.

"Run and find my lady," she snapped to the little maid. "I will open to the Queen myself. Volan, have the men see to the horses."

"There is nothing to see," the minstrel retorted lazily. "They have not ridden forty paces; the steeds could hardly lather from trotting a stable length."

"Impudence!" Earla muttered, but she dared not box his ears, for it would surely get back to the Lady Dione.

So the Bole went forward alone down the path from the little house and bowed deeply at the approach of the Queen of endlich-Erde. So dazzled was she by the sight of the splendid Capran that the old Bole could not see the mocking smiles on the attendants' faces. In any case, to Earla, servants had no faces at all.

"Your Majesty," she said, when the Queen was within earshot, and she curtsied even more deeply than before.

Amused, Shira nodded amiably and submitted—where usually she leaped in trews—to the aid of an attendant in dismounting.

Officiously, the Bole came forward and announced, "I fear my lady is not at home, but a maid has been dispatched to bring her at once."

"Thank you, Earla." Shira was a model of friendly condescension. The Bole stepped off the path and gestured to the Queen to precede her.

"Your men . . ." Earla started. "Shall I . . ."

Shira made a careless gesture. "They are very well as they are. Do not let the horses tread upon the garden," she called sharply to the men.

Earla, thrilled at this touch of homeliness in a royal person, fairly wriggled with delight. Her intercourse with kings and queens had been sadly limited in the democratic, indifferent port of Mar.

She was a little quelled by Shira's contemptuous glance around the little house, and thought again: How could my lady have chosen such a place?

But bravely she offered the Queen the courtesies of the house, steering her to the comfortable chair and hovering at her elbow with a glass of hemlock.

Shira at last took the wine from Earla's broad fingers and set it on a table at her side. "My lady," said Earla nervously, "should be returning swiftly now."

The Queen nodded, her oblique eyes raking the chamber. Her gaze caught the twined star-wheels above the door. "That is the wheel of Fahne, if I mistake not," said Shira in a tone of dangerous quiet.

Earla colored. The illicit connection was still a source of great pain to the tradition-bound Bole. She nodded miserably, still standing near the cabinet of wines.

"Shall I summon the minstrel, Your Majesty? He will while away the time for you with a little air."

"If you wish."

The Bole cried out the name of Volan, but there was no reply. "Where has the boy gone to?" Earla snapped. "Pardon me, my lady, and I will seek him out." She curtsied and, grumbling to herself, hurried from the chamber.

Shira looked about and, rising quickly, went to the chest of wines. The beakers, gleaming in the sunny light, were colored in the hues of the star-races, marked with small labels of silver. The Queen found the lavender one labeled "Dandelion," the wine Desmos had said was Dione's favorite, and unstopped it. Taking from her tiny carryall a vial of black glass, she poured the contents of the vial into the lavender beaker and stopped it hastily.

She thrust the vial back into her velvet carryall and was examining the *Emerald Table* when Earla returned.

"I beg your indulgence, Your Majesty," said the Bole uncomfortably. "The minstrel is nowhere to be seen. And I cannot think what has happened to my lady!"

"It is of no consequence," the Queen said easily, smiling, and the dazzled Bole inhaled her expensive scent of violets. "I shall return another day. It is my own foolish lack of care; it would have been well to send a message announcing my visit."

And she placed the book carefully upon the blue-clothed table. "Please tender to the Lady Dione my most affectionate greeting, and please say to her that we miss her sorely at the castle."

"Oh, I will, Your Majesty, indeed, I will," effused the Bole, fairly curtsying the Capran from the little house. And she stood for a long moment on the path, watching the royal departure of the little train and thinking how careless her own lady was of the visit of a queen.

Fahne the sorcerer jerked at the reins of his borrowed steed and leaped from its back onto the path before the little house, and one of the men led the horse into the stable to be rubbed.

The sorcerer, in three long strides, was over the threshold, asking curtly, "Where is she?"

Earla, with a stricken face, led him to a little bedchamber beyond. Fahne drew in his breath sharply and strode to the bed.

The small Marin lay with closed eyes, her face greenish-white, taking shallow, wheezing breaths. The sorcerer knelt down by the bed and leaned his head to her breast, listening intently, while his thumb on her narrow wrist marked her pulse's beat.

"It is weak and slow," he said to Earla in a strange, choked voice. Reaching into a pouch strung from his belt, he took out a sheaf of berry-bearing solanum and thrust it at Earla. "Quickly," he ordered, "you have water on the boil?" She nodded. "Then thrust these quickly in and soak them. When the water is black, bring back this potion for her to drink. Hurry."

When the Bole returned he took the cup from her hands and tenderly raised the Marin's head, giving her the cup of liquid to drink.

With half-opened eyes, Dione seemed to know him, for she drank obediently, and when she lay back on the gray-green pillows again, her face was alight with a feeble smile.

The Bole, sitting with Volan by the door of the small bedchamber, watched the sorcerer's unchanging scrutiny of the little Marin. The three were still—the lean man seated by the bed, the two by the door—until at last they heard the chimes of the castle tolling from a distance the Maeden-hour.

The sunlight in the room had changed from gold to nectarine when the sorcerer turned unsmiling to the minstrel and the Bole. Earla gave a moan of apprehension. "There has been no change," said Fahne.

Volan crouched unmoving in his chair, and the Bole saw that Fahne's cheeks were wet, his long-fingered hands shaking.

And suddenly her long-nourished enmity against the gypsy shriveled and died, blown away insubstantial as milkweed down in the storm of her emotion. He had saved the little Marin once, Earla reflected, had saved her from her fever. They had had so little time for joy, and now she might be dying—now, when in the blackness of his mind he did not even know she loved him.

An ache of compassion smote the Bole, and eerily she recalled the first visit of the sorcerer in Mar. Earla moved to the bed and touched the Marin's brow. It was still deathly cold, and her breathing was irregular.

"Will my lady die?"

Something stirred in the sorcerer's deep, dappled eyes.

"She must not die." Fahne stared at Earla, then he asked her, "What food and drink did your lady take before she was stricken?"

Earla told him, then added, "And a glass of wine—the dandelion wine."

"A wine that no other in the house would take," said Fahne. "There are no other Peisun."

"No."

He was silent for a time. Then he said, "In an hour, as well as this evening and tomorrow, she must be given the solanum." In the looking forward Earla heard his iron will as he handed her another sheaf of the black-berried branches, and she knew hope. Then she noticed that he pressed his fingers to his brow.

"Your head pains you," she said softly. "May I brew you some marjoram?"

"That would be very kind. I will stay by her to watch for any change."

Earla went to the kitchen to brew the tea. Volan remained, his cithara silent on his knees.

Fahne sat down again in the chair by the gray-green bed and stared at the little Marin. When Earla came with the marjoram, Fahne nodded his thanks and said, "Your lady must have taken the poison in the wine."

"Poison!"

The sorcerer nodded slightly, his face dark.

"It cannot be!"

"It is," he said grimly. "Who has been in the house?"

"Only the household—except for . . . the Queen."

"Shira." The sorcerer sounded thoughtful.

"But surely . . ."

The sorcerer's face closed up, and he said, "You had best pour out the wines and open fresh bottles."

Earla felt a thrill of coldness shoot up her arms, as if she had wandered into a house of ghosts.

A final ray of the sinking sun caught the crystal star on the caduceus medallion of Fahne, and the Bole watched it change before her very eyes, reflecting the colors of the dome above Dione's water garden in Mar. She looked into the eyes of the sorcerer, dizzied by their depths. He seemed to be looking beyond the boundaries of the little house.

Fahne knew below his feet the deck of a moving barge, and he saw a powerful man in scarlet lift a frail, green-clad figure from the other boat and bear it up the escalade into the somber palace. And he felt an aching anger to see her so near the Escor. Swiftly, other images succeeded the first, flashing before his inner sight: the little Marin in the bed of dragonfly silk, her fleeing fever; the green, hostile eyes of the man in scarlet; last, his own descent with the woman Earla into a sunken room like a peisun pool, a chamber like those he had seen in Sabbia, artifacts of the ancient pagans of Roma.

And now the voices, the Bole's and his own, came to him clearly: "The planetary order of the skies has destined her for me."

And then came Earla's shocked reply: "But you . . . you are a wanderer—a wanderer lacking property or land, a gypsy without title. What can you offer to my lady?"

"Your lady must come with me."

And then from a far chamber they heard the ripple of a cithara, moving with a graceful tempo. The cithara drowned out some hated name the woman had pronounced, the name of a man who would flout the ancient laws.

And Fahne heard his own voice saying, "Ever since the dawn of knowledge, since the first Chaldeans saw the whirling of the primal wheel of stars, the sea has always sought the calm of land, the earth has thirsted for the water."

The sorcerer awoke then to the present, and he was seated in the small house of Dione, where the twilight was falling. What strange tricks his brain was playing, he meditated, confusing the little Marin with the woman of his dream.

But he looked at the small figure on the ocean-colored bed with new eyes, and he felt Volan watching him.

The white woman of his vision and the Lady Dione . . . could they be one? She must not die. He leaned forward and touched her forehead. There was nothing now but to watch . . . and wait.

Gemelle's dancing blue eyes, waking, encountered the early morning sky through the transparent domed ceiling. There was no snow this hour, and in the waning winter, the Brisen sun had turned from a narcissus color to the warm yellow of a new rose. A flock of lilac birds passed. And the Twisan knew the clean fragrance of vanilla flowers, feeling Shabatu's sweet weight upon his chest.

He looked down, and his chin met her gilded head. Her scented hair was spread across his torso as she breathed quietly in her sleep. Its strands of silver-gilt were glimmering in the early light, and very gently Gemelle stroked it with his long, lean hand. How exquisite she was! She bore in her very person the glitter of the air, and to look upon her, for the Twisan, was to walk the high paths above the gaping people. In her arms was the way of the birds, and flying.

Gemelle pressed Shabatu close to him, and murmuring, she awoke. She shook back her golden hair and smiled up at the Twisan. Then she raised a wing-like hand, translucent as alabaster in the brilliant sun, and caressed his cheek.

He held her more closely and their bodies kissed. His strong, slender hand stroked her side.

But she made a small sound of protest, and his hand ceased its motion. "Gemelle," she said tentatively.

The Twisan heard the wheedling syllables and waited.

"Could we wait a little while before returning to Alioure?" she asked softly.

"Wait?" His flesh felt cold.

"Yes. You see"—Shabatu rubbed his lean chest—"Uras is so very alone."

Without responding to her touch, the Twisan replied, "I see that, of course. But I also see that to remain will entrap us."

Shabatu sat up, her gilded hair falling over her sweetly shaped arms. "That is absurd," she said coolly. "What difference will there be in a few days, a week?"

"Or a week or two . . . and then a circle," Gemelle commented.

"What is troubling you, my love?" The Waetergyt's remote blue eyes studied him.

"Just that—the few days, the week . . . the circle. And all too soon Uras will awaken in you some false sense of duty, some reason to remain in dernier-Brise forever."

"No, no!" She sought the shelter of his arm. "I swear to you that soon we will return to Alioure. But give us a little longer. Uras, you see, has no one else."

"Nor do I."

Looking up at her husband, Shabatu saw on his lean, humorous face a look that she had never seen before, a look of hunger and of fear. And she took his face in her hands, kissing him urgently to reassure him. But even as they came together with the magic that was the path of flying birds, the Twisan experienced a peculiar apprehension, and he could feel his wings beating against the bars of a crystal cage.

Mahar held up his hands for silence and the babel of the twelve men in the cavern ceased abruptly.

"So he has deserted you and gone to Mar," the Capran sneered, "for all his protestations. What more did you expect from the consort of the Queen?"

"What are we to believe?" One of the men was belligerent. "The understewards have sworn to us that the consort Desmos means to set us free."

Mahar laughed. "Set you free? What means has he to set you free, and what desire?"

"It is said," another intervened, "that he has gone to Mar to seek the aid of the Escors to battle Shira's army."

"You fool!" cried Mahar. "How many Escors do you think there are with weapon skill enough to best the soldiers of endlich-Erde? If the Peisun seeks the aid of the Escors, it is in a muddleheaded course—to add to the forces of Shira and put down our rebellion. Do you not see that?"

"But the Pfarren," said the first man, "have never lied. And the Pfarren have told us that Gonu himself made the proclamation of freedom."

"The Pfarren!" A fourth voice had risen, contemptuously. "Do you not know that the Pfarren have ever been the tools of the Crown? Do you not know that when Monoceros died and Shira took the throne, she promised great leniency to the priests . . . and they in turn have sworn new fealty to her?"

The first Capran serf retorted, "Sir Mahar has explained that. But I believe the Pfarren; they have never lied to us. I feel their oath to the Queen is part of their plot to aid us in our rising."

There was a tumultuous roar from the assembled men. Again the sly Mahar held up his hands. "We are defeating ourselves by quarreling among ourselves," he said firmly. "It is near the end of the Waetergyt, and we have sworn to storm the castle of the whore before the Circle of the Peisun. Are we together in this enterprise? Our number is great, and the carousing soldiers of the Queen have become ever weaker in their idleness. We can overcome them if we move now, and move with strength and determination. Are you content to let your freedom be lost forever? Or shall we move as we have planned—to show yourselves as men, free men, at last?"

The twelve listening men, aroused by the rhetoric of Mahar, shouted out, "We shall move! We shall be free men at last!"

And they dispersed to spread the news among their seven-score companions.

CHAPTER 7

"What is it, Pendra?" Shira inquired of the maid. A small expectant fire leaped in her oblique black eyes. This, then, might be the word so eagerly awaited, the word of the death of the Marin! There was a little quiver on her sensual red mouth.

"It is Gonu, Your Majesty, the highest Pfarrer."

"Bid him enter."

The high priest of endlich-Erde entered with hesitant steps into the bedchamber of the Queen. She lay back on her sumptuous pillows, her oblique, hot gaze holding a deceptive sleepiness. With embarrassment he looked away from her full, white breasts, almost exposed in the filmy gown she had taken no pains to cover.

"Yes?" she asked in a tone of unutterable boredom.

"There is grave news, madam, of the Lady Dione."

Shira raised her black brows in question, controlling an exclamation of triumph.

"She is dangerously ill."

"Ill!" The consternation in Shira's voice surprised the Pfarrer. He had not believed much love lost between them. But the Queen, who had expected to hear him say "Dead," cried out again, "Ill!"

"Yes, madam. The sorcerer Fahne is attending her, and I beg your leave to lend him my aid, and that of Orn."

Shira's beautiful face turned white at the mention of Fahne, and again Gonu was surprised and heartened at her seeming concern. "Of course," she replied tightly. "Lend him all support you can to aid the . . . cousin of Sir Desmos. And keep me well informed."

Gonu bowed his ancient head once and withdrew from the chamber.

Pendra was studying the Queen, and Shira snapped, "Why are you staring so? Have you no duties? No, wait, bring me a beaker of wine, at once."

And when the woman had fetched the wine, the Queen said coldly, "Leave me." Pouring the first goblet, she raged in silence: Ill! The bitch is only ill, and I must begin again! Draining the first goblet, the Queen quickly poured another, and she felt a grateful little flame coursing through her body, heating her vitals. His is not the only magic wand, she meditated sullenly.

Eleven-dark, the hour of the Capra, was tolling from the castle keep when Shira stole down the stairway of winding stone, her face rapacious as a bird of prey, flushed red from the beaker of wine.

She was dressed only in a flowing robe of thinnest tissue, and she gloried in the feel of her own bare flesh that heated her to visions of incredible lusting. The robe was a most peculiar garment with sightless slits that opened to expose the varied glories of her body. It had enchanted Desmos. A curse on him! she thought, and on his foolish cousin who has taken from me all I ever valued. Well, she would make Desmos the laughingstock of all the kingdoms, plant on his brow so many horns they would be as numerous as the hairs of his head!

The Queen laughed drunkenly.

Over her tissue gown she wore a long embroidered cloak mischievously wrought with the figures of nymphs and satyrs in obscene converse, a theme escaping the cursory eye.

A curse on Desmos! she reflected as she reached the bottom of the winding stairs. Then hearing the step of a guard, she slipped behind some heavy arras, smothering her laughter.

When he was gone, she darted down the stairway to the lower castle. A door beyond led to the barracks, where she knew this night the soldiers would be carousing.

Shira crossed the stableyard, hearing the distant shouts and raucous laughter of the soldiers. It was very late; there was only one tipsy guard outside the quarters of the officers. She moved nearer to him, and when she was standing in the light, the Queen parted her broidered robe and touched one of the slits in the upper part of the gown. She stood before the guard, who seemed unable to believe his sight. She saw his flat black eyes leap to her body. He licked his lips. Shira could almost hear the acceleration of his pulse. She parted her red lips and stared at him from under heavy-shadowed lids. His jaws fell ajar. He slowly nodded, then stumbled toward her and put his shaking hands upon her flesh. And motioning, he led her away into the dark.

His eyes looked mad, thought Shira, and she laughed aloud. There was a little dew of sweat upon his brow and his hands felt damp. "This cannot be." He pushed out his words; his throat sounded overfull.

Shira thrust herself against him, and he made a growling sound. Then she pulled him to the soil and began to bestow the legendary caress that had brought her an especial fame throughout the land of Erde.

When it was over and they lay drunkenly together in the dark, Shira began to laugh again, a wild and mad laugh that chilled the soldier's blood. Then rising unsteadily, she threw off his detaining hand and staggered toward the quarters of the soldiers.

The sun was young when Beta the serf, in her coarse stuff dress and shoes of straw, gathered up the egg- and chicken-rent and set out for the house of Dabih. Let Aspel scoff as he will, she thought practically; if a rebellion comes, then let it come. Meanwhile, I will stand in well with the steward!

Grasping the squawking hen more tightly under her arm, the servile woman made her way up the hill toward Dabih's house. The path commanded a view of the barracks of the soldiers.

"What good can come," she asked herself aloud, "of these foolish notions? Rebellion, indeed!" Drunken and idle as they were, she thought, the soldiers of the Queen would slay them all. What good were scythes against their swords and spears, their helmets and their armor?

Then as she toiled up the rise, an astonishing sight met

Beta's eyes: a woman with long, shining hair, falling disheveled about her shoulders, in a tattered robe that left a great deal of her white flesh bare, was running across the fields from the quarters of the soldiers. She had not seen Beta, but the servile woman had noted clearly the bruises upon her breasts and arms and the almost demented look in her oblique black eyes.

It was the Queen! The Queen . . . staggering naked in the morning light from the barracks of the soldiers.

A malicious joy filled the heart of the servile woman. How the others would roar with laughter when she told them this. Much good her silks and jewels and her crown would do her now, when her fine husband was told where she had been!

"Slept poorly, forsooth!" Cife the castle's chief cook hissed at Sebba, still smarting from the haughtiness of the Queen's maid.

They watched Pendra move in her stately fashion up the winding stairs.

" 'Her Majesty slept poorly,' " mocked Sebba the head kitchen maid. " 'Please prepare a tray for her chamber.' " She satirized the careful speech of Pendra.

"And I have supervised an entire meat dinner for the hall!" Cife grumbled. "Here, Sebba, fill these dishes: a little soup; some roast and veal pasties; some of the savory rice and rissoles; and there some pears and comfits. That should do."

"And a beaker of hemlock?" Sebba inquired dryly.

"It seems she has had a sufficiency of wine, from what the guards told Dabih." Cife sighed. "Poor Sir Desmos. It is all over the estate."

Ladling the rice, Sebba asked, "When does he return?"

"Soon, I think. He has been advised of the . . . indisposition of the Lady Dione." The cook paused significantly before the word.

"Do you think she really did it?" Sebba whispered.

"I put nothing past that one, Sebba," Cife replied in a low voice, looking over her shoulder. "Be still." She had caught sight of a man at the kitchen door. "That is one of the ushers from the house of the Marin."

As he entered, she called out, "I give you greeting. How can we aid you?"

The Bole touched his forehead to Cife. "I have come at

the behest of Earla, attendant to the Lady Dione, to seek some sheets and coverlets for Gonu and Orn."

"How does your lady, usher?"

"Not well," the man replied with a somber face. "It is not known if she will recover."

Cife made a clucking sound with her tongue and shook her head. "Poor, sweet lady," she said. "Go to the chamberlain, and he will give you what you require. And come back to the kitchen before you depart. I will give you broth to take to the little lady."

The Bole shook his head. "Fahne the sorcerer has said we can accept no food or drink from the castle."

Cife and Sebba exchanged a meaning glance.

"Go, then, Bole, and receive your sheets and coverlets."

After he had disappeared up the stairs, Sebba whispered to Cife, "They know, then."

The cook nodded. "And they will know the rest when the Bole returns. Hear him now, snickering with one of the men in the corridor."

"What will Sir Desmos do?"

"He can only put her from him, in the sight of all," Cife answered. She looked at Sebba with worried eyes. "What will we do then, Sebba? If the people drive her out, where will we go?"

"I shall go and wait in a tavern," Sebba said.

Cife was silent. For Sebba was young and comely, and she had not spent most of her days and nights upon the estate of Shira, who might not be much longer Queen of lower Erde.

The stronger sun of the Peisun Circle glittered on the gray-white parapet as Shabatu emerged with her basket of crumbs. It had become her delight to feed the lilac birds of the highest air in this high place, and they had come to know her, for they were gathering now and one of the bolder ones had lighted on her slender arm.

She had hoped to find Gemelle limbering his limbs on the cold stone, where now much of the snow had melted, but he was nowhere to be seen. He had sought much time alone of late, she reflected, sighing. But consoled by the presence of the delicate birds, Shabatu smiled and scattered the rest of her crumbs, looking out over the whiteness below, and to the peaks beyond. Already there were faint patches of pink on the lower elevations; the frost flowers were blooming.

Then she saw Gemelle climbing into the light; he had not seen her. Yet somehow she knew that this was like another morning, circles gone, when she had watched him thus.

And as on that other morning, the Twisan began to tune his agile limbs, a whirligig of yellow in the brightness. But this day his face was unsmiling, and a demon not of exhilaration, but of despair, seemed to cause him to leap upon the parapet and dance along its periled way. Laughing at death, but grimly, he began to cartwheel on that same small path at a dreadful height above the lowering snow.

As before, his foot slipped, and he hung by his steel-strong hands in the air. But again he pulled himself upward with painful care, ever so slowly upward by his sinewy arms, and with a gigantic effort he whirled over the ledge and landed cat-like on his ductile feet.

Shabatu cried out.

When he saw her, he went to her and took her in his arms. "Oh, Shabatu, Shabatu," he said breathlessly, "I was trying this time to die."

She put her slender arms around his narrow body and held him with all her strength. He could feel her wet cheek against his neck above his yellow tunic.

"I am dying here, you see," he said sadly. "Without my skills I shall become as dry and brittle as a bundle of old sticks, and I will shatter."

Drawing back a little, Shabatu raised her wing-like hands to cup his face and kissed him deeply. "Forgive me," she said. "I who was caged so long in a crystal cage have tried to cage another creature of the air. Forgive me. We will go to Alioure."

His face was alight, and he asked, smiling, "When? When shall we go?"

"Now, this hour," she answered softly. And taking his hand, she led Gemelle away from the parapet.

Fahne the sorcerer realized that he had not altered his upright position for more than an hour. Ramrod-straight in the chair by the bed of Dione, he felt the ache of taut muscles and the deep exhaustion pressing down upon his eyes. He leaned forward and peered at her again, placing his long, broad thumb on her fluttering pulse. Yes! Yes, it was a little stronger. Hope brushed at him with its fragile wings.

He expelled a trembling breath and leaned back in the chair; he let himself rest his head upon its soft back.

Fahne seemed to float away then to darkness, knowing the aquatic joy that is softness and repose. He felt upon his bare head the cool kiss of the small rain, and below him, he sensed the deck of a boat bounding gently on moving water.

He was quite alone upon the deck of a little boat, and the boat was drifting, without pole or sail, into a quiet harbor through no effort or will of his own, drifting magically and slow over calm, shining water toward an alien shore.

And even though the little rain continued to caress him, there was a light from the late sky, almost like the light of sunset, and he heard from the shore a haunting, dream-like air that seemed to proceed from the throats of water reeds, or from pipes of silk, so thin the music was, a rippling ecstasy that filled him at once with excitement and peace.

The small rain had the radiance of the sun and moon reflected on water; the rain, cognate with light, shimmered before him, making a glory of the sky and shore, a dazzlement of the water.

And there was an awesome still, then. The silk piping ceased and Fahne could hear the faint whisper of the rain, the lapping of water, and the odor of roses wafted to him from the nearing shore. A single bird called out, and the sound was so exquisite in the whispering silence that his throat pained him. He felt a sick excitement in his vitals akin to the moment when the heart seems to pause in the anticipation of seeing the beloved's face.

Then Fahne saw upon the shore, in the latening light, a long and graceful house of white touched with green, like the moon, with glimmering turrets of abalone and moonstone and mother-of-pearl, like the palaces of Mar. And there seemed to be no one living in the house, no one anywhere upon this island he had found, although the silken pipes began again, and peacocks wandered along the terraces.

The sorcerer looked upward at the clouds that were the upper waters, realm of Kun, the source of the fecund rain, then down into the clear green water by the shore, where there were multitudinous small fish, the birds of the nether regions, sinking with their penetrative motions into the water, which was the unconscious world, the house of dreams.

And as the boat drifted in to the shore, Fahne knew a sharp anticipatory aching in his inmost flesh. He stepped upon the shore; out of the shadows of the moon-like house a woman was emerging.

On her dark head she wore a gleaming crown of white, shaped in the crescent, symbol of water. She was slender and small, moving with an almost swimming motion over the soft, wet grass toward him, her white gown floating around her. In her hands she held a shining cup of moonstone; over it the lunar light moved on its ordered path like moonlight upon the sea.

And she was offering him the cup. He took it from her hands and held it to his lips. He handed it back; he could not see her face. There seemed to be a mist before his eyes, like a clinging spiderweb, and he brushed and brushed at it, trying to brush it away, for he longed to see her face.

"Her face," he whispered, "her face."

And Fahne the sorcerer opened his eyes to see the face of the little Marin, white and still upon her pillows in the bedchamber of the little house.

She was so thin and wan, he thought with pity. And the body of the woman in his dream had been roundly slender, and her step like the movement of silk, or the touch of rain upon the grass.

For an instant, before he felt the little Marin's brow again, the sorcerer wondered sadly if she had ever been, the woman of his ever-present dream.

A soft step at the door made him look up. Volan, the minstrel, with his brindled hair that so strangely blended the gold of Brise with the shadowy blackness of Mar, was stealing into the room.

Volan looked at the small Marin with an anxious face and whispered to Fahne, "Shall I stay so you may rest?"

The sorcerer smiled and answered, "Stay, Volan, but not so I may rest."

Volan sank down onto a stool by the sorcerer's chair and clasped his maimed hands around his thin knees.

Something in the shape of the minstrel's hands recalled to Fahne another place, a place of mist and candlelight, a cold hill, and a struggle in the dark. But what place it was, he could not yet remember.

What was it? he asked himself silently as he turned his gaze again to Dione the Marin.

CHAPTER 8

Desmos the Peisun faced Fomalhaut, the acting Lord Mayor of Mar, across the length of marble council table.

Fomalhaut tapped the green marble with his silver gavel, then began reluctantly, "Sir Desmos, you have been summoned before the Council of Mar because of the situation in lower Erde."

"The situation?" Desmos raised his wing-like brows in puzzlement.

"We have been advised—and let me say that I personally disbelieve it—that you are moving to take power in Erde with an eye toward conquering Mar."

Desmos repeated the last words in a tone of stupefaction.

"The ambitions of Monoceros are to be realized, after all," Madimiel the Escor broke in.

Angered, Fomalhaut banged the marble with his gavel. "You are out of order, Sir Madimiel. If you wish to present a motion before this Council, do so in the accepted fashion."

Mollis the Crabba raised his oval hand.

"Lord Mollis."

The Crabba spoke pompously in his thick prime-Marin. "The Council begs to hear from Sir Desmos of lower Erde." He pronounced the title with malice.

"Very well," said Fomalhaut. "Sir Desmos?"

The handsome Peisun arose and addressed the Council. "I deny the outrageous charge that I seek the precedence of lower Erde over my beloved country. My union with the Queen, although it has helped maintain the amity of our

nations, was entered into for purely . . . personal reasons."
He colored and resumed. "The Queen Shira is the ruler of
her country. I have sought only to guide her toward a
more . . . democratic rule in the noble traditions of Mar."

The Peisun Myrtillus asked for recognition, and he interposed quietly, "But with the best of intentions, Sir Desmos,
the interference of a Marin in the affairs of Erde could re-
sult in Erden malice toward the land of Mar."

"How so?" asked Desmos coolly.

"Mar is rife with rumor," Myrtillus answered dryly.
"And one of the rumors states that you plan a rebellion of
the people, a freeing of the serfs of lower Erde. As the
nominal leader of the Council, you perforce involve the
land of Mar in this action."

"If you view my honor so dimly," Desmos retorted, "I
will resign my position forthwith. It was only at the
request of Fomalhaut that I retained the title of Lord
Mayor."

The Peisun Fomalhaut looked apprehensive and shot an
irritated glance at Myrtillus. "Your leadership," he said to
Desmos, "has brought new civil peace to Mar. We would
be the poorer without your advisement."

The Escor Madimiel was recognized and said, "It was
your act, Lord Fomalhaut, that restored to the Escors their
hereditary rights."

"No," said Fomalhaut. "I opposed this course until Sir
Desmos showed me its justice."

Desmos warmed at his friend's courageous frankness.
There was a thoughtful silence over the assembly.

Lasca, the recently elected Peisun member of the Council, signaled to Fomalhaut for recognition and declared, "I
beg to know the source of the Council's information concerning Sir Desmos' activities."

Fomalhaut looked at Madimiel.

The Escor, annoyed, replied, "My kinsman the Lord
Mahar of lower Erde."

"Mahar!" Desmos said in a low voice to Fomalhaut. "He
is a bitter enemy of the Queen, and he likes me no better."

"I move," said Lasca, "that all references to such ad-
visements be stricken from the records of this Council."

"Do you cast aspersions upon the honor of my kinsman?" cried Madimiel.

Fomalhaut glared and pounded his silver gavel. "Cos-
mos!" he called sharply. Madimiel recalled certain unfor-

tunate statements that Fomalhaut had made relating to the
Escorpiuns' "poison rule." And the Peisun could see the
remembrance in the Escor's sharp green eyes.

"A motion is before the Council," said Fomalhaut. "A
vote must be taken."

The Crabba and the Peisun voted in favor of Lasca's
motion, the Escors vociferously against it.

Stinging from his defeat, Madimiel said, "I move that
Sir Desmos of lower Erde be required to resign his office."

After a long and angry debate, a vote was taken. The
four Escors and two of the Crabba decreed the resignation;
there were six nays from the other Crabba and the Peisun.

"We are deadlocked, then, good gentles," Fomalhaut
said wearily. "I pray that we adjourn this Council session
until the morrow."

There was a murmur of assent, and the Peisun Desmos
moved with Fomalhaut and the other eleven from the
Council chambers.

In the corridor a breathless page overtook Desmos and
his friend. "A missive for Sir Desmos," he gasped, "from
lower Erde."

Excusing himself to Fomalhaut and handing the page
a pewter piece, Desmos the Peisun tore open the letter.
The words were in the hand of Fahne the sorcerer. Desmos
looked up at Fomalhaut, and his face was sick.

"What is it, Desmos, my dear friend?"

"Look upon it, Fomalhaut," Desmos replied with disgust. "My cousin is near her death . . . and my wife, the
Queen . . . but look upon it yourself."

And Fomalhaut read the sorcerer's missive, uttering a
low outcry of disbelief. "You must return, then," he said
softly to Desmos.

"At once. I must return and face it all."

Compassionately, Lord Fomalhaut watched his young
friend disappear among the petitioners of the corridor.

Gonu the high Pfarrer and Orn the second Pfarrer
stepped into the garden of the little house. The morning
light of the Peisun that was so cool in Mar and frosty in
Brise was already warm and bright in endlich-Erde.

Gonu, the elder, loosened his robe of skins and wiped
the moisture from his lined brow below his square headdress. Both men were tall and lean, with a depth to their
flat black eyes that was absent from the other Caprans', a

look that cousined them to the Peisun and the Maeden, race of the sorcerer. But whereas the elder priest's long, coarse hair was the color of the trodden snow, the other man's was dark, and his demeanor was vital with the sap of youth.

The older man looked upon the fountain, with its dolphin form and column, sighing, "The sorcerer and the little Marin are so like in sensibility; he loves her and knows it not. I pray she will not die."

Orn replied, "He will join her if he goes on in this fashion; for two nights and days he has not lain down, nor has he taken food, only a little drink."

Gonu nodded. "He cried out to me, before you entered, 'Work all your magic on her! All my healing and magic have been in vain!' There is something more in this than her bodily ailment."

"Perhaps it is her dilemma," said Orn, "her agitation with the blackness of his forgetting. I feel that the time has come to press him to remember, Father Gonu. I am aware," he added hastily, "that you fear it will unseat his mind. But what if she died? His reason would truly be shattered then."

"There is justice in what you are saying, Orn. Yah, I think it may be the only way. Let us go to him now."

And they retraced their steps into the small house and into the room where Fahne sat stone-like in the chair by the Marin's bed, the skin below his reddened eyes halfmoons of darkness. Two deep, grim creases extended from his nose to the outer corners of his mouth, and his tawny skin was yellowish.

"Chronos!" Orn whispered. "He worsens."

Without replying, the elder priest went into the bedchamber and crossed to Fahne.

"My *zahne*," he said softly. "My son, Fahne."

Fahne looked up at Gonu with unseeing eyes.

"Come outside for a moment," Gonu urged. "Come into the garden for just a little while. It will refresh you. Orn will watch, or the young minstrel. You will be only a step away."

The sorcerer at first seemed not to understand. Then he shook his noble head. "No. No, I cannot leave."

"I beseech you," said Gonu. "If you fall ill yourself, what aid can you give?"

With an air of exhausted resignation, Fahne rose and

followed Gonu from the chamber, the priest Orn replacing the sorcerer in the chair by the bed.

Gonu saw at once that the sorcerer's tight face had relaxed ever so slightly when he breathed the fresh air as he moved into the sun-dappled shade of the garden.

"Sit down, my *zahne*," said Gonu, pressing the sorcerer gently onto a bench by the leaping fountain. Fahne stared into the glittering water, and the tears began to flow from his brindled eyes. "The world is meaningless," he said in a hollow voice, "and beauty but a painted picture that glosses over the ugliness and pain."

Sinking down beside him, the Pfarrer put a gentle hand on the sorcerer's arm. "That is the cynicism of exhaustion," he said quietly. "All has meaning, and beauty is triumphant. Ugliness and pain are only errors that must be eradicated by all the strength at our command. But meaning, my son, is everywhere," he said. "Look about you. The patient tortoise there, for instance, soothing himself with the water and the sun, speaks of the union of earth and water, the tie that binds you to the little Marin."

Fahne looked at the old man with dazed eyes. "Only the bond of compassion and friendship unites us . . . she is dear to my friend Desmos, and she is helpless in her ailment. That is all."

"Is it?" Gonu asked softly. "Think on it, Fahne; think on it deeply. We have rendered unto her all the healing and magic at our command. Has there ever been an invalid you have been unable to cure? Has anyone, for all the centuries, been immune to the arts in which you and I are skilled? There is a black agitation of the spirit here, an aching hollow in the little Marin that cannot be eased by herbs and runes, by ministering to her body alone. Do you not see what it is?"

"Desmos advised me," said Fahne in a low voice, "that she was waiting for 'a moment of revelation.' "

"She is waiting for the moment of love," Gonu replied. "Though I am an anchorite, and know not of my own flesh the appeasements of love, I have become conversant with the heart in my long days. She is waiting for the revelation of love," he said again, more softly. "Tell me, Fahne, of your dream of the lost lady."

And wearily Fahne recounted again some of his puzzling visions, repeating to Gonu the experience of excruciating pain that accompanied his half-remembrance.

"Try, Fahne," said Gonu urgently, "try now to remember, for the key to the little Marin's life is in the mists of your mind, and in your star."

"My star." Fahne took his medallion in his long-fingered hands and watched the glitter of its crystal star in the brightness of the Peisun morning. "The star."

"The star," Gonu reiterated, "that gleams with the wisdom of Solomon; the caduceus that denotes all knowledge, from magic to the solid presence of factual lore, the symbol of supreme strength and self-control. Do you really believe, with these weapons in your hand, that anything could defeat you? Look again on the star."

And Fahne obeyed, seeing the scintillating crystal darken and move, changing with the colors of the Marin, the colors of the sea that were in the dome above the little Marin's water garden.

Water garden! The words were shouted in the sorcerer's head, and with such an overpowering vibration that he feared his very skull would rend, and he felt in his brow such an excruciating pain that he could not but cry out.

Strongly, the Pfarren grasped his hand. "Remember!"

From somewhere Fahne heard the single word, rocking in his pain and helplessness. Then something seemed to burst, and a dizzying sequence of images whirled by before his inner sight—the little figure crumpling to the deck of the barge, and lying still upon the wide bed of dragonfly silk; the lady in the garden, with her sleeves of green; the white-skinned woman, naked on the red and yellow leaves, and pale by candlelight, tearing away the boyish shirt and hose; the lady with the face of mist who studied alchemy; the cousin of Desmos in the little house.

And the pain was gone.

"Dione!" the sorcerer cried, and leaping up from the bench by the fountain, he ran into the small house, seeking the chamber where the little Marin was.

Gonu sat quite still for an instant. Then he felt the happy moisture gushing from his old eyes and down his seamed cheeks. "Thanks be to Chronos," he whispered, "thanks be."

And he saw that two mounted men were galloping toward him over the fields. It was Desmos, and with him was another gentle-faced Peisun in rich raiment, with a wise and weathered mien.

As they drew near, and the younger Peisun leaped from his steed, Gonu rose and went to meet them.

"Gonu!" said Desmos. "This is Balik, the prime healer of Mar. How does my little cousin?"

The Pfarrer bowed his ancient head in greeting and replied joyfully, "I think, messires, that the crisis may be past. Come in with me and I will take you to her."

In the primary chamber of the little house there was an air of celebration. Earla was sitting with Dione for the nonce, and the little maid, overawed by the distinguished company, was serving them the wines of their races.

Volan, with heavy-lidded eyes—for he had slept almost as little as Fahne—had taken up his bird-shaped cithara and was playing a sprightly dance of magic Erde.

Fahne the sorcerer sat with a weary, yet tentative, air by the blue-covered table, with its bowl of acanthus and scarlet apples. He seemed almost comatose in his relief, yet he rested as lightly as a gladiator, ready at any moment to rise and return to the Marin.

Desmos looked upon the sorcerer with affectionate despair. "There is no way for us to make you rest," he said wryly.

"None," said Fahne, although his tongue was so thick with exhaustion he could barely speak. Desmos laughed.

"Never mind," he said. "Soon Balik will see to you."

Under the handsome Peisun's chaffing manner, the sorcerer could read his long, dazed agony concerning Shira, and despite his own exultation, Fahne was shadowed by the pain of his friend.

"I suppose," he added, "I must soon return to the castle."

There was a small, stricken silence, for everyone in the room, except for Balik, knew of Desmos' dreadful knowledge and greatly pitied him.

At last Fahne said, "I must go back." And with a compassionate glance at his friend, he returned to the outer chamber.

"Tarry for a moment longer, sire," said Volan. And he began to play a favorite air of Desmos and his cousin, the haunting "Westryn Wind." Yet as soon as he had raised his silver voice in the song, Volan was aware how indiscreet his choice had been, for to hear of having one's love in his arms again was paining the husband of Shira.

And, indeed, as soon as the air was done, the Peisun

Desmos rose with an expression of despair and said stiffly, "I must bid my cousin good-bye."

But the five men were arrested by a shouting from the garden. Desmos rushed to the door to meet the stolid Bole ushers of Dione running down the path.

"Messires!" one Bole was crying. "Messires!"

"What is the matter?"

"The serfs, messire, are rising! They are coming by the thousands across the fields toward the castle of the Queen!"

Desmos said to Gonu and Orn, "Stay here!" He ran down the path toward his mount. But the priests were following, calling to the stablemen to bring their horses.

"We will come with you, sire," Gonu called.

Desmos, pulling at the reins of his gray steed, repeated with exasperation, "Stay! The Lady Dione must have a guard."

Fahne, who had heard the shouting, was now on the path. "You cannot go alone," he called out to the Peisun.

"Do you mean to leave my cousin?" Desmos cried. "You must not leave her again. You must take her away now. She is no longer safe in lower Erde! Heed me."

He galloped away without another backward look.

"He must not go alone!" Fahne cried out to Gonu.

The old priest took his arm. "Sir Desmos will come to no harm, my *zahne*. Both the serfs and the soldiers love him. It is the Queen Shira who is in peril. Heed him. You have found your lost lady again, and her safety is all that should concern you now."

The sorcerer heard the truth in the old man's words. "You are right. Sir Balik!" he addressed the Peisun healer. "Can she be moved at once?"

"Indeed, there can be no harm in it. I will aid you. Call the men," he said to the minstrel, "and we will prepare a litter. You have a wagon?" Volan nodded. "Good. Then go, quickly."

The stunned Earla had come into the room and heard the exchange of Fahne and Balik. She shook the little maid, who had begun to squeal with fright.

"Silence!" The maid was intimidated into sniffling moans. "We have much to do, and swiftly."

And they hurried to the chamber of the Marin to gather up some of her belongings.

The sorcerer and Volan carried the litter of the Marin to the wagon. "It is not journey's end yet, Volan," Dione said weakly to the boy. But her sleepy green eyes, still heavy from many potions, turned to the sorcerer with joy.

And Fahne, as they handed her into the wagon, did not take his look from hers.

CHAPTER 9

When Desmos the Peisun reached the crossing roads that led to the castle, he reined in his nervous gray, exclaiming in horrified amazement.

Thousands of servile men—there must be four thousand, he estimated—were converging in the fields and heading for the hill to which the castle clung. They were bearing sticks and scythes, and before them on a shining black steed rode the sly young Lord Mahar. Behind him at the head of the shouting mass marched six serfs who apparently had been appointed as leaders. Desmos recognized two of them as men with whom he had held amiable converse.

He slapped the reins against the sides of his gray and took the side road to the castle. Whatever Shira's wrongs, he knew Mahar's hatred of her, and he could not allow her to be torn to pieces by the howling mob, for that was surely what Mahar would drive them to!

First to get her to safety, then climb to the keep . . . and reason with them. Desmos urged his gray up the little rise and was galloping toward the stables and the kitchen quarters when he heard a deep-throated bellow, then saw three serfs approaching, two brandishing stout sticks, one waving his scythe.

"Unseat the lord!" He heard one shout in guttural end-lich-Erden, and they were upon him, grabbing at the horse's reins, clutching at his legs to jerk him from his mount. With a mighty kick of his trained foot, the Peisun caught one of them in the groin, and the man collapsed, howling.

He leaped from his horse onto the second attacker and threw the astounded serf across his own shoulder. But the third was making a pass at Desmos with his swishing scythe. Ducking adroitly, the Peisun kicked out at the man, who fell, and Desmos snatched away the scythe and tossed it yards away, smashing at the peasant with his fists.

Then the breathless Peisun dashed into the kitchen quarters past the cowering, sobbing women, and up the stone stairs toward the quarters of the Queen.

Already in the echoing entrance hall were dozens of drunken serfs, tearing down the arras and trampling them, smashing at the armor with their sticks. One serf, with a flaming torch, had started burning a magnificent mural on the wall.

Sickened, Desmos unsheathed the short sword that he wore in lower Erde and ran toward the stairway that led to the upper floors.

The serf with the torch called out thickly, "Hold! No lord can pass!" Desmos faced him, holding out his short sword before him. The man threw the flaming torch at the Peisun and Desmos felt it ignite his sleeve; with one swift motion he slapped the fire out with his sword and, bringing it back, fetched the serf a mighty blow against the jaw. The man fell senseless.

Two more were on the stairs. Desmos rushed at them, butting them down and flailing away with his sword, and they fell back. The Peisun raced up the stairway into the chamber of Shira.

She was nowhere to be found; the dressing closet was empty, and her casque of gems had disappeared.

"Shira!" Desmos cried out, calling her name again and again. There was no answer, no sign of her or her maid anywhere on the floor of bedchambers.

Desmos heaved a deep sigh of relief. She must have fled, then, to safety. Now he must climb to the keep.

The journey to Erdemar, except for one near-incident, had been serene. At one point a band of serfs had passed above them on a hill, but apparently the little train had been unseen, for they proceeded undisturbed.

All went mounted except for Earla and the maid, who occupied the wagon with Fahne and the Marin. Therefore, a forced restraint shadowed a little the excitement of their reunion. Yet it was enough for the Marin to feel the sorcerer near, at last, and the dark lifted from his mind.

Shading her eyes with a white oval hand, Dione looked up at the sky above them; already the dry brightness of endlich-Erde was giving way to the peculiar light, half-sun, half-cloud, that characterized the borderland between Erde and Mar.

"Are we going to the hidden house?" she whispered to Fahne.

"Yes." He nodded, smiling, looking down upon her with such tenderness that her heart turned over.

"It will be no longer secret."

"No, but it is a secret shared with our friends. And the Marin healer is wholly in the confidence of Desmos."

At the mention of her cousin's name, an anxious look flashed into the green eyes of Dione. "Will he . . . be all right?"

"That brings me to . . . something in which you must aid me," he said soberly.

She looked up at him in question.

"I must return for a little while," said Fahne, taking her hand in his. "I had dreamed we would never again be parted, not even for a moment. But this . . . you see that I must aid him, I must leave you, for a little while, this one last time."

The tears were streaming down her face, but Dione nodded obediently and pressed the sorcerer's hand.

"When we come to the house, where you will be safe, I must leave you, but only for a little while," he repeated. "I swear it."

And when the train had reached the hidden house and Fahne had led them in, he saw that the little Marin was settled in the great bed, with its mist of blue-broidered curtains.

For a moment they were left alone. The sorcerer sat down upon the bed and took the Marin into his arms, kissing the top of her small head. "I must go soon," he said softly. "To part from you gives me such pain that to prolong our farewell is unbearable."

She did not answer, only giving him a long look from her green, dreamy eyes, returning his hungry kiss with equal hunger.

"It will not be long," he said. Then, rising with great reluctance, he strode from the chamber, stopping once at the door to look back. Soon she heard his step upon the stairs.

And Dione the Marin prayed for his quick return, for

with his departure all the light had gone out of the golden
room in the hidden house.

"A curse on the lily-livered bitch!" Shira cried aloud,
watching Pendra disappear into the thicket beyond the side
road to the castle. She will find out soon enough how
hazardous it is alone, the Queen thought with malicious
satisfaction.

She tied the heavy leathern pouch of gems to the saddle
of her gleaming mare and mounted with an agile motion,
easily astride in her boyish hunting clothes. A short cloak
concealed the fullness of her upper body, and her rich
black hair was stuffed into a broad cap of green.

Lashing the horse's side with her jeweled whip, the
Queen galloped away into the thicket toward the road to
Erdemar. As she jounced into the greening aisle of the
woods, Shira raged at the uselessness of the guard; the
fools had gone down like ninepins before the onslaught of
the serfs, and her mighty soldiers! A sneer twisted her red
lips. The varlets, stupid from their carousing, had only now
begun to trickle toward the castle. Why, she was a better
soldier! And she touched the jeweled dagger in her belt,
the hunting arbalest slung before her on the saddle.

As she galloped from the thicket into a clearing, she
was confronted by four drunken stragglers from the peasant
band. Whipping her mare into a frenzy, the desperate
Queen rode down on them, and two went down with
cries of pain. Another, swaying, stared stupidly at her, but
the fourth, a man who looked vaguely familiar, leaped for
the reins and, fighting with the terror of the mare, brought
the beast to a halt.

Looking down into his eyes, she recognized him as the
man she had encountered in the fields the afternoon she
had fled, half-naked, from the rejection of the sorcerer.

She brought up her whip and lashed him across the face.
"How dare you, varlet?" she cried out in a cold, hard
voice in which there was no fear.

The man yelped with pain and clapped his hand to the
bleeding cuts. But before she could gallop off, he yanked
her from the saddle to the ground. Shira fell with an astonished grunt, too stunned for a moment to move.

The serf threw himself upon her, shouting in the madness of his rage, "You were not so high that afternoon, my
lady!" He began to tear at her clothes.

Pretending submission, she became suddenly limp and smiled seductively at him. His hold gentled, his face alight with the disbelief in his triumph. Then he bent to her.

With a lightning motion, she drew her dagger from her belt. But he was too quick for her, and he had her wrist in an iron grip. His great fist smashed her on the side of the head.

As she fell into blackness, Shira heard him growling, "You will belong to me now."

"Stop! Stop!" Aspel bellowed to his grinning companions. Some were taking all the cressets they could find and setting them aflame; another was dragging from the bedchamber the sheets and coverlets and hangings, throwing them into a pile upon the floor of the corridor to set them aflame.

"What purpose do you serve?" Aspel cried out, but one of the men, laughing, made a pass at him with the flaming torch and set it to the fabric.

Desmos the Peisun, making his stealthy way upward toward the keep, felt his stomach heave with nausea. But he dare not pause now. He must reach the high tower, for there he could see the lay of the land. And there, alone and unaided, he would try the impossible—to speak to them, seeking an ear among the many who had called him a friend, and attempt to stop the rebellion.

A sound from the strongroom arrested the Peisun; it was the sound of a lone man's drunken laughter. Desmos edged silently around the arching door; in the strongroom, where in great casques the gems and coronets of the monarchs of endlich-Erde reposed, the Peisun saw the Lord Mahar.

The slender, sly-faced Capran had broken open a casque and was setting the crown of the late King Icorn on his narrow head. His back was to the door.

With a leap, Desmos was upon him, holding the point of his short sword to the Capran's back. Mahar's whole posture was that of amazement. He stood as still as stone, tensely waiting for the Peisun's next move.

"Throw down your arms!" Mahar did not respond. Desmos' blade pierced the tunic of the Capran, and he repeated coldly, "Throw down your arms! Now!"

The Capran's hand went to his sword, and whirling, he thrust with it at the Peisun. But Desmos' swift blade sliced the Capran's arm. With an agonized bellow, Mahar dropped his sword with a clang to the floor of stone.

He raised his uninjured arm to remove the crown.

"No," said Desmos with a strange inflection. "No, Mahar, do not remove the crown."

The Capran stared at him, bewildered.

"Leave Icorn's crown upon your head, and come with me."

Grasping his bleeding arm, the Capran stumbled ahead of Desmos up the winding stairs to the castle keep.

With his sword at the Capran's back, Desmos said, "I want them to see you as you are—the great liberator of the people, in a jeweled crown." The Peisun's voice was harsh with his disgust.

When they had reached the tower, Desmos dragged the bleeding Capran onto the topmost parapet. Mahar was sick with terror. He swayed perilously on the narrow, high path, the banners of Shira slapping at his knees.

Below them roiled the soldiers and the serfs. The steeds of the mounted soldiers were riding down on the men with sticks and scythes, and the air was terrible with the cacophony of pain.

Desmos kicked at a loosened stone of the tower, and it plummeted down among the struggling multitude, knocking a soldier from his mount.

Startled, the men below looked up. "It is Mahar!" cried a serf to his fellows. "Mahar, the people's leader!"

"See your leader now!" bellowed Desmos with all the might of his lungs. "Your leader wears a crown! You have traded your Queen for a tyrant! Mahar lies! It was all lies! Mahar has deceived you!"

An unbelieving shout rose up from the men below and they resumed their ugly battle. The scythe of a peasant raked a mounted soldier's limb, and his fellow ran the peasant through. The man gave a terrible scream as he fell, and the serfs around them moved in on the mounted soldier.

Again Desmos raised his voice in the throat-tearing bellow that threatened to rend him: "Listen to me, my friends! I have been your friend! Listen to me now!"

Incredulously, the Peisun saw one peasant raise his head: it was a man he had spoken to amiably, many times, in the fields. And he saw the man hold up his hand and turn to a man near him. The soldiers, temporarily at bay, were driving back another cluster of serfs behind them.

Soon a dozen men were looking up at Desmos, hypnotized by the sight of the jeweled crown gleaming on the head of the wounded Mahar. And then another dozen peasants had gathered, looking upward at the Peisun.

Miraculously, there was an instant's pause in the screaming struggle, and sensing his advantage, Desmos stood upon the parapet, holding out his arms.

"Look at your liberator now!" Desmos cried out again. "Wearing the crown of Icorn!"

Now there were more peasants gathering below to listen to Desmos. Two mounted soldiers moved toward them, and the Peisun shouted, "Hold! I command you, spare them! Shira has gone, and I am the commander of your army now!"

The officers, seeing Desmos gain control, held up their swords, ordering the soldiers in the field to halt.

Desmos was blinded for a moment by the moisture of relief streaming from his brow into his eyes. Dizzy with triumph, he swayed perilously upon the parapet. Then he gathered his forces.

"I pray you, return to your houses! This pillage and this slaughter can gain you nothing—nothing! I will meet with your leaders in the castle, and we will plan the way to seek your freedom. I pray you, disperse!"

A great murmuring swept the peasants in the field. One of the peasant leaders appointed by Mahar shouted out, "It is true! Mahar told us there would be no more crowns, and now he wears one upon his head!"

"Mahar is a traitor! Listen to Desmos!"

Now the men were dispersing into two separate camps. A sweating, hard-eyed serf bellowed at the first speaker, "How do we know this is not a trick? Desmos is a lord, and the husband of the whore!"

Cries of assent rose from the men behind him, and the peasants of the other group began to mutter among themselves.

"He speaks true!" one cried. "Desmos is the husband of the whore, and he has wounded our leader, Mahar!"

"Let us go up to the keep! Let us slay him!"

A hundred peasants began to move toward the castle, and again the soldiers closed in.

Then from a great distance Desmos saw like a speck of

blue a figure upon a chestnut steed. It seemed to be a man in the teal-blue of the Maeden, and as the speck grew larger, the Peisun recognized the form of Fahne the sorcerer, his tawny hair flying in the wind as he galloped toward the turbulent field in front of the castle of the Queen.

Fearless and alone, the sorcerer rode in among the serfs and soldiers, and distantly Desmos heard someone cry out, "It is Fahne—the magic-maker!"

Both serfs and soldiers parted to let him pass. The Peisun looked upon the scene, astounded. It was true, then, Desmos thought with elation—the man of magic inspired such an awe in the people that they did not threaten him now, even the hard-bitten soldiers of the Queen.

Calmly, the sorcerer came riding upon his great chestnut-colored horse. He galloped past the soldiers with their arms and the workers with their sticks and scythes. No one stood in his way as he rode toward the bridge above the moat.

Desmos heard the shouting die, and an eerie stillness fell upon the multitude below him, broken only by random low murmurings from some of the men.

He saw Fahne turn his steed and face the motley crowd before the castle. In all his days, the Peisun had never dreamed of such a sight—hundreds of armed and angry men who moments before had bellowed for each other's blood, standing silent before the lone mounted figure of the sorcerer.

And Desmos knew then the astonishing power of the sorcerer, the power he had for so long curbed amiably, diverted into the uses of healing, into harmless feats of legerdemain to please a sleepy lord before his fire. The Peisun watched him breathlessly, praying that his spell over the multitude would not break; once it did, there was no saving him! Desmos' heart fluttered in his throat.

But Fahne sat on his mount serenely and began to speak to the men immediately before him; the Peisun could not hear his words at all. The crowd moved in; they seemed to be transfixed by the sound of the sorcerer's quiet voice and the sight of his brindled eyes.

Then as his voice rose, the Peisun heard him calling, "Listen to the Peisun Desmos. He is your friend. If you listen to him now, you will be free. If you do not, you will die at each other's hands, and all will be lost. I have never lied to you. I have come among you as a healer and a friend, is this not so?"

There was a wave of assent from the men around him, and one called out, "He has healed our people and never done us harm. He is a friend of the Peisun, and no friend to the Queen. Listen to him, and to the Peisun!"

So weakened was he by his strain that the Peisun Desmos nearly fell. But he bent all his strength to one last mighty effort. Again he held his arms wide, and the people listened.

"Go back to your houses now, I pray you. I will descend and meet your leaders in the castle entranceway."

The six men appointed by Mahar looked at each other in hesitation. At last with one accord they waved to the people of the field. "Go home!" one cried in a loud voice. "Go home, and we shall meet upon the morrow in the fields!"

Dazed, the soldiers watched the men with clubs and sickles moving away in four directions from the field before the castle. Desmos took the arm of Mahar and led him away from the parapet.

Fahne dismounted and walked with the six men across the bridge into the castle of the monarchs of lower Erde.

CHAPTER 10

In peculiar contrast to the ruined chamber, the morning sun was stealing through the high vaulted windows when Fahne and Desmos, spent, sat down.

The pale early rays caught fragments of shattered armor and gleamed on the splendid arras pierced and torn by the workers' scythes. Deep scratches scarred the polished wood of the massive central table where they had drawn tall carved chairs.

Desmos felt his bone weariness. Glancing at Fahne, he saw that the sorcerer was almost numb with his exhaustion. He had tended the wounds of Mahar and overseen the care of a hundred men before he would pause.

And the Peisun had explored, with the few servants remaining, the whole of the castle, to help put out the fires and reassure the women.

Now Desmos' green eyes rested sadly on the wreckage. Then he said, "Perhaps it is as well. These are cruel souvenirs." He sighed and took a sip of strawberry wine. "But much has survived," he added, smiling for the first time in many days. "They did not reach the cellars."

"My thanks to Hermes for that," replied Fahne, and he quaffed a goblet of valley-lily. He stretched out his aching legs. "And now there is no one left to rule. How strange it is!"

The Peisun nodded. "Shira is nowhere to be found. So now there are no more of them. The male line on both sides has perished in battle. Poor Icorn never knew that it would come to such an end."

"You will remain, then?"

"I must, for a time. There will be a myriad of dangers. Should the armies strengthen in Erde and find them leaderless, a general could wear the crown." Desmos shuddered. "Uras of dernier-Brise will be of great aid in helping form a people's government. And, of course, there is the Council of Mar. Who knows what winds will blow from upper Erde and Sabbia? In any case, someone must steer the course until then."

"I do not envy you, my friend."

Desmos filled his glass and said wistfully, "What a leader you would be, Fahne."

The sorcerer laughed and made a gesture of negation. "Not I, Desmos, never. Whatever aid I can bring you I will with gladness, but the ways of leaders are not my ways." After a brief silence, he said with hesitant gentleness, "I beg you, remain not too long alone. There will come a day when the hollow in your heart will be filled again."

Blessing his friend's discretion, the Peisun replied in a melancholy tone, "I fear I have been hollowed out too deep to quickly fill again and soon."

The sorcerer's brindled eyes were full of compassion. "Do not despair, Desmos. When my own life was most empty, and the drought of an eternal desert within me, your sweet cousin appeared to refresh me and give me new hope. And then, in my black forgetfulness, the light returned—I am alive again now, at last. It will be so for you. I know it."

"I wish I shared your hopes."

Rising, Fahne clasped his friend's shoulder with his broad, long-fingered hand and said, "I must leave you."

"So soon?" Desmos cried. Fahne looked away from the desolation in his green, dreamy eyes, the eyes so like Dione's.

"You have not closed your eyes these many nights, and you have journeyed to and fro and labored like a man of the fields with us. And yet you will ride this same day to Erdemar." The Peisun shook his head and gave Fahne a rueful glance.

The sorcerer's face, shadowed with sleeplessness and drawn down in grim, exhausted lines, lightened at the sound of "Erdemar." He said, "Even though the courier has gone to advise her of my safety, I cannot rest until I have reached the hidden house. So many circles have intervened"—there was an edge of excitement in his voice— "that to spend this time away from her . . ." He paused, unable to express his longing further.

"Then at least, my friend, let one of the men drive you in a wagon," Desmos said. "Your fine steed, Merddyn, can walk along without your constant burden on his back."

Fahne grinned. "I accept with gladness."

Desmos rose and they walked together to the corridor. The Peisun took the sorcerer's arm. "How can I speak my gratitude?"

"Do not speak of it. It was you from the beginning who saved the people. We will meet anon in Erdemar."

"Anon," Desmos repeated.

He clasped the sorcerer's hand once more and then watched him stride down the corridor toward the lower floors that led to the stables.

Then Desmos retraced his steps across the floor of echoing granite to the wreckage of the Council chamber.

He stood for a moment looking about him. The sun brightened and its light was ghostly on the broken armor and the tattered arras.

Then resolutely the Peisun took up a pot of ink and carried it to the massive table. Searching for a quill and paper in the chaos, he sat down and began to write in the lonely stillness, drawing up the charter of the republic of endlich-Erde.

The wheel of stars was moving to its end and its beginning; the late-March Circle of the Peisun would soon descend into the sector of the Ramm, the young equinox. The city of Alioure in premier-Brise was even brighter with the nearing of spring. And Uras' courier from dernier-Brise, who had never been in Alioure before, was dazzled.

Seeking the house of Gemelle, the courier blinked at the swift commerce upon the streets of ice. The towering structures of Hermes-glass reflected the strengthening sun like enormous mirrors. The place seemed one great looking glass to the messenger; he shadowed his pallid eyes. And the people! They flew about on their bladed shoes like winged creatures, quick and light as aliens from a fairyland.

The courier waited for a silvery sleigh, drawn by snowy horses, to go by and skated awkwardly across the glassy street. The small shining house before him, then, must be the house of Gemelle, brother-in-law to the Baron Uras.

He made his perilous way up the walk and rang a small crystal bell on the door of the shining house. A man with narcissus-colored hair, in matching yellow raiment, opened the door and smiled, accepting the missive from him. The courier received with thanks a piece of silver and returned to the brilliant street.

"Shabatu!" Gemelle called out, and the fragile Waetergyt, with her ice-blue robe flying about her, ran with grace down the white-painted stairs. Her movements were so light in her soundless slippers that she seemed to float like thistledown.

The last few weeks of happy peace, alone in the house with Gemelle, had given her pallid face a new glow; there was a color in her skin like the frost blooms of the lower mountains, and her remote blue eyes, like winter morning, rested with affection on her slender husband.

"There is word from Uras," said Gemelle, holding up the grayish missive, with its silver seal of dernier-Brise.

When Shabatu reached the bottom stair, the Twisan encircled her with his sinewy arms. She raised her white face for his kiss, and her fall of hair, bright as silver-gilt, glittered about her shoulders. Gemelle felt its feathery softness with his slender hand.

He put his arm around her narrow waist and led her into the sunny dining chamber. Its furniture and appointments were all of crystal, scintillant in the sun that streamed through the transparent window-wall. The inner walls of Hermes-glass reflected the lovers' morning-colored hair, the yellow garments of Gemelle, and the frost-blue robe of the Waetergyt.

They sat down at the crystal table and Shabatu poured out Gemelle's blue marjoram and violet tea for herself, saying, "Read Uras' letter."

The Twisan sipped his tea and tore open the silver seal. He read to Shabatu the news of endlich-Erde and of Fahne the sorcerer.

"So that is where he has been."

"And they will be together at last. Poor Uras. But I am happy for Dione. Her face was always so sad in Brise. And you have found again your old friend and companion."

Gemelle laughed. "And we have dismissed entirely the matter of a fallen kingdom!"

"Monarchs have never meant much to you," Shabatu countered. "Nor to me," she added, then took his hand.

"I must say that affairs of state make strange companions," the Twisan said. "To think that Uras will be aiding the cousin of Dione and the friend of the sorcerer."

He raised the wing-like hand in his and kissed it fervently. "How good it will be to see Fahne again. Would you object to a journey to Erdemar?"

"Of course not. But will they not journey, perhaps, to Alioure?"

"I have a feeling," Gemelle said thoughtfully, "that it will be a while before they care to journey."

Earla the Bole had not enjoyed a good quarrel since the death of Chiton the Lord Mayor of Mar. Therefore, it was with the excitement of a war horse hearing bugles that she entered the fray with the ancient servants of Fahne.

The aged pair who leisurely tended the unfrequented house had received the party from endlich-Erde in a wondering flurry. So many years had gone by since the hidden house contained all these.

But the Bole was in her glory, arranging quarters for

Gonu and Orn, the Marin healer and the minstrel, grumbling at the ushers and the maid.

She quickly made a militant survey of the place, from attic to cellar, poking into the outbuildings, sniffing at the strange smells of the alchemical chamber as Fahne's ancient house-man stood by like a grizzled watchdog above the sorcerer's treasures.

But that evening, when Dione had regained some of her strength, she chided the Bole for her discourtesies and a modicum of peace was restored, with the previous chain of command.

Fahne's servants, glowing with their restoration to power, showed their devotion to Dione in countless ways, and the Marin soothed Earla in turn by pitying the couple's age.

"We must try," she said with sweet mendacity to Earla, "to forgive them their little ways. You are, after all, so much younger."

And the Bole, her very vigor renewed by this declaration, held her peace.

It was therefore a morning of serenity Dione awoke to in the bed with broidered draperies. The mildness of the late-March Peisun sun gilded the misty curtains of the great bed. She recalled with a stab of longing the nights she had lain there with Fahne, smelling the earthy scents of sun and cedar from his tawny skin—that odor that seemed native to the Erden and that so thrilled the pallid Marin like herself, ever hungering for the solidity of earth.

Dione yearned for his presence so that she felt a wave of actual weakness wash her body, as if her blood were melted snow, coursing coldly through her veins. If he should die, if he should die!

And suddenly all the parted circles, the nights of emptiness and days of solitude, and the endless waiting through the blackness of his recall gathered themselves into one enormous stone of pain she no longer had the strength to raise: it was crushing, crushing her, and she began to weep, a bitter, desolate weeping.

The sound of her mourning brought the faithful Bole into the room, and Earla parted the misty curtains, taking the weak Marin into her broad arms. "I pray you, my lady, weep not," Earla begged with passion. "He will come home, he will come home, I promise you. I have prayed

to Aphrodite so constantly these many circles . . . for your
joy and for your forgiveness."

"Forgiveness?" Dione asked feebly, her voice muffled on
Earla's bosom.

"I tried," said the Bole, stroking the Marin's tangled
hair, "to part you from the sorcerer—first to mate you with
the mad Vanand and then the cruel Monoceros. I tried to
turn awry the very order of the wheel of stars." Earla's
voice broke. "Forgive me."

Gently the Marin pushed the Bole away and looked up
at her. "I forgive you, Earla."

Then she lay back on the pillows, and sighing, she
added, "Nothing has import now except that he live. I
cannot endure much more."

And, indeed, thought the Bole, the little Marin could
not; she looked like the dry stem of a flower ready to
break.

A tapping at the door aroused the women. The little
maid, a timid, ill-aspected Peisun, crept into the room and
handed a missive to Earla. "A courier from lower Erde,"
she said softly, then withdrew.

Dione cried, "Give it to me!" And snatching the missive
from the Bole's wide hand, she ripped it open, her desperate glance darting down the page.

With a gasp she lay back on the pillows, clutching the
message to her breast.

"What is it, my lady?"

"He lives, Earla! He lives!" And the smile that transformed the Marin's face was Earla's full forgiveness.

Few, still, in the border country of Erdemar knew that
the thicket far from the winding road was not a thicket
but a house. So magical was the blending of walls and
trees that no one glimpsing it from the crossingways could
know a house stood there.

And so on this gray and golden evening of misty sun
habitual to Erdemar, the woman seemed to materialize
from the very woods. The lovely dark-haired woman in the
peacock-colored gown, her face as white as milk, stood before the green-and-russet expanse. She watched the wagon
pause at the crossingway and saw the tall, lean man in the
teal-blue of mittel-Erde leap out. He raised his arm to her
in greeting and began to run.

With an almost floating motion, the woman started toward him, her peacock-colored sleeves spread out like wings, over the descending field of lavender and harebells, roses and clove-scented gillyflowers.

For a moment the man was struck with fear that the woman was only a chimera, that when he touched her his hands would encounter painted air, that he would awaken from this as he had from the fleeting visions in his time of blackness.

But now she was near, and his starved sight fed upon her face and neck and hair; in the latening sun her black hair glimmered so blackly it was almost blue; her heart-shaped face had the silken texture of a water lily.

Around her neck on a fragile chain was the little crystal star.

As soon as the courier had delivered into her hands the word of Fahne's well-being, all Dione's weakness had fled, and she had arisen swiftly to array herself in the peacock-colored gown, the gown of their flight last Maeden Circle, for she knew that he soon would come.

When she looked up now, in the field of flowers before the hidden house, she saw a different man from the one in the motley barge: this man, too, was tall and strong, his bare arms as powerful as oaken branches, and the hands rising to embrace her were broad, yet sensitive, a healer's hands. On his face was the same look of gentleness and power; his hawk-like nose and generous mouth were unchanged, as well as his tawny beard and hair. And around his neck he wore still the caduceus of Hermes, god of all wisdom; in its center was the six-pointed crystal star of magic, the Star of Solomon.

But his deep, brindled eyes—the eyes that reflected the tinctures and lore of other places—had been hollowed more profoundly with deeper passions, and filled with a tender wisdom wider than before. The dappled colors of those wondrous eyes had so intensified that the Marin was stricken with their beauty—she saw the Kani's turquoise, bright as flame; the winged blue of the Twisan, like the winter sky; the rich brown-black, like velvet, of the Capran's earthiness; and, green as emeralds now, the mordant brightness of the Escorpiun ascending.

There was no word in any tongue with strength enough to greet him.

The impact of their meeting bodies nearly toppled them.

When they had come to themselves in the twilight and Fahne could see again the broidered mist of draperies around the bed, he whispered, "I would we soon were wed. I like not the ambiguity of your state, when I would honor you before the world."

She moved closer to him without a reply. He looked down at her in question. "Would it please you to be wed in Mar?"

Dione asked softly, "Can only Anunitum join us in the rite of the Maeden and the Peisun?"

He stroked her hair, giving a low laugh. "I thought to be wed in the silver city would give you joy."

"I have no joy in contemplating another journey. I think of all the journeys we have made apart, and of the day of the fair, when my momentary whim almost cost us everything." She shivered and hid her head under his arm. He tightened the pressure of his grasp.

"We will be wed in Erdemar."

"Then it is journey's end," she said with delight.

"The journey never ends," he answered gently. "But it matters not." After a little silence, he said, "Once I called this house, and then your water garden in the land of Mar, 'temenos'—the garden in the center of my self. But where we are together lies the garden. You are temenos."

They heard the four long chimes of Maeden-hour.